FRANCES PARKINSON KEYES
*brings romance and revolution
to the diplomatic corners of the world.*

*MICHAEL TRENT—An empire-builder who
couldn't wait for success in the foreign
service—even if it cost him his wife.*

*DAPHNE DAINGERFIELD TRENT—Shy,
provincial, beautiful, her marriage brought
her face-to-face with terror and tragedy.*

*ALONZO LOOSE—Michael's diplomatic
superior. He couldn't have Daphne—so he gave
her husband to another woman.*

*VIVIENNE deBLONVILLE—A married
hellcat who played at drawing-room love.*

*ROSEMARY TRENT—The beguiling
daughter who stepped innocently into her
father's greatest mistake.*

Avon Books by
Frances Parkinson Keyes

ALSO THE HILLS	19687	$1.50
VICTORINE	20438	$1.25
ALL THAT GLITTERS	09548	$1.25
BLUE CAMELLIA	05611	$ .95
CAME A CAVALIER	16568	$1.50
CRESCENT CARNIVAL	08896	$1.25
DINNER AT ANTOINE'S	09480	$1.25
FIELDING'S FOLLY	06197	$ .95
GREAT TRADITION	06312	$ .95
HONOR BRIGHT	09852	$1.25
JOY STREET	09712	$1.25
PARTS UNKNOWN	06148	$ .95
QUEEN ANNE'S LACE	06064	$ .95
RIVER ROAD	19208	$1.50
ROSES IN DECEMBER	06262	$ .95
ROYAL BOX	05694	$ .95
STEAMBOAT GOTHIC	09613	$1.25

Frances Parkinson Keyes

Parts Unknown

 AVON PUBLISHERS OF BARD, CAMELOT, DISCUS AND EQUINOX BOOKS

AVON BOOKS
A division of
The Hearst Corporation
959 Eighth Avenue
New York, New York 10019

ISBN: 0-380-00152-7

First Printing, December, 1962
Tenth Printing

AVON TRADEMARK REG. U.S. PAT. OFF. AND
FOREIGN COUNTRIES, REGISTERED TRADEMARK—
MARCA REGISTRADA, HECHO EN CHICAGO, U.S.A.

Printed in the U.S.A.

CONTENTS

To Lelia Montague Barnett
In Whose Hospitable Home
This Book Was Begun
And Whose Friendliness
Facilitated Its Progress

FOREWORD

In "Parts Unknown" I have followed my usual practice, based upon a precedent set by far more eminent authors, of using names which are regionally characteristic, both at home and abroad. As far as I know, however, there is not the slightest resemblance between any of the characters I have created and individuals, either living or dead, who have actually borne these names. In instances where there has been a reference to a personage who is not a fictitious character —as in the case of John Jacob Rogers, for example—a real name has been used. In all other instances, such personages are imaginary.

I have taken certain slight liberties with the time element. For instance, though there is now an American missionary hospital at La Paz, this was not established until shortly after the period when my hero and heroine are supposed to have lived there.

St. Peter's-at-the-Crossroads, like Solomon's Garden, has its prototype in reality, though its name has no connection with any specific church. My own interest in the ancient crossroads churches, so characteristic of the part of the South which I know and love the best, was greatly stimulated through reading the delightful book entitled "The Crossroads Church—A Virginia Institution," by Mr. H. S. Brock, a member of the *New York Times* editorial staff.

The old epitaphs described on page 210-11 are actually in the Glebe Burying Ground of Augusta County, near Staunton, Virginia. The stories of Floretta's funeral and of Moaning Moore and the hidden flag, are true ones, though they have been shifted from the locality in which they actually took place; while the ghostly harpists are still said to play on a plantation which I have often visited myself.

Many queries have come to me regarding the characteristics of a "flounder house." These were always built with a high flat blank back and a roof which sloped down at a sharp angle with pillars supporting an upper gallery in the front. The theory is that the settlers who built these houses intended to duplicate their construction on the other side in which event the high blank wall would have become the center of the house and would, of course, have the necessary intersections in it. But for some unknown reason this was never

7

done and the "flounder houses" which have survived the ravages of time are all as they were originally built. Alexandria is the only place of which they are typical, though there are two or three in Charleston and two or three in Fredericksburg.

I am greatly indebted to Mr. J. Montgomery Farrar, Advertising Manager of *National Aeronautics,* and himself an experienced military aviator, for the technical information which facilitated the preparation of Chapter XVII and served as a safeguard against inaccuracy of detail. In spite of the considerable amount of flying I have done myself, and my deep interest in the general subject of aviation, I could not have satisfactorily achieved this chapter without his help.

I am similarly indebted to Miss Doris Fleeson, Washington correspondent of the *New York News,* for her help in the preparation of Chapter XXII. Miss Fleeson, who in 1937 was the winner of the prize awarded by the New York Newspaper Women's Club for the best reporting done by a New York newspaperwoman during the previous year, was the only woman accredited as a correspondent on the official trains of both presidential candidates in the campaign of 1936. Although I wrote Chapter XXI myself, I could not have done so without Miss Fleeson's informative cooperation; and in mapping out Chapter XXII, I asked her to do the actual writing, recognizing her superior fitness for this, and myself temporarily assumed an editorial role. I am very proud to hail as a collaborator a journalist for whom, both personally and professionally, I have the greatest admiration.

F. P. K.

PART I

The Dream and the Desire

CHAPTER 1

MICHAEL TRENT swung his Ford almost savagely off the Highway Bridge and tore along over the River Road toward Alexandria at a pace which defied all speed limits. The rate at which he was traveling rendered him oblivious, for once, of the ill-smelling dumps on his left and the sprawling railroad yards at his right, both of which, under ordinary circumstances, offended his Midwestern sense of sanitation and order. "These slovenly Southerners!" he had frequently exclaimed with contempt, before he had a special reason for ceasing to speak of Southerners contemptuously and beginning to speak of them admiringly. Now he was blissfully unaware of his surroundings until a motorcycle cop whizzed up alongside him, blocking his progress.

"Say what's the great idea?" inquired the policeman with a harshness which brought Michael back to the consciousness of many mundane things, including the smell of the dumps. "You ain't out aimin' to make a few angels today, are you?"

"No, I'm aiming to go to see one," Michael reported with a disarming grin, as he shut off his engine. "Haven't you got a girl yourself, officer? If you have, you might let me off. I know I was going too fast. But I've got a lot of ground to cover and the best news ever to carry."

The policeman grunted, and glanced covertly at the face of the persuasive young man in the ramshackle car. It was an agreeable face, frank and fresh-skinned; the hazel eyes had a twinkling light in them, and the mouth parted over amazingly white teeth. But the brows were unexpectedly heavy and much darker than the crisp hair; and there was a hint of hardness in the square chin. While it was the face of a man who would not choose to pick a quarrel, still it was the face of a man who would not hesitate to fight, and fight

9

hard, if he were pushed to it. The policeman decided not to push him.

"Well, I might let you off, seein' as how you've got such a good alibi," he said with less gruffness. "But if I recollect right, I've seen you before. You ain't got a face I'd forget easy. Seems to me like the last time me and you met up, we had a little argument about you being parked in front of a hydrant. And that time, if I ain't mistaken, you told me you hadn't even saw the hydrant, when you parked your car, because you was on your way to pay a call on a certain party. And that was right here in Alexandria. What I'd like to know is, are you always in such a hell of a hurry? And are you always on your way to see certain parties, scattered from one end of the state of Virginia to the other? You say you've got a long ways to go this time."

Michael laughed outright, and leaning farther from his car window, addressed the officer with a still greater show of candor. "There's only one certain party," he said confidentially. "When you and I met before, in front of the hydrant, she was here in Alexandria, visiting her cousin. Now she's in King George, where she lives. If you really feel you've got to give me a ticket, let's have it over with, so I can get along down there. But I think it's only fair to tell you that I've studied law. I'll put up an awfully good plea in my own defense, to save ten dollars. I need it to get married on."

He was still grinning and already reaching toward the switch. He moved swiftly; his long fingers, the policeman noticed, were square at the ends, very brown, and firm even in their flexibility. The officer drew back a little.

"All right, all right," he said hastily. "But remember, the third time you'll get pinched, that's all there is to it. No amount of soft soap won't let you off. Get along with you, and give my best to King George!"

Michael wasted no time in acting on the officer's suggestion. He was off like a streak toward Accotink past stretches of forest where the oak leaves still clung to the skeletal branches and sunshine dappled the depths, bordered by small tortuous creeks which gurgled as they foamed and rippled out of sight. He hardly saw Pohick, Aguia and Stafford Court House as he sped through them; but at Falmouth he stopped at a scrubby little station to buy gas, before turning off into the narrow country road skirting the Rappahannock. Somehow the drowsy, dilapidated old town, unglamorous even in the glow of autumn light, had always puzzled and intrigued him. Now, even in the midst of his preoccupation, it challenged his attention.

"Strange that the first million dollars in America should

10

have been made in a place like this," he muttered to himself as he paid for his gas, carefully counted his change, and felt in his pockets for a package of cigarettes, doubly elusive because of its flattened condition. "If it could be done here, you'd think it could be done anywhere. And if Basil Gordon could do it, I don't see why I shouldn't do it too."

A slight grimness crept into his cheerful soliloquy. It was conceivable that he might have made his million too, he reflected as he wound his way farther and farther into the country, if he had only stuck to law. He had been elected to *The Review*, he had graduated with honors, he had even had an offer from the most exclusive firm in Boston, which did its scouting in the senior class of the Harvard Law School with mingled caution and haughtiness. But to the mutual amazement of this firm and himself, he had declined the offer. There had been something about his father's face, when Richard Trent had suggested that before Michael "settled down" they might go around the world together, that he had been impelled to meet—a mute confession of loneliness, an unexpressed hope, a forced, pathetic heartiness. Looking into Richard Trent's honest, pitiful eyes, Michael had found he could not suggest that the older man should go back to the nondescript little house in St. Louis, where he had lived completely alone for years, and leave his son free to dig into pleasant bachelor quarters on Beacon Hill. And because Michael had not been able to do this, he had lost his chance of becoming a junior partner in the exclusive firm, and he and his father had set sail on a small freighter bound for Kobe.

And then, like a fool and a dreamer, he had succumbed to the charm of the life which he had consented to live only temporarily and only to please his father. When he was back in Boston, after his year of exile, he found that he did not want to stay there. He had outgrown all its traditions and limitations. He sat continually on a bench in the Common, like any common loafer, thinking yearningly of the deer at Nara and the sampans on the Yangtze and the golden pagodas of Burma. He strained his ears for the sound of temple bells and his sight for a vision of high peaks. He hungered for curries and goulashes, and thirsted for Turkish coffee and iced Asti. And finally his urge for these things overpowered him, and he flung caution to the winds and snatched at the one opening which seemed to offer a chance to recapture them.

Well, the chance had come and no one should wrest it from him now. The pudgy Congressman as whose secretary he had been slaving since shaking himself free from the shackles of

11

Boston, had served his purpose. Now that his own feet were firmly on the first rung of the ladder, he did not propose to be bullied and browbeaten again by Horatio L. Tittmann of the Eleventh Missouri District, or any of his ilk. The year in Washington had not been wasted, but the capital was only a way station for him. He was really headed for Batavia, Capetown, Edinburgh, Montevideo and other points north, south, east and west. Meantime, he had met Daphne Daingerfield.

He had accepted the tickets to the Annual Southern Ball without enthusiasm, though with unimpeachable civility. He had never given the Honorable Horatio L. Tittmann occasion to say that he had been lacking in courtesy, and to do the Congressman justice, he never had said it. Mr. Tittmann appreciated Michael's abilities, and would have been overjoyed to keep him indefinitely at the head of his office force, if Michael would have consented to remain there. Indeed, it was partly with the hope of "making things pleasant" for his secretary that Mr. Tittmann had offered him the tickets which he had been badgered into buying by the wife of a colleague from Arkansas, the Honorable S. J. Quigley, Jr. The Congressman had pressed the tickets into his employee's long, lean fingers with a pompous little speech.

"You should get about more, Trent, you really should," Mr. Tittmann had said impressively, "Of course, it is highly commendable for a young man to work as diligently as you do. But social contacts are not to be despised either. Here are two tickets for the Annual Southern Ball. It is one of the outstanding events of the season here. You will find all the best families of Virginia represented at it, not to mention those of numerous other states. Find yourself a pretty girl and take her. That won't be hard for you, eh, Michael?"

Mr. Tittmann had slapped his secretary heartily on the back as he brought his genial remarks to a close, and had been surprised to feel Michael's hard shoulders stiffen slightly under the impact. Once or twice before he had detected a tendency toward aloofness in this otherwise promising young chap. Mr. Tittmann deplored such an attitude not only because Michael was his subordinate, but also, as he frequently said to Mr. Quigley, because he had a feeling that the fellow might go far. Yet he had a hesitancy which he could not explain, about saying anything on the subject to Michael himself, which the secretary might conceivably resent.

Michael had not taken a girl to the dance—indeed, up to that point, he had met comparatively few girls in Washington, and none who had intrigued him. And his first impression of the function had been that if it represented a gathering of the fine flower of the Southern aristocracy, then this

12

flower was beginning to wither on its stem. An astonishing number of old ladies were present, whose thin and faded hair escaped from their nets in wisps about their wrinkled necks, banded in rusty black velvet, and who were wearing dingy collars of duchesse lace, cameo brooches and Paisley shawls. Some of them were shepherding flat-bosomed daughters, who did not look as if they needed watching, to ward off seduction. Others were accompanied by aging escorts, whose broadcloth was rather shiny at the seams, and whose linen, in some instances, was not above reproach. After looking over this collection of antiques, Michael had made up his mind that the evening was a total loss and that the sooner he went back to his bare bedroom in Georgetown and his perusal of *Commercial Geography,* the better. And then he had caught sight of a girl, whose sapphire eyes were looking longingly out toward the sedate dancers on the half-filled floor, and had stopped short.

She was seated in front of the palms near the entrance, beside a withered spinster whose cameos were the largest, whose collar was the most bedraggled, and whose shawl was the most voluminous of any he had observed. The girl herself was wearing a blue dress, the color of her eyes; it was bright and crisp, but clumsily and conservatively cut. Michael involuntarily found himself wishing that it might have been more revealing; he was instinctively aware that a glimpse of the girl's budding breasts would disclose even greater delicacy of skin than her cheeks and throat, and that her figure, slender as it was, must melt into beguiling curves. She held her head rather high, her small chin tilted; her hair, soft and dark, waved over her forehead and partially concealed her small ears. Like her skin and her eyes, it was arresting; there was something cloudlike about it. In spite of her general air of ethereality, the dignity of her carriage gave her the effect of height. At one and the same time she seemed elusive and seductive.

Suddenly she became aware of him. The color in her cheeks deepened and spread until it suffused her neck and disappeared beneath her laces in a rosy glow. But her blue eyes, after the first startled second, looked steadily into his own. Michael walked straight over to her.

"I'm so glad to see you again," he said easily. "I don't know whether you remember me or not, there was such a crush around you all the time. But I met you, for a moment, yesterday at Mrs. Quigley's party. My name is Michael Trent. I'm Representative Tittmann's secretary. May I have this dance?"

The ruse was as blatant as it was hackneyed; but Michael

13

did not care. The only question was whether the girl would meet his challenge, and something told him that she would.

"I'm afraid you've made a mistake," she said. Her voice was a little hesitant, but it did not sound affronted. "I don't know Mrs. Quigley" she went on after a moment, while Michael wisely awaited developments. "I wasn't at her party. But I did read about it in the paper. It must have been lovely."

"It was." Michael, who had not been there either, still spoke easily. "And I could have sworn I met you there. You haven't a twin sister, have you?"

"No, I haven't any sisters at all."

The elderly spinster, who had been slowly gathering her forces while this interchange of words had been taking place, now asserted herself. "My young cousin is a complete stranger in Washington," she said frigidly. "She has no acquaintance here whatsoever."

"Well, that does seem a pity, doesn't it? Especially at a dance! But I'm sure she'll make any number of them, in no time at all. Meanwhile, if you'd let her—or shall I go and find an usher to present me properly?" Michael, who did not know any of the ushers, concluded handsomely.

"Oh, Cousin Georgie, that isn't necessary, is it really? It would be all right for me to dance with Mr. Trent, wouldn't it? I've been thinking, if I could have just one dance, it wouldn't be quite so bad!"

The elderly spinster opened her lips to protest again. But she was too late. The girl was already on her feet and the next instant Michael had swept her away. He did not bring her back again until suppertime, when he had the tact to invite Miss Georgina Fairfax to join them. The old lady was almost famished by that hour, for she had followed her usual practice of economizing on the evening meal if she were going out later on, and Michael catered to her appetite solicitously. Her plate was first heaped with diced veal masquerading as chicken salad, potato chips and stale rolls, all of which were replenished; then with Neapolitan ice cream and crumbling ladyfingers. As her hunger subsided, Miss Georgina began to regard Michael less belligerently than she had at first. Besides, during the interval while he had been dancing with Daphne, she had contrived to ascertain, from another relative who was not dancing—being one of the flat-bosomed maidens aforementioned, so seldom lured upon the floor— that there really was a Congressman Quigley of Arkansas whose most particular friend was a Congressman Tittmann of Missouri, who in turn had a secretary named Michael Trent, coming from St. Louis. Miss Georgina did not recog-

14

nize the existence of Arkansas on the map, socially speaking; but she believed there were a few reputable families in St. Louis, though she could not recall that any of them was named Trent. It was always possible, however, that her memory, which was not as good as it once had been, was slipping.

Michael, meanwhile, had also obtained a certain amount of information during the dancing interval, though the acquisition of this had not been his main preoccupation, as it had with Miss Georgina. He had found out that the name of his entrancing partner was Daphne Daingerfield, that she was an orphan, and that she lived with her uncle, Roger Daingerfield, who was rector of the famous old church, built in the form of a Maltese cross, called St. Peter's-at-the-Crossroads. Just now she was visiting her kin, the Fairfaxes, in Alexandria, which she generally did once a year. She spent a week or two with Cousin Georgina and a week or two with Cousin Tyler and, occasionally, an additional week or two with some of the other cousins. She didn't know whether or not she would stay for these additional weeks this year. She had gone to Stuart Hall in Staunton, and she had loved it there, but she hadn't graduated. Michael gathered that the difficulty had been financial rather than scholastic, though Daphne did not actually say so. Since her return to the rectory, her uncle had taught her himself, as he had previously done. He was a great scholar as well as a real saint, and he was very fond of her and very good to her. He had no children of his own. His wife, Daphne's Aunt Vinnie, was sickly. Daphne relieved her, as much as she could, of household cares and parish duties. But Dr. Daingerfield thought that Daphne should get away from these occasionally, because it was rather quiet for a young girl in the country, and King George County was all country. So that was why she came up to Alexandria, which was very pleasant, though not really so very gay either, for an annual outing. And oh, she did love to dance——!

There were very few evenings after that, during the next month, when she did not do so. Michael amazed Mr. Tittmann, the morning after the Southern Ball, by frankly admitting that he had been thinking over their conversation, and that he realized his employer was right in saying that he ought to get about more; he would be glad to go anywhere that Mr. Tittmann would suggest. Mr. Tittmann, overjoyed because his words of wisdom had not fallen on deaf ears, presented his secretary with his tickets to numerous other benefits, and to the Congressional reception at the White House, which he had been in Washington long enough to despise. He introduced the young man to the Quigleys, who did invite him to the next party they gave, and were soon urging him wholeheartedly to come to their home as often as he could and bring anyone with him that he liked; the latchstring, they said, would always be out, and they knew he would not mind taking potluck. Having gone thus far, Michael had no difficulty in attracting the notice of the well-known widow of a former Senator from Missouri, who entertained lavishly in the pseudo-feudal castle which she had erected on a prominent point of land, and who, in her later years, had developed a passion for dancing; twice a week, at least, her overstuffed drawing rooms, hung with ponderous paintings, were cleared for this pastime; and she soon began to depend on Michael's regular attendance at her parties. Not to be outdone by this dowager, another, who was still richer, threw open her ballroom for daily dancing, and welcomed young and old to disport themselves amongst its baroque splendors. It was astonishing how easy everything was made for Michael, and how easy he, in turn, made everything for Daphne.

Miss Georgina watched her with compressed lips as, night after night, Daphne Daingerfield dressed to go out with Michael Trent. But after the old lady's first futile protest, she did not try to remonstrate with her young relative again. For Daphne had turned on her with unexpected fire, and had made a declaration of independence.

"I'm sorry you don't think Michael is a suitable escort for me, Cousin Georgina; but somehow none of the reasons you've given me for thinking so is very convincing. I can't help it if you've never heard of any Trents in St. Louis. I suppose it's just barely possible he never before heard of any Fairfaxes or Daingerfields in Virginia. Oh, I know it isn't the same thing, that he should have, but then— He's clean, isn't he, and decent? He doesn't swear, he doesn't drink, he doesn't——"

"But my dear child, we take all those things for granted in any man."

"Well, maybe we do, but sometimes there isn't any special reason why we should. I've seen men, right here in Alexandria, who drank too much. Besides, to go back to Michael, he's good-looking and he has good manners. He's intelligent and well educated. He has something to say for himself."

Miss Georgina, though startled by Daphne's warm defense of the interloper, managed to remark dryly that he had almost too much to say for himself.

"Perhaps, but I'm tired of men who do nothing but mumble. I like the way Michael Trent laughs. It's so open and friendly. I like the way he moves around. As if he owned the earth, or meant to some day. I like the way his eyes crinkle and the way his hair curls and the way his teeth shine. I like the feeling of his hands."

"Daphne!" exclaimed Miss Georgina in horror.

"Well, I do, Cousin Georgina. There's something so strong and warm about them. He doesn't just slide them into yours. He grips with them. You know the French don't talk about *shaking* hands. They say '*serrer la main.*' That's what Michael does. And when I'm dancing with him, he holds me so firmly. I don't like to dance with men who are limp and languid any better than I like to talk with men who mumble."

If Daphne had only spoken to Michael himself in the same vein that she spoke to Miss Georgina, he would have been spared many anxious moments; but she never did. She accepted his invitations willingly, even exuberantly; and after she left Alexandria and went back to the old rectory she welcomed him cordially whenever he motored down to see her. There was a little room with dormer windows, where a small spool bed fitted snugly under the eaves and a Chippendale mirror hung over a lowboy, which he soon found was always ready for him if he could spend the week end at St. Peter's-at-the-Crossroads, instead of merely staying for the Saturday night supper which was so leisurely and so ample a meal. Mamie Belle, the old black servant, always laid a place for him with an alacrity surprising in one of her size; she knew his favorite dishes intuitively, she beamed with pride when he praised them and became effusive when he gave her a quarter for a tip. Dr. Daingerfield conversed with him, gravely and courteously, about crossroads churches, which it transpired were characteristic of colonial days, though it was seldom that rectories were adjacent to these. Mrs. Daingerfield smiled on him, sweetly if wanly, invited him to inspect the jonquils which were her special pride, and played to him on the harp, which was her special preoccupation. And Daphne herself took him to call on her county kin, and sat beside him in the great square pew near the ancient gray font and went walking with him through the quiet woods. But still there was a certain detachment about everything that she and her aunt and uncle and their servant did and said, as if they were pleasantly aware of the obligations of hospitality and yet disinclined to bestow the favors of intimacy. Michael was perpetually conscious of the unspoken words, "So far you may go, but no farther." And, with increasing determination that verged on desperation, he yearned to go farther, and farther still.

17

For it was eight months now since that memorable night when he had met Daphne; and in all that time she had contrived to keep their relationship impersonal. Every time he felt that she was almost within his reach, she escaped him after all. Daphne! Her sponsors in baptism must have been gifted with prophetic vision when they named her that. She constantly eluded him, and he could not run the risk that his own urgency might in the end be his undoing. It was only when he spoke of his work, of his high hopes and vaulting ambitions, that Daphne would sit quietly beside him, slipping her fingers into his, and listen, with an attentiveness that had in it elements of excitement, to his tales of the career which he meant to carve out for himself.

For she too had her dreams of far horizons. Provincial and circumscribed as her existence had been in many ways, the natural barriers which hedged her in had never fettered her spirit or blinded her vision. She too longed to climb high mountains and sail over wide seas, to merge in the throngs of Continental cities and mingle with the teeming millions of China and India. She too could see the distant splendor of Bagdad and Athens, Carcassonne and Granada, with clarity, in detail, as if they were close at hand. She too longed for a life full of change and color, for brief sojourns in strange abiding places, between long journeys. The ancient rectory with its mellow paneling and musty books was a prison for her, just as the austere offices of Boston's best law firm had been a prison for Michael. Only in this lay Michael's opportunity.

For a long time Daphne's rebellion against her surroundings and her eagerness to range the world, had alike been mysterious to Michael; but he had seized upon both with unquestioning avidity, conscious that they were pregnant with promise for himself. Then, on the day when he had pelted down to the rectory to tell her that he had passed his examinations for the Consular Service and that, consequently, his drab days as Mr. Tittmann's secretary were numbered, she had spontaneously spoken to him of much that he had never known before. She had insisted that they should celebrate his success by giving a party, and her aunt and uncle and Mamie Belle had seconded her warmly. So, as there was no telephone at the rectory, she had climbed into his car, and together they had made a circuit of the County, stopping at house after house to invite all her kin to come the following evening at eight o'clock to St. Peter's-at-the-Crossroads. And, as they made their rounds, she had told him, for the first time, something about her parents, in the intervals between accepting hospitality quite as lavish as that which she meant to proffer.

"I want to begin by going to Solomon's Garden and Barren Point, Michael. I always think of the Brockenbroughs and the Tayloes first, when I am going to give a party, because I have a specially tender place for them in my heart. They have always been so wonderful about my father—careful to tell me that he was charming and brilliant and never to say that he was dissolute. You see, he was the black sheep of the family. He ran wild at the University and was expelled and then he ran wild all over King George County and was ostracized. And then he ran away to sea, which, of course, was the very height of wildness. He was forever forging beyond the outposts of civilization. Once when he was knocking around in Argentina, he came across two very old maps in a pawn shop. One was a map of North America and the other was a map of South America, and both of them had 'Parts Unknown' written across a great blank expanse in big black letters. He emptied his pockets to buy those maps because they meant so much to him. Afterward he carried them with him wherever he went and hung them up whenever he had a place to put them. He used to say they fortified him in his resolution that no part of the world should be unknown to *him*."

"Where are they now? They must be very valuable!"

"Oh, I have them. I don't know whether they're valuable or not, but I love them too. They hang in my bedroom. I'll show them to you someday. That is, I mean— Well, my father was very gifted really, much more gifted than Uncle Roger; but he didn't make good use of his talents to become a serious scholar, as Uncle Roger did. He drifted from place to place, not just bumming his way along, but doing odd jobs of all kinds when he could get them, and writing and writing and writing in his spare moments. He didn't write theses and essays and things like that, but little songs and sketches and stories. I have a trunk full of them in the attic. Some of them were published and—some of them were suppressed. I don't think they're so very wicked, that is, if you think of them the way he probably did. But, of course, customs in the Near East and the Straits Settlements are not like those in King George. So the family brought pressure to bear, and just when Father thought he saw the end of hard times, the big newspaper which had ordered a series of articles on Sumatra and Borneo from him canceled the assignment. Father took it very hard, because I was a baby then and he needed money. My mother was a young Irish girl he had met in Singapore, a nursery governess at Government House.

She was very sweet and he was madly in love with her, but she wasn't what the Daingerfields considered a suitable match, and that made more trouble still. I wasn't even born in Virginia. I was born in Bali. I don't often speak of it because Uncle Roger and Aunt Vinnie are so sensitive about it. I—I am afraid my father drank too much, also. But he didn't drink himself to death, as some of the family has said. He died of dengue fever. Then my mother died too. She had nursed him devotedly and, of course, she had to take care of me too, and there was so little money! It was all very dreadful! I wish I could remember what she looked like. There are some old snapshots, but they're very poor. I know, though, she had blue eyes and black hair, too, because my father wrote a poem about them. And *her* name was Daphne. No Daingerfield ever had a name like that—they're all Annes and Marys and Harriets. Aunt Vinnie calls Daphne a 'fancy name,' but she doesn't mean to be unpleasant about it—I was sent back to Virginia in care of the captain of a freighter."

Their arrival at Solomon's Garden interrupted her narrative; and though Michael, intrigued and excited by what she had told him, tried to lure her into saying more later on, she was no longer in the mood for confidences. But she had said enough to build his hopes of winning her higher than they had ever been before. Since they both had a streak of Irish in them, they had at least one bond in common; the bars between the aristocrat and the plebeian, which he had seen as separating them, were knocked down at one blow by her disclosure about her mother; and with such a heritage as she had revealed, it was no wonder that she was straining for liberation. Somehow he would strike off the shackles which bound her, and set her free except from himself——

He had pursued this purpose persistently; yet spring had merged with summer and summer had flowed into fall and still she had continued to retreat to the rectory, eluding every advance that he made. Now, at last, he believed she could do so no longer. His pulses were pounding, his thoughts racing, as he tore along. The spires of Fredericksburg, black against a vivid sky, were only dark pointed pencils in the distance now. No other cities, not even any villages, lay along his route from here on; merely a cluster of houses around a church and a store, and far from the main road, the half-hidden porticoes of a few great mansions located in the dim seclusion which the early landowners had loved; aside from these only the fields and the forests, clothed in the quiescence of autumn, the pastures gray and undulant, the trees unstirring. But the air was soft, permeating even the dead roots with its warmth, as if for one lingering moment summer had

20

come back again; and above the drab ground the heavens slowly spread a panoply of glory. Overhead they were dyed a deep amethyst, which grew more and more glowing as they approached the horizon. At the west, the sun hung suspended in space like a golden ball; at the east, the moon, equi-distant from the earth's rim, no less round, no less huge and radiant, formed a disk of silver, instead. Bathed in their joint glory, the atmosphere took on a supernal quality. Throughout the land which had lain so still, magic was suddenly unleashed.

It was when he became conscious this had happened, that Michael also became conscious of Daphne, standing bare-headed and motionless beyond the wicket gate which led to the churchyard.

CHAPTER 2

HE CAME up to her so quietly that his footsteps made no sound on the spongy soil. Her face was averted from him, her eyes fixed on the twin luminaries which had transfigured the tranquil countryside with their splendor. Her detachment from him seemed more complete than ever before. But even her immobility was provocative, her figure a shining silhou-ette, her hair a mesh of enchantment. As he spoke to her, the very sound of her name seemed like an incantation.

"Daphne!" he whispered. "Daphne—darling!"

She looked around slowly, and met his eyes without even that slight startled interlude which still so often preceded the gaze of untroubled candor with which she regarded him. For an instant, after he had called to her, he feared lest he might have frightened her, looming up so suddenly before her in the dusk. He had not sent word that he was coming; and as it was midweek, not week end, she had all the less reason for expecting him. But she gave no evidence of any sort of fear; rather there seemed to be a certain expectancy about her, an air of recognizing and meeting the inevitable.

"Yes, Michael?" she said. There was a questioning inflec-tion in her voice, but it had no insistence in it. In fact, its very tranquility was a shock to him, and for a moment he groped for words to go with what he had come so confidently to say. "I came out here partly to meet you," she continued, as ready phrases still eluded him, "and partly to look at the sky. I couldn't see it really well from the house, or even from the garden, and it is all so wonderful—the sun and moon

21

together like that, each low in the sky and barely above the earth. I never saw anything like it before! Did you?"

"Yes, once. When father and I were going through the Suez Canal. They shone over the desert, on either side of it. I've never forgotten."

Daphne drew a deep breath. "You never could, could you? Over the desert! And were the sands silver, Michael, or golden? I mean, did you feel the sunshine was the stronger, or the moonlight, as you looked at them?"

"I'm afraid I have forgotten that part. The sunshine, I guess. Sunshine is always stronger than moonlight, isn't it?"

"No, not always. Not moonlight like what we'll have to-night. I think that's stronger—more powerful—than any other light in the world."

"Well, you'll have to show me later on. Remember I'm from Missouri!" He laughed, trying to speak nonchalantly. But his mood was not nonchalant, and he knew hers was not either. "What was it you said when I came up to you, Daphne? That you had come out here partly to meet me? But you didn't know I was coming!"

"Yes, I did. That is, I felt that you would. I can't explain why, but I did. I've felt that way all day long. As if there was some special reason why you should. Is there?"

"Yes. Daphne, I've got my appointment!"

"You've got your appointment!"

"Yes, my appointment as Vice-Consul. In La Paz. I'm leaving for Bolivia by the first boat!"

Again she turned away from him, and again, after she had done so, something about her pose and her immobility struck him as intangible. But this time he was not to be thwarted. He spanned the distance between them in one step and seized her hand.

"Daphne—you know what I'm going to say, don't you? I can't leave you behind—you've got to come with me!"

She did not try to draw away her fingers, but neither did she move her head or answer him. Importunately, he put his free hand on her arm.

"Daphne, look at me! Tell me you understand! Tell me you'll come! I have tried to be patient; I have tried to wait until you were ready to love me! But we can't go on like this forever! And I can't put the world between you and me!"

"Doesn't your career mean more to you than anything else in the world?"

"No—not unless you share it with me! Not unless I have you too! You know you're only putting me off again when

22

you ask me a question like that! Don't be so cool and col-lected, Daphne—or so cruel either!"

"I don't mean to be cruel, and I'm not cool—you know that. As for being collected—one of us must hold back, Michael! If we were both always rushing in where angels fear to tread, what would happen to us?"

"We'd be up among the archangels by now, in the seventh heaven of bliss!"

She laughed, and her tone was not without tenderness as she did so. She had spoken whimsically, just a few mo-ments earlier he had attempted to speak nonchalantly, but with more success. Now, still without freeing her fingers or detaching his hand from her arm, she began to walk slowly through the graveyard and past the church toward the house.

"Uncle Roger and Aunt Vinnie have gone to Solomon's Garden to have supper with General and Mrs. Brocken-brough," she said as they went along. "They didn't seem to share my premonition that you would be down tonight, and I didn't mention it to them. And Mamie Belle has had the misery all day. She's in her own cabin. Strangely enough, she didn't have the premonition either—usually it's she that has them first. Or perhaps she really has been too miserable to bother with premonitions. But anyway, we'll have the eve-ning to ourselves. We can go in and have supper now, if you like, or we can stay outdoors, while it's so lovely, and go in later on. Just as you prefer."

"I'm not hungry," Michael said, almost sullenly.

"Well then, shall we sit in the gazebo? It's so warm, I'm glad I left the big swinging seat there. Of course, we don't have to swing——"

"Daphne, if you think you can put me off tonight by joking——"

"I'm not going to joke with you, Michael. I'm going to talk to you."

"Well, what are you going to say?"

She pushed aside the overhanging ivy at the entrance of the little summerhouse and went in. She did not answer him until she had settled herself imperturbably in the corner of the wide, cushioned settee, and he had taken his place, still somewhat sullenly, beside her.

"I'm going to ask you, first of all, just how you think Uncle Roger and Aunt Vinnie could get along if I left them? She *is* delicate, you know. And he's as impractical as a child of six."

"But great heavens, Daphne, you're not going to stay single all your life so that you can live at St. Peter's-at-the-

Crossroads and look after your Uncle Roger and your Aunt Vinnie!"

"I think, perhaps, I ought to stay somewhere near them, whether I stay single or not. Of course, I want to get married—and of course I want to marry you. But I haven't forgotten that they took me in when I was a forlorn little baby with no place else to go. I haven't forgotten that they scrimped and saved to send me to a good school, even if they couldn't afford to keep me there. I haven't forgotten that they've surrounded me with loving kindness all my life. I think I owe them something in return. Even if I didn't want to be helpful to them, I'd think that. But I'm grateful to them. And I'm fond of them."

"But you're fond of me too!"

Nothing that Daphne had said, nothing that she might say later on, would matter much now that Michael had heard her utter the words, "Of course, I want to get married—and of course, I want to marry you!" His arm was around her now like a band of steel; and if his lips were not pressed, equally hard, against hers, it was only because he realized, even in his exultation, that these must be kept, not for kisses, but for argument, at least a little longer. He had not watched Daphne throughout eight months, like a hawk, for no purpose. He knew that since she had begun to unburden herself to him at last, she must be given free rein to have her say, or he would get nowhere with her in the end. But whatever she said he must be prepared to combat; and that he would never be able to do, if he drank even a little of the heady draught for which he had thirsted so unutterably and which she had so long withheld from him.

"Yes, I'm fond of you too," Daphne answered, with complete simplicity. "But that isn't enough, is it?"

"Enough for what?"

"Enough to get married on."

"I don't know why it isn't."

"Oh—I thought people had to eat and drink and have shelter and wear clothes and keep warm and pay doctors' bills and educate children."

"I'll have a salary."

"How much?"

"Twelve hundred a year, to start with."

"Is that enough?"

"No, I don't suppose it is. But we could manage, somehow. And probably in a year or two I'll have more. I'll be promoted and then I'll get——"

"Well, how much will you get then?"

"Daphne, I never would have believed you'd be so mer-

24

cenary! I thought you knew what it was like to do without!"

"I'm not mercenary and I do know what it means to go without. That's why I'm asking you these questions. If I were a rich girl, I wouldn't have any idea of the value of money. And if I were a mercenary girl, I wouldn't care whether I wrecked your career or not. I'd let you keep your nose to the grindstone to get me what I needed and wanted instead of leaving you free to soar!"

"You won't wreck my career. You'll help me build it."

"I don't feel so sure about that either—even if it weren't for the money, I mean. I think a consul's wife ought to know more than I do. I think she ought to be able to speak languages, for instance—not just a little schoolgirl French, but German and Italian and Spanish. In La Paz, you have to speak Spanish."

"But good gosh, you could learn to speak Spanish!"

"Ye-es. If I didn't have to learn too many other things at the same time. I don't even know how to dress very well. Miss Flippen, who helps me make my clothes, does the best she can, but even so, our combined efforts don't show up very well in Washington, or even in Alexandria. You have to dress for dinner every night on a boat, don't you? Not to mention going out to parties almost every night if you live officially in a capital? Well, I have just two evening dresses to my name, as you ought to know by this time. You've seen me wear them often enough. And they're both nearly a year old. I don't think they'd so much as last until the ship got to La Paz."

"The ship doesn't go to La Paz—that's inland, thirteen thousand feet above sea level. It's the highest capital in the world. The boat goes to Antofagasta, in Chile. From there you have to take the railroad, which is pretty nearly perpendicular."

"Well, you see I didn't know that either. I don't even know geography, which is just as bad as not knowing how to dress. I'd keep making stupid slips like that and embarrassing you before important people. You've lived in Boston, Michael, you're used to girls who know a lot. They don't so much, in Virginia."

"Daphne, darling, I don't care a tinker's damn whether you know how to read and write! You've got more charm in your little finger than any girl I ever saw in Boston has in her whole body!"

"All right, I'll cut off my little finger and let you take that with you to La Paz. I mean to Antofagasta first and then to La Paz. I'd cut off my whole hand if I thought that would do you any good. But I won't cripple *you*."

25

It was going to be harder than he had foreseen. Michael realized that now. He tried a different tack.

"I think my father would help me a little. He always has managed to, somehow. The money part wouldn't be so hard, if he did."

"Then don't you think it would be fairer to take him instead of me? I—I could stay here and—and study geography and Spanish and wait for you until things were a little easier for you and I were a little better prepared to be a credit to you. I wouldn't mind at all, really I wouldn't. I'd be perfectly contented. And your father would jump at the chance of going with you, Michael. I've been thinking about him too, as well as about Uncle Roger and Aunt Vinnie. He must be lonely, terribly lonely. And he's been so wonderful about everything. Resigning from the position he had when your mother died, because he'd promised her on her deathbed he'd take care of you himself. And saving his small capital to send you to a good school and a good college and then making it possible for you to study law as well. That year you and he spent going around the world together is the only one he's been with you much, since you were twelve years old. And he hasn't had anyone else. He's lived all alone and done for himself and gone without and never complained. It isn't as if he were a young man any longer, either. You told me that he was over forty when you were born. That makes him nearly seventy now, doesn't it? Why don't you send him a wire tonight, telling him you're going to La Paz and asking him to go with you? He'd be the happiest man in the United States if you did! He hasn't a thing to tie him in St. Louis, you know he hasn't. I believe if you'd only asked him, he'd have come to live with you in Boston or Washington or anywhere else. Only you never did ask him. And he didn't want to be a nuisance to you or a hindrance. Any more than I——"

She bowed her head. In the moonlight which now coated the landscape with silver like a fine film, Michael could see the expression of her face—tremulous, lovely, sacrificial. His own voice shook as he tried to answer her laughingly.

"Sweetheart, you're mistaken, utterly mistaken, about everything! Why Dad isn't lonely—he's lived by himself so long he'd be frantic inside of a week if he had to put up with anyone else fiddling around him! And as for leaving St. Louis, he'd be like a fish out of water if he did that! He was tickled to death to get back there after we'd been around the world. It was I who wanted to go on tramping, for ever and ever. And that's what you want to do too, you know it is! You know you're simply spellbound at the very sound of the names of places like Samarkand and Isfahan and Casa-

26

blanca. Why, you weren't contented here before I was in the picture at all—you were simply straining to get out of the rectory and out of the country and out of Virginia! You ate up Washington in great big gulps, and as for a place like Berlin or Budapest, you'd try to swallow it hook, bait and sinker. Contented, my hat! You'd cry your eyes out after I was gone! But you'll love La Paz—we'll both love it! It's one of the most picturesque places in the world. And Dad will keep thinking how grand it is that he's able to help us go there, and watch for the mails to come in, with funny postage stamps and queer postmarks on the envelopes."

He stopped abruptly. Daphne had not raised her head, she was still sitting in the same position as when he had begun to talk, with the same expression on her face. Then Michael knew that all his levity had been lost on her, that not a single word he had said had made any difference.

He glanced away from her, looking impatiently out across the garden to the meadows and woodland beyond it. He understood now what she had meant when she said that moonlight could be more powerful than any other light in the world. It was uncanny, this silver radiance that brought the trees into sharp relief against the lustrous sky, and lay as glittering as snow across the fields, and merged into pools of black onyx under the clumps of box. The summerhouse itself was surrounded by bushes and overgrown with ivy; the moon played tricks with its lattice work, making bright designs of it on the flagstones beneath the swinging seat. It was all fantastic and unreal, just as Daphne's arguments and objections were fantastic and unreal; and it was beautiful beyond belief, just as Daphne herself was beautiful beyond belief. Beads of perspiration gathered around his mouth and stood there, and the thought flashed through his mind, "This heat is uncanny too! That's what's the matter with me! Here I am, sitting out in a garden late in November, and instead of being half-frozen, I'm burning up! But tomorrow this unseasonable warmth will be gone, the air will be crisp and I shall be chilly, and then I shall feel sane and natural again." The heat did seem to him like part of these strange supernal patterns; and yet he knew it was not because of the unseasonable warmth that he was burning up, but because of frustration and anger and unappeased desire.

"Daphne," he said at last, trying to speak reasonably and steadily, "you know I love you very much. You know I want you very much. But you don't seem to know that I need you very much too. When I started down here this afternoon I felt as if I couldn't wait to get here. Not only because the chance I'd worked so hard and waited so long for had come

27

at last and I wanted to tell you about it, but because I thought you'd understand what you mean to me. Because I thought you'd turn to me when I told you. Because I didn't dream you'd fail me. Because I thought you'd make this the happiest day of my life."

He paused, and waited for a moment, hoping that she would help him to go on. But the hope was vain.

"Won't you come with me, Daphne?" he asked again.

For a long time she did not stir or speak. Then at last she looked at him.

"No," she said in a low voice. "I can't do that. I've told you why, Michael, already. At least I've tried to. It seems to me you don't understand, either. We don't understand each other. So probably it's better that we shouldn't try to talk about it any more. Because we mustn't quarrel the last time we see each other before you go away. We must part— lovingly. Because we do love each other and both of us do understand that. And though I won't go with you, Michael, I'll wait for you. As long as you want me. As long as I live——"

Her lifted face was close to his as she finished speaking. He bent over her.

"It isn't waiting I want," he said. "Don't you realize that? Don't you realize I've never even kissed you—that is, not in a way that counts. Do you expect me to waste my life and yours—just in waiting?"

His voice was not steady and reasonable any more, it was not even gentle. But if Daphne noticed its sudden harshness she gave no sign of this as she raised her face higher still.

"No one has ever kissed me in a way that counts," she said. "Yet— But I knew you would, of course, before you went away. I knew we'd kiss each other before you left me tonight. I've known all day that was inescapable."

"Inescapable! So you still *want to* escape me!"

"Yes—up to a certain point."

"But you're willing to yield a point at last? Just because I'm part of a pattern made by the moonlight? Just because you've had a presentiment all day that I was coming?"

"Those things do count too, Michael. But they're not what I meant. I meant I knew—I've known for a long while that we belonged to each other—and that sometime——"

What she had said was true. Her very lips were virginal. As they quivered under his own, he felt the full freshness of their undrained sweetness; then he was aware that they were growing warmer, less hesitant, more responsive. She was not eluding him any longer. She lay relaxed in his arms, her soft hair fragrant against his cheek, her soft breast pulsing against

28

his heart. His dazzled brain was shot through by bewildered questions: Should he, after all, have kissed her first and reasoned with her later? Could an argument be both answered and averted by an embrace? Was the last way that he would have dared to seek the only one by which he could win her? He did not know, even now. But he did know that to Daphne the hour seemed as inevitable as it was overwhelming, that in the end, she had not been able to prevail against her fate. While he took, avidly, all that she would give him, he knew that in her prodigality she herself was fulfilled.

PART II

By the Waters of Babylon

CHAPTER 3

MISS GEORGINA FAIRFAX lay prostrate upon her canopied bed in a state of complete collapse.

Her cousin Tyler, who had been hastily summoned by Dr. DuBose, kept leaning forward from the winged chair drawn up at her bedside, to press her limp hand from time to time, and to murmur words of encouragement in her muffled ears. It was not unprecedented for Miss Georgina to collapse. She did so regularly, from shame, every time a Republican was elected to the Presidency of the United States, and from exaltation, after the Biennial Conventions of the Daughters of the Confederacy. Dr. DuBose had learned to cope with these attacks, competently and unaided. Indeed, sometimes Miss Georgina "felt one coming on," and walked over to his office to tell him so; then returned to her own house, undressed, and lay down to await his professional visit.

But this one seemed to be more serious. There had been no planned preliminaries, and it was certainly indicated that a member of the family should be summoned. Tyler happened to be the first with whom the doctor could make connections and Tyler responded promptly, with some twinges of conscience. He had been rather urgent in his insistence that his cousin should call upon a very charming widow who had recently moved to town, apparently without any valid reason. Her name was Mrs. James Crofts, which conveyed nothing to Virginia, and she was a Philadelphian, entirely without Southern affiliations; yet she had seen fit to establish herself in Alexandria. She had bought a house which had originally belonged to one of the Lees but which had later been desecrated as a rooming house, and had spent a great deal of money on its restoration. She had employed a local contractor and a local architect, both of whom were loud in her praises; she had not once quibbled over their estimates, and their bills had been paid by return mail. The local tradesmen were equally enthusiastic about her, for similar reasons. She set an abundant table, and lived in a generally lavish way. The rector of Christ Church was the next to join in the paeans about her; she proved to be an Episcopalian in good standing who went frequently to services and promptly pledged herself to regular donations.

All this could and did occur without even making a dent in Alexandria, socially speaking. But presently the case of Mrs. Crofts began to assume new and alarming aspects. Several prominent bachelors and widowers who had not darkened the door of Christ Church except when weddings or funerals took place there, since anyone could remember, began to develop devout tendencies; and in no time at all they had contrived to be presented to Mrs. Crofts by the rector. Within the week, they had one and all called to pay their respects to her, and the next step was inevitable: They suggested, at first hesitantly and then with mounting insistence, that their mothers, sisters, aunts and cousins should call upon her also.

Tyler Fairfax had been one of the earliest victims and one of the first to urge that the existence of Mrs. Crofts should be recognized. For some time Georgina had succeeded in putting him off. She reminded him that her finances were at low ebb, and confessed that she did not possess a pair of fresh white gloves; without these, she could not, of course, make a formal first visit; it was never done. Tyler endeavored to surmount this difficulty by going straight to the Boston Store and buying two pairs of white gloves for Georgina. But when he presented them to her, she told him that she had caught a bad cold at the meeting of the Garden Club the day before, and throughout the following week she remained in her room, denying herself to all visitors, even to her nearest of kin.

At last Tyler, losing all patience, invaded her stronghold and told her brusquely that as far as he could see she was neither sneezing nor sniffling, much less coughing, and that there was no reason why she should not call on Mrs. Crofts that very afternoon. He carried his unpleasantness so far as to intimate that Georgina had been dishonorable in accepting the gloves if she did not intend to put them to the use for which they were designed. This insinuation, base as it was, had the desired effect. In cool and injured tones, Georgina told him that if he would withdraw, she would rise and dress herself for the ordeal.

Only a few hours had elapsed since this painful scene had taken place. And now here was Georgina back in bed, in the most serious state of collapse Tyler had ever seen. It was no wonder that his conscience smote him. Obviously she had been really ill, or the effort she had made would not have prostrated her so completely. Or else, something had happened during the course of the call to upset her. This contingency was almost equally alarming, and it presented grave potentialities to Tyler's troubled mind. But until his cousin was calmer, he could not question her.

At last he saw signs that her hysteria was abating, and with a few preliminary pats, spoke to her soothingly.

"There, there, Georgina," he said softly. "You are beginning to feel a little better, aren't you? I am very much distressed, indeed I am, to see you in such a state. Was Mrs. Crofts— Did anything unpleasant happen in the course of your call?"

Georgina moaned slightly, but made no other sound until Tyler had repeated his question. Then, with little gasps between her words, she began to speak.

"No—not—not exactly. But I think you should have warned me beforehand, Tyler, what sort of a person Mrs. Crofts is."

"What sort of a person!" he echoed in genuine astonishment. "I'm afraid I do not understand you, Georgina."

"You might have told me that she is a lady. I did not doubt that she was considered one in Philadelphia. But I had no reason to suppose that she would seem so similar to a Southern gentlewoman. Of course, her accent is unfortunate, and she employs white servants, which is regrettable. And I do not approve of dressing gowns, that is, for drawing-room wear— The one that Mrs. Crofts had on was made of gold brocade, about the same color as her hair, which I trust is not dyed. But I am forced to confess that in spite of this frivolous confection, Mrs. Crofts' appearance was, on the whole, ladylike, and her manner left nothing to be desired. No doubt she was very grateful to me for calling, but she was not effusive about it. She offered me tea, and it was served with considerable elegance. While we were drinking it, the butler came in with a telephone message, asking her to dine, informally, at the White House this evening and remain for moving pictures afterward. Of course, it is a calamity to have a Republican as Chief Executive of our country; but still, an invitation to the White House cannot be considered negligible, under any circumstances, and this one seemed to be very cordially, if rather too casually, extended. It moved me to extend one myself. I asked Mrs. Crofts if she would care to come in to tea after our next meeting of the Colonial Dames which, as you know, is to be held here at my house.

I thought it would be a privilege for her to meet some of the members, and with such an arrangement I should not have to prepare two sets of refreshments. After I had asked her, however, I received a severe shock. She smiled rather strangely, and divulged the fact that she is herself a member of the national organization. If I had known that she was a Colonial Dame, I should have called long ago."

"Well, well!" murmured Tyler. He knew that the explanation was inadequate, but at the moment he did not know what else to say. "Of course, it is too bad that Mrs. Crofts has not been more suitably received," he went on after a moment, "but I am sure everyone will hasten to make amends for that now— You are feeling a little better, aren't you, Georgina? Now that you have relieved your mind, I believe your attack will pass. I——"

"Relieved my mind! How can you say such a thing, Tyler? You have not even given me a chance to tell you what has caused my prostration! You have kept me talking all this time about Mrs. Crofts!"

"But I didn't know of anything else that *could* have caused your prostration!" exclaimed Tyler, his bewilderment mounting again. "Do you mean to tell me that you have had another shock this afternoon—besides discovering that Mrs. Crofts is comparable to a Southern gentlewoman and that she belongs to the Colonial Dames?"

"I have been trying to tell you so, Tyler, for the last hour! When I came home, after paying the call, feeling very much exhausted—remember I was not equal to going out in any case and did so only because you insisted——"

"Something has happened *since* you came home?"

"Tyler, if you will only allow me to tell you, instead of interrupting me every minute! I was standing in the vestibule, taking off my new white gloves before touching the doorknob, when a very vulgar noisy boy came rushing up to me with a telegram. I managed to open it, but then I fainted dead away! When Dr. DuBose arrived he had to carry me upstairs!"

Tyler, biting his lips to keep from asking who the telegram had been from and what it had contained, tried to possess his soul in patience.

"The most terrible thing has happened that has occurred in our family since Larry Daingerfield ran away to sea. And this is a case of like father like daughter."

"Has Daphne run away to sea, Georgina?"

"Oh, Tyler, how can you jest at a time like this? Of course, she has not run away to sea. But it amounts to the same thing. She has married that common young man, Michael

33

Trent, whom I have always disliked and distrusted! Married him without ever having been engaged to him—unless there was some sort of a secret understanding between them which, of course, does not count! Without being the recipient of a shower or assembling a trousseau or inviting her kin to the wedding! Indeed, I doubt if there *was* any wedding in the real sense of the word. How could there have been when all this has happened so suddenly? And now on top of everything else she wants to bring him here to stay at this house!"

"Daphne is *married!*" gasped Tyler in his turn. "To Michael Trent! Are you sure?"

"I suppose there is no question that the ceremony, in a way, is legal," moaned Georgina, "since Roger is a clergyman. But the heirlooms which every bride in the family has worn for five generations are *here!* The wedding dress and the second day dress that belonged to Daphne's great-grandmother are both in my attic this very minute. I have never even entrusted the recipe for our bridecake to Vinnie, she is so shiftless. If she were not, she would never have allowed this calamity to occur! Oh, Tyler, I think I shall die of the disgrace!"

"There, there, Georgina! Nothing really disgraceful has happened. It isn't disgraceful to get married."

"No—not exactly. Though you know my feeling that a gentlewoman of real refinement prefers to remain single. However, if two persons enter into the holy estate of matrimony 'reverently, discreetly, advisedly, soberly and in the fear of God' I admit they are acting honorably. But Daphne and this upstart have done nothing of the sort. They have entered into it lightly and unadvisedly, in spite of the warning contained in the prayer book. They have not even remembered the Declaration of Independence."

"The Declaration of Independence!" echoed Tyler, groping for the connection.

"Have you forgotten our great Jefferson's immortal lines about 'a decent regard for the opinions of mankind'? Daphne has shown no decent regard for the opinions of mankind. She has acted impetuously and improperly! She has flown in the face of all our most sacred traditions!"

"Well," said Tyler, clearing his throat. "Well." To a certain degree he shared Georgina's viewpoint, but he was more tolerantly inclined, and he was, moreover, extremely fond of Daphne. "Perhaps there is something we do not quite understand about this," he murmured. "We must not judge her too hastily or too harshly."

"I am only too sure, Tyler, that there are *a great many things* we do not understand! That is the worst of it!

"I mean," said Tyler, growing rather red and speaking more stiffly, "that some unforeseen contingency must have arisen. Why, for instance, does Daphne wish to come here to stay? There must be some special reason——"

"If you can call it a reason——"

With a lingering gesture, suggestive of both reluctance and repugnance, Georgina drew the telegram slowly from under her pillow and permitted it to flutter from her fingers into Tyler's hands. He clutched at the yellow sheet just in time to prevent it from falling to the floor and spread it out before him.

"MICHAEL AND I WERE MARRIED THIS MORNING"

He read, still incredulously:

"MAY WE STAY WITH YOU PENDING DEPARTURE FOR BOLIVIA
                    DAPHNE DAINGERFIELD TRENT"

"Well," said Tyler again. "Well." This time he did not stop with clearing his throat. He swallowed hard. Involuntarily, he began to feel conscious of a certain sympathy for Daphne, and even for Michael. "Poor youngsters!" he thought. "They must be hard-driven to ask for hospitality which they know will be grudgingly given. I suppose there is no money at all. I shall have to look into that without letting Georgina know. They mustn't feel trapped, if I can help it. But I am afraid, somehow, they feel that way already." Aloud he said slowly, "You know, Georgina, that Michael Trent has been trying for almost a year to persuade Daphne to marry him. He seems to have succeeded at last. And apparently his success is connected in some way with the career he is so determined to pursue. He told us weeks ago, you will recall, that he had passed his examinations for the Consular Service. I suppose his appointment to some foreign post was only a matter of time after that. Evidently the appointment has been made without our knowledge. I confess I never thought of such a remote place as Bolivia as a possible post. But I can understand that a young man who was very much in love would not wish to leave his sweetheart behind if he were going so far away."

"Perhaps you can, Tyler, perhaps you can. But remember Daphne has never acknowledged that she was his sweetheart. *I* cannot understand how any well-bred girl would permit an importunate suitor to override her wishes."

"It may be just possible it wasn't necessary to override them," replied Tyler, whose mounting sympathy for Daphne was making him feel more and more exasperated with Georgina. "Perhaps it was only necessary to clarify them. Michael Trent may have done this, somehow. I think Daphne was attracted to him from the beginning and that she is now much attached to him, even though she never has admitted it."

"Then why should she admit it *now?*"

"Good God, Georgina, why shouldn't she? There has to be a breaking point sometime, for almost everyone, and Daphne must have reached hers! You wouldn't have had her send the boy off alone to the ends of the earth, would you, if she wants him? Have you answered her telegram saying that of course they may come to stay here?"

Georgina had begun to cry. "No," she said between sobs. "I haven't answered it. I haven't told her they may come here. I haven't room for them. You know how cramped I am for space! And I think you are very coarse, Tyler, to talk as you do, and very unfeeling as far as I am concerned. I——"

"Certainly you have room for them!" Tyler retorted, interrupting her brusquely. "What is the matter with the guest chamber where Daphne has always slept? It *is* too bad that our grandmother was such a fool as to tear down half her house after the War because she had no slaves left to take care of it. But I think you are using her folly as an excuse for inhospitality once too often! How many rooms do you think a young couple need on their honeymoon? I am going straight out, Georgina, to send Daphne a wire telling her that she and her husband will be welcome!"

Tyler addressed his telegram to both bride and groom and put into it all the cordiality of which he was capable. Indeed, he succeeded so well in making it sound hearty that Michael, reading it over Daphne's shoulder, exclaimed gratefully, "Good for the old codger! I didn't know he had it in him!" But Daphne was not deceived. The message had been a long time coming through; there had been no swift spontaneous response to her own; and it was signed by Cousin Tyler and not by Cousin Georgina. As clearly as if she had been at the bedside, she knew that Cousin Georgina had spent the intervening hours in a state of collapse and that she was the cause of it. The knowledge added another burden to her troubled heart and kept her silent and subdued throughout the drive north.

Michael, singing one rollicking tune after another, and reverting, at regular intervals, to "I'm on My Way to Dublin

36

Bay," hardly noticed her silence. He interrupted himself only to turn and kiss her between each song and to make sure that his shabby plaid robe was tucked firmly about her. The unseasonable heat had passed as quickly as it had come. The roads were frozen into hard ruts, and the wind whistled shrilly through the flapping curtains of the car, which would not fasten tightly enough to keep the sleet from cutting across their faces. They had made an early start, for Michael had an appointment at the State Department that same afternoon; it was essential that they should reach Alexandria before lunch. Michael made good time, pushing the ramshackle little automobile swiftly ahead in spite of the sleet and the frost; he had always contrived to get speed out of it, and he could do so still, though it had reached the stage where it would hardly hold together. He did not mind jerking and jolting, and it did not occur to him that Daphne might find it trying. He drew up dashingly at Miss Georgina's front door and made a breezy entrance, rattling on gaily through a meal which, without his banter, would have been oppressive. Then he kissed Daphne again, quite comprehensively, at the foot of the winding staircase in the presence of Miss Georgina, suggesting that she should get unpacked and settled while he was gone, and departed for Washington in the highest spirits, slamming the front door after him with such gusto that the knocker resounded as loudly as if someone had been rapping on it.

"Michael is apparently not aware that a lady always lies down after lunch," Miss Georgina remarked stiffly, as the iron gate at the foot of the flagstone walk creaked and clicked. She was a good deal shaken by her vicarious experience of his farewell kiss and her voice was reproachful in proportion.

"Why should he be?" Daphne retorted defiantly. "He's never lived with a lady before. And certainly he couldn't judge by Aunt Vinnie, because she lies down practically all the time, when she isn't playing the harp. Besides, I'm not tired. I think his suggestion's a very good one. I'll have our room all in order by the time he gets home."

"The room was in perfect order before you arrived," Miss Georgina said stiffly. "And the towels on the rack nearest the tub are yours and—and your husband's. I hope you will caution him about not going out into the hall without putting on some sort of a dressing gown, and to try the bathroom door to make sure it is locked whenever—whenever he has occasion to enter it. The latch sticks a little.—I shall lie down now, as usual, for an hour, but after my rest I will come to your room. I wish to have a little talk with you."

"Oh, Cousin Georgina, don't be silly! Of course, you know that I meant I would have *our own things* in order in our room! And please don't speak about Michael as if he were a savage! As for 'a little talk'—well it's too late for that now, isn't it, considering that I'm married already?"

"I was referring to some plans for your entertainment," Miss Georgina said, still more crushingly. "I will leave you now, Daphne. And I hope that while I am resting, you will reflect on your very unbecoming manner of addressing me and be prepared to apologize to me on my return. I am afraid that your recent associations have not had the effect of softening your speech."

Certainly she had been very rude, Daphne reflected with genuine regret, as she unbuckled the straps of Michael's Gladstone bag with inexpert fingers. She would willingly say she was sorry; she would prove to Cousin Georgina that she meant it. Meanwhile, sorting clean clothes from soiled ones, her heart sank again. Michael's belongings were in very bad condition. His collars were frayed, his socks had large holes in them, his trousers were shiny at the seams and there were buttons missing from his coat. Well, at least she could mend and press. That would help a good deal. But not enough. She knew he needed a complete outfit, shirts by the dozen, fresh ties, well-cut suits.—As for her own things, they were fresh and whole, but they were very shabby and there were so few of them! When she had finished her unpacking, she sat down at the high old secretary and began to do sad little sums. She continued to do them until Miss Georgina, refreshed by her nap, came in to see her; and after the elderly spinster, somewhat mollified by Daphne's candid contrition, had left her, she went back to her figures again.

She was still bending over them when Michael flung open the door without knocking, and charging across the room, caught her up in his arms. His face, pressed hard against her cheek, was cold with autumn air and wet with rain; but she could feel the glow underlying the hard, ruddy surface, and instantly she was aflame herself, her troubles consumed, her fears forgotten. When Michael released her, lingeringly, it was she, unconsciously, who prolonged the embrace.

"Well, look at the lady learning how to love!" he said jestingly. "I'll say I've an apt pupil!—See, sweetness! I've brought you a little present."

He shrugged swiftly out of his overcoat, picked up a package shaped like a cornucopia, which he had tossed down on the bed as he came in and handed it to Daphne. It crackled under her fingers as she untied the dingy scrap of string with which it was fastened, and fell open to disclose some small shaggy chrysanthemums, already slightly wilted.

"Oh, Michael, how lovely! But you know you shouldn't have done it!"

"I bought them from a pushcart man on the corner of Pennsylvania Avenue and Seventeenth Street. They didn't cost much. I'm afraid they're seconds, not very fresh. But I knew you'd scold me if I went to a florist. And I just had to bring you something."

His voice shook with the impulsion under which he had acted. He put his arm around her again.

"Have you been lonely while I've been gone?" he asked tenderly.

"I've missed you dreadfully, Michael, every minute. But after her rest, Cousin Georgina came in to see me. Of course, she is bristling with reproaches. Yet she really wants to do the right thing by us."

"Just what is the right thing, in her mind?"

"She wants to give a party, a—a sort of wedding reception. She couldn't resist the temptation of saying the last of the mint has just been frozen and that it's still a little early for eggnogs. But it will be a nice party, just the same. She thought next Tuesday would be a good night for it."

"Well, we could squeeze it in then. We don't need to go to New York until Wednesday. We're sailing Thursday. I've just found out."

"Thursday! Of next week?"

"Yes, on the *Santa Laura.*"

"I don't think Cousin Georgina realized we were going so soon. I imagine she thought we would be here about a month. I reckon everyone in Alexandria thought so. She says lots of people are planning to give parties for us, even Mrs. James Crofts, who has only just come here to live. And, of course, all the Fairfaxes expect us to drop in at the different family houses in succession every Sunday after church for drinks, before coming back here for dinner."

"But, good God, darling, if we'd had a month to spare we could have done everything differently!"

"Yes, I know. But Cousin Georgina doesn't.—She's offered to let me wear my great-grandmother's second day dress to the party. She wouldn't have done that unless she were trying hard to be pleasant."

"What is a second day dress, Daphne dear?"

"Oh, Michael, you're awfully ignorant, aren't you, about the South? Almost as ignorant as I am about Bolivia! A second day dress is just what it calls itself—a dress for a bride to wear on the second day. On the first day—her wedding

39

day—of course, she has always worn a white dress and a veil; but a special dress has always been provided, too, for her to wear—afterward. My great-grandmother's is made of garnet-colored grosgrain and there is garnet jewelry to go with it. I've always thought it showed great sensibility to give a bride a dress on purpose for her second day."

"The idea intrigues me," Michael answered with obvious interest. "I didn't realize there was such a survival of the celebration of consummation, anywhere in America. Of course, in the Near East, you still—" He broke off, aware of the deep, spreading flush that always made Daphne doubly enchanting in his eyes; and rather tardily, a thought struck him that had not entered his mind before. "I suppose there's an ancestral wedding dress as well as an ancestral second day dress, isn't there?" he asked. "You'd have worn that too, wouldn't you, if we could have taken time to have a regular wedding? It would have meant a lot to you, wouldn't it, to wear that first, instead of beginning by wearing the second day dress?"

"Yes, it would have meant a lot to me. But there are other things that mean a lot more."

She spoke so steadily that he himself was shaken, and tried, by changing the subject, not to let her know how much.

"Whatever have you done to this room?" he asked glancing around him. "It seemed to me sort of cold and stiff when I brought the bags up. But you've made it look lovely!"

"I've only moved things around a little and lighted the fire and folded the shutters. I—I hope I'll be able to make our room look homelike, Michael, wherever we are."

"Well, if you can make our cabin on the *Santa Laura* look homelike, I'll grant you've got a gift. I've just seen the boat plan."

"Oh, Michael, show it to me!"

He plunged his hand into his pocket and drew out a paper. Daphne unfolded it and spread it over the polished surface of a piecrust table.

"Ours is number four," said Michael, indicating a small rectangle, ringed in red. "It's a minimum fare stateroom. Of course, that's all I'm allowed. I can't kick at that—I expected it. What does appall me a little is the rule about spending money. It seems there's a provision for tipping the deck steward, but no one else. Now why the deck steward, do you suppose? If there was only one provided for, you'd think it would be the table steward or the room steward or the bath steward, because we do have to have food and beds and baths. But we don't really have to have deck chairs. In fact, I don't see how we possibly can."

"We don't need them. We'll walk on the decks a lot and go inside when we have to sit down."

"Well then, let me see.—The table steward and the room steward will have to get at least five dollars apiece from both of us, and they ought to get more—it's a long trip, over two weeks. But we'll say five apiece, that makes twenty. The bath steward five between us, that makes twenty-five——"

"Isn't there a stewardess, too?"

"Oh, gosh, yes, I'd forgotten about her—you know, I've always traveled with Dad before. Well, you'll have to give her five dollars, too; more if you're sick and need any special service."

"I don't believe I'm going to be sick. I'm going to love every minute of it so much that I couldn't be."

"Well, just in case—there's thirty dollars for tips. Then we'll have laundry and I've been cautioned to go easy on that. I heard of one fellow who got into trouble over three pairs of socks on an expense account."

"I'll wash things out in the basin."

"You can't wash out white duck suits in the basin," said Michael, a little grimly. "And that's what I'll have to wear, going through the tropics."

"Have you got any white duck suits, Michael?"

"One or two, left over from my trip around the world. They were pretty well gone, though, when I got home, and I'm not sure just where they are now. I'll have to do some shopping in the morning."

He turned away from her, thrusting his hands into his pockets and jingling his change and keys about. There was an embarrassed silence while both of them stood thinking the same anxious thoughts.

"Perhaps I can get some clothes on credit," he said. "I've never run up bills at the stores here, but I shouldn't wonder if I could. After all, I'm still a Senator's secretary. And there's one good thing, Daphne. I'm not in debt anyway."

"Yes, that's one good thing."

"And I'm going to sell Penelope."

Penelope was his battered Ford, which he loved as much as if it had been alive. Daphne winced.

"Do you have to?"

"Yes, I guess I do. I couldn't take her to La Paz, anyway. Maybe I can get enough for her to cover the tips. Then we can save the money Dad's wired us for some real emergency."

"Oh, and Michael, Cousin Tyler has given us some money too! After you had gone I found a package on the dresser that I hadn't noticed before. It was a little fancy bag with ten twenty-dollar gold pieces in it. He would think it was unsuitable to send us a check, but gold doesn't seem the same to him.

"I can't see the difference. But it's money, anyway. A lot of money! Let's be thankful for that."

"I am thankful. And for Uncle Roger's present too. I know that represents a real sacrifice."

Michael knew it also. He had not been going to St. Peter's-at-the-Crossroads regularly for eight months without learning something about the pitiful economies that were practiced there. He knew how deeply the Daingerfields depended on the garden as a source of food, that a sudden storm or a long drought was a calamity to them. He knew how often fires went unlighted because of the scarcity of wood. He knew how greatly in arrears the rector's small salary always was. Yet after that strange, hushed service, in the chilly church, empty except for the necessary witnesses, at which Roger Daingerfield had pronounced Michael and Daphne man and wife in a voice that shook and broke, he too had given the bride a "little fancy bag" with gold in it. The sum—sixty dollars—had seemed a strange one to Michael until Daphne had told him that her uncle's parishioners had "made up a purse" for him on his sixtieth birthday, and that he had put the money away for the time of bitter need which must accompany his old age. Now his little nest egg was gone in order that the bride whom he had tremulously given in precipitate marriage might not be utterly undowered.

Michael realized that Daphne's reference to her uncle's sacrificial gift was as light as she could contrive to make it, that there was no *arriére-pensée* of reproach for himself in her words; but he flinched a little as she spoke, and again their mutual sense of embarrassment overcame them. Strange, Michael mused inwardly, that the financial adjustment to marriage should make them so self-conscious when the physical adjustment had been so spontaneous. In the triumph of primal possession he had forgotten that Daphne was inherently shy. Now, as he watched her standing mutely beside him, her sudden self-abandonment seemed doubly dazzling to him. He drew her down in a great winged chair, and buried his head in the white breast which was no longer veiled against his kisses.

"Daphne," he said at last, a little brokenly. "I don't know just what I've got you into. I know you're afraid, that you've been afraid all along. That makes what you've done so glorious. Because it means so much to a girl like you to take such a terrific plunge. But I'll never let you down, darling, as long as I live. I'll make everything up to you. I don't see yet just how, but I will. And even if I don't know what I've got you

42

into, I do know that everything will come out all right. I'm sure, I'm sure." Desperately, he added to himself, "I'm not sure; how could I be? When I say I am, it's only bravado, like my whistling and wisecracking and slamming doors! I know we're going to be poor, I know we're going to be homeless, I know we're going to be strangers in a strange land. If I'd left her alone she'd be in the rectory still, remote and safe. She wouldn't have had to come with me, whether she felt it was wise or not, whether she thought it was right or not. She could have waited for me, the way she wanted to." Contrition for his own ruthless urgency, compassion for Daphne's ultimate defenselessness under the force of it, swept over him. Then, as remorse seemed to submerge him, he heard her saying, "I'm not afraid any more. I don't care what you've got me into and I know you'll never let me down. But you haven't got anything to make up to me, Michael, because I'm not sorry for what we've done. I belong to you of my own free will. I couldn't live without you. I thought—beforehand—that I could, but now I know I couldn't. I'll go with you to the ends of the earth and I'll never complain. I don't care how hard things are for us. I don't even care any more whether we've made them hard for someone else. Only promise me that we'll be together—like this—always—always—always——"

Her voice trailed away into silence. The fire flickered softly on the hearth. Except for the sound it made, the shuttered room was steeped in stillness.

CHAPTER 4

"I AM SO sorry. Every room in the Quinta is taken. Abelina doesn't speak or understand much English, so perhaps she couldn't make that clear to you."

"Yes, she did. I don't speak or understand much Spanish, but she did. And I asked her if she wouldn't call you just the same. Because I thought if I could explain to you how desperately my wife and I need a room that maybe you'd manage to stow us in somewhere."

The sprightly, white-haired woman, framed in the doorway of her rose-colored stucco house, looked appraisingly at the insistent young man confronting her from the paved veranda, and then permitted her gaze to wander briefly across the garden. Beyond the gate stood a dilapidated *coche,* the dispirited horses attached to it slumping in their tracks, the *cochero* somnolent on his perch, a drooping figure surrounded by shabby luggage dimly visible on the back seat. The *patrona* had been obliged to steel herself against such spectacles hundreds of times since she became the proprietor of the Quinta Bates. But somehow this time she could not help hesitating; and seizing upon her moment of indecison, the young man began to press his case.

"I've been hearing about the Quinta Bates ever since I left New York," he said eagerly. "I've been told over and over again that the Quinta and the sunsets are the two principal sights of Arequipa. But that's not why I'm so stubborn about staying. I'm not thinking of the sightseeing." He laughed, rather mirthlessly, and then plunged on. "We've had a terrible trip. My wife has been deathly sick all the way down. And if I'd known what it would be like, disembarking at Mollendo, I'd have been sure I couldn't get her off the boat."

"Was it so very bad?"

"Bad! We came up to the roadstead in a heavy fog early yesterday morning. By and by the fog cleared away, but the sea was so rough that we had to stay at anchor for hours. At last lighters were lashed to the *Santa Laura* and we were lowered down to them in baskets. There was a terrific swell and we were drenched to the skin. At last we got to that 'Grand Hotel' made of corrugated iron and set right out in the middle of a sand heap, where the rooms all open out on one long porch and plumbing is practically nonexistent. There was a painting in our room of some sacred subject, very gory and realistic, hanging just opposite the bed. And this morning I woke out of a sound sleep with the feeling something was wrong, and there was my wife sitting up beside me, shaking all over, and looking at the picture with a queer fixed gaze. I looked at it too and it was twitching and turning around before our face and eyes. I don't wonder she shook. It gave me the creeps too."

"There must have been a slight earthquake," remarked Mrs. Bates philosophically; but the tone of her voice was sympathetic, and after a fleeting glance which took in the activities of an Indian woman who was squatting on the veranda languidly occupied with her weaving, the *patrona* looked again in the direction of the drooping figure in the dilapidated *coche*.

"Well, maybe you'd call it slight in Peru, but it was our first one and it looked pretty big to us," Michael retorted, following the direction of the *patrona's* eyes. "It was just barely daylight, but presently we could see the two stiff-backed chairs and the center table in the room twitching, too,

44

and feel the bed beginning to quiver. We sat still—of course there wasn't anything else we could do—and Daphne clung to me tight. She didn't scream or moan or anything like that, but she didn't speak either. I knew she was simply paralyzed with terror."

"Yes. The first experience with an earthquake is apt to be terrifying."

"She's hardly spoken all day, since then. She's kept trying to, but the words just won't come. And she was even sicker on the train than she'd been on the boat. Oh, Mrs. Bates, can't you find some little corner where you can tuck her away? It doesn't matter about me. I can sleep on the lawn or the porch or anywhere! But I can't take Daphne to another filthy hotel, where there isn't any way of making her comfortable or anyone who speaks English or—or any woman who'd be good to her. Do let me go back to the carriage and bring her up!"

"I told you the truth when I said I didn't have a free room, Mr.——?"

"Trent. Michael Trent. I'm the new American Vice-Consul, on my way to La Paz."

"Oh! Well, as I said, Mr. Trent, I haven't a free room. But certainly, under the circumstances, I must try to do something for you and your wife. I will send Pepi out to get the bags and I will show you the upper terrace. You may take Mrs. Trent there for the present. She can rest on the chaise longue, and I will send you some tea. While you are having that, I will see what can be arranged. Perhaps some of my other guests would consent to double up for a night or two. In an emergency, people generally try to be obliging."

She was all alertness. Within ten minutes, the *cochero* had been dismissed, the bags had been brought in, and a well-laden tray had been set carefully down on a little carved table beside the cushioned seat where Michael had deposited Daphne among the pillows. The swarthy serving-woman who had brought up the tea leaned over her solicitously.

"*Un poco de te, Señora?*" she asked in slow guttural Spanish. And as Daphne, whose face was ashen and whose eyes were still closed, did not move or answer, Michael began to pour it out.

"It's piping hot, darling," he said in a voice that he strove to make cheery. "I'm sure, if you could manage to drink a little, you'd feel better. And there are some cunning little cakes too— Do try one of those! You haven't eaten a thing all day."

With an effort that was obviously great, Daphne slowly opened her eyes and tried to sit up. Michael, perching pre-

45

cariously on the edge of the chaise longue, smiled encouragingly and handed her a steaming cup.

"There!" he said, still more heartily. "If you don't say that's the best tea you've had since you left the Rectory, I'll eat my hat!"

"With all those cakes right under your nose? Not to speak of that beautiful thin bread and butter? Why, Michael! You better save your hat to eat until after we get to La Paz."

"She's trying to play up to me," he thought desperately. "She's bound to make me believe she feels better. But she's sick, she's desperately sick still. I wonder if Mrs. Bates can get us a doctor, one that can give her some relief? That doctor on the boat—!" Indignation welled up in Michael as he remembered the helplessness of the ship's surgeon in the face of Daphne's racking nausea. Aloud he only said, "All right, dearest, I will. That is, if you'll eat two or three of the cakes with me now. And about a dozen slices of bread and butter!"

She began to sip the tea slowly, a little color creeping into her face as she did so; but though she took a piece of bread in her hand, she crumpled it between her transparent fingers without tasting it. Then, as if already exhausted by the effort she had made, she leaned back and closed her eyes again.

"Daphne! You've simply got to look! Something wonderful is happening!"

The enthusiasm in his voice roused her from her torpor. She saw, at first vaguely and then with a wonder which stirred her numbed senses, that a miracle seemed to be transfiguring the horizon. All afternoon the sky had been banked with heavy clouds; now these were becoming gradually translucent, and a strange lambency shone behind them. Then they parted slowly, forming in light ephemeral masses above and below three towering mountain peaks which were covered with glittering snow and bathed in rosy color. Gradually the band of radiance mounted; the lower clouds grew gray; the upper ones turned pink; the mountains assumed a still more dazzling quality. And finally the heavens themselves seemed all aflame.

"It's—it's like a celestial vision, isn't it?" Michael muttered, with the trace of bashfulness which often overcomes otherwise bold young men when any reference, however indirect, is made to supernatural things. "Not magical, like the sun and moon that we saw hanging opposite each other above the bare earth in Virginia. But heavenly. I remember that at Garoet, in Java, Father and I used to see sunsets that made me feel the same way—queer and wuzzy inside! But the mountains there couldn't compare with these!"

"My father wrote sonnets about the sunsets in Java," Daphne said slowly. "He and my mother went there too, you know—on their honeymoon. I always hoped——"

"Why, of course, we'll see those together someday, darling! My very next post might be in Java, who knows? But I think these sunsets right here in Arequipa are going to be good enough for our honeymoon, don't you? Though I'm afraid I can't write sonnets about them!"

"People don't have to write poetry, Michael, when they're living it."

"Daphne, do you really feel that way? That we're living it? When you've been so sick and frightened and wretched? After the sea swell and the earthquake and everything?"

"Of course, I do. Those are just passing incidents. They haven't any lasting importance. They slide by like the dreams which never can affect realities."

She smiled and slipped her fingers into his. All her attention was apparently concentrated on the splendor surrounding them; and to both of them, words seemed superfluous as the quietude of the evening continued to infold them. It was their hostess' voice which recalled them to the complications of the situation which had ceased to menace them.

"That sunset is gorgeous, isn't it? But then, nearly all sunsets in Arequipa are gorgeous! And there's no better place to see them than on my upper terrace. I advise you to spend every afternoon here. You've just missed the biweekly train for Puno, so you'll have the benefit of at least three more such spectacles before you can go on to La Paz."

In their absorption, they had not heard the *patrona's* approach. Now, to their astonishment, they saw that she was standing near them, her air of alertness undiminished, a kindly smile on her face.

"Don't move," she said, as Michael sprang to his feet. "I'm happy to tell you that I have everything arranged for you. Lady Brereton, the mother-in-law of the British Minister to Bolivia, Mr. Halliday, has kindly consented to move into her daughter's room. Lady Brereton has been visiting in La Paz, and now she and Mrs. Halliday, who is going with her to Mollendo to see her off, are spending a few days with me at the Quinta before she sails. It is always persons of that type to whom I turn in an emergency. They are much more cooperative than parvenus.—Mrs. Halliday says she can be out of her room within half an hour and within another half hour Abelina can have it ready for reoccupancy. You would like to go to bed as soon as possible, wouldn't you, Mrs. Trent?"

"Please—if I may. And don't think of sending me up any dinner."

"Well—" The *patrona* appeared to ponder for a moment. Then she added impersonally, "Sometimes it is easier to retain food at night than at any other time—that is, if nausea comes from natural causes. Hasn't anyone told you that, Mrs. Trent?"

"No.—You see, I've never taken an ocean voyage before, at least since I've been old enough to remember it. So I don't know much about seasickness. But it can't last much longer, can it? That is, we've been ashore more than twenty-four hours already——"

"There is a sensation not unlike seasickness called *soroche*, which sometimes overcomes travelers in these regions," the *patrona* said, still thoughtfully. "But usually it does not attack its victims until they have reached a higher altitude than this.—And then, of course, there is what is called pernicious vomiting."

"Is that caused by high altitudes, too?" inquired Michael, anxiously.

"No," said the *patrona* smiling faintly. "It may occur in almost any altitude. But it usually yields to time and treatment.—Mr. Trent, I really think your wife is feeling better now that she has rested and has had some tea. Why don't you leave her with me for a little while and go for a stroll around the city? I promise that I will take the best of care of her, and have her all comfortably settled in bed by the time you get back. It would never do for you to arrive at your first post without being able to describe the places where you have stopped along the way! And besides, when you come in, you can give Mrs. Trent so much pleasure by telling her what you have seen—which ought to include the Cathedral and the Compania and the colonnades around the Plaza at least. This is a sleepy old city, but it has a great deal of charm."

"Oh, Michael, please go! I do feel better! And I should love to hear all about Arequipa!"

He protested, though not very vigorously, and then rose with a qualm of conscience at the realization that he was not actually reluctant to go, since Daphne was in such good hands. It was days since he had left her side; and this close confinement had sometimes given him a fettered feeling. At first unconsciously, and then involuntarily, he had missed the hearty masculine companionship with the ship's officers which he had so greatly relished in the course of his trips with his father, the long drinks and late poker games in the smoking room, the competitive sports on the boat deck. There had even been moments when his anxiety and his passion had themselves seemed to him like instruments of enslavement,

48

when he had rebelled against the forces which drove a man to take a mate and then made a victim of him no less than of her; and though he had been ashamed of these moments, he had not been wholly able to escape them. Now that his anxiety and his passion were alike assuaged, he was eager to move about again, swift and unshackled, to see strange sights and encounter peculiar people. Even in Mollendo, he could have forgotten the prevalence of sand and corrugated iron, if he could have wandered freely along the wharfs watching the huge steam cranes lifting and depositing merchandise with ponderous precision; if he could have poked about among the great warehouses where wool and hides and minerals were stacked, awaiting export. And during the drive from the Arequipa station to the Quinta Bates, he had been intrigued by the slim cassock-clad figures on every side and the black-robed women with long soft veils wrapped about their heads and floating away from their faces, who slipped quietly along the silent streets or stood silhouetted against stucco houses that were colored bright blue and rich yellow. He had sensed the pulse of the life beating behind the blank façades of shuttered buildings, as he caught glimpses of flowering patios beyond grilled gates, provocative with the promise of hidden beauty. He had thrilled to the melancholy refrain of reed pipes, played by barefoot Indians meandering along the cobblestone streets, to the raucous commotion in the market place and to the sweet sound of church bells. His personal history, like the history of the world, was repeating itself; his yearning for the unknown was again self-assertive, more demanding, more dominant than ever.

He bent over to kiss his bride with a resurgence of bounding spirits, and then asked the *patrona* the most direct route to the Plaza. She told him, rather tersely, and then watched him swing buoyantly out of sight before she turned again to look at the girl lying on the lounge beside her. Her voice was noticeably softer when she spoke again.

"My dear," she said gently, "would you think I was impertinent if I asked you how long you have been married?"

Daphne's lips parted and then closed again as a wave of color momentarily overspread her white face. But after a moment she answered the *patrona* with complete tranquility.

"No, I should think you were taking a kindly interest in me."

"Very well, then. How long have you been married?"

"I was married just this last fall—not long before Michael and I started for South America. He didn't want to leave me behind, when he found he was coming here."

"I see. But how did you feel about it yourself?"

49

"At first I thought we ought to wait until we had a little more money. We are both poor. But later on I realized that didn't matter—compared to other things. I felt just as he did about it. I couldn't have borne it if he had left me."

"I see," said the *patrona* again, still more gently. "I really do, my child. I couldn't bear to be 'left behind' either, when my husband struck out for a Bolivian mining camp. It was there that I began to take 'paying guests' because we were so short of money. And I managed to make a go of it. Fortunately I always had good health. But it takes a great deal of endurance for a woman to win through strange and trying conditions if she isn't strong physically. And I'm afraid you're feeling very ill."

"Yes, I'm feeling very ill just now. But I'm sure I'll be better before long."

"Mrs. Trent, haven't you thought—that there might be some contributing cause to your illness?"

"Oh, yes! I know I'm going to have a baby. I understood what you meant when you spoke about pernicious vomiting, even though Michael didn't. I overheard my Aunt Vinnie speaking of it once to Mrs. Brockenbrough, a neighbor of ours in Virginia. They were discussing the condition of Honor Bright, Mrs. Brockenbrough's granddaughter, who had recently married Jerry Stone. They said if her 'morning sicking' didn't develop into 'pernicious vomiting' she would be all right; and that was before her little girl, Millie, was born, so I gathered what they were talking about. Well—my morning sickness is developing into pernicious vomiting, isn't it? But I'm sure I'm going to be all right, anyway."

"I hope that you are, my dear. However, now that you do know you are going to have a baby, don't you think you would be wiser to turn back, after all? To go where you can have comfortable surroundings and good care? Because La Paz isn't the best place for——"

"*Now* that I know!" interrupted Daphne. "But, Mrs. Bates, I—I *have* known, from the beginning! I mean—women do, intuitively, don't they? But I haven't told Michael yet. I thought it would be better to wait until we were all nicely settled in La Paz and then—" she caught her hostess' look of incredulity and went on, somewhat defensively, "It didn't occur to Michael that I might have a baby. I mean, he didn't reckon that out—how it would affect us, if I did. He was in love with me and he was bound and determined to marry me. That was all he thought about when—when we did get married. It was all he *could* think about—just then. He couldn't think about risks and consequences."

"But you thought about them!"

50

"Yes, I thought about them. And they frightened me a little at first. That's why I hesitated so long before I finally gave in. I knew I would have to take them—the risks and the consequences both. But later on they ceased to frighten me so much. Because I knew I'd be able to take them. Because I knew I'd have to."

She raised herself from the pillows among which she had been lying and swung her feet slowly to the pavement of the terrace. Then, rather unsteadily, she rose. She swayed a little when at last she managed to stand upright, but as she faced her hostess, she gave the effect, strangely enough, not of instability but of essential steadfastness.

"Michael must be enjoying his stroll," she said conversationally. "He's been gone over an hour. I'm so glad he's having something to divert him at last. This trip has been much harder on him, in lots of ways, than it has on me. He was so sure that everything was going to be easy and pleasant, so unable to face facts as they really were." The *patrona* rose, in her turn, and Daphne laid her fingers lightly on the elder woman's arm. "Didn't Solomon say that there were four things too wonderful for him to understand and that one of these was 'the way of a man with a maid'?" she asked softly. "I was brought up in a rectory, so I read the Bible from cover to cover dozens of times and I seem to remember something of the sort. And Solomon was a very wise man! I'm sure you're very wise too, Mrs. Bates—as well as very kind. But you mustn't try to understand—about Michael and me. You must just accept us the way we are and be our friend, if you will. And not worry about me. Solomon said something about fires and many floods too, and that they couldn't quench love. They won't quench ours—fires and floods, or whatever corresponds to them in Bolivia. At least they won't quench mine. And I believe if a girl can go through them unscathed, she can take a man through them safely with her!"

CHAPTER 5

MR. JEROME BLAKE, the American Consul at La Paz, was an apologetic man with a strong sense of duty and no personal attractions whatsoever. His nose was pointed and shiny, and even redder than his bald head. His beady eyes were obscured by glasses which were continually slipping out of place. His legs were thin and his stomach was protuberant.

But all these handicaps, insurmountable as they appeared, could not disguise the childlike quality of his friendliness. He emanated good will even toward persons who little deserved it, and continued to trust a deceiving world in spite of multitudinous proof that his confidence was misplaced.

For some months he had been struggling along at the Consulate with no help beyond that which he could wring from a stolid Indian clerk who viewed his work with the same impassiveness that he viewed the world at large. This had meant a considerable struggle for Mr. Blake himself, but he had not complained; and when he was finally advised that a vice-consul had been appointed to replace poor Matthews, whose career had terminated so tragically the summer before, his relief on receiving these tidings was shot through with fear lest some of his reports had seemed slipshod to the Chief of the Latin American Division, or lest one of the Congressmen junketing down the West Coast had complained of the paucity of his reception when he took the much vaunted "side trip" to Bolivia. Mr. Blake could not bring himself to believe that succor was being sent to him for the simple reason that he was so desperately in need of it. His optimism, great as it was, did not extend that far. And as he prepared to welcome his new assistant, he fretted inwardly lest his own removal to another post, which should not now be far distant, would be merely a transfer and not a promotion. And on account of Edith, he needed a promotion so desperately——

Not that he had ever blamed Edith. She had been led to hope for better things, when she married him, than he had been able to give her; and now that her mother was so pleasantly settled in Paris, it was perfectly natural that Edith should join Mrs. Brattle there for an extended visit. But if he himself could only have a post in Paris, or anywhere on the Continent for that matter, he might reasonably look forward to a reunion with Edith, whom he loved devotedly and who felt nothing but impatience and irritation, as far as he was concerned. And no wonder! He had been sent, since their marriage, to Barbados, to La Guayra, to Penang, and now to La Paz. And it was only since they reached La Paz that Edith had concluded that she could not stand the Service any longer.

As soon as Jerome Blake had heard of Michael Trent's appointment, he had decided to ask the young man to share his house in the Sopocachi with him. Not that it was much of a house, or likely to prove alluring as such. But it did contain two bedrooms, one of which was now vacant; and if Michael Trent felt disposed to move into this and share expenses—well, it would be less lonely for both of them and it would cut costs considerably. By pooling their resources, they might even be able to buy a little coal and have a fire in the living room occasionally. So far, though the fireplace was rightly regarded as an asset and an ornament to the otherwise nondescript little house, it had stood cold and empty. With coal at eighty dollars a ton, Mr. Blake had simply not been able to manage—though he had heard from Justo, his houseboy, and Celestina, his cook, that coal could sometimes be bootlegged for as little as forty dollars a ton. He did not approve of bootlegging, on general principles, but he was almost prepared to compromise with his conscience in this respect, if such a compromise would assure him the company of Michael Trent.

At all events, it was obviously indicated that he should invite the Vice-Consul to come straight from the station to the Sopocachi; and for days—before his departure, still dazed with sleep, for the Consulate early in the morning, and after his return from it, completely fagged out, late in the evening —he had admonished Justo and Celestina to put the house in order against the coming of his guest. In spite of all these admonitions on his part and a great show of excitement on theirs, it still remained in the same state of dusty clutter in which Edith had left it. At last, despairingly, he tried to do a little cleaning himself, after the members of his modest retinue had departed to their own shacks for the night. But for all his efforts, he was unable to make any impression on the prevailing disorder. He could only hope that Michael Trent would not notice such things much. After all, a great many young men did not.

Intermittently, he also worried lest Michael Trent might be a man of means, able to afford a baroque mansion on the Prado, and bent on spending his leisure in playing bridge for high stakes with wealthy Bolivians. In that case, small economies and stodgy companionship would not appeal to him. But this contingency was not one of those which gave Mr. Blake the greatest concern. It was the Diplomatic, rather than the Consular Service, which the youthful scions of millionaire families usually selected in choosing their career; and exceptions to this rule were so few and far between as to be negligible. Of course, if the new Vice-Consul were a youngster—the dispatch had given no intimation of his age—it was probable that he would prefer tennis at the Club to golf at La Paz Alto; and next to Edith, golf was Jerome Blake's great passion. It would have delighted him to reveal the unique and lofty links to his assistant, to be magnanimous in respect to handicaps until the boy got used to the queer course and the high altitude. But if the more vigorous sport had the greater appeal to him, that could not be helped. In any case, there would doubtless be days when he would be glad to go Dutch treat to the Hipodromo for the races, or to jog down to Obrajes for a game of *sapo*.

On the whole, Mr. Blake's reflections were hopeful. Relief from the pressure of work he would inevitably have, he pondered, looking across the dingy office to the corner where the Indian clerk sat stolidly in front of his high desk, staring into space; and a certain amount of human intercourse would be almost inevitable too. When he opened the door of his nondescript little house in the evening, he would not find it empty as well as cold. Whatever else happened, he would no longer be consumed by the desolate loneliness peculiar to the solitary exile.

The first jolt to his comforting anticipation came in the shape of a second dispatch from the State Department regarding the new Vice-Consul: Mr. Trent, it appeared, had married shortly after his appointment; his bride was accompanying him to his post. Mr. Blake could not suppress a pang of disappointment at these tidings. Bridegrooms, he knew, were apt to be preoccupied; files and invoices were not of paramount importance to them. Probably he would not have as much practical help as he had counted on after all. He would be obliged to continue to drive himself and prod the Indian. And certainly he would not have as much companionship as he had counted upon. Doubtless Mrs. Trent would veto his plan for joint occupancy of the house. He remembered that a similar plan had been proposed to Edith when they first went to La Guayra, and that she had promptly had hysterics. The empty bedroom which might have suited a bachelor so well would be cramped and crowded for a couple. They might be glad to make shift in it for a few days. But at the earliest possible moment they would seek out cozier quarters where they could be by themselves.

Characteristically, he swallowed his own feeling of frustration and redoubled his efforts to make his house presentable. It was certainly very shabby. The "mission" furniture in the living room, the "golden oak" in the dining room—he knew that these were alike hideous. So were the bed of tubular brass, the "chiffonier" and the "vanity" in the dreary little guest chamber. He tried to think of ways in which he could soften their ugliness by supplementing them with native products. There were beautiful things to be had in La Paz— ancient inlaid *baguenos* and carved *armarios*, bright woven textiles, soft furs, hand-hammered silver. Mr. Alonzo Loose, the Minister, had bought quantities of these; the Legation, as a result of his lavish spending, had taken on a sumptuous aspect. But luxuries such as these were not within the limits of Mr. Blake's means. His governmental salary was not supplemented, like that of the fortunate Mr. Loose, by a large income derived from the manufacture of a popular patent medicine.

He was still dwelling with distress upon his inability to mitigate the unattractiveness of his home, when another disturbing telegram came in. It was from the *patrona* of the Quinta Bates; and though Mr. Blake's personal acquaintance with this lady was slight, being limited wholly to the impressions he had gleaned while he and Edith were waiting for the biweekly train between Arequipa and Puno, on their way to La Paz, he attached great weight to her words. Not for nothing had he heard her described, over and over again, as "the best loved woman on the West Coast." He knew her make-up and her mettle; he knew that she was not given to idle fears herself and that she did not nonchalantly scatter alarm to others. Therefore her message was doubly upsetting:

"GREATLY CONCERNED OVER CONDITION MRS. MICHAEL TRENT"—he read with troubled eyes—"URGE PROPER PREPARATION CARE VERY SICK WOMAN ON ARRIVAL TRENTS LA PAZ NEXT MONDAY."

If the *patrona* was concerned about the condition of Mrs. Trent, this must indeed be serious. Yet apparently the bride and groom were planning to continue their journey together with the least possible delay, doubtless—Mr. Blake knew so well how these things worked out—partly because Michael Trent himself was obligated to report at his post at the earliest possible moment and did not want to be separated from his wife, and partly because he simply could not afford to leave her behind. A sojourn at the Quinta Bates necessitated by waiting for the biweekly train, could be charged up against an expense account, and the item would be allowed to stand. But if it were prolonged beyond three days, that would be a different matter. It would have to be paid for out of the vice-consul's own pocket; and Mr. Blake knew, from bitter personal experience, how empty a vice-consul's pockets were likely to be. Still, he believed that Trent would somehow have managed to leave his wife under the watchful eye of Mrs. Bates, no matter how greatly he might miss her and no matter how hard pressed he might be for money, if he had been able to visualize the hardships to which she was about to be subjected.

If young Mrs. Trent were already seriously ill, she would certainly be desperately so by the time she reached La Paz, for the journey from Arequipa was a grueling one. Yet Jerome Blake, who was sympathetic rather than resourceful, could not see how he was to go about the process of making "proper preparations" for her reception under these painful circumstances. He knew nothing positive about conditions in Bolivian hospitals, but he was inclined to believe the worst of them; and even if they had been excellent, it was unthinkable that a girl who did not know a single word of Spanish could be made comfortable in an institution where no one spoke anything else. There was a Methodist Mission in La Paz which maintained a small clinic of spotless cleanliness, though inadequate equipment; but he found, upon inquiry, that every bed in this was filled. He saw nothing for it but to follow his original plan of taking both Mr. and Mrs. Trent directly to his own home.

He had hardly reached this conclusion when still another dispatch reached him. It had been sent from Juliaca, and it was signed by the Marquese Bonatelli, Italian Minister to Bolivia, who had recently been home on leave. Mr. Blake hardly knew this functionary by sight, for their paths very seldom crossed; one was a glass of fashion and a mold of form; the other was a plodder and a drudge. In spite of his general distress over a situation into which it appeared that the Marquese had now been precipitated, Mr. Blake was conscious of momentary and involuntary gratification that something had at last occurred to bring him into the elegant Italian's orbit. But the text of the telegram was certainly very alarming:

"HAVE EXHAUSTED MY SUPPLY OF OXYGEN IN MINISTERING TO NEEDS OF YOUR COUNTRYWOMAN MRS. TRENT. HAVE AMBULANCE WITH PHYSICIAN MEET TRAIN WITHOUT FAIL."

Dimly Mr. Blake remembered that he had heard Mr. Loose jest over the fact that the Italian Minister was a sissy and a "fraidcat," who never traveled without small tanks of oxygen stowed away amongst the multitudinous crested luggage with which he surrounded himself. The Marquese, as far as anyone had heard, had never been attacked by *soroche*, but despite his apparent immunity, he believed in preparedness; wherever he went in the highlands, there did oxygen go also. And for once, at least, it had apparently been fortunate that this was the case. Indeed, Mr. Blake reflected somewhat grimly, it might have been just as well if Mr. Loose himself had been traveling about with small tanks of oxygen, instead of taking his ease, as he had now been doing for several weeks, at Viña del Mar.

Mr. Blake, retracing his steps to the Methodist clinic, and pausing on every street corner to get his breath, tried not to be vindictive about Mr. Loose. He knew the American Minister for exactly what the man was—a lax-living, loud-mouthed politician, who had bought his way to a diplomatic post because he hoped it might prove a steppingstone to the Senate, and who in spite of a fat contribution to the campaign fund had been relegated to Bolivia when he had asked for England; a bully who browbeat his subordinates and gratuitously insulted the reserved and sensitive people to whom he had been sent as "Envoy Extraordinary and Minister Plenipotentiary." Heretofore Mr. Blake had always endeavored to make excuses for his chief, both to himself and to those others who cursed him more or less openly or maintained a conspicuous silence when his name was mentioned. Now he found it hard to do so. If the luxuries of the Legation had only been available for the sick girl, her sufferings might have been assuaged and her chances of recovery enhanced; but there were many reasons, aside from the Minister's temporary absence, why the Legation would not be a suitable place for her.

In his absorption, Mr. Blake had reached the clinic before he realized it. Now having paused again so that he would not pant between his words when he addressed the Director, he entered and stated his errand apologetically.

"I'm so sorry to trouble you again, Dr. Smiley. But it appears that Mrs. Trent, of whom I spoke to you yesterday, is even more seriously ill than I thought." He produced the Marquese's telegram, conscious that in the case of the missionary, the message, rather than the signature, would appear impressive. "You're quite sure you haven't a free bed?"

"Quite sure, Mr. Blake. In fact, we're dreadfully over-crowded already."

"Dear me, dear me— It is sad to think of all the sorrow and sickness there is in the world, isn't it? But I assume you can meet the train and furnish an ambulance?"

"I can meet the train, of course. And I can see that Mrs. Trent is carried on a stretcher to your home. We have no modern ambulance."

"I shall be very grateful; very grateful, indeed, Dr. Smiley, for anything that you may do to help."

He went out into the street again, feeling slightly cheered. Even though there was no bed available at the clinic, Dr. Smiley had promised him that Miss Finch, one of the missionary nurses, would devote as much time to the care of

Mrs. Trent as her other duties would permit. In fact, she would come to his home before the arrival of the travelers, and assure herself that the best possible preparations had been made for the comfort of the invalid. She had been in La Paz for some time already; she got on well with native servants. Dr. Smiley was confident that she would be very helpful.

Mr. Blake felt confident of it too, but again his anxious mind reverted to the condition of his house. It had been painful enough to his pride to think that his assistant was to be a witness to its derelict state, doubly painful that a bride should be brought into it—for Mr. Blake still cherished the sentiment that everything should be made bright and beautiful for a bride. Now that a missionary nurse was to penetrate to its unclean recesses, it seemed almost more than he could bear. Nurses, Mr. Blake reflected, were always "poison neat." Miss Finch would see the dirt in all the corners, and she would probably spend most of her time scrubbing, instead of ministering to the needs of Mrs. Trent.

Meanwhile he felt impelled to do something for the bride himself. In the morning, of course, he would buy flowers and see to it that Celestina placed these about in empty preserve jars. The flowers in La Paz were exquisite, especially the sweet peas, and so cheap that he frequently permitted himself to indulge in a bouquet even when he was all alone. Indeed, a bunch of sweet peas in the middle of a dining-room table lent so much grace and color to his lonely meals that he had come to count upon its presence. This time he proposed to purchase quantities of the fragrant blossoms instead of a single bunch. But flowers, no matter in what profusion, did not seem to him sufficient to show his sympathy for this sick girl whose first journey into a far country had been such a hideous ordeal. Something more substantial, something more enduring, should be offered her as well. He decided to go on a shopping expedition, and since it was growing late, to do so immediately. The dazzling light of midafternoon, reflected from the snowy peaks of Illimani and flooding the city with its brilliance, had already begun to fade. Surely it could not matter much if, for once, he deserted his office and visited some of the slitlike shops, intersecting the thick walls flanking the narrow streets, where such curiously-wrought silver and such rich bright silks were sold.

He had hardly come to his rash decision, when he became aware of the guttural importunities of an Indian vendor who was confronting him. The man cut a colorful figure, the coarse woven poncho flung over his shoulders, and the peaked knitted cap, with long eartabs, being both bright orange, the white strip on his trousers shining in sharp relief against their dark texture. But it was his wares, rather than his costume, which arrested Mr. Blake's attention. For over his arm were folded two tawny vicuña rugs, and these he now extended toward the Consul with a movement which was at one and the same time tempting and insistent.

Involuntarily, Mr. Blake stopped and put out his hand, plunging it into the soft fur. This was extraordinarily fine and silky, and the skin itself, as he touched it, was supple beneath his fingers. He had never owned a vicuña rug, though he knew of hardly a household besides his own in La Paz that did not boast at least two or three of these, used alike as coverings for floors or furniture. Suddenly he visualized the tubular brass bed transfigured by such a spread, its sagging mattress concealed, its tarnished metal redeemed. The sheets which Miss Finch put upon it would be snowy, he felt sure of that; and he would not even put it past her to contrive that his dingy blankets should be washed also before Mrs. Trent's arrival. Then if on top of these, a vicuña rug could be triumphantly overlaid—even though there was no time to have this lined with brocade, according to custom—why, there would be a bed worthy of a bride after all!

Digging his fingers still deeper into the fur, he raised the rug that lay uppermost slightly from the Indian's arm and asked the usual cogent question.

"*Quanto?*"

"*Cinquente,*" the Indian responded with equal brevity.

Mr. Blake had never been good at bargaining. If the man was asking fifty bolivianos for his rug, it was probably worth about forty; and even so, the sum, translated into dollars, was a formidable one. His limp wallet, carefully carried in an inner pocket, contained very little more than that, the office safe, half as much again; and somehow their combined contents must be made to last until his next remittance came in. He did some mental arithmetic, slowly and painfully: There were the wages of Justo and Celestina to be met, ridiculously low, but so eagerly awaited that they must not be even a day in arrears. There was *toquia* to be bought for the kitchen stove, cheap too, but without substance, so that the supply must be constantly renewed—after all, what could one expect, if one used the dried dung of an animal for fuel, instead of cleancut wood or hard heavy coal? There were canned goods, meat and flour to be procured, and the cost of these was exorbitant, for all had to be brought from a great distance. Moreover, if the Trents arrived with their own funds exhausted—as Mr. Blake shrewdly suspected would be the case—he might have to help tide them over until another pay check arrived; and if there were three *patrones,* instead of one, to wait upon, Justo and Celestina might demand higher wages, while certainly more *toquia*, more meat and flour and canned goods would be required.

Mr. Blake could not and would not deceive himself as to any of these phases of the situation, or overlook the fact that the Methodist Mission also operated on a shoestring and that the services of Dr. Smiley and Miss Finch must be recognized and rewarded. And still he continued to stand on the street corner, digging his fingers into the long silky fur of the vicuña rug. When at last he withdrew them, it was to take the limp wallet slowly from his pocket, and to count the fifty bolivianos into the Indian's grubby hand.

He experienced a moment of fleeting fear lest, after the transaction had actually been made, he might be overwhelmed with worry, submerged by a sense of guilt. Instead, he had hardly transferred the rug from the Indian's arm to his own, when a feeling of exaltation swept over him. Timid as he was, he had proved to himself that he could do and dare, even as braver men; poor as he was, he proved to himself that he could experience the pride of possession, even as men who were rich; limited as he was in every way, he had proved to himself that he could indulge in a generous gesture, even as men who do not need to stint themselves in prodigality. As he strode down the street, forgetting that he was short of breath, and pausing only to dispose the rug in neater folds, he became for the first time in his life a personage and a power in his own eyes, with the rug as the symbol of his new freedom and his nascent prestige.

But he was still far from guessing how much more it would come to symbolize in the months that lay ahead.

CHAPTER 6

DAPHNE TRENT lay in the tubular bed under the vicuña rug, her cloud of hair dark against the freshness of her white pillow, the shadows under her long lashes dark against the transparency of her white skin. Between the paroxysms which shook her spasmodically, she lay spent and still, a wasted figure of prostration and immobility. Yet in her was centralized the metamorphosis which had revolutionized the life of Jerome Blake.

In justice, he kept reminding himself, he should have ascribed part of this metamorphosis—perhaps even the major part—to Michael and not to Daphne. In the first place, if Michael had not come to La Paz, Daphne would not have come either—that much was incontestable; so the mere fact of her beneficent presence in the Sopocachi was due to Michael. Moreover, the atmosphere of the office had altered quite as much as the atmosphere of the house; and this improvement, also incontestably, was entirely due to Michael. In spite of his natural anxiety about his bride, he had scarcely seen her shifted from the stretcher at the train to the brass bed in the dingy guest room and safe in the hands of the capable Miss Finch, when he suggested to Mr. Blake that they should go down to the Ayacucho and take a look around the Consulate; and when Blake had reminded him that it was almost closing time at the office in any case, and that they might very well wait until the next morning before getting down to business, he had persisted in his purpose notwithstanding his superior's leniency.

It so happened that Muñoz, the Indian clerk, was just slinking out into the street as they approached the dark doorway over which the shield with the spread eagle was reassuringly fastened; he had mistakenly depended on the Consul's absence throughout the afternoon and had taken the rare occasion for which he doggedly watched to cut short his laboring hours—or rather the hours in which he was supposed to labor. He was recalled to his duties in a voice of authority, which Jerome Blake scarcely recognized for his own as issued from his lips; but he was instinctively aware that his Vice-Consul would despise him for any lack of discipline where this was indicated. With Muñoz, dazed and cowed, at their heels, they mounted the steep dingy steps to the office and Jerome Blake unlocked the door and threw it open with an air into which he endeavored to instill both a note of welcome and a note of bravado. They crossed the threshold, and from that moment onward Michael possessed himself of his surroundings.

It was not that he was lacking in respect to his chief, at least not outwardly; indeed, he deferred to him in all things. He asked whether it would not be a good plan for him to get the dingy stairs scrubbed, the dim brass polished and the dusty windows washed; but when all this had been done once, and the place had assumed aspects of cheerfulness and tidiness which hitherto it had never achieved, he seemed to take it for granted that he was expected to give the orders and supervise the activities destined to maintain it continually in this shining state. He asked if it would not be a good plan for him to run through the files, to familiarize himself with the contents of the office correspondence and accounts; but

61

as he ran through them, he put them in order, and after that he kept them in this condition. He asked if he could not relieve Mr. Blake of the routine letters which did not need to be dictated, casually remarking at the same time that of course he could take dictation whenever the Consul desired to give it to him—for stenography was one of the mysteries he had solved during his apprenticeship with Representative Tittmann; but it presently appeared that he put practically all letters in the routine class and those which Mr. Blake was called upon to dictate were few and far between. He asked if he could not receive callers as they came in, thus protecting Mr. Blake from cranks, bores and bullies; but so undisturbed did Mr. Blake's hours soon become, that it was evident Michael classed ninety per cent of the office visitors in these groups, and intended to shield his chief from them. His high-handed methods gave no offense to the callers in question; on the contrary, from the hearty handshakes which Mr. Blake beheld at a distance and the hearty laughter that came echoing over to his own corner, it was evident that Michael was affording satisfaction alike to touring Americans and resident Bolivians, missionaries and drummers, officials and magnates. Even Muñoz, inside of a week, had become his willing slave. The Indian no longer sat stolidly on his high stool, staring into space; instead, his eyes were turned in the direction of Michael, alert for orders.

Visas, invoices, reports, bills of lading—none of these seemed to balk or disturb the new Vice-Consul. He had acquainted himself beforehand with what should come into Bolivia and what should go out of it, the cost, the importance, the amount of every major export and import. In an unbelievably short time, he not only knew how many Americans were doing business in La Paz and what the nature and extent of their business was, but he had been to call on them all, to assure them that he was entirely at their service and to urge them to take him at his word. Men whom Mr. Blake had hardly known by sight before Michael's arrival, were soon coming continually to the office, calling the boy by his first name and haling him into their homes. Nor did this cordiality apply to the American colony alone; once their first distrust had been assuaged and their first reserve broken down, Bolivians, in their more formal fashion, began to make him welcome also. Language did not long remain a barrier to him, for he sopped up Spanish as a sponge sops up water. He played expert bridge, and he could play it practically all night, and still turn up at the Consulate, full of vim and vigor, on the stroke of nine every morning. The climate had no adverse effect upon him whatsoever; he took an immense amount of exercise without even getting out of breath, and while his golf was good, his tennis was better. He enjoyed excursions to Obrajes, and showed unlimited enthusiasm for *sapo*. He dropped in at the Strangers' Club every day or two and went to the races every week; and wherever he went he became a favorite as well as a familiar figure.

Indubitably he worried about his wife; for while he forged ahead with rapidity which had in it a hidden quality of ruthlessness, she continued to lie under the vicuña rug, shaken by spasms which increased in frequency, struggling harder and harder to breathe, and sinking deeper and deeper down into her well of exhaustion and anguish. Indubitably he worried about his finances; for he had arrived in La Paz literally penniless, and eagerly as he had grasped at Jerome Blake's suggestion of shared expenses, even this fortuitous arrangement did not enable him to keep abreast of the current cost of living. But he seemed to have the happy faculty, in which the Consul himself was so totally lacking, of immersing himself in the preoccupation of the moment to the exclusion of all others. He did not go in a vicious circle from work to worry and back to work again, like his unfortunate superior. As he bent over Daphne, to kiss her good-by in the morning, his heart was wrung at the sight of her suffering; but during the course of his brisk walk to the office, his anxiety became submerged in the intensity and variety of other interests. On market days he never failed to pause in the Plaza San Francisco; and his progress through the adjacent avenues and alleys, where even the sidewalks were strewn with strange foodstuffs and bright crockery, became a mere saunter. The clatter and commotion of the throbbing scene made his own pulse beat more quickly; he felt impelled to become a part of it, in some small way at least, to bicker and barter and banter. The stately trains of llamas, coming in caravans to the capital from distant inland valleys, and bearing as their burdens rice, coca leaves, coffee and bananas, had an irresistible fascination for him; he could not take his eyes off them as they swung slowly past him, mincing, exotic and arrogant. The *Chola* girls, in their brilliant costumes, affected him even more poignantly; when a black-eyed, brown-skinned half-breed, still young and comely, brushed by him, he had an almost irresistible impulse to lay his hand on the puffed sleeves of her braided velvet jacket or on the full folds of her short brocade skirt. The hats, fashioned like undersized derbies, which these girls wore perched high on their glossy heads, intrigued him especially; he observed that though these had no visible fastenings, they never blew off, no matter how shrilly the wind whistled through the narrow streets.

"I'm sure they're kept on by suction from within," he remarked over and over again, jocosely, to Jerome. "I suppose the heads of those girls are complete vacuums."

Jerome knew that if it had been Edith who was lying sick almost unto death in the Sopocachi, he himself would not have been able to give so much as a passing glance at *Chola* girls, much less to jest about them; he would have gone by them with unseeing eyes, his thoughts still concentrated on the cold clean room which he had left behind him. Indeed, he did this even though it was Daphne and not Edith who was lying in the room. Nevertheless he did not doubt Michael's devotion to Daphne; he knew that he and the youngster were made of different stuff, and that the youngster's stuff had the stronger fiber. He did not question which had the finer.

At the office, no less than on the Plaza, Michael threw himself with intensity into his surroundings. Probably that was why he so quickly seemed to have taken possession of the headquarters where he was merely a subordinate. Jerome had never been able to get up any real interest in dull commodities like cement, linoleum, wickerware and foodchoppers, though he recognized that the distribution of these in Bolivia was, in a general way, advantageous to American business. Michael, on the other hand, seemed to get a thrill out of the very thought that Bolivians might become the beneficiaries of such products; and when it came to a question of sewing machines, automobiles and plumbing supplies, he waxed vociferously enthusiastic. The most intricate questions concerning expenses, estates and extraditions with which the Consulate was called upon to cope, were quickly unraveled under his strong and skillful touch. The driest letter, as he tapped it out on a new typewriter, the arrival of which had marked a red-letter day for him, took on punch and individuality. He wrote vigorously:

"CONSULATE OF
THE UNITED STATES OF AMERICA
LA PAZ, BOLIVIA

January 14, 19___

New York Cotton Exchange
  60 Beaver Street
    New York, N. Y.
SIRS:
  Reference is made to your letter of October 20, inquiring regarding cotton production in Bolivia.

Cotton has not been grown in Bolivia in important quantities. The lack of adequate means of transportation between the growing regions and the principal centers of population has prevented increases in production. However, a project for the installation of a cotton mill in the neighborhood of Santa Cruz in the region where cotton is planted, if it is realized might well mean substantial increases in Bolivia's yearly cotton crop.

Cotton is planted in Bolivia during the spring months (September and October) and harvested in the fall (March, April, May). The cotton season may vary to some extent according to the region of the country where the crop is planted.

Cotton is not exported from Bolivia and the figure of 20,000 pounds is the amount of domestic raw cotton consumed by the only cotton mill in Bolivia during the year ended June 30, 19__ and may be taken as the amount of domestic production of lint cotton during the current season.

> Very truly yours,
> MICHAEL TRENT,
> American Vice-Consul."

Sometimes, when he came in late at night, he dropped easily down, without taking off his overcoat, into one of the mission chairs drawn stiffly up on either side of the inadequate little living room fireplace, lighted a well-seasoned pipe, and chatted with his chief, who always waited up for him. These conversations usually took place on the rare occasions when Michael had lost at cards, instead of leaving a party in funds, as he almost constantly contrived to do. Among Jerome Blake's many anxieties were those aroused by his Vice-Consul's gambling proclivities; the Consul was convinced that if Dr. Smiley and Miss Finch realized they were being paid from the proceeds of Michael's winnings over the bridge table and on the race track, their missionary souls would revolt against such tainted money. On the other hand, if Michael did not win, they would not be paid at all, and that was a cause of even deeper concern. He tried not to let the youngster see how worried he was on the occasions of these midnight conferences when Michael himself broached the subject of money.

"I don't see how those bigwigs in the State Department think a man and his wife can get along on twelve hundred a year in a place like La Paz, where the food comes in by the pint and the fuel by the ounce. They must expect us to live on the interest of our debts."

"Those bigwigs in the State Department take it for granted that when a fellow lets himself in for a consular appointment in La Paz or anywhere else, he has a private income to supplement the twelve hundred. They don't think in any other terms. If they did, they wouldn't and couldn't be bigwigs in the State Department. But no matter what they thought, it wouldn't do any good unless Congress appropriated more money for consular salaries. You know that as well as I do."

"But hell's bells, Congress is always appropriating money for pine blister and grasshoppers and boll weevils—millions and millions! Why shouldn't it appropriate something for consuls?"

"Maybe it will someday. But these changes take time."

"Time! Hasn't Congress had time, in a hundred and fifty years, to find out that a consul needs to eat?" Michael reached for a dog-eared pamphlet entitled "The American Consular Service," which lay on the golden oak table beside him, and began to read in a singsong voice:

" 'The Consular Service is charged with the duty of protecting the interests of the Government and of American citizens abroad and with extending and protecting American trade in foreign countries. . . .

" 'An exceptional opportunity is offered by the Consular Service to young men who wish to serve their country abroad and assist in the protection of the interests of the Government and of their citizens, in the expansion of American trade, and in the promotion of good relations with the peoples of other countries. . . .

" 'Consular officers are expected to endeavor to maintain and promote all the rightful interests of American citizens and to protect them in all privileges provided for by treaty or conceded by usage; . . . . to ship, discharge, and under certain conditions, maintain and send American seamen to the United States; to settle disputes between masters and seamen of American vessels; . . . . to act as official witnesses to marriages of American citizens abroad; to aid in the enforcement of the immigration laws . . . .; to protect the health of our seaports . . . . ; and to take depositions and perform other acts which notaries public in the United States are authorized or required to perform.

" 'When disasters occur in his consular district, an officer is required to report to the Department of State whether Americans or American interests have been affected in any way, and to point out any steps which should be taken by those interested. . . .

" 'A consular officer's duties bring him into contact with the leaders in his consular district in every important activity, governmental, professional, commercial, and otherwise. As the representative of his Government, he is expected to maintain a good position in the community, and to that end his adaptibility, balance, tact, and integrity are important factors in his success.' "

He closed the pamphlet and threw it back on the table. "And that's only the beginning of what a consul's supposed to do and be! Isn't he worth as much to the Government as a boll weevil?"

"It isn't the boll weevil that's important to the Government," Jerome said patiently. "It's the cotton and the cotton growers."

"Well, isn't he as important as the cotton growers? I'd say he was! But as far as I can make out, there's only one Congressman that's consul-conscious! My old friend Tittmann certainly wasn't—Conservation of Wild Life Resources and Cross Licensing and Pooling of Patents were his specialties! But there's a man from Massachusetts, named John Jacob Rogers, who seems to have us on his mind. He knows we're getting a raw deal."

"Yes. I knew he'd introduced a bill to merge the Consular Service with the Diplomatic Service and call the combination the American Foreign Service. I understand that if it had gone through, there would have been better salaries, and post allowances, and even living quarters provided in some places. Also a sort of shuttling back and forth, which would have been all to the good as far as the morale is concerned. For instance, a vice-consul in Bahia might have waked up some morning to find he'd been appointed a third secretary in Berlin, with all the perquisites of a diplomatic position and, on the other hand, a secretary in some soft spot like Madrid might have waked up some morning to find he'd been appointed a consul in Bombay and that he'd got to get down to making out ship's papers and fighting cholera epidemics instead of bowing and scraping around a palace."

"Rogers thinks all appointments, even to the highest offices, should go to career men and that politics should be wiped out of the picture entirely."

"Speaking of political appointees—you haven't happened to hear, have you, when our own revered Minister is getting back from his latest little holiday?"

"No, but it's bound to be soon now. He's been gone seven weeks already."

Michael laughed, rather grimly, and rose, tapping his pipe against the side of the fireplace, and emptying the bowl into the cheerless hearth. "Well, the longer he stays away, the better suited I'll be," he remarked. "It's nothing to me that the entire annual leave is supposed to be thirty days, and that the Honorable Alonzo Loose hasn't been at his post for that long since I've been here! By the way, has that distinguished colleague of his, the winsome wop, been around this afternoon with one of his customary offerings?"

"Yes, with some very beautiful roses and some Ecuadorian pineapple. Daphne's been holding one of the flowers in her hand, and she sipped a few teaspoonfuls of the juice. Miss Finch thinks even that will help."

Michael did not answer immediately. It had been evident, from the beginning, that Daphne had made a profound impression on the Marquese during the course of the momentous journey when he had emptied his precious oxygen tanks in her behalf. Since then he had hardly let a day go by without calling in person to inquire for her, his flexible cane tucked jauntily under his arm, his well-gloved hands filled with bouquets and tidbits. Michael resented both the personal aspects of the Italian Minister's interest and the fact that Bonatelli was able to give it substance in the form of Asti Spumonti, tropical fruits and exotic blooms which he himself could not afford to purchase. Still, it was undeniable both that Daphne derived pleasure and benefit from these offerings, of which it would have been selfish to deprive her, and that the Marquese's notice had had wide repercussions of which it would have been impolitic to deprive himself. It was possible, of course, that Lady Brereton's sympathy might have taken concrete form in any case, since this had already been aroused in Arequipa; and the favor of the British Legation, however lightly bestowed, was never negligible anywhere. But Lady Brereton, though adequate in her intentions, had not begun to be as assiduous in them as Bonatelli, nor had she heralded the reasons for them half as widely. To the Marquese, more than to any one person in La Paz besides himself, Michael owed much of his social success there; and he was not unmindful of this nor of the far-reaching consequences which it might have.

"I'm very glad," he said without much heartiness, shivering as he spoke. Then he added, "Gosh, but it's cold! How much more money did you say I'd got to win before we could buy half a ton of bootleg coal?"

"I didn't say. You know very well, Michael, that I don't approve of your gambling. But——"

"But you realize that if I don't gamble, we're going to
68

starve and freeze, so you don't make too many objections! That's the long and the short of the matter, isn't it? Listen, Mr. Blake—you don't suppose Daphne is as cold as we are, do you? I can't get her to talk about it.—Of course, she doesn't talk much anyway. But when I came home to lunch today I was afraid——"

Jerome Blake followed the train of thought through to its unwelcome end. In the middle of the day, Daphne was feeling her very worst; so it had been agreed that Michael should always go home at that time, though it had never been Mr. Blake's practice to do so. He had feared that Celestina might rebel at the preparation of an extra meal, and had formed a habit of carrying a small Thermos jar filled with lukewarm coffee and some tough sandwiches to the office with him. But he soon observed that Celestina, like everyone else, was fawning at Michael's feet, in spite of the fact—Jerome did not realize that it was because of this!—that Michael had sent several dishes back to the kitchen with the curt comment that they were unfit for consumption, and had threatened to dock her wages every time she burnt anything. Her cookery had now taken a distinct turn for the better, and she especially exerted herself to make Michael's midday meal attractive and appetizing. But in spite of all her efforts and of Michael's own faculty for throwing off trouble, these noontime interludes must inevitably be extremely painful. Jerome could understand that, though he was not a witness to them, as he continued to eat his dreary picnic lunch at the office in order that Michael might not feel hurried about getting back to work, if Daphne needed him.

"I suppose she's bound to be cold, when she's so undernourished," he admitted, after duly pondering the question, "even if her room weren't cold anyway. I know Miss Finch does the very best she can, with hot water bottles and blankets—and, of course, the weather isn't really severe now. But when winter comes——"

" 'When winter comes, can spring be far behind?' " quoted Michael bitterly. "I'll say it can! Listen, Mr. Blake—how long can a woman hold out when she's cold all the time and suffering all the time and doesn't eat anything? There's a limit, isn't there, to the lengths she can go?"

So it was there after all, the dread with which he himself was obsessed, but from which he had supposed Michael was mercifully more or less free. The consciousness that the boy was suffering too came as a shock to Jerome Blake; and as if he had read the Consul's thoughts, Michael broke into impetuous speech.

"You thought I didn't worry much, I suppose? Because I

get out such complete reports and never add up my invoices wrong! Because I take in the sights of the city! Because I play bridge half the night and spend every Sunday afternoon at the race track! Good God, can't you see that the better I do my work the quicker I'll have a chance of getting Daphne out of here? That is, if she doesn't die before I can get her out! Can't you see that if I never have any exercise or fresh air or diversion, I'll go under too? Can't you see that every boliviano I win represents a lump or two of that coal we haven't bought yet? Can't you see that I know I've dragged my wife down to hell after I'd promised her that everything would be all right, that I'd cherish her and shield her and comfort her if she'd only trust herself to me? And what did I do instead? I got her with child and carried her off to the ends of the earth so that she could starve to death by inches!"

He strode from the room, slamming the door after him. Jerome Blake sat still, fettered with mounting fear, torn with inner tumult. Day was breaking before he rose at last from his Morris chair and tiptoed across the floor in his stocking feet. When, still shaken and white-faced, he tried to talk to his Vice-Consul the next day, Michael met his eyes with an expression of defiance; it was plain that he would brook no reference to the scene which had taken place the night before. But that afternoon, as he left the office, he submitted to his chief a résumé of the latest outbreak of hostilities between the Bolivians and the Paraguayans in the Chaco to which Mr. Blake felt not a word need be added before it was slipped into a diplomatic pouch; and when he came home at two o'clock the next morning from a soiree at the Brazilian Legation, he brought with him the money to buy a ton of coal.

Jerome Blake, reflecting on all this, admitted freely to himself that Michael had indeed brought great changes both into his design for living and into his outlook on life. But in spite of all that Michael had done, in the last analysis it was still Daphne who had wrought the major metamorphosis.

Every day, when he returned from the office, he went into her room and sat at her bedside until dinnertime. Without even a passing regret, he gave up golf in order that he might be able to spend these hours with her. True, it had once meant a great deal to him. But it had come to mean nothing at all. Without a second thought, he declined the invitations which he now received far more frequently than at any previous time in his consular career. He was not so dull that he did not recognize the fact that these invitations were due, indirectly, to Michael, since no one could be so flagrantly lacking in savoir-faire as to disregard the existence of the American Consul entirely, if the American Vice-Consul were to be made the recipient of countless flattering favors. He felt no resentment over this phase of the situation, though he was not misled by it. Instead, it seemed to him right and fitting that Michael, who had such great social graces, should show himself from one end of the Prado promenade to the other, while he, Jerome, kept vigil beside Michael's wife.

It was true, as Michael had said, that Daphne spoke very little; there were days when she did not speak at all. But she never failed to look up at Jerome, with a faint smile, when he came into her room, or to stretch out her transparent fingers in farewell when he left it. Presently, he became aware that she looked forward to his coming and regretted his departure, that there was something steadying and solacing in his presence. It was the first time in his life that anyone had ever given him such a feeling. His mother, whom he had worshiped as a child, had not done so, nor had Edith, whom he still adored. He ceased to see himself as they had done, beady-eyed and sharp-nosed, thin-legged and big-bellied, and began to see himself as he slowly sensed that Daphne saw him. Looking straight past his ridiculous physique she beheld him not as a monstrosity, but as a courteous and considerate host, a faithful and friendly companion, a fellow countryman in a far country, an ally and a sympathizer.

Although she did not talk to him, he soon found it easy to talk to her. He never forgot to begin by praising Michael; and he watched, with a stab of excitement, for the light that came into her dark-ringed eyes as he did so. There was a great deal that he could say in Michael's favor; but even if there had not been, he would have extended his remarks on this subject indefinitely, for the mere purpose of watching that strange luminance, which he himself had never caused to come into any woman's face. After he had said all he possibly could about Michael, he went on to tell her the news of the day—what he had read in the papers, what he had seen on the streets, what had come up at the office. Eventually, when he could think of nothing further to tell her, he read aloud to her, either from the *Saturday Evening Post*, to which he always subscribed, no matter how low his finances were running, or from a battered volume of Robert Browning's poems, which had been left in the house by a previous occupant.

By the time he had begun to grow hoarse from reading, Daphne had usually begun to grow drowsy. It was then that Miss Finch watched for her chance to slip a few spoonfuls of "nourishment"—as she invariably called it—between Daphne's pale lips. The evening was her best time, and she also seemed a little better on alternate days. Jerome Blake

71

prayed for the coming of evening, and of alternate days, on Daphne's account.

After he had had his dinner, which was still frequently a solitary one because Michael was out so much, he talked to Miss Finch about Daphne before the nurse went off duty for the night. Dr. Smiley was so hard pressed all the time, at the hospital, in the countryside, and here and there about the city, that he could not often pause for much conversation. Indeed, he did not come to see Daphne every day. He said there was nothing much he could do for her at the present stage, and that Miss Finch would advise him immediately of any change for the worse in her condition. Personally, he hoped that when a change did come, it would be for the better. Very often, even in bad cases of pernicious vomiting, he had seen such a change take place during the fifth month.

"The fifth month!" Jerome Blake had echoed in bewilderment.

"Yes. When the quickening begins, you know. The general system seems to adjust itself to pregnancy, about that time. Often quite suddenly and satisfactorily."

Mr. Blake did not know, never having heard much about quickening, which to him was just one of those Biblical expressions not much used in genteel modern society. Besides, he felt the fifth month to be intolerably remote and said so.

"Won't she starve to death before then?"

"Well—she was very slender, of course, to start with. In this case that was a great disadvantage.—I've seen plump women live on their own fat for a long time. But she has a great deal of will power—will power and courage. Besides, she loves her husband and she wants the baby. All that helps. Really, Mr. Blake, there's no immediate cause for concern. If her heart holds out and she doesn't catch cold, she'll be quite all right yet. And we mustn't meet trouble halfway or cross bridges until we come to them."

Mr. Blake hoped that Miss Finch had told Daphne about the quickening, and that the possibility of earlier relief than she had counted upon might give her fresh courage. He longed to speak to her about it himself, on the chance that the nurse had not; but he could not bring himself to discuss it with either of them. He did, however, finally broach the subject to Michael in the course of one of their midnight conferences.

"Dr. Smiley thinks that Daphne may begin to feel better by April or May," he said hesitatingly, as Michael started to tap his pipe against the fireplace, preparatory to leaving the living room.

"By April or May!" Michael exclaimed, turning around in

astonishment. "Why April or May? That's when the weather gets really cold, isn't it? Not that I believe she'll mind a little extra cold, any more than she's minded these frightful thunderstorms we've been having! They shake the whole house, just like an earthquake."

"Yes, I know. Well, you see—Dr. Smiley says that when the quickening begins—about the fifth month—and I thought——"

Mr. Blake blushed profusely in the dim light. He felt like an evil-minded old gossip who had taken obscene delight in counting off months by the finger method. And from the look on Michael's face, the Consul feared that the boy regarded him in the same way. He too had colored, as Mr. Blake had never seen him color before, quickly and violently. It was a moment or two before he spoke; and when he did so, it was in a hard voice through lips closed in a hard line.

"Well, let's hope Dr. Smiley is right," he said tersely, and walked away without another word.

When Jerome went into Daphne's room the next afternoon he found, to his amazement and delight, that she was already better than he had ever seen her. There were two pillows under her head, and though there was no real color in her face, it had partially lost its look of transparency. And she not only smiled at him. She spoke to him.

"I have some news for you today," she said joyously. "Michael brought home a can of clam chowder with him last night. One of his big business friends gave it to him. He opened the can right away and heated the chowder while he was getting undressed, and kept breaking crackers into it and talking to me all the time he was feeding it to me. I was so sleepy by the time I had finished that I don't remember anything after he took the bowl away from me and put his arm around me. And when I woke up this morning he was looking down at me and laughing, and telling me I had been a good girl at last and hadn't spit up any of my supper."

Daphne laughed herself at the memory of this speech, and Jerome, his conscience smiting him because of his injustice to Michael laughed with her.

"I am sure this is the beginning of the end," Daphne went on cheerfully. "The end of all the awful sickness, I mean. It really has been awful, hasn't it? I know I never could have stood it so long, if it hadn't been for you and Michael. You see, when he's left me in the morning I've kept saying to myself, 'Somehow I can stand this until Michael gets home at noon.' And then, when he's left me after he's had his lunch, I've kept saying, 'Somehow I can stand this until

73

Jerome comes in to read to me.'—You don't mind if I call you Jerome, do you, even if you are Michael's chief?—And then, when you've left me at dinnertime, I've kept saying, 'Now I can stand this until Michael comes to bed.' Each time it's been only a little while that I've had to stand it alone.— I say alone, because though Miss Finch is kind and all that, she doesn't really count. It's men who count at a time like this—men like you and Michael."

Men like Michael and himself! In her gratitude, in her generosity, she was coupling him with Michael! It was almost more than Jerome could bear.

"Perhaps you ought not to try to talk any more, just now," he said, speaking a little gruffly in an attempt to hide his feelings.

"Oh, yes, I ought! I want to talk. I want to talk about hundreds of things, to make up for all these weeks of silence. You won't stop coming in to see me every day, will you, just because I'm better? Of course, pretty soon I'll be well enough to get up, and then you'll take me out to see La Paz. Michael says it's a wonderful city, that it reminds him of clustered jewels lying in a deep agate bowl. In a way, I feel as if I knew what it is like already, from his descriptions and from the presents he's brought me. Of course, the presents have been just little things he's got at the market.—In fact he said he'd found most of them at a fete that was called The Feast of Little Things— the *Fiesta de las Alacitas*—is that the way you pronounce it? And the Italian Minister has brought me lovely presents too. But neither Michael nor the Marquese has given me anything to compare with this rug."

She stretched out her hands and pulled up the vicuña rug. Its fawn-colored fur bushed out, soft and silky, against the bed-jacket of featherstitched cashmere which she was wearing and which was blue like her eyes. Then she patted the rug into place, and ran her fingers over it, smoothing it down.

"It's beautiful," she said softly. "Beautiful. I don't know anyone except a man like you, Jerome, who would have thought of giving me anything like this. I'll take it with me, wherever I go, as long as I live, as a reminder of your loving-kindness and all that it has meant to me."

When Jerome Blake left Daphne's side that evening, he went into his own room and shut the door and locked it. Then he knelt down beside the empty bed which had once been Edith's, and gave thanks because Michael Trent had brought his young wife to La Paz, and that she had invested with grace and glory his own sacrificial gift.

CHAPTER 7

DURING THE year and a half which he had spent—intermittently—at La Paz, the Honorable Alonzo Loose, Envoy
Extraordinary and Minister Plenipotentiary of the United
States of America to the Republic of Bolivia, had seldom
darkened the door of any member of his staff. To be sure,
his staff had consisted most of the time only of Jerome Blake,
except for the brief period when Stillman Matthews had been
Vice-Consul in La Paz; and Stillman Matthews had lived
with the Blakes. So there had been very little latitude as to
the hearthstones to which the Minister might have condescended. He had gone once to a dreadful Sunday dinner with
the Blakes and the spindling young Vice-Consul who was
their "paying guest"—the Honorable Alonzo sneered as he
recalled the term—when the rest of the company had consisted of Dr. and Mrs. Smiley and two elderly spinsters—the
cousins of a Congressman from Kansas—who were touring
South America in search of ruins, but who, Mr. Loose
thought grimly, had only to look in their own mirrors to
achieve this end. The occasion had been far from successful.
Mrs. Blake had already reached the peevish and pouting stage
which preceded her departure for Paris and made no effort
to ingratiate herself with her visitors. Mr. Blake, ill at ease
over her attitude, miscalculated his measurements when he
mixed the cocktails, and in his agitation did not even notice
that he had used one part gin and two parts vermouth. Dr.
and Mrs. Smiley were total abstainers in any case, so they
did not suffer through this blunder; but the Honorable Alonzo
who liked his liquor, took it as a personal affront. If the
drinks were bad, however, the food was even worse; Celestina had never turned out a more horrible repast, which was
saying a good deal; and as Mr. Loose was addicted to
costly viands no less than to rare vintages, the tepid soup,
the tough beef, the unflavored vegetables and the burnt pud-
ding seemed to him like insult added to injury. Stillman
Matthews, as usual, shivered and stammered; the interval
which elapsed between the time when he began one of his
rare remarks but before he actually achieved a sentence,
became an endurance test not only for himself but for everyone else at the table. The elderly spinsters gushed about
Cuzco and Tiahuanaco. Before the rest of the group had

75

finished the muddy coffee, which Justo, clad in a soiled jacket and ragged trousers, offered them on a sloppy tray, Mr. Loose had risen, snorting with resentment, and had taken an indignant departure.

Shortly after this Edith had made her escape and the unfortunate Matthews had succumbed to severe *soroche* in the course of an excursion to Potosi. Having been brought back from there in a state of complete collapse, he had never risen again from the tubular brass bed in which, already unconscious, he had been laid down to die. Mr. Loose had not been among those who attended his pitiful little funeral; and when he heard that Jerome Blake had induced the new Vice-Consul and his wife to assume occupancy of the room which Matthews had so tragically vacated, and that Mrs. Trent had not once been out of it since her arrival, he said, sharply and shortly, that he believed Blake's house had a curse on it, and that he, for one, would never enter it again.

He was out—not only out of the Legation but out of the city—when the new Vice-Consul called upon him; and as he never bothered to return the visits of his subordinates, he did not even know Michael by sight until the Trents had been in La Paz for some time. Then it slowly dawned upon him that everywhere he went he seemed to run up against a personable young man who was a stranger to him but who was apparently a general favorite. One evening when he had dropped into the Strangers' Club for a drink before dinner, he inquired idly as to the identity of the newcomer.

The British Minister, in whose society he liked to be seen, happened to be the person to whom he put the question. Lord Brereton stared at Mr. Loose for a moment through his monocle before he answered.

"It's the American Vice-Consul, Mr. Michael Trent," he said in what seemed to Mr. Loose an unnecessarily dry tone. Then he added, with increasing heartiness, "A very stout fellow too. My wife met him and Mrs. Trent in Arequipa and took quite a tumble to them both. We've been wanting to give a dinner for them and all that. But poor Mrs. Trent's been having a most beastly time. Terribly ill, don't you know. When she gets better, we shall be carrying her off to the country with us, I hope. Charming girl, my wife says, delightful, really."

Mr. Loose pricked up his ears. One vice-consul more or less, whether dead or alive, meant very little to him, even a vice-consul who had succeeded in becoming *persona grata* at the British Legation. But charming girls, whether married or unmarried were another matter. He kept an eye alert for these.

"Look here, what's-your-name," he called out in the general direction of Michael. "I hear you're my new Vice-Consul. Come over and let me have a look at you."

Michael, who was playing bridge at an adjacent table, laid down his cards and his cigarette, excused himself to his partner and his opponents in a pleasant voice which, without being raised in the least, had extraordinary carrying qualities, and crossed the room.

"Good evening, Mr. Minister," he said, still very pleasantly.

Mr. Loose shot a glance at him from under beetling brows. Undeniably the boy was very good-looking. Undeniably his manner left nothing to be desired. Yet Mr. Loose was uncomfortably conscious that everyone present regarded both the summons, and the manner in which it had been delivered, unpardonable, and that Trent, as well as himself, was responsible for this attitude. He raged inwardly, but having called the Vice-Consul to his side, he could not very well avoid continuing the conversation without appearing ridiculous.

"You might drop in at the Legation sometime," he remarked, for lack of anything better to say.

"Thank you, Sir. Is there any special time that would be convenient to have me call?"

Mr. Loose was not unaware that his frequent absences from his post formed a topic for considerable comment. Into Michael's wholly respectful question he read the inference that it was hard to find him at home, which was perfectly true.

"Well, come to dinner tomorrow night," he said ungraciously. "Nine o'clock."

"It's very kind of you, Sir. But I have an engagement to dine at the Presidencia tomorrow night, so I hope you'll excuse me."

Mr. Loose, who himself had never been invited to dine at the Presidencia, or indeed to go there at all except on the most formal of official occasions, stared at Michael unbelievingly. Then he observed that one of the foursome from whom he had wrested his Vice-Consul was the President's favorite nephew, Horacio Rodriquez, who was himself a member of the Chief Executive's household, and the sole heir to an immense fortune derived from the tin mines of his maternal grandfather. This gilded youth, to whom bridge was as the breath he drew, called to Michael now.

"*Ven Miguelito, ven!*" he exclaimed impatiently. "Ve are vaiting." Michael bowed to Mr. Loose.

"If you don't mind, Sir?" he said politely. And turned away.

77

The memory of this encounter rankled in the mind of Mr. Loose throughout his next vacation. But what Lord Brereton had said about the unusually charming girl lingered in his memory also. On his return to La Paz, he decided to call at Mr. Blake's house and make her acquaintance. He rang up the Consulate.

"Hello, hello! Damn the fool telephones in this hellava hole! Hello, I say!"

"American Consulate, Trent speaking," came back an even voice to him over the wire.

"Oh, hello, Trent, howarya? How's the wife?"

"She's much better, thank you, Mr. Minister."

"I thought I might drop in and see her some day soon. She must be lonely. Cheer her up to have a little company, perhaps."

"It's kind of you to think of her, Mr. Minister. She doesn't go out at all yet, but she's generally able to receive callers late in the afternoon."

"I'll be around, I'll be around," said Mr. Loose condescendingly.

When he alighted from his limousine, in front of the little house in the Sopocachi where he had vowed never to set foot again, he was both astonished and amazed to find that the entrance was very much blocked with cars already. This had been no part of his plan. Still less was he prepared for the scene which met his eyes as he entered the living room after handing over his hat and coat to Justo, who was now immaculate in white duck, and whom the Minister did not recognize as the same boy who had slopped the coffee about.

The unredeemed ugliness of the mission furniture had vanished. On the walls of the living room there were now some very fine portraits, and on the floor there was an Aubusson rug. The mantel, above the brightly burning fire, was adorned with vases of Sèvres porcelain, and the astral lamps, which were scattered about between bowls of flowers, shed a lambent light upon well-rubbed mahogany and gleaming damask. In the farther corner of the room, a tea table, set with a silver service, was drawn up beside a chaise longue on which a young and very lovely girl was reclining, dressed in a rose-colored negligee and partially covered by a vicuña rug. Mr. Loose could see her graceful hands moving about among the tea things, and the cloud of dark hair above her bent head. But he could not instantly discern her features, because the room was so full of persons who obscured his view of her. Near the door, the representative of a great typewriter company was standing deep in converse with the

78

representative of a great automobile company, and just beyond them a petroleum king was talking to Lady Brereton. Lord Brereton himself, together with Horacio Rodriquez and the two sisters of the Brazilian Chargé d'Affaires were playing bridge in front of the fire; and the head of the German brewery and his wife, who were experts themselves, were closely following what appeared to be an exceptionally intensive game. On the window seat the Bishop of La Paz and the Director of the Antofagasta-Bolivia Railway were contentedly ensconced. Beside the chaise longue, his rapt gaze riveted upon it, sat the Marquese Bonatelli; while beaming on all and sundry as he circled about with a laden tray of highballs, was Jerome Blake, his sharp nose shining like a headlight in front of his flat face, his expression significant of supreme satisfaction.

So self-absorbed did this group appear to be, that it was actually a moment or two before anyone realized that Mr. Loose was standing, stunned and neglected, on the threshold. Then the girl on the chaise longue, more intuitive than the others, looked up quickly, and he was aware of the luminance in her eyes, even before he heard her speak. She signaled to Jerome Blake.

"We have another guest, Jerome," she said softly. "Won't you tell Michael? I think he's in the kitchen, mixing more cocktails." She turned back toward the Minister, and he noticed the exquisite lines of her white throat, and the way her small head was set on her sloping shoulders. "This is Mr. Loose, isn't it?" she asked, raising herself slightly on the chaise longue and holding out her hand. "Michael told me you might call and I'm so glad you did. Will you have tea or a highball or a cocktail? I'm afraid the cocktails have given out, but there will be a fresh supply in just a minute. You know everyone here, don't you, Mr. Minister?"

Mr. Loose did know everyone there, but not with that degree of intimacy which would lead him to expect any of them to drop into his house, late in the afternoon, for cocktails, cards and conversation. His progress was not much impeded as he stepped across the Aubusson rug toward his hostess, nor did the Marquese seem in the least disposed to yield his own point of vantage to his American colleague. Quite unperturbed by the general coolness of his reception, Mr. Loose seated himself on the chaise longue, experiencing a feeling of pleasure from the inevitable contact with Daphne Trent's feet before she drew them away a little.

"Pleased to meet you, I'm sure," he said with unmistakable sincerity. "I'd like a Scotch and soda, if you can guarantee your Scotch."

"It's some that Lord Brereton was kind enough to bring us, so I am sure I can.—Jerome, do you know just how Mr. Loose likes his highballs? No? Well, suppose you let me mix his drink for him."

"That's what I call the right idea," remarked Mr. Loose, settling back more firmly on the chaise longue. "Fine!" he announced a moment later, smacking his lips. "Just fine! I guess you've had experience in mixing highballs before this."

"I make mint juleps better. But there isn't any mint in La Paz."

"Delighted to raise some for you in my greenhouse," announced Mr. Loose, with a generous wave of the hand. "I'll send my gardener over to talk to you about it. No, I'll come with him myself, and then we'll be sure to get everything just right. Have a little conference, eh? Some day when you're not quite so busy."

He winked at her over his glass and then permitted his gaze to wander, with renewed admiration and astonishment, around the room.

"I'd say you'd been making quite a few changes about the place," he remarked, inviting explanation.

"Oh, Mr. Blake has been so kind! He said he didn't mind in the least having me put my own things around, that he'd like to have me. And, of course, a bride does like to have her own things, doesn't she?"

"All these your things?" Mr. Loose inquired, with ever mounting surprise. "I'd say you had pretty good taste in antiques, if you ask me. Where did you buy 'em all?"

"Oh, I didn't buy them! I couldn't have afforded to do that! But most of the Daingerfields and the Fairfaxes too have more furniture than they know what to do with, and I am kin to them all. So when I got married they just turned to and cleared out their attics and gave me whatever they happened to find. I didn't have much of anything myself to start with, except those two old maps over there, marked '*Parts Unknown*' and that big breakfront bookcase."

"Oh!" said Mr. Loose a little blankly. He had never heard of either the Daingerfields or the Fairfaxes, and antiques which were inherited instead of bought were not part of the pattern of his life.

"It means so much, doesn't it, to have the Government let you take your furniture with you free when you go to a post? I was simply delighted when I found that out at the last moment, because furniture was about all I did have. We couldn't get ours unpacked right away, because I was too ill to attend to it.—But it seems doubly good to have it all in place now! I had the most wonderful time, lying lazily on

80

the sofa, and suggesting to Michael and Jerome where I would like to have things put. But, of course, we worked a plan out all together. It was Michael who liked the idea of putting my grandmother's portrait over the Sheraton settee, but it was Jerome who thought that the miniatures would look well, all grouped together, on either side of the Chippendale mirror."

"May I offer you a chair, Mr. Minister? I'm afraid you're not very comfortable where you are."

Michael had apparently finished preparing the fresh supply of cocktails. As usual, his perfectly agreeable voice had the effect of penetrating to every corner of the room. Mr. Loose rose hastily, with the feeling that he had been pricked, in a vulnerable spot, with a small sharp weapon.

"Oh, hello, hello!" he said. "I didn't see you come in. Very pleasant place you've got here."

"Mr. Blake has made it very pleasant for us. We're extremely grateful to him."

"Well now, I'd like to make things pleasant for you, too. We must set a date for you and this pretty girl here to come to the Legation. The sooner the better, the sooner the better."

"I'm so sorry, Mr. Minister. Dr. Smiley doesn't think it's best for Daphne to go out at present. She's had a pretty long hard pull, and she doesn't stay up all day, even now."

"Well, bring her over for the week end. Delighted to have her. There are plenty of bedrooms in the Legation. And there's nothing like a bed, you know, to set a pretty woman off." Mr. Loose drained his glass. "How about it?" he inquired, turning to Daphne with another wink.

"It's awfully kind of you. But I'm afraid I couldn't, just now. I'm trying to be very careful."

"That's right, that's right! 'If you can't be good be careful, and if you can't be careful, be as careful as you can!' My motto exactly!"

"I'm trying to be very careful," Daphne repeated softly, "because I'm hoping to have a baby. I've been so terribly ill that I was afraid I mightn't. But now I believe everything's going to be all right. I'm sure you'll understand, Mr. Loose, and not urge me to do anything that wouldn't be good for me just now."

An infinite tenderness had settled over her lovely face. Mr. Loose, in spite of himself, caught his breath and swallowed hard.

"Oh, yes—I—I see! Very thoughtless of me, very! Well I hope that later on——"

"Later on, I'll bring the baby to see you. That *will* be fun, won't it?"

"Won't it?" echoed Mr. Loose, speaking rather blankly again. And then, to his utter amazement, he found he meant what he said.

He did not linger very long afterward. Daphne Trent had been grand to him, there was no denying that. She—well she was a lady, if he ever saw one. He had not seen very many, that is, not the way he had seen her. But Mr. Loose, who was not a stupid man, even though he was an ignorant one and a coarse one, did not need to have anyone tell him when he had blundered even worse than usual. He took Daphne's hand, and held it in his for a minute, and she did not draw it away. She looked at him with her big clear eyes, and then she thanked him for coming and said she hoped he would come again and that he wasn't to forget about the mint and about the "rain check" on her visit to the Legation. After that, he shook hands with Michael, who said nothing at all except, "Good night, Mr. Minister." He forgot to say good night to Jerome Blake. And apparently everyone else forgot to say good night to him. The Marquese bent over the chaise longue again, the bridge players were absorbed in a no trump bid, doubled and redoubled, the bishop and the Director were discussing the impending Ascension Day holiday from both the ecclesiastical and the transportation standpoint, and the big businessmen were congratulating each other on the way things were looking up.

Mr. Loose hesitated for a moment on the threshold, just as he had when he came in. Then he went out into the street, where a light snow was now falling and where the cars of all the other guests were still parked against the curb.

"The damned insufferable bounder!" he heard someone saying angrily as he stepped into his limousine.

But it was a man's voice. It was not Daphne Trent's. So he did not care very much. He knew he was a bounder, and he also knew that while he had bought his way into the American Diplomatic Service, there were some other things which he could not buy.

CHAPTER 8

AFTER AN autumn which had been unusually cold the winter gave promise of being a mild one. The gentle snow, which began to come intermittently in early May, fell no more heavily or frequently as the month advanced. Most of the time the sunshine was dazzling, and in the middle of the day it emanated warmth as well as brilliance. As Daphne grew steadily stronger, Dr. Smiley encouraged her to stay out in it as much as she could.

It was a handicap, of course, that she had no car of her own, for she could not do much walking. She thought of Penelope, sacrificed to pay the shipboard tips, with a fresh sense of bereavement. But all the diplomats and most of the other consuls had automobiles, not to mention the prosperous members of the American colony and the wealthy Bolivians with whom she was coming more and more constantly into contact. There was always a car at her disposal, whenever she chose to use it; and though she could never bring herself to ask for favors, and felt hesitant about accepting them too often even when they were offered, she took a short drive nearly every day, because she knew it was good for her to do so, and because it was so important, not only for her own sake, but for Michael's and the baby's, that she should be well and strong.

The city had the same fascination for her that it did for Michael, and like him she was able to submerge her sense of adversity in her sense of enchantment, though less boldly and buoyantly. She reflected, with endless joy, on what he had said about La Paz—that it was like a cluster of jewels lying in an agate bowl. She thought that if she were only a poet, like her father, she would write a sonnet of which this description would be the keynote; she resolved to try to do so anyhow, even though she knew she had no gift for writing. She did not repine because she could not go to the *Fiesta de las Alacitas* herself; she listened enthralled while Michael talked to her about it; and she kept the grotesque, potbellied figurine of the Ekeko—the Bolivian manikin symbolic of favorable fortune—which he had brought home to her, on her bedside table, where she could lean over, from time to time, and touch the peaked cap with which he was crowned, and the tiny pots and kettles and knickknacks with which his tunic was strewn. He reigned over the microscopic chairs and tables of silver filigree, the infinitesimal riding boots and saddles, the miniature ponchos and shawls which had also come from the Fiesta and by which he stood surrounded. She told Michael she was sure he would bring good luck to them, just as he did to all the peasant families where he was regarded as the dispenser of prosperity and happiness and the inseparable companion of the home. She said that the next year, during fiesta, they would buy the baby an Ekeko of his own, instead of a rubber doll.

About the time she began to take her daily rides, a famous travel writer came to La Paz, who labored under the delusion that all her own observations and experiences were of unique value. She called upon Daphne, and talked to her with pitying condescension.

"It seems such a shame that you aren't seeing anything of the real Bolivia. Now *I* have spent six months near the Cordillera Real. I went from there into dozens of native huts, and got to know the way the Indians actually live. I made a thorough study of llamas and alpacas. That's the *only* way to see a country, you know—through its aborigines and its animals."

"I like the Bolivians that live right here in La Paz," Daphne said composedly. "They're so courteous and cultured and such marvelous linguists. I haven't been made uncomfortable, not once, because I don't speak Spanish."

"Indeed! Well, I never waste my time making social contacts," Miss Peake remarked, staring at Daphne. Then she continued, more belligerently, "I always go straight to the root of things. For instance, I made this trip on purpose to see the celebration of Todos Los Santos and the Carnival: all the special ceremonies that follow a death among primitive people—so picturesque and gruesome—and the votive dances that end in orgies of drink and sex. There's nothing like them anywhere else in the world, nothing!"

"There's nothing like the tiers of colonnades around the patio of the Presidencia when they're filled with flowers, just as the Hanging Gardens of Babylon must have been," Daphne replied, with continued tranquility. "And there's nothing like the white marble statue of Queen Isabella with the white marble mountain glittering behind her."

"The white marble mountain?" inquired Miss Peake, bristling with incredulity.

"Yes, Illimani, you know. Don't you think it looks as if it were made of white marble? Except at sunset, of course—then it looks as if it were made of rose quartz. I love to stop on the Prado and watch Queen Isabella while the light is fading. She seems so serene and real as she stands there—not like an image at all, but like the embodiment of the old Spain which made the new Spain possible. There's something imperishable about her and Illimani both—some dazzling quality of purity and permanence. I think they share in heavenly harmonies. Don't you, Miss Peake?"

"I hadn't thought about it at all," replied Miss Peake, abruptly, which was all too true. She felt very much affronted that young Mrs. Trent, who had hardly been outside her own front door since she came to Bolivia, had discovered something which a seasoned traveler and trained observer had missed.

Daphne did not exaggerate when she said she did not feel as if the statue of Queen Isabella were an image. Not that she had any objection to images—indeed, as she began to penetrate to the dim naves, smelling of stale incense and guttering candles, which lay beyond the carved façades of the ancient churches, she discovered silver-crowned virgins and stiff-robed saints that held her spellbound with amazement and admiration. But they did not affect her as poignantly as the Castilian Queen. She formed the habit of pausing beside Isabella almost every day, of looking at her from every angle and in every light. And one afternoon, as she stood beside the shining pedestal, the Honorable Alonzo Loose came up and spoke to her.

He had never called on her a second time, nor had he renewed his invitation to the Legation, which was located not far from the statue which so enthralled her, and which was conspicuous, even among the ornate houses lining the Prado, for the number of balconies and turrets with which it was decorated, the massiveness of its doors, and the intricacy of its carvings. She knew it very well by sight, and was not without a certain amount of curiosity to see the treasures which it was said to contain, and which Mr. Loose was reported to have combed both Bolivia and Peru to secure. Indeed, she would have welcomed an opportunity to talk with him about his antiques, for he had touched her heart by his unqualified admiration of hers. But this opportunity had never arisen either. She still went out very little socially, and then only to small early parties which she could leave at any time and she felt tired and which did not overtax her strength; and the American Minister, though scrupulously accorded every courtesy of a strictly official nature was seldom included in gatherings of this sort. So altogether their meetings had been few and far between.

"Good afternoon," she said with genuine cordiality as he approached her. "Are you coming to look at my statue with me?"

Mr. Loose glanced from her to Isabella and smiled. "So that's your statue, is it?" he inquired, with more understanding than Miss Peake had revealed. "Well, I can see how you'd like it. And I guess Queen Isabella would've liked you. I guess she wouldn't raise any objection now, if she knew you'd appropriated her monument."

"The mountain is mine too," Daphne went on, much encouraged, and indicating Illimani, which the Andean glow was slowly transfiguring from glittering white to fiery rose.

85

"I'm sure the mountain and the statue belong to each other, and if they do, and one of them belongs to me, the other does too! Do you see what I mean?"

"Yes, I guess I do," Mr. Loose remarked thoughtfully.

"I'm so glad. I tried to explain to Miss Peake, but she didn't understand at all. All she cares about is animals and aborigines."

"Well, I guess animals and aborigines are all that care about her," responded Mr. Loose shortly. "That is, if they do. From what I've heard, the Indians hurry to their huts and the llamas take to the hillsides as soon as they hear her coming! My God, what a woman! And she wanted to come and stay at the Legation! She said it would be an 'ideal center' for her while she was writing her next book."

"Did you encourage her?"

"Did I encourage her! My God, she didn't need any encouragement! But I told her it wouldn't do, it wouldn't do at all, me being a bachelor and all that. And then she was tickled to death at the idea that she might be compromised. I guess she's been hoping vainly for a good many years that her reputation would be ruined—I wouldn't like to say how many. That's always the way, Mrs. Trent. The women you invite to your house won't come, and the ones you won't invite are forever trying to batter down the door. What's a poor man going to do?"

Daphne laughed. "You might invite me again sometime," she suggested. "I do go out quietly to tea almost every day now. When you asked me before, it didn't look as if I would be able to this winter."

"Would you come quietly to tea with me, this afternoon?" the Minister inquired, with increasing interest.

"I'd like to very much. We could walk over to your house from here easily, couldn't we? Then perhaps later on you would send me home in your car, and I could let Lady Brereton's, which she kindly loaned me, go now. And when we get to the Legation we could telephone Michael, and tell him where I am, and ask him to join us, if he hasn't an engagement for bridge. Couldn't we?"

"Well, yes, we could do all of that, if it's what you'd like."

"I'd like it very much," Daphne said again. "You don't think I'm presumptuous, do you, making suggestions myself?"

"I think you're just as cute as you can be," Mr. Loose replied, smiling more broadly than ever. "I can't say I'dda thought, myself, of inviting your husband too, when you were just going to drop in on the spur of the moment, so to speak. But it's all right by me, if you'd rather. Only I guess you'd better call him up yourself. I haven't ever been able to get the hang of the telephone system on this continent. It bothers me so that I break out in a cold sweat every time I pick up the receiver."

Daphne laughed and said she would be glad to telephone. But when she returned to the drawing room, after doing so, Mr. Loose noticed at once that her manner had altered. It was no longer companionable and carefree; it was restrained. Her eyes were troubled and her lips were trembling a little. Mr. Loose was concerned.

"You haven't begun to feel sick, all of a sudden, have you?" he inquired.

"No—no—I'm perfectly all right. But I don't believe I want any tea, after all, if you don't mind."

"Well, how about a glass of champagne? I've got some mighty good Heidsieck, vintage of——"

"Thank you ever so much but I really don't want anything. I'll just look at your beautiful antiques for a few moments, until Michael comes to get me."

"Oh, he's coming to get you, is he? Didn't have a bridge game on then?"

"Well, he did, but he said he'd come and get me just the same. Oh, Mr. Minister, I—I'm dreadfully sorry."

"I see," said Mr. Loose. He spoke slowly instead of shortly this time. But he spoke kindly too. "So your husband thinks I oughtn't to have invited you to come to tea with me, does he, and that even if I did, you oughtn't to have accepted?" he inquired. "Well, don't you worry, Mrs. Trent. There isn't any harm done and there wasn't any intended. But I see how he feels. He's heard some ugly stories about me and some of them are true. And he thinks I was pretty fresh the day I came to your house. I don't know but what I'd feel the same way, if I was in his place. I don't lay it up against him any, the way he feels. But I'd like to be friends with you, if I could. With you and with him both. It wouldn't do either of you any harm and it might do both of you good someday. I've taken a liking to you and I've got quite a variety of interests. Seems as if we ought to be able to figure out some way we could be friends."

"Oh, I'm sure we can!" Daphne exclaimed impulsively. "And I like you too, Mr. Loose. Everything will come out all right I'm sure. It's just that Michael——"

"I know, I know," Mr. Loose replied reassuringly. "Now don't you worry, Mrs. Trent. Because worrying is the very worst thing you can do right now. Don't you worry a mite. Because everything is going to be okay."

Daphne replied, quickly, that of course she knew it was.

But inwardly she did not feel so sure. Michael's behavior, during the five minutes which he spent at the Legation, was more formal and frigid than she had ever seen it. He declined a Scotch and soda. He declined to look at Caspicara's wood carvings, or the silver censers that had come from Cuzco. He declined the offer of the Minister's limousine, although Lady Brereton's car had already been sent away. He hurried Daphne away from the Legation so fast that she slipped on the steps, and scarcely spoke to her during the course of their walk to the Sopocachi. But the door of their bedroom was hardly closed behind them when he burst out into angry and violent invective.

"Don't you know what that man's reputation is? Couldn't you see for yourself the sort he is the day he was here? What do you mean by meeting him in the street and going to his house with him?"

"Michael, I didn't meet him 'in the street'! How can you say such a thing? I was standing looking at Isabella and Illimani, the way I do almost every afternoon, and he happened to go by and——"

"Oh, he *happened* to go by, did he? Well, I'll bet my bottom dollar that he's seen you mooning around that statue day after day, and has just watched for a chance to come and pick you up. All he had to do was to look out of his window! And I'll say you *gave* him a chance! Do you suppose anyone who saw you go into his house would believe for a moment that the meeting was accidental?"

"I don't see how any sane person could possibly believe anything else. He was kind and cordial, that was all."

"Oh, *that was all*, was it? Because I got to the Legation in double quick time, that was why it was all!"

"Michael, *you're* not acting sane. I like Mr. Loose. I can see that he's got faults and failings, but I like him, just the same. And I think he's lonely, almost as lonely as Jerome was when we came here. Of course he doesn't have to worry about money, like the rest of us, but money doesn't keep a man from being lonely. It must be awful to go into a room and feel that no one is glad to see you."

"There are plenty of darn good reasons why no one is glad to see him. If he lays his filthy hands on you, I'll throttle him!"

"He hasn't the least idea of laying his hands on me, and they're not filthy. But even if they were, you know there isn't any kind of a man who would insult a woman who's going to have a baby."

"You don't look like a woman, and you don't look as if

you were going to have a baby. You look like a silly little softie who's easy prey."

"You're not going through life imagining that every man who speaks to me is going to make love to me in the next breath, are you, Michael?"

"I suppose that's meant to be a dirty dig. Well, if you must know, I don't trust any man too far. And I don't trust you too far, either! Why should I?"

"Oh, Michael—I knew you'd say that to me someday.— But I didn't think you'd say it to me *now!*"

In an instant his rage had evaporated. He tried to take her in his arms, to beg her forgiveness, to tell her he knew he was a cad and a beast. She would not listen to him, she would not let him touch her. She was beside herself with shame and grief, sick with sorrow, racked with weeping. And she was imprisoned. There was no escape for her, no place where she could go to cry out her heart in secret. The four walls of her room closed in upon her, fettering her to Michael, who had insulted her and stricken her. If he would not leave her, she could not make him. She must suffer his presence, as she had suffered so many other things already. Overwhelmed, she threw herself down on the bed and turned her face to the wall. Then she was startled by the sound of soft insistent knocking at the door.

She heard Michael go to it and open it, heard Jerome's voice, strained and terrible, on the other side of it. Then Michael went out, closing the door after him, and afterward only muffled sounds came to her for a long time. She knew that something dreadful must have happened, that Jerome must be in trouble too. But no trouble, it seemed to her, could be as annihilating as her own. She lay still sobbing softly, her face turned to the wall, for a long time. Then, as she gradually grew calmer, she was ashamed of the selfishness which caused her to stay there, when there might be something she could say or do to comfort Jerome. She sat up slowly, wiping her eyes and smoothing her hair back into place. Then as she swung herself off the bed, she heard Michael come back into the dark room.

"Daphne," he said tensely. "Daphne—we've got to forget our quarrel and everything that caused it—right away. Because Jerome is in desperate straits. We've got to stand by him together—it would simply add to his anguish if he knew we were struggling against each other. You're—you're big enough to forgive me, aren't you, Daphne, for Jerome's sake, even if you can't for my own?"

"What has happened to Jerome?" Daphne asked, ignoring his question.

"He heard from the State Department. He's got his transfer."

"But he's been hoping for a transfer!"

"Yes—to Paris! He says *I'll* get that! He's being transferred to Tegucigalpa."

"Oh! I am sorry! I know he did have his heart set on Paris. But still——"

"But still you think he might stand up under a disappointment like that, even if it were a bad one! Well, he would, of course—except that he's had another blow, right at the same time—one that's a good deal worse."

"What else's happened?" Daphne asked fearfully. But she knew, even before Michael told her.

"He's heard from Edith. She's made up her mind to cut away from him for good and all. She says it's no good, that she simply can't stand the Service. She's divorcing him."

Late that night, as they lay with their arms around each other, Michael and Daphne began to talk about the effect that Jerome's transfer would have upon themselves. Dinner had been taken, untasted, from the table, and they had stayed with him throughout the dreadful evening, trying to think of something to say which might comfort him, while he sat hunched in his chair, incoherent with pain, his head bowed, his hands clasped limply in front of him. But at last he had tried to thank them for their sympathy, and had risen and walked wearily away to his own room. For a long time afterward, they had not been able to think or speak of anything except his ruined prospects and his shattered life. Then Daphne had laid her cheek softly against Michael's in the darkness.

"Michael—we won't be like Jerome, whatever happens. No matter where we're sent, no matter what else we lose, we'll always have each other."

He held her hard. "God bless you, darling, for saying that, tonight," he said huskily. Then after a moment he added, "It's going to be rougher sledding for us than ever, you know, after Jerome goes. I don't know how we're going to manage."

"We could move to a boardinghouse."

"If we did that, you'd have to go to the hospital when the baby is born, which would be a lot more expensive than having it here. And there'd be the cost of moving and all that. I don't believe we'd save much in the end. Besides, it wouldn't be fair to leave Jerome stuck with the lease and you'd be awfully uncomfortable in a boardinghouse. You couldn't have any of your own things that you love so much around you either."

"I know, but I wouldn't mind giving those up, if it would help. But if it wouldn't— Perhaps we could get someone to come here and share expenses with us, the way we have shared them with Jerome. Perhaps Miss Jane Peake would take Jerome's room. She wants to find a place to stay while she writes her book on Bolivia."

"She isn't going to spend the next two years writing her book on Bolivia, is she?"

"No, but I suppose she'll spend the next two months doing it, at least. Even if she only stayed two months, that would tide us over a little."

"It's an outrage," Michael said hotly, "that we should be lying here wondering how we can keep the wolf away from a five-room house. It's an outrage that you should have to beg for a ride every time you need a little fresh air. It's an outrage that we should never be able to invite anyone in for dinner, and that we couldn't even ask anyone to drop around in the afternoon if the drinks we served hadn't all been given to us. It's an outrage that I should have to gamble to pay your doctor's bills! Why don't you say you told me so, Daphne? It's a marvel you haven't before this, and I don't see how you can keep from saying it now! You did tell me so, and I wouldn't listen to you. It's all my fault that we're in this dreadful mess."

"No, it isn't. It's my fault too. I don't believe it's going to be so very dreadful. Anyway, I'm glad you didn't listen to me."

She spoke with sincerity as well as tenderness. But Michael felt her tremble a little.

"Yes, you do. No, you aren't. Why are you trembling, if you aren't afraid and aren't sorry?"

"I'm not trembling. That is, not exactly. I'm—I'm shivering a little. I've been cold, sort of, all day."

"You mean, colder than usual?"

"Yes. I've had little creeping chills running through me ever since morning. I hesitated whether to go out or not. But it was such a lovely day——"

"Shall I get up and heat you some milk? You know you didn't eat any supper! Or would you like a hot water bag?"

"I don't want any milk. But I would like a hot water bag."

Michael rose, put on his bathrobe, and warmed some water on a small electric heater in the bathroom. When he got back into bed he could hear Daphne's teeth chattering.

"I think I'll put my bathrobe on too, Michael, if you'll

give it to me," she said. "We'll pretend we're Eskimos, settling down in our igloo."

"We don't need to pretend anything. We'll just face the fact that I'm an American vice-consul in the service of the richest country in the world."

For the next hour he was intermittently conscious that she was still shivering, and eventually he persuaded her to take a hot drink, after all. Then they both fell asleep, and when he left her the next morning she was still sleeping, the deep slumber of exhaustion and spent emotion. He was careful not to disturb her, moving about as quietly as possible; and before he left the house he scribbled a little note, which he laid on her bedside table, saying he hoped she would stay in bed, and keep warm and quiet; he would telephone later in the morning to find out just how she was. Before he had done so, however, Dr. Smiley telephoned him.

"I don't want to disturb you unnecessarily, Mr. Trent, but I'm rather concerned about your wife. I've just been to see her and she's quite feverish. She tells me that yesterday she had chills all day long. I'm afraid she's caught a bad cold."

"I'll go home at once."

"Suppose before you do that you let me come to the office. I'd like to have a little talk with you, and I'd rather not run the risk of having her overhear us conferring about her. She might get the idea that something was seriously wrong."

"Well, is there?"

"I'm afraid there is," the missionary answered, and hung up the receiver.

"Dr. Smiley's been to see Daphne. He says she's very sick," Michael said, turning from the telephone to Jerome, who was sitting at his desk, engaged in emptying out its drawers and dividing their contents into pitiful little piles.

"That's what he says, anyway," Michael repeated doggedly, and began to pace up and down the office.

When Dr. Smiley arrived there, a few minutes later, he looked very grave. "You know I told you, sometime ago, that Mrs. Trent would be all right if she didn't catch cold and if her heart held out. Well, she has caught cold. She has a very bad cold indeed. And I don't like the way her heart is acting. You don't know of anything, do you, that could have made her feel very badly about something, that could have given her a severe or sudden shock?"

"Yes!" Michael and Jerome exclaimed together. They were not thinking of the same thing, but as they looked at each other they both felt like murderers. "What can be done for her?" they asked, also in unison.

"I hardly know what to advise. Usually, when my patients

92

contract severe colds, I try to get them out of this altitude as quickly as I can—down to the coast, if possible. Of course, it isn't always possible. It's a long expensive trip. But it's a great safeguard against incipient pneumonia."

"Has Daphne incipient pneumonia?" Jerome and Michael asked, still speaking together.

"Well, no. Not—not yet. But she was a very sick woman, as you know, for months. Her vitality is greatly impaired. And now she has this bad cold; she seems to be suffering from the results of some kind of a shock."

"Who would take care of her, if we could get her down to the coast?"

"Well, of course, there are doctors in all the ports. Not American doctors in every case, but Peruvian and Chilean doctors. And hospitals or nursing homes of one sort or another. And consuls or consular agents. The British are more fully represented than we are, and they are very helpful in cases of this kind."

"And how much would it cost to get her—well, to Arica? That's the nearest place, isn't it?"

"It costs about twenty-five dollars each way for one person. But she couldn't possibly travel alone. I should have to send Miss Finch with her—unless you could go yourself, Mr. Trent?"

"I could take her," Jerome Blake said suddenly. "I've just been ordered to another post, Dr. Smiley, so my expenses would be paid—that is, what I spent on them would be refunded to me. I can leave at once, on the next train, if necessary. Michael could send my things after me."

"Yes, of course, I could. Only——"

The three men looked at each other. Then Michael broke into a short ugly laugh.

"Only I shan't have enough money to pay *Daphne's* fare to the coast until the first of the month! And though your expenses will be refunded, Jerome, they won't be advanced! I don't suppose, if we pooled what all three of us have in ready cash at this moment we'd have enough among us to send her! So what are we going to do? Let her die because we haven't? I'm damned if I will!"

So swiftly that the missionary and the Consul were only half-aware of what he was doing, he had rushed past them, down the dingy stairs and out into the street. He was still coatless and hatless; but he did not notice the snow falling on his hair or feel the sharp wind blowing on his face as he plunged along toward the Prado. And when he reached the American Legation, he pounded on the massive door until an astonished servant came and let him in.

Afterward, he told Daphne how very kind the Minister had been to him, that he had not shown any resentment or surprise at the sight of Michael. He had turned at once to the telephone, which he so heartily hated, and had spoken, first of all, with the Director of the Arica-La Paz Railway. Would it be possible, he had then asked, in a tone which implied that of course it was possible, for him to have a private car put at his disposal immediately? Yes, naturally, to be attached to the next train out.—It had not seemed to matter to him that there was no regular train running until Thursday. He had said that there must be a special train provided for that night. It did not seem to matter to him, either, that the only private car available belonged to the Director himself, and this functionary had just offered it to the President of Bolivia for an official trip—When the details about the car had been settled, Mr. Loose called up the Central Bank in La Paz. He should want quite a large sum of money sent down to the Legation at once, he said. Well, five thousand bolivianos would do for the moment probably but to be on the safe side it would be better to make it ten. He would have the check to cover the cash ready for the messenger when he arrived. Then the Minister had put his hand on Michael's shoulder, and had said they were going to reverse the usual order of things—that he was going to stay in La Paz and look after American interests there, but that he was going to send his staff down to the coast on indefinite leave but on full pay. All that he wanted to see of Jerome Blake and Michael Trent was their heels. And when Michael had broken down entirely, and had tried to apologize to him and explain to him and thank him all in the same shaken breath, the Minister had cut him short and had told him to be off to his wife, and to thank God that he had her——

Michael did thank God that he had her. But it was a long time before he told Daphne about all this—not until after Jerome was settled at his lonely post at Tegucigalpa and Edith had her divorce and Jane Peake's book was written. The special train never started for Arica after all, and the ten thousand bolivianos that had been dispatched from the Central Bank were returned, still intact, to its vault. For Dr. Smiley had not known when he went to talk with Michael that Daphne had had a sudden fall and an exhausting walk as well as a severe chill and a strange shock; and when he went back to the little house on the Sopocachi to tell her that she was going on a journey, he found that it was already too late to send her. Afterwards when she groped her way back from that valley of the shadow to which every travailing woman descends alone, she returned from it alone also, her anguish unassuaged with joy that a son had been born into the world.

For the child which had so nearly cost her own life had never breathed and she had never looked into his face.

PART III

Danger Zone

CHAPTER 9

SHAMEEN LAY still and shimmering under the summer sun. The shadows formed by the rich foliage of the banyan trees fell deep and tranquil along the waterfront. The narrow bridges, arching over the canal and leading into the native city, were both deserted; all its clamor, all its confusion, rose far beyond them. The foreign colony, untouched by its uproar, relaxed in the restfulness of the siesta hour.

Daphne Trent, languid with warmth and well-being, slipped between the linen sheets of her big bed and drifted from daydreams into drowsiness and back into daydreams again. The silence of the house was in itself soothing, permeated, as it was, with that element of emptiness which brings with it such a sense of seclusion and detachment. Michael had gone back to the Consulate immediately after an early lunch. The cook and houseboys, having removed the last traces of this with their usual deftness, had noiselessly withdrawn to their own quarters. Even Ah Luk, the amah, after Rosemary had cuddled contentedly down in the crib and Richard had been settled in his cradle, had disappeared, as she always did at this time, to some retreat of her own. The cradle was drawn up close beside Daphne's bed, where she herself could minister instantly to his smallest needs, if he made any such known. But the baby boy had reeled away from his mother's breast in that state of infantile stupor which follows utter repletion, and now slumbered profoundly, his mouth still moist with milk, his chubby arms extended, his pink fists closely clenched.

How healthy and happy they all were, how fortunately favored, Daphne mused thankfully, turning on her cool pillow and settling down more deeply into that charmed state of semiconsciousness which lies between sleeping and waking.

How prodigal China had been in her bounty to them all! In Bolivia, she and Michael had been called upon to cope with one exigency after another—poverty and pain, death and disaster, had dogged their very footsteps. Despite the fascination which La Paz held for them both, they had never been free to abandon themselves to its spell. To the very end of their stay there, it had seemed as though they were fated to battle against adversity. Rosemary had been less than a week old when Michael's orders for a transfer had come through, with instructions to report forthwith at his new post in Canton; and Daphne, still spent with travail, had perforce left her bed to dismantle her home and move her belongings. There was no one to take the responsibility from her slim shoulders. Justo and Celestina, stunned at the prospect of losing their *patrones*, stumbled stupidly about, accomplishing nothing; the butler sent down by Mr. Loose from the Legation did not know where anything was or where anything should go; Miss Finch was called away on an emergency case; Michael was kept confined to the office, for fresh disturbances had broken out in the Chaco, and he was busy explaining the nature of these and the menace they brought with them to his successor at the same time that he endeavored to clarify the routine of office work. Though she was able to rise above her own exhaustion, Daphne was never free from fear of the effect it might have upon her baby. The potential loss of a second child was a calamity which she thought she could not face; yet horror lest she be forced to face it haunted her day and night.

The baby had come strong and healthy into the world, this time; but she ceased to gain from the time that her mother rose, so prematurely, to meet a new emergency; and by the time the little family was on its way to Arica, she had begun to lose. Michael, appalled, himself, at the prospect of fresh disaster, kept constantly assuring Daphne he felt certain that as soon as they were at sea, the little girl would be better.

"You'll be able to rest on the boat, darling. The stewardess can help you take care of Rosemary. And maybe the ship's surgeon will be able to suggest something that will do you both good."

"The stewardess! The ship's surgeon! You remember how much good they were, don't you, when we came south?"

Michael did remember, only too well. But he tried to make light of the recollection.

"Well, this isn't the same ship. Probably we'll get something better this time."

He knew in his heart that probably they would not, and he shared Daphne's dismal foreboding that she would be forced to wean the baby. When this presentiment had been fulfilled, he tried to console her by viewing the situation from another angle.

"You'll be ever so much freer, darling. You and I will be able to do things together, if you're not tied down—we haven't done many so far, you know."

"Yes, I do know. But who is going to take care of Rosemary, while you and I are off 'doing things together'? I can't just dump her down anywhere, you know, and trust to luck she'll be all right until we get back. Besides, I loved nursing her. And I'm afraid I'll be a good deal more tied down, fixing formulas and boiling bottles, than I have been so far."

It was all too true. Moreover, the condensed milk which was the only thing that the surgeon could offer, disagreed violently with the baby. When the ship docked at Callao, Daphne and Michael sped off at once to Lima, taking Rosemary with them in a basket, and consulted the most eminent specialist they could find. They saw neither the Torre-Tagle Palace nor the pleasure pavilion of La Perichole nor the Sanctuario of Santa Rosa. They sat endlessly in the physician's waiting room with the basket between them, and finally hurried back to the boat much poorer but very little wiser than they had left it. The Consul, Mr. Yauvey—a super-annuated widower, whose false teeth kept slipping—to whom he thought "might do" and had incidentally made it suggestion beyond vaguely mentioning the name of a doctor whom he thought "might do" and had incidentally made it quite clear to them, at the very moment of meeting, that he was not "in a position to entertain."

At Panama, where they stayed for a few days while waiting to transship to a Pacific bound steamer, they fared much better. The Minister there, a friend of Mr. Loose, had sent them a cable inviting them to stay at the Legation. They found this exceedingly well-staffed, and permeated with dim charm, in spite of its disadvantageous location; and Mrs. Perry, the Minister's wife, won their hearts by her tact and resourcefulness. Rosemary was at once turned over to a capable trained nurse who, Mrs. Perry informed them lightly, was a regular member of the Legation household; and though Michael and Daphne were both inclined to doubt this, they could not challenge her veracity by saying so. Immensely grateful for even temporary respite, they danced lightheartedly at the Union Club and went for a day's outing on Tobago Island; but they had hardly put out to sea again, when they realized that such improvement as Rosemary had made had been ephemeral. She attacked her bottle avidly, only to struggle against it a moment later; she wailed most of the day and fully half of the night. The heat in the small minimum fare cabin was terrific, and the more unendurable to its caged occupants because they had, by this time, become accustomed to the crisp climate of La Paz. They had no bathroom; their basin was cluttered with jars of boric acid and lime water; a makeshift clothesline, on which Michael kept continually hitting his head, was suspended across the room; the atmosphere reeked of curdled milk and drying diapers.

Inevitably, tension succeeded tedium and irritation, discomfort. The moment came when Michael tripped over the sterilizer as he sprang out of bed just before dawn after a sleepless night, determined to escape for a breath of air before the other passengers began to infest the deck.

"Damn that thing! It's always in the way—I'm forever stumbling over it! Can't you put it somewhere else?"

"Well, where exactly?"

"I don't know! Hell's bells, just listen to that kid! I should think she'd split her throat.—I suppose you know the two old maids in the next cabin have complained——"

"Yes, the purser told me. But, Michael, what can I *do?*"

"I don't know. But whatever you do, I hope to God you won't have another baby!"

"*You* hope I won't have another baby! Well, what do you suppose *I* hope? If you'd had two of them, within a year of each other, you might have some idea how I feel about it! But don't worry—there won't be another a year after Rosemary! Nor two nor three nor four years after, either!"

"What're you trying to do, tell me you're tired of me?"

"I'm tired of everything and everybody! I wish I were back in my own room at the rectory—with the door locked."

It was their second serious quarrel, and in a way it left deeper scars than their first one, because no precipitous calamities came crowding in, as in the other instance, to heal the breach between them. They were still resentful, still estranged, when they reached San Francisco, where they were obliged to effect a superficial reconciliation for the benefit of Michael's father, who, to their utter amazement, was waving to them eagerly from the dock.

"Couldn't miss this chance of meeting my granddaughter!" he called to them through cupped hands. "What's the trip from St. Louis to the Coast nowadays—nothing, positively nothing! Daphne—my dear—do you realize I've never seen you before either?"

He was trembling with excitement and emotion as he hurled himself against the gangplank; his form was as frail as Michael's was vigorous; but he forged his way ahead of far more stalwart passengers; and from the moment that he first lifted Rosemary into his arms, she nestled down against his shoulder as if she had found the first secure haven of her troubled little life. Richard Trent regarded her with welling anxiety and affection.

"Why the dear little girl! Glad to see her old granddaddy, isn't she? Knows he'll look out for her, doesn't she? I had to look out for Michael when he was a baby, Daphne. You see, his mother——"

There was no doubt about it, the bond between the old man and the young child was as strong as it was immediate. Two days later, Michael made an impetuous suggestion to his father.

"Look here, Dad—why don't you come on to Canton with us?"

"Why don't I—Michael, I never thought of such a thing! I thought if I could just get a glimpse of you all, while the ship was in port——"

"Yes, I know. But why don't you think of it? You could afford to come, couldn't you?"

"Yes—yes—I suppose I could. It doesn't cost me much to live, Michael, these days. I'm a little ahead of the game. But I've been thinking I ought to make you more of an allowance. I'm afraid you've had to do a good deal of scrimping. And now you have this baby——"

"Well, we can take all that up later—I believe it's cheaper in China than it was in Bolivia, anyway.—It couldn't be more expensive, that's certain! And there's nothing to keep you in St. Louis, really, now is there? Besides, we've been wanting to have you come to visit us, for a long time! Why we spoke of it, almost as soon as we were married."

"Well, Michael, I don't know, I don't know. It's good of you to suggest it. But Daphne might not feel the same way about it."

"I'm sure she would. But we'll ask her."

"It's better for young couples to be alone, Michael."

"Well, I don't know," Michael said in his turn. And from the tone of his voice Richard Trent knew that there was something amiss, though he was too wise to pursue this knowledge to its source.

But at least there was no lack of warmth in the manner with which Daphne seconded Michael's suggestion; and in the last analysis, Richard Trent really needed very little persuasion to go on with them. As if his presence had brought beneficence with it, the voyage to the Orient was calm and beautiful; and Rosemary, whom he constantly kept cradled in his loving old arms, ceased wailing and began to smile and gurgle and coo. He had no patience with modern methods of baby feeding. He whipped a reliable old patent powder briskly into warm milk, stirred the mixture slightly, and presented it without more ado to his grandchild. She sucked it in with relish and began to gain. He insisted that her basket should be placed in his cabin, where there was plenty of room—it was not the first time, he reminded Michael and Daphne again, that he had looked after a baby at night. He hoped he had not reached that stage of dotage where he could not still do so, especially with a baby like Rosemary, who needed practically no looking after. He even could, and very frequently did, give her a bath and reveled in doing so, remarking that of course Michael had been a very fine baby, very fine indeed, but that after all Rosemary was exceptional.

As they neared Yokohama, he outlined a plan which admitted of no argument, since obviously he took such delight in it: He had seen Japan inside out, he said, when he and Michael had been there together a few years before. Now Michael must show it to Daphne, and he would take care of Rosemary meanwhile! They must hurry off the boat the instant it was tied up and be on their way to Kamakura to see the Daibutsu at dusk; then early the next morning they must take the day train for Kyoto, which would give them a chance to see the Japanese countryside; and in the ancient capital they must make the rounds of the temples and palaces and tea gardens. They would even have time to get out to Nara to feed the deer before they hastened to Kobe to rejoin the ship. They could hit only the high-spots, of course—but after all, what else was so well worth hitting? And as to the expense—well, the trip was to be his birthday present to Michael. He had had the money laid by for a long time.

There was no gainsaying him, and with the approach to Shanghai he told them a similar story; only it appeared it was Daphne's birthday he had been planning for this time, and a young lady's birthday must be celebrated differently. She must go shopping, he explained, while their ship, which had entered the turgid waters of the Yangtze early in the morning, made its slow way up the mighty stream, churning off into the Whangpoo later in the day amidst the craft of every conceivable kind that choked its passage—junks and sampans, tugs and gunboats, freighters, sailing vessels and ocean liners. She must buy quantities of soft brocades—blue to match her eyes, pink to match her cheeks, green because it would look so cool just now, yellow because it would look so warm later on—and have them made up, overnight, by a skillful Chinese tailor. She must have quantities of embroidered underthings and a big embroidered shawl and a string of amber and a string of jade. Her china and her household linens, probably, she would prefer to buy in Canton; but still, if she found anything along those lines that suited her in the meantime, she was not to stint herself——

Actually, the sums which he squandered upon her were not large; but he produced the effect of prodigality and Daphne returned from her shopping expeditions in Shanghai to look at him with shining eyes.

"This is my trousseau," she said gratefully. "I didn't have any before, you know."

"I know," he said, and added, "let's begin gettings things for Rosemary's trousseau right now. I have a feeling in my bones she's going to make a great marriage and an early one. How could she help it? It's evident she'll be a beauty and she'll have every chance."

It was true that the baby was beginning to give promise of loveliness. Her fuzz of fair hair already showed a tendency to form ringlets; her lashes were long, her eyes wide, her cheeks dimpled. Richard Trent, who professed to be a prophet, declared that when she grew up she would have her father's coloring and her mother's winged look, and that the combination would be irresistible.

"She's a little princess," he insisted, "and all the good fairies have come to her christening. Why, Prince Charming will be battering down the door of her rose-bower before you know it."

"I'll keep the door to Rosemary's bower well guarded," Daphne retorted. "In fact, I'll keep all the gates leading into the garden locked while she's growing up."

She spoke lightly enough; but something in her tone caused her father-in-law to glance at her shrewdly.

"I shall help you to do that," he said, "until the *real* Prince Charming comes—with the very best credentials presented in the most suitable and respectful manner. But we must have her properly equipped to greet him, when he does come. I think we might at least start a string of pearls for her, a very small string, don't you?"

They started the small string in Shanghai, added a bead when they reached Hongkong, and after that kept on adding to these, one at a time, out of Canton's abundant supply. From the first, Richard Trent roamed freely about the native city, choosing the time when Rosemary took her nap, or after she had cuddled down for the night, to do so. He made friends with the merchants on Jade Street and the proprietor of the Pacific Café and with the river people, among whose boats he seemed, from the first, entirely at home. He became a familiar figure as he rode about in his rickshaw and sat in

102

the window of the famous restaurant and sailed his own sampan, his snow-white hair and white pointed beard, his neat black coat and trim trousers setting him apart from the glossy-pated, smooth-faced, silk-clad figures which swarmed about him. Indeed, he was the only member of the household who established bonds of any sort beyond the Island of Shameen, where the foreign colony dwelt and the island across the river where the missionary college was located. Michael, to be sure, saw the Chinese who came to his office, to whom he was courteous and who were courteous to him in return; but they never came to his home, nor did they suggest that he should come to theirs. Daphne's outlook was even more limited; it was confined to the park where she took an occasional walk, and the houses and gardens which flanked her own, in a long row facing the waterfront.

She had moments of regret that this was so. In La Paz she had lived among the Bolivians and they had been her friends; in spite of the handicaps of her health, she had learned their language and their customs and had quickly felt at home among them. Here she was utterly cut off, utterly a stranger; never once had she penetrated beyond the smooth mask of a Chinese woman's face, or spoken to her in her own tongue; never once had she sat with her, intimately secluded in her courtyard, at the hour of tea, or joined with her in the celebration of some festival. She knew that she was missing something precious and beautiful through this segregation; but she was told that it was inevitable, that Europeans who had lived all their lives on Shameen had never had enough contacts with the Chinese to really know them; and gradually she came to take the lack of *rapprochement* between the two races for granted.

It was the easier for her to do so because her existence was otherwise so complete, so smooth-running, so generally satisfactory. Her house was a comfortable one, with large rooms, high ceilings and long verandas; her own ancestral belongings looked beautiful in it; and these were supplemented, from time to time, by the gifts her father-in-law made her, which were by no means confined to jars of ginger and trinkets of mother-of-pearl, but ran to ivories, porcelains and carved teakwood. Her domestic staff, small though it was according to Chinese standards, was double the size that she had ever had at her command before, and its efficiency was a never-ending source of joy and wonder: The food was perfect, the service was perfect, the pattern of life was perfectly ordered. She did not lift her hand to perform any menial task, yet there was never so much as a rumpled doily in the house or a petal out of place in the garden. Her tea was brought to her bedside, her

103

bath was drawn for her, her clothes were laid out, freshly laundered and neatly mended, for her to put on; her one concern with the kitchen was to approve the menus as these were submitted; her sole responsibility for Rosemary, a nominal supervision of what the amah was doing much better than she could do it herself. Her every need was forestalled, her every wish anticipated.

With the mechanism of domestic duties thus completely lifted from her shoulders, and the financial strain of running her household greatly relieved by her father-in-law's cooperation and the low cost of living, she was entirely free to devote her unlimited leisure to the pursuit of pleasure; and she quickly discovered that on Shameen it was not necessary to pursue pleasure either very hard or very far. It came out, easily and alluringly, to meet her. She made a round of formal calls and these were formally returned; then a ceaseless round of gaieties began. Very often she met a group of other women, as agreeably idle as herself, for bridge before luncheon; their households, like hers, ran on greased wheels; there was nothing to harass or detain them. After luncheon came the siesta, undertaken not so much to eliminate fatigue as to guard against it. Then there was more bridge, or dancing at teatime, or tennis for the more energetically inclined, of which Daphne was not one, for she still preferred dancing to any other form of exercise; and she, who had never had her fill of it before, was having it now. The dancing at teatime was interrupted, to be sure, by the cocktail hour and by dinner; but after dinner it began again, and it lasted, night after night, until the stars grew pale and the teeming river woke to fresh life and activity.

Richard Trent excused himself from most of the pursuits in which his daughter-in-law immersed herself and in which he was always courteously invited to join. He had lived a solitary life too long, he said, to enjoy the ceaseless chitchat of Shameen society. He was less scornful concerning the faculty circle of Canton Christian College; but he really preferred to be wholly free, when he was not occupied with Rosemary, to ride in his rickshaw around the native city, to sail among the river people, to stroll along the Bund and to feast on the famous pigeons of the Pacific Café. Michael, however, who took his office work very much in his stride, entered into the rounds of gaiety with the same zest as Daphne. To be sure, since his bridge was better than hers, they seldom played at the same table; and since her dancing was better than his, they never were partners for long. Besides, he insisted on having a set of tennis every day, so while he was on the courts, she went to tea dances without him.

The result was that though they were equally occupied as to their avocations, they gradually, indeed imperceptibly, began to find diversion and excitement not in being together, but in being apart.

Neither one was directly responsible for this or indeed instantly aware of it. The shipboard quarrel had never had a sequel. Their courtesy toward each other, artificial for a few days after the altercation occurred, became spontaneous again after Richard Trent's arrival had eased the strain between them; they wholeheartedly enjoyed their holiday in Japan, and they shared in their satisfaction with Shameen. But some of the glamor had faded from their feeling for each other, some of the glory had gone out of their relationship. The words spoken in anger seemed to have crystallized in their consciousness, and with the cold quality of crystal, these still lay between them, where once they had been so close together. When Michael told Daphne that he had been ordered to the interior on special business, she realized that it was pique because she had not been included in the expedition rather than sincere sorrow over their first separation, which caused her to resent his impending departure.

The day before he was due to leave, when his belongings were already strewn about, preparatory to packing, a dispatch was brought to Daphne. It was from Mrs. James Crofts, who had kept up an intermittent correspondence with her ever since her strange honeymoon in Alexandria, and who herself was prone to shaking the dust of that historic city from her pretty feet, once in so often, in order to range here and there over the earth's surface. It appeared that she was now taking a world cruise on a luxury liner which was soon to stop in Hongkong. She suggested that Daphne should join her there, as her guest, go on to the Philippines with her, and take a local boat back either directly from there or after briefly visiting Java, Bali and Sumatra also. Daphne read it aloud with an impetuous exclamation of delight.

"Too bad you can't go," Michael observed briefly.

"Too bad I can't go! Of course I'm going! Why shouldn't I go?"

"Well, I'm going to be gone. Perhaps for some time. I don't know how long it will take to check with the Chinese Control and straighten out these taxation tangles, not to mention all the other things I have to do. Don't you think one of us ought to stay and look after Rosemary?"

"You know perfectly well your father and Ah Luk will look after Rosemary with a microscope. If you have any doubt of it, why not ask for permission to have your assignment postponed? You could go up the river anytime, and I won't get another chance like this as long as I live."

"Some day it may dawn on you that vice-consuls don't challenge their superiors' orders; they execute them, if they know what's healthy. What's more, if I hit the bull's eye in my report on this trip, it will have a pretty direct bearing on my future. And I intend to make it a knockout. I want to get to Europe for my next post, and I want to get there before senility sets in. I'll have hard enough work wangling that anyway, now that the Rogers Bill has been defeated again, without passing up any chances to improve my record."

"Well, if you're aiming to get to Europe for your next post, I think it's all the more desirable that I should go to Bali while we're in this general part of the world. After all, I was born there. My father and mother lived there. You know how I've longed to see it. And Java too——"

"Yes. I seem to have some recollection of a plan we had of going to Java together. To look at the sunsets, the way we used to do at Arequipa. That was the idea once, wasn't it?"

"Michael, we can't afford to have another quarrel. Is there any prospect that you could take me to Java yourself—any in the world?"

"No, I don't suppose there is—not any in the world. I suppose everything that gives you pleasure, from vicuña rugs to Java junkets will be presented to you by someone else indefinitely."

Daphne crumpled up the cable between her fingers and walked out of the room. She knew that back of Michael's inexcusable speech lay real regret because he had not been able to load her down with gifts. He was just the sort of man who would have delighted in decking his wife out with rare jewels and fine furs and costly laces, in seeing her installed in the most costly suites on steamers and at hotels, in facing her across a long table which glittered with silver gilt and painted porcelain and was lined on either side with distinguished guests. He could not do any of these things, and he was straining at the leash because this was so; therein lay his bitterness, not in anything which she had done or left undone. But his words burnt just the same. Before he could catch up with her, she had dashed off a cable to Mrs. Crofts saying she was sorry she could not accept the merry widow's delightful invitation; and it was only when Mrs. Crofts, who was not used to being so easily thwarted in a plan she had made, actually took the night boat from Hongkong to Canton and confronted Daphne indignantly in person, that Daphne was persuaded to change her mind and go on the junket after all.

It was Richard Trent who aided and abetted Mrs. Crofts's

efforts at persuasion and turned the scales in her favor, for Michael, before her arrival, had already started off for the interior, curt and cool when the moment for leave-taking came. The memory of the casual brevity of his farewell rankled in Daphne's breast all through her own holiday. How was it possible, she asked herself resentfully, that a man should kiss his wife like that, when so short a time before no caress had ever been long and ardent enough to satisfy him? Had she begun to lose her allure for him already? Again her pride was piqued and, safeguarded by Mrs. Crofts's engaging presence, she experimented lightly to see what the effect of her charm would be on the men whom she met. Up to a certain point the results of her experiments were reassuring; then they became alarming. Her cheeks flushed every time she remembered an encounter which had taken place in the garden of the Malacañan Palace at Manila, near the end of a late and elaborate party.

"Good Lord, what are you carrying on so for? You asked for it, didn't you?"

"I thought you were a gentleman."

"Well, I thought you were a woman of the world. Apparently we were both mistaken. Shall we go back and join the other guests? It would rather seem as if we were wasting each other's time, here."

She did not go on to Java and Bali, but took the first Hongkong-bound boat she could catch after this episode, leaving Mrs. Crofts slightly puzzled, but too preoccupied with a suave Spaniard she had just met to feel affronted. Daphne kept to her berth through the greater part of the short passage, declining, almost sulkily, to mingle with the other passengers. She felt out of sorts with the world and everyone in it. But as her ship began to nose its way into Hongkong harbor, moving with difficulty toward the dock because of the myriad small craft flying fluttering pennants which crowded around it, the glimpse which she caught of the Peak from her cabin window proved too provocative to resist, and she went out on deck to watch the shifting pageant.

She had not remembered that it was all so lovely, that the harbor gave such an impression of gentleness and generosity, and that the encircling hills sloped down to meet it in such a gentle and generous manner. Along the waterfront the buildings were clustered closely together; but beyond them was a stretch of unbroken green; and above this were houses, scattered about on the heights, and so precariously perched that they produced the effect of the chamois she had seen in pictures, couchant, yet ready to leap at any moment from crest to crest. When she first went on deck, late in the afternoon, the harbor and the hills looked soft and smooth; then the sun seemed to dodge behind one of the mountains, spilling such radiance around it as it vanished, that Daphne wondered whether the pot of gold itself had not been emptied to form the molten mass. As this radiance faded, the harbor and the hills darkened to black velvet and the lights began to come out—clustering along the waterfront, clambering over the mountainside, like the buildings they illumined; and in the mysterious sky above them a luminary more brilliant than all the others suddenly sparkled and shone.

"What is that gorgeous star?" Daphne asked a ship's officer, who was strolling past, one eye on the progress of the ship, the other on her.

"That's a planet, Madam. Venus."

"Oh! And that little dim one tagging along beside it—is that Cupid?"

He laughed, and they fell into casual conversation. She felt better for her pleasantry, better to be out in the air again, chatting companionably, than she had while she had been shut up alone in her stuffy little stateroom. When, a few minutes later, she was joined by her father-in-law, she greeted him with unalloyed enthusiasm.

"I seem to be forming the habit of meeting the boats you're on, Daphne," he said, half-apologetically. "Well—when your cable came in, saying that you'd decided to start back to Canton instead of going on to Java, I thought perhaps you weren't feeling well, or something. Anyway, I wanted an excuse to return to Hongkong—we didn't see much of it when we passed through before, you know. I thought we might spend a few days at the Repulse Bay Hotel and do a little sightseeing—that is, if you would like to. I have Rosemary and Ah Luk with me. And I've heard from Michael that he isn't leaving the interior for nearly three weeks, so there's no need of hastening back on his account."

He handed Daphne the letter. She had not received one of her own, but she forebore from mentioning this, in spite of the twinge of resentful jealousy that shot through her as she opened the envelope and unfolded the big sheets of sleazy paper covered with Michael's bold black handwriting.

"*Dear Dad*—(she read)—
I have a chance to send off mail on a boat that's going downstream today, and I think it may interest you to hear something about the trip, because I've found it immensely interesting myself, so far.
Of course the accommodations are awful. I share a

108

stateroom with an explorer who's bent on finding out all about insect life in the Orient and I should think he could learn plenty without even going ashore. Our beds are pretty densely populated, and what doesn't come out of the mattresses comes in at the windows instead. The food is about on a par with the quarters. On the other hand, there's plenty of excellent Scotch Whisky aboard and the beer wouldn't be bad either, if it were only cold enough. I'm glad I was warned to bring plenty of silver along, for Canton paper money isn't acceptable and it would have been pretty tough if I couldn't have kept myself in drinks.

My fellow passengers, beside the explorer, are (1) a student who has a job with a reconstruction company, (2) three young aristocrats who hold degrees from Columbia and Oxford who are returning to their native heath after a prolonged absence, (3) a war-lord with a plain wife and two pretty concubines and (4) five missionaries with thirteen children among them. These children are without exception the most obnoxious kids I ever saw and make life miserable for everyone except their doting parents. There's so little free space that it's hard to escape them except when they're asleep. They're always underfoot and generally yelling.

One of the missionaries insists on holding a service every day and passing tracts around. I usually manage to be in the middle of a bridge game when this takes place. (The Oxford boys could lick the pants off Whitehead any day.) I must say though that his wife has a very good voice. She sings well, without any accompaniment, and persuades groups to sing with her. There's something quite poignant about it. She must have been lovely to look at once, though she's a wreck now. Too much malaria and not enough money. Missionaries are paid even worse than consuls. Perhaps the Boards that send them out have even a hazier idea of their necessities than Congress has of ours or perhaps the Boards—like Congress—think it all doesn't matter much anyway.

The countryside is attractive—wooded and mountainous. I've seen quite a few tribespeople and two opium caravans. And I've found an English club everywhere we've stopped so far, even when there were only a dozen other buildings in the place. It's extraordinary how these Britishers dig themselves in——"

Daphne folded the sleazy sheets and handed them back to her father-in-law without reading any farther. Not a word of regret over their separation! Not a single reference to her! It was insufferable!

"Oughtn't we to be getting off?" she asked a little stiffly. "Everyone else seems to be going ashore."

It was pleasant at the Repulse Bay Hotel, but there was not much to do there. Daphne enjoyed the day's outing they took to Macao, finding in the little Portuguese island-city an individuality which made it beautiful as Latin cities, rather than Oriental cities, are beautiful. Wandering through its courtyards and churches, its parks and plazas, she was poignantly reminded of much that she had loved in La Paz and that she now missed; and in the casinos she found excitement in the strange swift gambling. But on the whole she was restless, even a little bored. She was glad when they were aboard the *Fat San* on their way up the river, a blue and placid stream dotted with jewel-like islands, which wound its way along through verdant hills and pastures overhung by a soft warm haze. Her malaise melted away in the balminess of the atmosphere, and she stretched out luxuriantly on a long chair to doze, only to spring up in alarm when two Sikh policemen, blue-clad, white-turbaned, strode suddenly past her, large muskets held firmly in their capable hands, their piercing eyes darting in every direction. The next instant they had been joined by two others, and then by two more; and Daphne, glancing apprehensively in front of her, saw that they seemed to be patrolling the entrance to the second-class quarters, which was formed by a padlocked iron gate standing amidst a row of sharply pointed iron bars surmounted by barbed wire.

"Father!" she called, fearfully. "Just look! Is anything the matter?"

Richard Trent, who was stretched out in a chair beside hers, laid his fingers on his lips to indicate that she must speak more softly or she would rouse Rosemary who, as usual, had cuddled down in his arms and gone to sleep.

"No—no," he said reassuringly. "But as I understand it, these boats are always guarded nowadays. Just as a precautionary measure."

"But six policemen! On this tiny boat!"

"Well, it seems that some of the bandits who are said to infest the river region used to 'plant' a few of their number in the second cabin, so that at a given signal, those on shore and those on shipboard could unite. I believe they did this quite effectually, two or three times. Not lately however. Everything is very peaceful, just now."

"You didn't come down to meet me because you thought the trip was dangerous, did you, Father?"

"Of course not, Daphne! What an idea! Would I have brought Rosemary with me if I had?"

"Well, I met some people in Manila who told me they thought conditions in Southern China were very 'unsettled' just now. They said there was no telling what the Kuomintang might do—that's what it's called, isn't it, this new national movement?"

"Yes, that's what it's called. It's very active, there's no question of that. But I doubt whether it's as evil an influence as it's been represented to you. Only it's like fresh leaven working in old bread."

He began to talk to her about the political situation, with clarity and calmness. She listened to him intently. In La Paz, Michael had sometimes told her about the Chaco disturbances, or the smoldering resentment which Bolivia felt at having been deprived of its last port; but since they had come to China, he had been strangely silent on public questions. Once, with irritation, he had said that he wished the United States had a policy like Great Britain—not just in regard to salaries and post allowances, he was all through fuming about those—but in regard to the zoning of its foreign officers. How could a man who was jumped from Bolivia to China and who, for all he knew, might next be bounced away to Sierra Leone, really know anything about any one country? Whereas, if his field of concentration kept him in the same region—It seemed to Daphne a logical complaint and she would have been glad to have him enlarge upon it. But after his momentary outburst, he had said, with slight sarcasm, that he mustn't make her late for her tea-dance by talking about statecraft, and had gone out himself, swinging his tennis racket.

She regretted his attitude, and because of this regret, drank in the more eagerly all that her father-in-law had to say. She thought she understood for the first time now what the vision of Sun Yat Sen had been, what his true followers were trying to do. But when she told him so, instead of looking pleased, as she had expected, he shook his head.

"Don't ever presume to say you understand the Chinese, Daphne," he cautioned her. "Not even if you should live here for years and years. The Latins, yes—I believe you have already comprehended something of their psychology and caught something of their philosophy. But I doubt if you will ever probe the Oriental mind, even if you try to do so as earnestly as I have, even if you admire it as much as I do."

Because she was so enthralled, she protested against his

pronouncement and urged him to tell her more. She had not moved from her seat when the sudden thickening of water traffic made her aware that they were approaching Canton. Up to then, there had been only a stray sail in sight once in awhile; but now they were surrounded with even more congestion than at Shanghai, by a river life that was merrier than that too, fluttering its pennants, singing its wares, waving its greetings.

"There's no sign of ill feeling here, at any rate," Richard Trent remarked, smiling. He rose and stretched himself, shifting Rosemary expertly to his shoulder as he did so. Then he walked over to the rail to wave a greeting, in his turn. "How can a great group of people living like this be so carefree and so gay and so kind?" he asked, looking back at Daphne. "Families of seven and eight who have no other home, crowded together in sampans hardly bigger than ordinary rowboats, washing their rice and their laundry side by side in the same stream. Look at those little stoves in the rear with smoke coming out of them—they constitute the kitchens, I suppose! And the small cubbyholes that are so brightly decorated are the parlors, no doubt!"

There was no further chance for conversation at the moment. The thickening of water life had been followed by the thickening of land life. The scattering villages had given way to brick buildings crowded together, warehouses, factories, foundries, shops. They were passing Shameen, with its border of banyan trees along the river and the narrow canal at its side. They could see the flags floating from the consulates and the gunboats lying at anchor; then they were opposite the Bund with its bright breadth, its tall department stores and solid banks and spacious clubs forming a jagged skyline. The *Fat San* came to a standstill, churning up water all around it, and their own launch, flying the Stars and Stripes, came chugging out to meet them.

Daphne was glad to be back in Shameen, glad of her own cool comfortable house, glad to watch Rosemary, who was walking very well now, as she toddled from room to room, glad to listen to her father-in-law's dissertations on the Kuomintang and the stories of his experiences in the native city and among the river people. But she was still very restless. She had passed the point where she was satisfied to lie in bed late in the morning, to go from the bridge table to the dinner table and from the tea-dance to the supper-dance. The trivial chatter of her circle bored her. At the college there were women who had some of the new books sent out to them or who kept up with their music; they had a serious purpose in life, and when they spoke they had something worth while to say. But on Shameen the feminine talk revolved mostly around clothes, bargains, petty rivalries and small scandals, with a certain amount of obstetrical detail thrown in.

It occurred to Daphne for the first time that doing the same things over and over, no matter how pleasant these were, might become as monotonous as doing nothing at all, that seeing the same circle of people, however delightful, day in and day out, might eventually produce the same feeling. She had the sensation of riding on a merry-go-round, gaily companioned, but never getting anywhere. At last she said so to Richard Trent.

He did not answer her at once. For a wonder, she had been dining at home, without guests, and they were sitting together, in the cool of the evening, on the long veranda overlooking the little garden at the back of the house. Rosemary had just been carried off to bed, waving to them sleepily, over Ah Luk's shoulder, and babbling "Bye-bye" in her soft small voice. It was very still and peaceful.

"I thought you might come to feel that way, eventually," he said at last. "It's natural for young people to crave gaiety, especially if they've been deprived of it at the very age when they need it most. It was pretty lonely for you, as a girl, at St. Peter's-at-the-Crossroads, wasn't it? And then, of course, in La Paz you were sick so much—I haven't begrudged you your fling, Daphne, and Michael has wanted you to have it too. He's wanted to have it himself. But I've known in the end it wouldn't suffice."

"What will suffice then? I've got more now than I've ever had in my life before!"

"No, my dear, you haven't. Because you're not getting as much from Michael as I believe you did once. And you're not giving him as much. We can't get a great deal in this world, you know, that's worth while, unless we give a great deal. When you and Michael were giving each other the very best that each of you had in you, it didn't matter if you were deprived in other ways, because you two had so much to offer in ways that counted more."

"I should be glad to give Michael whatever I could," Daphne began. But she was too honest to go on. She knew that her bounty, like Juliet's had once been as boundless as the sea, as far as Michael was concerned, but that later she herself had set limits upon it. "—if I were sure he wanted it," she ended rather lamely. "I'm not sure, Father, that he wants anything."

It had seemed easy and natural, from the beginning, for her to call Richard Trent "Father." He spoke to her like a father now.

113

"Are you sure that he doesn't?" he asked gently.

In her turn, she did not answer immediately. He seized upon her silence to go on.

"Why did you name the child I love so much 'Rosemary'?" he asked, with apparent irrelevance. "Do you know, you have never told me? It does not sound to me like a family name. Did you give Rosemary her name for a whim?"

"No," Daphne answered in a low voice. "I named her for the baby I lost. Not literally. Of course, that baby was a boy. But Rosemary means remembrance. I named her for him so that the memory of him should always be kept fresh and beautiful."

"It was a lovely thought. But you are not planning, are you, Daphne, that the memory of the son you lost should take the place of a living son for you?"

"The choice wasn't mine, Father. It was Michael who said——"

"I know what he said. He has told me, in great shame and contrition. But in spite of what Michael said, hastily and cruelly, I believe that the choice has lain with you, my child, and not with him. He has felt he could put no pressure upon you, perhaps because of his wicked words, perhaps because he had done so, to his sorrow, in the past. I do not know. He has not told me that part. But I know that it must have been very hard for you, my dear, that your second child was born so soon after your first; that your first was born—as it was. And it is natural that you should feel as you do. Nevertheless, Michael remembers too, and some of his memories must be both sad and bitter. If you can, be generous to him."

"If I thought——" Daphne said quickly.

"Try to think, my dear. You could not choose a better place than China in which to do so—the Chinese were profound thinkers centuries before our own country had any civilization at all. They have made both an art and a virtue of contemplation. It might prove worth your while to cultivate the art and practice the virtue, even if you had to give up a few bridge parties and tea-dances to do so."

"Father! That isn't fair!"

"Perhaps not, Daphne, perhaps not. You must forgive me if I have said, or if I ever do say, anything that is not fair. I love you dearly, I want above everything else to be just to you—just and friendly and kind. But sometimes I have wondered—I have been sorry, as I am sure you have been sorry, that you have seen nothing of the Chinese, that these vapid, idle, frivolous Europeans should have absorbed all your time. Especially—to go back to the subject we were discussing a little while ago—because it seems to me you might have

114

found a Chinese lady more congenial to you than many of your present companions. Certainly more helpful. She would not have talked slightingly to you, as I have reason to believe some of them have done, about maternity, for instance. In China that is still a woman's great career. She neither shuns it nor dreads it. That was your attitude at first too, Daphne— in spite of the diversity of anguish which it brought to you. Do not think for a moment that I am unmindful of all that you have been through. But I am puzzled as to why you now strive against your manifest destiny, when once you went out to meet it with your head high and your arms held out in welcome."

"I've told you, Father, that Michael—besides, you don't think that is all a woman is for, do you? To have a baby every year?"

"Daphne, you know I do not. Nor will you. Your life will not be so ordered. Maternity, great as it is, touches only one phase of marriage, which is far greater still. Marriage is made up of diverse elements—the spiritual and the mental no less than the physical. But they form an indivisible trinity. Any attempt to sever them results in disaster, for where one begins and another ends, none can say. Could you tell me, if you tried, whether it was your quarrel with Michael that caused your estrangement, or whether it was your estrangement that kept your quarrel alive?"

"No—no. But——"

"Dear child, I have said all I can to you. You must decide for yourself. But again let me beg you to ponder these things in your heart."

The next day Daphne resumed the same old round into which she had been swept so soon after she had come to Canton. And yet it was not quite the same. For even though she had little time to think during the crowded days, she did so during the empty nights. She was not sleeping well, and brief as these actually were, the hours between her return from the festivities of the evening and the moment when the amah brought her early morning tea to her bedside, seemed to stretch out in endless watches. As she tossed restlessly from side to side, troubled reflections filled her anxious mind. If there was banditry on the lower river, what was the condition of its banks as it wound its way to the interior, where Michael was? Might it not be infested with danger— If there were no menace in the state of Canton, why were the gunboats always anchored so portentously in front of Shameen? Did five nations send warships to guard a place that was safe? Instinct told her that they did not.—She could not discover anything on the smooth surface of the island which could give her an instant's anxiety. Yet deep down in her heart she worried over what she could not see.

Nor was this all. As the nights dragged their slow length through, the visions which Richard Trent had conjured up peopled her lonely chamber. She saw herself again, not in the cavernous darkness but through a film of moonlight, heard her own voice as it had sounded when she had said to Michael in the garden, "I've known for a long time that we belonged to each other. I've known this was inescapable." It was true, yet since then she had forgotten, or striven to forget, how irretrievable was their union.—She saw herself again, not shrinking away from her fate, but rising to face it defiantly, as she had when she quoted the Biblical phrases with which she had silenced the *patrona* of the Quinta Bates—"Many fires cannot quench love, neither can floods drown it." Yet after all, she had permitted the fires of mere anger to quench it, the floods of silly tears to drown it. Not wholly, to be sure, but almost—so nearly that Michael and she had both reached that danger point at which complete annihilation, complete shipwreck, came so easily and so quickly——

At last she felt she could bear it no longer. She wept, without shame and without restraint, in the darkness. Then she slipped from between her sheets, and knelt down beside her bed, as she had not knelt since she left St. Peter's-at-the-Crossroads.

"Oh, God, give me another chance!" she prayed, almost as a child might have done. "Just one! Don't let me lose him! Don't let him stop loving me! Punish me in some other way, if I've sinned! I know I have sinned. But I can't stand it if he doesn't need me, if he doesn't want me—anything else but not that! Send him back to me, send him back to me soon, safe and strong. Please, God!"

Even after articulate words failed her, she did not immediately get back into bed. But finally she rose from her knees and lay down again, vaguely comforted, vaguely reassured. Then she drifted off into light slumber. She was roused by the consciousness of unaccustomed sounds, hushed yet close at hand. There was someone entering the house, someone coming up the stairs, someone opening the door of her room. Her first impulse was to scream, to summon help, to flee while there was yet time. Then suddenly she knew what had happened, knew before she felt Michael's hands groping for her in the darkness, before she heard him whispering with his lips against her own.

"Daphne, darling, I've come home! I didn't frighten you, did I, coming to you this way—not really? Forgive me if I did! But I couldn't wait until morning to get to you, and I felt you'd know it was I. I felt almost as if you had called me. Oh, Daphne, I've missed you so, I've longed for you so unutterably! Tell me you're glad I'm here, tell me you do love me still in spite of everything I've said and done to forfeit your love! Let me hear you say we'll never be separated again, never, never, never——"

It was almost a year later when Daphne told Richard Trent that she was frightened. He looked at her in surprise. They were seated again on the veranda overlooking the garden, where she spent a great deal of time in those days. Nothing could have been more peaceful, nothing could have seemed more secure than the tenor of her life.

"Frightened, Daphne? Of what? What can you possibly have to fear?"

"That this won't last. It's too perfect. Everything about my existence. Not just one element in it, but every essential."

"Oh!" Richard Trent said slowly. "Well, perhaps it won't last, Daphne, perhaps it won't. But you're having it now. That's the fact to hold fast to. Because nothing can rob you of that. You know the old proverb, don't you? 'God gave us memories so that we might have roses in December.' When December comes to you, my dear, the perfume of your memories should make life sweet for you still." He touched her lightly on the arm. "You haven't been listening to silly stories about bandits, have you, Daphne, or worrying about the Kuomintang?"

"No, Father. I haven't even thought about them lately. I've had so much else to think about."

"And you're not dreading what's coming to you so soon now, are you?"

"Oh, that! No, Father, not the least in the world. I know that everything is going to be as right as rain this time!"

None of them had doubted that the expected child would be a boy, and in Daphne's and Michael's minds at least, there had been no question of what he should be named. Richard Trent had tried to dissuade them, at first; but when his grandson was put into his arms, his opposition to their loving plan melted away into thin air. Another Richard Trent—one who would fulfill his dreams and do the deeds he never had! His namesake! His heart seemed to dissolve in him with joy as he looked down at the newborn baby.

"Richard Trent, Second," he said softly to himself, when he thought no one was listening. *"Second!* Well, anyway, I was the First—and he is my child too as well as Daphne's and Michael's—the child of their flesh but of my spirit—they know it also. That's why they have named him as they have——"

Daphne's prophecy that everything would be right as rain had more than been fulfilled. Laughingly she said it was "hardly decent" to have a baby so easily—or that one should gain so fast and grow so prodigiously. If she had had her own way, she would have tried to be up and around in no time. But everyone who did not actually insist that she should "take things easily" at least encouraged her in languor; and she fell easily back into the line of least resistance, even after she left the hospital. Ah Luk brought her baby to her to be nursed at six in the morning; but after that she drifted off to sleep again, and woke only in time to watch him being bathed, at her bedside, before his next feeding and her own breakfast. Through the morning she lounged on the upper veranda, sewing a little and occasionally receiving a caller, though there were not many visitors in those days whom she really cared to see, and she made her leisurely convalescence a pretext for prolonging the seclusion of her halcyon days. Michael came home to lunch, and she went down to this; but immediately afterward, when he returned to the office and her father-in-law went out in his rickshaw or his sampan she sank unresistingly back into slumber again. Later in the afternoon, when she had bathed and had her tea, she played with Rosemary until dinnertime, or challenged Richard Trent to a game of cribbage; and when they were through with dinner Michael read aloud to her.

"I'm getting to be the laziest white woman on Shameen," she said once, to her father-in-law. "And that's saying a good deal."

"It makes a difference whether a woman is lazy from sheer stupidity and sloth or because she's pouring out all her vitality for the well-being of her child and building up reserves of strength for herself toward the future," he answered with his quiet smile. "I think you may rest assured that your seeming indolence is creative. Besides, tranquility becomes you, Daphne. You're growing lovelier every day."

It was true. Her figure had filled out a little, her skin had taken on new luster, her hair more sheen; even the clarity of her eyes seemed intensified. What her father-in-law told her so calmly, her husband told her with a fervor that brought quick color into her cheeks. But there was infinite tenderness in his attitude toward her in these days. He knew, as his father had said, that she was pouring out all of her vitality for her child, and that she was storing up future strength for herself. His love for her spent itself in solicitude.

118

It was because he was so careful never to disturb her, never to break in upon her rest or rouse her from sleep that she was slightly startled when she opened her eyes, on the still summer afternoon that had faded far away to the background of her consciousness, and saw him standing beside her. He had never come upon her unaware a second time, and the sight of him, so unexpectedly close to her, sent a swift daggerlike thrill darting through her, recalling, as she did, the night when he had returned, without word or warning, to reclaim her. Was it night again now? A time for love rather than rest? She knew she must have slept a long while. Half a dozen times, at least, she had wakened just enough to know there was no need for her to wake, and then had drifted off again from daydreams to delicious drowsiness, from drowsiness to deep abysmal slumber. The siesta hour must long since have been over. And yet the house was still, almost uncannily quiet. There was no light tinkle of teacups, no sound of softly padding feet; only in the distance she could hear something that sounded like a muffled roar. The room was not bathed in blackness, but the shades were drawn and the light in it was very dim. She sat up slowly.

"What is it, Michael?" she asked sleepily. "Did you want me?"

"I always want you. I always have. I always shall. Remember that, Daphne, won't you, whatever happens?"

"Yes—yes—what has happened?"

"There's trouble in the native city. Oh, God, Daphne, there's no time to break this to you gently! Our servants have deserted us—even Ah Luk—that's why the house is so quiet. I've had to fight my way here from the office. There's been a riot—a—a massacre. The Cantonese are on Shameen already. In another hour—Daphne, don't ask me to tell you details now—every minute you waste may mean your life— Rosemary's—the baby's! The gunboat's waiting—I've got to get you on it!"

She leaped out of bed, thrust her feet into slippers, threw her dressing gown around her. Then she snatched the baby, still sleeping, from his cradle and ran from the room. By the time she reached the stairway she met Michael, who had left her as quickly as he had come to her, calling over his shoulder that he was going to get Rosemary. They rushed down the stairs to the sharp crackle of rifles and the blare of machine guns; and dimly she recalled that one of her visitors had told her that while she had been in the hospital there had been disorder during a procession, some sniping, bad blood afterward. But Michael had never mentioned it to her, so she had not questioned him or thought of it as serious, with the

119

possible aftermath. Neither Michael nor her father-in-law—her father-in-law—her father-in-law—. Suddenly she stopped dead in her tracks.

"Michael!" she cried. "Where is Father? He's coming on the launch too with us, isn't he?"

"No—he—he's staying with me."

"Staying with you! But, Michael, you're not staying yourself, are you?"

"Daphne, dear, don't stop to talk to me now. You know that soldiers and missionaries and consuls don't desert their posts."

"You're sending us away from you—and staying here to be killed yourself?"

Her knees had crumpled suddenly underneath her. By the landing at the waterfront, she could see the launch bobbing up and down, she could hear its shrill whistle above the crackle of the bullets and the blare of the machine guns, coming closer and closer. But only dimly, only like something distant and unreal. Nothing but the figure of Michael, with Rosemary in his arms, was vivid and substantial. Then she saw him set Rosemary on her sturdy little feet, felt his arm go around her own waist, steadying her, supporting her, heard his voice, comforting her, yet compelling her.

"Daphne, don't let yourself go—not—not now! After you get on the boat it won't matter—you can break there, if you have to. But you've got to make the launch—you and the children. There are other women and children on it already—women and children whose husbands and fathers could get to them more quickly than I could get to you. Every moment you hold them up, you're endangering their lives as well as your own."

"What about Father's life? What about yours?"

"Run, Rosemary, run!" she heard Michael saying encouragingly. "Run to the launch—that's the girl! Let Daddy see how fast you can get there! The launch is going to take you out to the gunboat, and the gunboat is going to take you down to Hongkong to have a lovely time!" The child hesitated an instant, flung her chubby arms around Michael's neck and kissed him resoundingly. Then she bounded off toward the stone steps against which the river was still lapping lightly. The launch was making the chugging sound which presages departure, its whistle was blowing sharp and angry blasts; but they did not drown out Michael's voice as he went on speaking to her.

"Father was killed this afternoon. He was riding in his rickshaw, among the people he loved. He was pulled out of it and slaughtered by the mob—he was an easy mark in his black clothes. I didn't want to tell you, I wanted to spare you that. But you've got to go, I've got to make you. So I have to tell you. You can't save his life by staying, it's too late for that already. But you can save his namesake—the 'child of his spirit.' You and nobody else. If you don't come with me now, Daphne, you'll be false to him and everything he taught us."

Somehow she found her feet. Somehow she covered the narrow strip of ground which still lay between her and the launch. Michael was half-carrying her already, and as they reached the waterfront, he lifted her up and swung her over the railing with her baby still clutched to her breast. But before she dropped, safely, on the other side, she saw his eyes shining down upon hers, and heard him speaking to her once more.

"Remember, darling—whatever happens—nothing can really separate us now."

The launch shot forward into the water. Michael stood on the waterfront, with the flag on the Consulate floating out behind him.

PART IV

"Hope Deferred"

CHAPTER 10

THE MEMBERS of the Board of the Foreign Service Personnel were seated in the private office of its chairman, the Honorable T. Gilbert Morgan, Assistant Secretary of State. He was a very precise man whose personality dominated his nondescript headquarters. A long succession of Assistant Secretaries of State had failed to leave any visible imprint on the high white walls, the large blank windows, the frayed mouse-colored rugs and the slippery leather furniture in the apartments assigned to these functionaries. But even if the accessories of which Mr. Morgan made use had been blotted from view, one glance at his smooth hair, his expressionless face, his tight collar and his immaculate clothes, would have convinced the casual caller that his desk would be uncluttered, his blotter spotless, his inkwell shining and his papers arranged in neat piles; also that the only ornament in view would be a framed photograph of his wife in correct but conservative evening dress. Such a portrait did indeed dominate the desk of the Assistant Secretary of State and it was one which was characteristic of Mrs. T. Gilbert Morgan, who had seldom been seen in Washington society after dark without a tiara, and who still ordered her corsets from the same firm which had made them to measure for her nearly half a century earlier. It was a standing jest among the pert young sprigs in the Department that she slept in both, and that the Honorable Gilbert had never been inconvenienced by either.

At Mr. Morgan's right was seated Mr. Joel Grimes and at his left was seated Mr. Ambrose Estabrook, both of whom also ranked high in the Department. Mr. Grimes was aged and spent; Mr. Estabrook was young and vigorous; both beat themselves in vain against the impassivity of their chairman. At the moment, Mr. Grimes was thinking longingly of his dog, his hearthstone, his carpet slippers and his pipe. Mr. Estabrook was thinking of a governmental overthrow in Athens and wondering if his lieutenant, Hillary Faulkner, would give him a ring if anything arose during his absence, or whether Mr. Faulkner would seize upon this as a pretext for making an independent decision. The Honorable T. Gilbert Morgan was perfectly well aware of what was passing in the mind of each and was entirely impervious to it.

"Well, gentlemen," he said at length, glancing down at the small memorandum pad which lay before him, "I take it we have practically finished our labors for the afternoon. We all seem to be agreed that Mr. Finnegan should remain in Bahia but that he should be promoted from Class II to Class I and that Mr. Emory should be transferred from Bangkok to Lisbon without promotion. Before we part, however, we might briefly consider the case of Mr. Michael Trent, about whom there seems to be some difference of opinion."

Mr. Grimes sighed, but said nothing. Mr. Estabrook, with scarcely a proper pause, seized upon the opportunity created by his superior's silence.

"I really feel very strongly about Michael Trent, Mr. Morgan," he said earnestly. "It seems to me that if anyone deserves a break, he does."

"I'm prepared to listen to your views, Mr. Estabrook, though I'm not sure I share them."

"I realize you don't share them but I think you know them already. Michael Trent has played into hard luck ever since he entered the Service. He has no private fortune and the La Paz post would have been an endurance test for him under those circumstances, even if he hadn't had his wife's illness to contend with. But he made good in it. He didn't whine and he didn't whimper. The Bolivians and the Americans both liked him. He ran the office efficiently, he wrote excellent reports, he got trade results. Loose came to swear by him and Loose is one of his biggest backers now."

"I am aware that Mr. Loose thought highly of Michael Trent. But after all Mr. Loose has now been retired to private life, so his opinion is comparatively negligible. Besides, if I may say so, his judgment was never marked by the greatest delicacy of perception."

"He's had enough perception to pile up twenty or thirty millions," retorted Ambrose Estabrook, "and even if he has been retired to private life, his campaign contributions are still pretty substantial. I doubt if he's resigned to permanent retirement. But quite aside from all this, Michael Trent made good in Canton also. And his experience there was ghastly. His father was killed almost before his eyes. His wife and

123

children were wrested from him and taken off in a gunboat. He lived for six months under conditions which were simply appalling. I don't think any of us here begin to realize what our officers went through in Canton during the autumn after the Shakee riots. There wasn't a woman left on Shameen, or a servant. They did all their own work—washing, cooking, cleaning. They went with baskets to a local godown to get the ice and vegetables that were run up from Hongkong—otherwise they wouldn't have had any. Their living conditions were unspeakable. Their lives were in constant peril, both from disease and from sharpshooters. The strain was terrific. The——"

"Mr. Estabrook, I do not wish to interrupt you. But as the hour is getting late, I must remind you that Mr. Grimes and I, no less than yourself, have given due attention to the report on the Chinese situation."

"That's so, that's so," remarked Mr. Grimes, rousing himself for the first time. "The reports were distressing, Mr. Estabrook, I agree with you there—in fact I could hardly bring myself to read all the details. But I looked over the digests, I assure you. I did indeed."

"Well, then," Ambrose Estabrook went on, with a determined effort to keep his contempt for his colleagues from revealing itself in his tone, "I think you will agree with me, Mr. Grimes, that it's time that this boy had something good coming to him. He's had a terrifically long pull. What about that vacant secretaryship in Berlin? I believe Trent would do well in Berlin. And he's exactly the kind of man Representative Rogers had in mind in planning for the consolidation of the Consular and Diplomatic Services."

"Mr. Trent, like yourself, is a Harvard man, I believe, Mr. Estabrook? Indeed, if I am not mistaken, he is a member of the same club to which you belong and which you both joined as undergraduates—though, of course, Mr. Trent came along sometime after yourself."

"Well, yes. But Trent isn't what's generally called a 'typical Harvard man,' though I suppose I am. He isn't a Bostonian or even a New Englander. He didn't go to Groton. He——"

"There is a very general feeling, as you know, Mr. Estabrook, that too many Harvard men have been appointed to the more desirable posts. The public doesn't pause to inquire where such men come from, or where they prepared for college. They are conscious only of the University background, which always seems to make itself felt—sometimes rather arrogantly, not to say objectionably. Don't you agree with me, Mr. Grimes?"

"Why, yes, Mr. Morgan, I do, on the whole I do. There has indeed been a good deal of criticism. Now if Mr. Trent had only gone to Columbia, or even to Yale, the matter would be much simpler, very much simpler. But as you say, Harvard—" He looked rather piteously from Mr. Morgan to Mr. Estabrook and back to Mr. Morgan again. He did not wish to seem to insult the University from which Mr. Estabrook had graduated and in the councils of which he stood high, and yet at the same time he knew that Mr. Morgan, who was a graduate of the University of Chicago, must be conciliated. He himself was a product of Union, and felt duly humbled in the presence of the others. "Harvard is inopportune, slightly inopportune, just at this juncture," he concluded lamely.

"Well, then," said Mr. Estabrook, his voice slightly edged with irritation, "why not keep him here in the Department? He'd fit in well, either in the Latin American Division or in the Far Eastern Division. And I have reason to believe that he'd be very glad to be stationed in Washington for a time. I happen to know that his wife has recently inherited a fine old place in Alexandria. They are living in it now. That is, most of Mr. Trent's leave so far has been spent in St. Louis, settling his father's estate—what little there is of it. But Mrs. Trent has been in Alexandria—she and the two children. She's very happy there. It's her ancestral home."

"I do not think, Mr. Estabrook, that we can take into consideration the ancestral homes of the wives of our Foreign Service officers in deciding where these shall be stationed."

"Well, I think we might stretch a point and consider Mrs. Trent in some slight degree!" Ambrose Estabrook exclaimed, his annoyance no longer under complete control, "especially since there's absolutely no question of her husband's superlative qualifications. She lost her first baby in La Paz. She left there with her second one when the poor kid was a fortnight old. Her third one was born the week of the Shakee demonstration. She refugeed with these two youngsters in Hongkong while the worst of the trouble in Canton was going on. But she was taken off Shameen almost by force and she was the first white woman to go back there. She's stood by her husband through thick and thin, and he's had it thick and thin both. I'd be glad to see her able to live like a lady, for a little while."

"Mrs. Michael Trent appears to inspire such sentiments in the minds of most of the men who see her," remarked Mr. Morgan dryly. "Undeniably, she is very alluring." Then, as Ambrose Estabrook flushed angrily, and seemed about to break out into further impetuous speech, the First Assistant

Secretary of State raised a warning hand. "I think we had better not go into that, however," he said. "Let us confine our discussion to the merits of Mr. Trent and not stray toward the attractions of Mrs. Trent. I admit that the young man is above the average in ability. At the same time, his record has not been flawless. In one instance at least he has been guilty of grave indiscretion. He has been known to state that he considers British methods preferable to American methods in some respects—in the zoning of Foreign Service officers, for instance. I think you will agree with me, Mr. Grimes, that such a remark, coming from an American Foreign Service officer, is very unfortunate."

"Why, yes, Mr. Morgan, I'm certainly amazed that——"

"Well, I'm not," broke in Ambrose Estabrook, hotly. "I'm sure he said it—if he did say it—when he was almost desperate. I know the Far East, gentlemen, better than either of you do—if you'll permit me to say so. I served my own apprenticeship there. I know what Michael Trent went through in Canton, even before there was any question of a revolution. He was in charge of passports, he was responsible for issuing visas. Nine-tenths of all the Chinese who come to this country originate in Canton or its vicinity. Nine-tenths of the ones who want to come will go to any lengths to get a visa. They'll lie, they'll forge, they'll bribe. They're especially strong on bribing—and Michael Trent isn't a rich man, as we said before. The pressure put upon him through bribery must have been pretty hard to withstand. And he did withstand it—completely and comprehensively. That's more than we can say for all our men, I'm sorry to admit, gentlemen. But it puzzled him. He couldn't follow the workings of the Oriental mind. He couldn't understand why a people which in so many ways is so civilized and so cultured should take graft as a matter of course. He felt that if he'd only had more experience in China, he might have grasped the situation better. Possibly he said so—impetuously or confidentially, to friends."

"Or to his wife? It's just possible, isn't it, Mr. Estabrook, that his remark may have been made to his wife, and that in spite of the fact that she seems to be such a paragon that she may have been so ill-advised as to repeat what he said—confidentially or impetuously, to friends? However, we will not pursue that point. The main point is that if Mr. Trent were to remain in China longer, he would come to know the Oriental mind better, would he not? Which is just what he has said himself that he would like to do?"

"You'd send him back to China—when his father has been slaughtered there?"

126

The Honorable T. Gilbert Morgan rose, drawing a neat line across his memorandum pad. "*I* shall not send him back to China, Mr. Estabrook," he said coldly. "I do not need to remind you, I hope, that majority opinions prevail on this Board. You have expressed your opinion concerning Mr. Michael Trent very clearly and, if I may say so, very forcibly. But Mr. Grimes has not yet expressed his views. He has hardly had an opportunity. And I am afraid that I must now bring this very interesting conference to a close. Mrs. Morgan and I are going to the White House for tea this afternoon and it is time for me to join her. But we do not need to make an immediate decision. Mr. Trent still has another month's leave coming to him in any case, which at our discretion may be extended. I should not disapprove of such an extension, under all the circumstances. We can therefore carry over the consideration of his next appointment until our next meeting. I wish you good evening, gentlemen."

Ambrose Estabrook went down the steps of the State, War and Navy Building feeling slightly sick. It was not the latest news from the insurrection in Athens which had upset him—that, it appeared, was dying down as quickly as it had flared up, and Hillary Faulkner had not taken too much upon himself in regard to it either. But this business about Michael Trent was certainly very bad—unbelievably bad. It didn't seem possible that Morgan could use his power to break the boy, to punish him for one peccadillo instead of rewarding him for all his pluck and all his perseverance. Yet that was the sort of thing that Morgan had done before and that he might do again. It was the sort of thing in which he seemed to delight. Ambrose felt sure that as a boy, the First Assistant Secretary of State had pulled off the wings of flies and trapped defenseless rabbits.

Well, Michael Trent was neither a fly nor a rabbit; he could not be permanently maimed, he could not even be seriously injured. But he could be given a severe setback, he could unjustly be made to suffer acutely. What he needed now, to build up his morale, was a boost. There must be some way of seeing that he got it. Ambrose decided to leave no stone unturned that would help him to find this way, though lately he had been trying to avoid any action which would publicly proclaim his distrust and dislike of the Honorable T. Gilbert Morgan and his contempt for Joel Grimes. There had been so much gossip floating around Washington and percolating through to the country at large regarding a "split" in the State Department, an alignment of certain high ranking officers against certain others, that he knew it was the course of prudence to refrain from a rash move which

127

would give color and substance to such reports. At all events, there was nothing he could do about it at the moment. Indeed he did not have anything at all in mind to do at the moment. He had not been invited to the White House to tea or anywhere else to tea, for that matter. Since Constance, his wife, had died of typhoid fever in Singapore, he had rather lost heart for merrymaking; and gradually his friends had ceased to urge him to join them in jollification. But he had lost none of his driving energy and he did not wish to linger aimlessly in the vicinity of the State, War and Navy Building, the sight of which, looming ponderously up toward the blue sky, was obnoxious to him. Its ornate bulk, unredeemed by simplicity of surface or detail, had never seemed so hideous to him before. And it was a beautiful day. He felt as if he would like to go somewhere or do something. As he unlocked his car and turned on the engine, it occurred to him that he might motor out to Alexandria and find out whether Daphne Trent were at home.

The cherry blossoms were already in bloom, and as he skirted the Speedway and saw their rosy reflection in the Tidal Basin, his irritation began to pass. In spite of the oppressiveness of some of its public buildings, there was undeniably a quality about Washington in the springtime which gave a man a lift. And the minute the Potomac was crossed, there was a consciousness of brooding peace as well, as if the essence of the South had come stealing up the stream. It was too bad that the new bridge and the Memorial Highway were so long in building—when they were finished the ride along the river would have elements of quiet magic in it. But even without such an approach as the broad boulevard would eventually give it, the quaint little city toward which Estabrook was bound had its own self-contained charm, and it appeared that outsiders were becoming more and more aware of this. There were signs of restoration and renovation on every side. The slight shabbiness, the slight decadence of an earlier era, which had succeeded the one of splendor that had come earlier still, was yielding everywhere to signs of prosperity and progress.

Estabrook glanced up at the weird wax figure, about which he had heard so many conflicting legends, that kept its strange watch over the empty spark plug factory; then he slowed down, as he went by an imposing array of colonial dwellings, which had once sheltered the Lees, the Fairfaxes, and other famous families. It was certainly a great stroke of luck for the Trents, he reflected, that Miss Georgina Fairfax, whose death had been as timely as that of Richard Trent had been tragic, should have willed her beautiful flounder house to Daphne. Her father-in-law had also left her a small legacy, and she had immediately converted this into cash and put the cash into her home. Layers and layers of dingy paper, coat after coat of drab paint, had been scraped away; the exquisite woodwork, the pale cool walls of the house had been revealed afresh in all their pristine beauty. Weeds and underbrush had disappeared from the neglected garden, and its high sheltering wall, crumbling into ruin, had been solidly rebuilt. Pansies and primroses were blooming between low hedges of dwarf box, daffodils and tulips were swaying in the spring breeze, blossoming bushes of quince and forsythia were clustering in the background. They all contributed to the charm of the plot, singularly secluded for a garden in the heart of a city.

The gate clicked as he opened and closed it, with a distinctive sound which he had learned to like. He had scarcely shut it, when he saw that Daphne was directly in front of him, bending over her flower beds in such absorption that she did not instantly notice his approach. Then she straightened herself suddenly and looked directly toward him, her wide blue eyes framed by a flushed face and tumbled hair.

"Oh, Mr. Estabrook!" she exclaimed. "I'm so sorry I didn't hear you! But I'm awfully glad to see you. I've just got hold of two new millstones—I mean two old ones—well anyway, two more—and I've been trying to figure out the best place to put them. They're beautifully imbedded now, and I've been wishing someone would come along, so that I could show them off. Will you take a look at them? They're in the rear, near my new kitchen. Perhaps you'll let me show you that, too. Or do kitchens bore you?"

"Not at all. I have a great predilection for kitchens."

"Well, you'll lose your heart to this one then. It's the kitchen of my dreams—big drainboards on either side of a shiny sink, countless cupboards, a gleaming white range——"

She broke off with sudden shyness.

"I don't suppose a leading light in the State Department, like you, could possibly care about such things," she said. "But they make me happy, the same way that music does, or mountains—I had a pet mountain in Bolivia, did I ever tell you? I pretended that it belonged to me. I missed it ever so much, after I left it. But now I don't miss anything. I'm so happy to be at home again, that I couldn't."

"I thought you were the young lady who wanted to see the world?"

"Well, I did. But I have seen a good deal of it now. Enough to know there's nothing in it that can compare with Virginia!"

He laughed, but did not contradict her as she led the way

129

to the millstones. "I think they look nice, don't you?" she asked a trifle anxiously. "I have an extra reason now for wanting them to be exactly right. I've just been elected to the Alexandria Garden Club. I'm tremendously pleased."

"Of course you are," agreed Ambrose Estabrook gravely.

"I've had the magnolia tree trimmed since you were here," Daphne went on. "But I've gone about that very cautiously. I'm sure it is a tree with a soul. Cousin Georgina told me she had heard from her mother that all through the War Between the States it didn't bloom once. And—it didn't bloom while Michael and I were in China, either. But now it is covered with beautiful buds. You must come out next week and see it again—it will be a mass of glory then.—Will you sit out here in the garden while I mix you a mint julep? I never saw the mint as tender and fresh and green as it seems this spring! Or will you come into the parlor? I have the new gilt cornices up over the gold-colored curtains and those are pretty too."

He knew from her voice that she wanted to show him the newly decorated drawing room. So he followed her willingly into it and saw that she had made it very charming, carrying out a scheme of white and gold most effectively. The library too, on the other side of the small square entrance hall, had undergone improvements since his last visit. There was a great globe near the wing chair drawn up beside the fireplace; and close to a sunny window, an ancient reading stand. The walls were lined with old books, the paneled mantel surmounted by a mellow portrait. Daphne looked at him, inquiringly, almost like a child waiting to be praised, and Ambrose Estabrook smiled.

"It's all immensely successful. Don't let some member of the 'Foreign Legion' talk you into selling it. Outsiders are swarming in here these days like locusts."

"*Talk me into selling it!* Why, Mr. Estabrook, I'd cut off my right hand before I'd sell it!"

There was no doubt about it, she had tears in her eyes. She loved this house and the garden which surrounded it as she loved human beings. They were infinitely precious to her, and now that she had come into undisputed possession of them, she regarded this as permanent. Moreover, her own nature was undergoing a form of joyous expansion, because of them, which had in it elements of poignancy.

"Wouldn't you like to come upstairs, too?" she asked, with growing self-confidence. "The gallery is very pleasant. I think the children are having their supper there right now. But perhaps you don't like children?"

Ambrose Estabrook did not especially like children, but not for worlds would he have told Daphne Trent this. He went with her up the narrow staircase, glanced, at her suggestion, at the beautiful four posters and lowboys in the rooms on either side of the hallway and followed her out on the gallery. In one corner of it, a little girl was sitting at a small white table; and as she put down the silver mug which she was draining, Estabrook saw, with surprise, that her eyes were flecked with gold, like her father's, and that her hair was golden too, as his must have been when he was a child, and that even her delicate skin had a golden tinge, but that in spite of this extraordinary coloring, it was Daphne whom she really resembled. She slid at once from her seat, and without prompting or urging, dropped a quick little curtsy and held out her hand.

"How do you do?" she said politely. "I am very pleased that you came to see us."

"I am very pleased that I could come, Rosemary. Your name *is* Rosemary, isn't it?"

"Yes, and I haven't any nickname and neither has my little brother. His name is Richard."

"Where is your little brother?"

"Mammie is giving him his bath. She helps me take mine first, because then I can start supper by myself. Richard can't. He spills what he puts on his spoon. He can't wash himself, either. I can wash everything except the middle of my back, and Mammie says lots of big people don't wash the middle of their backs. But I shall, when I get big. I like to be clean all over.—Would you care to have some of my supper?"

"Thank you very much. But your mother has promised to make me a mint julep."

"Sometimes she lets me scrape the frost off the goblets with my fingernails," observed Rosemary. "May I tonight, Mother?"

"Yes, darling, if you like. But sit down again now and finish your supper. I'm sure Mr. Estabrook will excuse you. We'll go and have a look at Richard."

Unselfconsciously, the child curtsied once more, slid back into her seat and picked up her mug. As Estabrook held the door open for Daphne to re-enter the house, he spoke impetuously.

"What a beautiful little girl! And what charming manners she has!"

"Yes, hasn't she? She has always been like that. My father-in-law insisted that she was a little princess, a sort of fairy changeling."

"And it's a queer thing, she has your husband's coloring, but she looks like you."

"Father said that too—though she's much lovelier than I

131

ever was. And she's bright too. She's doing awfully well at kindergarten, and in Mrs. Callaway's dancing class. And she goes to Sunday School at Christ Church. She's fitting into the pattern of life in Alexandria as naturally as if she'd always lived here."

"And as if she were always going to!" Ambrose Estabrook thought, with a sudden wrenched feeling about his heart. It was evident to him that Daphne was hopefully assuming that her husband would be kept in America, that her stay in Alexandria would be indefinitely prolonged. Everything she was doing—the reclamation of the garden, the renovation of the house, the installation of the little girl in school—pointed to this. Again, as when he had walked down the steps of the State Department, he felt slightly sick. Then he heard a joyous shout, and saw that a little boy, still wet from his bath, had escaped from his nurse and rushed across the hall, hurling himself headlong into his mother's arms.

He was not as beautiful as his sister, Estabrook noticed instantly, though in coloring he was very like her; but he possessed some indefinable quality which the little girl lacked. In the dim light of the hall, the hard-headed diplomat who was accustomed to facing facts and was not given to indulging in fancies, could have sworn that the child looked as if he had a halo around his head. He seemed to radiate joy and light. Smiling at the stranger over his mother's shoulder, he diffused an essence of happiness and trustfulness. Daphne looked at her visitor across his bright head.

"Do you know that phrase in the prayer book about 'a child of grace and an inheritor of the kingdom of heaven'?" she asked softly. "I always think of it, whenever I take Richard into my arms. It describes him completely. Rosemary has looks and poise, but he has something more. I don't know yet what, but something. He's his grandfather's namesake, you know."

"Yes, I do know. And I see what you mean."

"I'm rather hoping," she said more lightly as she led the way down the stairs, "that my next child will be an American. My first one—my first two—" she amended with a momentary return to gravity, "were little Bolivians. And Richard is Chinese! So I think it would be nice——"

"Of course, no matter where a child is born it is legally an American if its parents are American citizens. You know that."

"Yes, of course, I know that. But it doesn't seem quite the same. Perhaps I should have said I hoped he would be a Virginian!—Will you be comfortable, do you think, in the drawing room, while I go to mix the mint juleps?"

He would be entirely comfortable, Estabrook assured her, as he established himself on the loveseat, covered with gold brocade, that was placed at right angles to the fireplace, a piecrust table, on which a crystal bowl of daffodils was standing, beside it. It was unthinkable, he kept telling himself, while he waited for Daphne's return, that this family should be needlessly uprooted. Morgan must see the young mother and her beguiling children in their own home, he must be made to realize.—Surely if he once came into contact with Daphne's charm and Daphne's candor, even the First Assistant Secretary of State would not be able to resist them! When she came back, bearing the frosted goblets on a silver tray, he asked her a precipitate question.

"Do you go out much in Washington, Mrs. Trent? It doesn't seem as if I'd seen you there a great deal."

"No, I haven't been out there a great deal. You see, Michael has been in St. Louis most of the time since we came back to the United States, and I've been terribly busy trying to get settled here, so that everything would be comfortable and look attractive when he came home. He's been delayed longer than he foresaw. He had a chance, unexpectedly, to sell his father's house—the quarter of the city it's in has changed a great deal, there's a large brewery going up there. Michael has always said that St. Louis is mostly breweries and convents, anyhow. He was glad to sell the house. Aside from the consideration of money, I mean. He doesn't feel about it as I do about this place. His father's soul was what mattered, the house was just a shell. And now that's empty. The soul has escaped. The soul of the people who lived here has been captured."

"I understand what you mean.—Do you write poetry, Mrs. Trent?"

"Why, no! I've never written a line of anything in my life! What made you ask?"

"Because, more than once, when you've been talking to me, you've given me the feeling that I was listening to poetry. When you first described La Paz to me, for instance, as 'a cluster of jewels lying in an agate bowl.' "

"That was Michael's phrase."

"Yes. But you interpreted it. And just now when you were talking about souls—first about the souls in trees and then about the souls in houses, you gave me the feeling again. Trees and houses have souls of course. But most people don't know it or can't put their knowledge into words."

He stopped, suddenly embarrassed. It was not like him to talk so intimately to anyone, now that Constance was dead, to reveal that he was touched and moved. Moreover, he had

133

been switched from the subject he had especially desired to pursue. Unconsciously, Daphne continued to sidetrack him.

"Perhaps you guessed that I have always wished I could write poetry," she said in the shy voice which he found so entrancing. "When I said I'd never written a line in my life, perhaps I gave you the wrong impression. I—I have tried. But the words don't come when I try to put them on paper. Only when I speak them. But my father did write poetry. Quantities of it. Among other things."

"What became of the things he wrote?"

"I'm afraid that some of them were lost. And some of them were printed in newspapers and thrown away. And some of them tied up in bundles and locked away in an old trunk at St. Peter's-at-the-Crossroads."

"Have you read them?"

"Not for a long time. And not many of them. I've always meant to. But you don't do such things thoroughly, you know, when you're a young girl. And I haven't been back to St. Peter's-at-the-Crossroads since I was married. Uncle Roger and Aunt Vinnie have been here to spend the day with me and to see the children, but I'm waiting for Michael to take me to see them."

"Don't wait too long," said Ambrose Estabrook involuntarily.

Afterward he was bitterly sorry that he had said it. He saw a look come into her eyes that was not shy, but startled, as if her sweet sense of new-found security had been shattered. She did not lose it again throughout the evening, though this was a very pleasant one. Before they had finished drinking their mint juleps, her Cousin Tyler Fairfax came in with his friend Mrs. James Crofts, who seemed to grow more fascinating every year. Without much difficulty, they were persuaded to stay for supper, and after supper there was a rubber of bridge. When it was over Ambrose Estabrook heard himself promising, without forethought, to dine at Mrs. Crofts's house the following Sunday; and soon he was commuting more or less regularly to Alexandria. He had not realized that life there was so gay and leisurely, and that it was so easy and delightful to fit into its pattern. But it afforded fewer and fewer opportunities for quiet calls on Daphne, as his circle of acquaintances there widened, and his participation in its festivities came to be taken more and more as a matter of course, not only by Daphne's relatives and intimates, but by Daphne herself. So it was some days before he had a chance to press the point which he had already tried to make, without success.

134

At last, however, he found the occasion of doing so. She had set up a gay striped umbrella now, over a painted table, in the corner of the garden where the millstones had been laid, and had grouped chintz-cushioned wicker chairs around it. The place was a restful one in which to spend a late afternoon. The magnolia tree, heavy with fragrance and foliage, was in bloom now; so were the purple iris, the snowy bridal wreath, the first pale-pink roses. Daphne and her children were embowered by them all.

"You've been to call, Mrs. Trent, haven't you, at all the proper places? I mean at the White House, and on the wives of the Secretary of State and the Under Secretary of State and on Mrs. T. Gilbert Morgan?"

"I'm afraid I haven't. You see, I haven't any car yet. I've been waiting to find out whether I'd be able to afford one after I'd finished paying for the house. And I think I can. But I've never learned to drive one, anyway, and all that makes the problem of calling a little difficult. I thought, after Michael got here we'd go together."

"Well, try to do it as soon as you can, won't you? I don't need to remind you, after your foreign experience, that some people set great store in the observance of such formalities. I know the Morgans do, for instance."

"Yes, I suppose they do. I will go, Mr. Estabrook, I really will. I'll look at cars this week. And I think Michael will be home almost any day now. But you see I've been so busy and—and so happy right here. Fixing over the house and getting Rosemary started in kindergarten and making sure that Susie's cooking would stand up under the test when the head of the family came home. Moaning Moore is the old fashioned type of mammie—I know how to get on with that!— But training a modern maid is a great responsibility and Susie is nothing if not modern."

"Moaning Moore!" exclaimed Estabrook.

"Yes.—It's a quaint name, isn't it? It's a little doleful, but I don't mind that. Moaning Moore's mother was my grandmother's mammie, who curled her hair and embroidered her pantalets and taught her to 'observe the courtesies of gentility'. Her name was Moaning too—Moaning *Tombs!* So a generation has made some progress toward cheerfulness! But Moaning Tombs was a wonderful woman, just as her daughter is. During the War Between the States my Great Uncle Andrew had a flag of the finest rep silk made at home for his regiment, but before it was finished he was sent to Fort Donelson, so the flag was left with my grandmother. After the fall of the Fort he made a hasty retreat South, but he sent a message to my grandmother telling her to

135

present the flag to the first Confederate company that passed by the plantation. As the whole region was occupied by Federal troops, it was quite a problem to think of a safe hiding place for this treasured ensign. So Mammie offered to keep it. She wrapped it up carefully and put it in the bottom of her cedar chest and covered it with carpet rags."

"Yes? And then?"

"Then one day a searching party of soldiers came along looking for hidden valuables. They ransacked the big house and then they went into Moaning Tombs' cabin and opened her wardrobe and threw the contents on the floor. They didn't find anything in the wardrobe so next they demanded the key to the chest. Moaning Tombs didn't dare decline to give it to them. But when they began to rummage, she rolled up her eyes and put her hands on her hips and began to moan. I reckon she lived up to her name. She kept saying, 'Mah Lawd, mah Lawd! I thought you Yankees was the friend of niggers! I thought you done come to protect us. Mah Lawd, mah Lawd!' At last the officer in command couldn't stand her moaning any longer, and he told his men to 'let the old nigger's rags alone.' So the flag was saved."

"And what happened to it eventually?"

"Oh, eventually, my Great Uncle Andrew came back and got it himself. He was the kind who would. He lined up his entire force in front of the big house and had a flag-raising. And Grandmother went out on the balcony to see it and took Moaning Tombs with her. She addressed the troops formally and told them that she herself had brought the flag to them from its hiding place in the cabin of a faithful negro. At that point Mammie placed her hand on her heart and made a profound bow and began a speech herself. 'That was me, Gentlemen,' she said. And three rousing cheers went up for Mammie——"

"It's a delightful story—in fact all your stories are delightful, Mrs. Trent. But you didn't tell it to me by any chance, did you, with the idea of changing an unwelcome subject? We were talking, as I recall it, about the advisability of more contacts in Washington."

"But, Mr. Estabrook, there's so much to do right here in Alexandria that I never need to go into Washington for amusement! I don't think it's awfully amusing anyway. I heard someone describe it a little while ago as a place where you talked to people you didn't know about something you didn't know anything about. That seems to me a good definition. Here it's different. You know yourself how pleasant our mint julep parties and bridge games and buffet suppers are, and what a way they have of prolonging themselves indefinitely, so that you drift from one to another. Then some of us have taken to going down regularly to Kettlands' for sea food every Thursday—it's a quaint old tavern, we must take you there too—and Mrs. Crofts has just bought a houseboat, which I don't believe you've seen, and which is ideal for warm evenings on the river. And then there's the Garden Club and Section B at Christ Church and the Colonial Dames——"

"It's charming, all of it. It's complete of its kind. But if you'll permit me to be very frank, Mrs. Trent, I'm going to tell you candidly, it's not the kind of a life that will affect your husband's future very much. Or rather, it may do exactly that. What I should have said was, it won't help to advance him very much. And I'm sure you don't want to leave any stone unturned that will do this."

"But I'm not *hurting* his prospects, am I, Mr. Estabrook? Why, I can't be! I haven't done anything!"

"That's just the trouble. Try to do something. Go out in Washington society. Make an effort so that you will know people and understand what they're talking about. Register in their minds—as an individual and as a wife of one of our most promising young Foreign Service officers. You had some contacts when you were here as a girl, didn't you— with the Quigleys and the Tittmanns and other Congressional families, for instance? Get in touch with them again!"

"Do you really think, Mr. Estabrook, that the Tittmanns and the Quigleys are great social assets, that they'll help advance Michael's interests?"

Daphne spoke solemnly, but Estabrook was conscious of light satire lurking behind her words. He answered her seriously.

"They're not social assets in the usual sense of the word. Of course I know that as well as you do. But it's a mistake to underestimate any Congressman's influence, even that of a pretty uncouth Congressman. Don't forget that Tittmann liked Michael well enough to give him his first chance and that he probably still likes him. He might be disposed to give him another. Besides, you know Senator Stone, don't you? He's spent a lot of time, off and on, all his life, in your neck of the woods, and his sister-in-law, Honor Bright, on whom he dotes, is practically a next door neighbor of yours in King George County. You couldn't have a better friend at court! But as far as I know, you've never yet asked her to darken your door!"

"I know that Honor isn't in the mood for leaving Solomon's Garden, any more than I'm in the mood for leaving Alexandria. But when I go down to visit Uncle Roger and

Aunt Vinnie at St. Peter's-at-the-Crossroads the next time, I'll go over to see her too."

"Yes, I hope you will. But it seems to me every time I see you, you've postponed that visit to Solomon's Garden again! And you might at least try to get Honor and that good-looking husband of hers up here. Why, you wouldn't even have invited *me* here, if I hadn't taken the trouble to seek you out. You're all so satisfied with your own little charmed circle here in Alexandria that you don't ever want to leave it and you don't greatly care whether anyone comes to enlarge it. But I'd heard such glowing accounts of both you and your husband from Mr. Loose, the last time he passed through Washington, that I was determined to meet you. Besides, I'm interested in Mr. Trent as a Harvard man and a fellow club member and a Foreign Service officer who's made good in a post where I was stationed myself as a youngster. He did better in it than I did—a great deal better. But he had an advantage over me—he had a wife to look after him, and a home, when he was on Shameen. I lived at the old Victoria Hotel—the 'morgue,' we used to call it. The walls there used to get so damp, in summer, that there was blue mold on them. And three men on my corridor died of cholera that same spring." Estabrook saw Daphne wince, and knew that he had been thoughtless and cruel to speak of Shameen, that any reference to it was horrible to her. "Forgive me," he said slowly, "and get all the joy you can out of Alexandria. I know you need it. I know you deserve it. But just the same, don't neglect the White House and the State Department. You can't afford to."

She promised that she would not, and the next morning she went over her accounts with great care and decided that she could afford a car. That very afternoon she made the rounds of the agencies, inspecting various inexpensive models and inquiring as to arrangements for driving lessons. That evening, however, a telegram came in from Michael, telling her that he would be home the following day; and in her joyous preoccupation at the prospect of seeing him again, she completely forgot that she had failed to complete any kind of a transaction.

Eventually, she made up for the oversight. She bought the car, and soon handled it so expertly that even Michael complimented her on her mastery of it. Together they went and left cards at all the appointed places; but nobody happened to be receiving when they called, and though later they were invited to several official garden parties and went to these also, they were completely swallowed up in the crowds of indifferent strangers who swarmed about them. The official season was almost over, Congress was soon to adjourn, practically everyone was making plans to leave the capital for the summer, and Mrs. T. Gilbert Morgan had already gone. It seemed futile and foolish to Daphne to try to pursue a penetrative campaign under these circumstances, in spite of Ambrose Estabrook's warning, especially since Michael himself did not urge it. He too preferred to stay quietly in the garden, to romp with the children, to read aloud to Daphne, to play a quiet rubber of bridge, or to lie stretched out on a steamer chair on the tiny deck of Mrs. Crofts's houseboat. He did not even go out to the Bellehaven Club for golf. Daphne could not remember that she had ever seen him so listless. It was as if something had snapped, as if the energy and enthusiasm which had long appeared inexhaustible had been slowly but surely drained away.

At first his mood seemed to Daphne natural enough. She had expected that he would be depressed and exhausted when he first returned from St. Louis. He had been under a strain there which must inevitably have been devastating, not so much in itself, but because of the memories it evoked and the associations which it brought to an end. But she had not foreseen that once he had got away from there it would take him so long to recover. She reproached herself, openly, for not having gone there with him.

"You couldn't have been in two places at once, darling," Michael reminded her. "It meant more to me to have all this ready to come to, in the end, than it would have meant to have you in St. Louis. And we wouldn't have had any place to put the children there—that is, not any good place. Besides, I wanted to be alone. I wanted the feeling that there was something between Father and me in which no one else had any part, not even you. You don't mind, do you, Daphne?"

"Of course not, Michael. I know just what you mean. But I'm afraid you were terribly lonely."

"Well, I was. I stayed alone in the house, all alone, as you know. The way Father used to when I was away at school and college and—afterward. But I wanted to do it that way. I wanted to re-create for myself what his life must have been. Solitary and sacrificial."

Michael sank into a reminiscent revery, from which Daphne wisely did not try to rouse him. At last he went on of his own accord.

"I didn't mind selling the house. As I said before, that was just a shell, and when it was empty it was meaningless. But I found I felt differently about the furniture. Father's bed, you know, and his books. The desk he always used. The silver and china and drawing-room set that my mother had had when she was a bride. I've had them all sent on by freight. I hope you won't mind that either. I don't know just what we'll do with them here. You have this house beautifully furnished already, and anyhow, they wouldn't be suitable for it—there's nothing colonial, though some of the pieces were inherited and are pretty good early Victorian. I hadn't realized before that this period had its own attractions."

"Of course, it did. I'm sure I can use all the china and silver anyway—I didn't have as much of those as we needed. And we can put the furniture out into the Quarters, until we decide what we would like to do with it. We might even fix up the Quarters, in ante-bellum style, which would be perfect with early Victorian furniture, and rent them."

The Quarters consisted of a long low building at the rear of the garden which had contained the old kitchen and smokehouse and the rooms for the slaves. Daphne had taken no steps, as yet, toward renovating these; but she had seen the possibilities of what could be done with them, and her fingers were fairly itching to get at the task. She was delighted at the thought that Michael had given her a reasonable pretext for doing so.

"Well, let's just store the furniture there, for the present," he said disappointingly. "After all, we don't know how much longer we'll be here—perhaps only a month or two. You might get halfway through your renovation and then have to leave it uncompleted. In that case you couldn't rent the Quarters, and everything you'd put into them would be a total loss."

"But don't you believe, Michael, that we're going to stay here, that you'll be assigned to the State Department next?"

"I don't know what to believe. I haven't had a hint all this time. In fact I haven't heard a word from the Department, officially, since I got the notice saying my leave had been extended. I know that my name didn't even come up for consideration at the last meeting of the Personnel Board. And still it was one of those sessions which Morgan is forever talking about, that last indefinitely. He gloats in going around Washington with a martyred air saying to everyone whom he can buttonhole, 'I must get back to the State Department. The Board of Foreign Service Personnel will be having an all night meeting.' I hear that Faith Marlowe called his bluff once, and asked him if he couldn't possibly get through with the meeting in seven or eight hours, if he had hot coffee and sandwiches served at midnight, and whisky and soda at two A.M. But he glared at her without answering. He doesn't

140

appreciate her at all. He's obsessed with the idea that woman's place is not in the Senate, but in the salon."

"But Mr. Estabrook likes you very much. Why didn't he try to bring up your name?"

"He did try. But Mr. Morgan doesn't like me at all. That's the answer in a nutshell."

"Why, what about Mr. Grimes? He'll have the deciding voice, if there's a difference of opinion, won't he?"

"That poor old derelict! His voice never decided anything —he never raises it! It's his master's voice that counts. And unless I'm very much mistaken, Morgan is his master. Two or three men, acting together, might be stronger than he is. But not any one man, acting alone. Certainly not Estabrook. The Back Bay era is over at the State Department. This is the era of Lake Shore Drive."

"But don't you believe Mr. Estabrook is trying to get two or three men to act together—trying indirectly I mean? Don't you believe he's making an effort to bring pressure to bear upon the Personnel Board from outside?"

"Yes, I believe he is. But it's a question whether he'll succeed. Anyway, there's nothing I can do about it."

This, as Daphne realized all too well, was not a normal attitude for Michael to take. Hitherto he had always felt there was something he could do, whatever happened, whatever was at stake. And now nothing really disastrous had happened and so much that was vital was at stake! Apathy, like weariness, was unnatural in Michael. But Daphne could not bring herself to put pressure upon him. There was something too pathetic about his spent state.

Hitherto, she had always leaned on him. Now she was aware that he was leaning on her. He was turning to her for solace, for refreshment, for refuge. She sensed his loneliness if she left him even for a little while; he wanted to know that she was near him, within the sound of his voice and the reach of his hand. But he did not make love to her and for hours on end he did not even speak to her. It was enough for him merely to know that she was there. She learned that anything in the nature of curiosity irritated him, that all exertion wearied him and that passion was numb or dormant in him. But occasionally, on his own initiative, he confided in her.

"I'm glad you put your nest egg into this house," he said to her one day, when an expansive mood was upon him after a long period of repression. "You've made it wonderfully attractive. God, but it was awful when I first saw it, what with the chocolate-colored wall paper and the brick-red paint and the knickknacks and the antimacassars—not to mention the bay windows and the stained glass! Now it's exquisite, it's unique. I believe you've made a good investment. If you should ever care to sell it, you'd get a big price for it."

"I don't think I shall ever care to sell it," she said, speaking more quietly than when Ambrose Estabrook had made a similar suggestion to her. But she was pierced by a sudden pang. "Why should I?" she asked, still striving to keep her voice calm. "This is our home."

"Oh, I don't know! You might feel it was the sensible thing to do. Foreign Service officers don't have homes, you know, only dwelling places—that's all they're entitled to. After all, I've sold my home."

"You sold the house that used to be your home. It wasn't any more. You said yourself that was different."

"So I did. But you might come to feel differently about this. If we leave here, in a little while, for South Africa, for example, wouldn't it be foolish to hang onto it if you got a good offer for it?"

"I don't think so. We would always have it to come back to."

"Yes—after we'd been to Finland and the Canary Islands and New Zealand! Ten or fifteen years from now!" He looked at her, and saw an expression of concentrated tranquility, which he knew represented supreme self-control, on her face. "Forgive me, darling," he said, reaching over and taking her hand. "I didn't mean to be a kill-joy and a calamity-howler. But I was all in when I got here, and now this endless waiting is getting me. I'm what you'd call 'whipped down,' in King George County hunting vernacular!"

"We're waiting in a pleasant place anyway. If we were sent off, it might be to a very unpleasant place. Do you remember the Perrys, who were so nice to us in Panaria? Mr. Perry has been transferred, and I had a letter from Mrs. Perry the other day that doesn't sound as funny, the second time you read it, as it does the first." Daphne turned to the desk in her breakfront bookcase and produced the letter. Michael took it listlessly. He read:

"Dear Mrs. Trent,
"I cannot resist writing again to tell of our experiences, which finally at supper tonight reduced us to gales of laughter in spite of the fact that I have been in tears most of the day. We moved into our house last Friday and found that every variety of insect . . . had made their homes here ahead of us. Several cans of flit, plus creolin, etc. left us in comparative privacy from the winged invaders, but the house was screenless and the windows are about eight feet high, so we had to hurry

142

a herd of carpenters out here to remedy that defect.

"*We have finally acquired two servants, one cook from Trinidad and a little Andean Indian maid. They were the only two out of twenty-odd applicants who were able to present clean bills of health. The cook is a perfect wizard when it comes to frying bananas; Jim brought a jar of imported jelly home tonight and kept it in his pocket telling me that he had it just in case we got fried bananas again. Sure enough when dessert time came, the fried bananas put in their appearance and it seemed so funny that we really had our first good laugh in a long while!*

"*This morning I found the cook (who comes highly recommended) paring a corn on her toe, in the kitchen, with a bread knife. Wouldn't you love to have dinner 'chez nous'? Just before dinner we were sitting in the living room, which is quite a way from the kitchen. All at once we heard the maid shout at the top of her lungs from the kitchen 'La Comida esta servida.' And so it is—with fried bananas!*"

Michael handed the letter back to Daphne without a smile. "No, it isn't funny," he said grimly. "But I'd rather hear we were going to be shipped off to some spot where conditions were like that than not to hear anything. If I only knew what was going to happen to us, I wouldn't be so low—or so edgy. Of course there's no reason why you should sell the house, now anyway. We're not too badly off. I haven't talked much to you about finances, have I? I should have, long before this, and you've been an angel not to pester me about them. Well —with my salary and my cleared inheritance we can count on about five thousand a year."

"We can be very comfortable on that, Michael, considering that we have the house besides, if we're careful."

"Yes, if we're careful!" he exclaimed, suddenly speaking with resentment again. "If we don't send the children to first-class schools or do any elaborate entertaining! If you never go to a good dressmaker, and I never belong to a good club! If you don't have any more children and I don't have a surgical operation or a long illness! If we don't try to save anything for the future! Under those circumstances, we can be fairly comfortable, I suppose!"

"Michael, dear, we're ever so much better off than when we started."

"Yes—because your cousin and my father have died—not because I'm a member of the American Foreign Service, en-

143

titled, as such, to a decent living! I feel as if every cent I touch was blood money!"

He jerked himself out of his chair and began to pace up and down the small garden. Daphne watched him with a heavy heart. "He's commencing to feel caged already," she said to herself. "He isn't contented here in Alexandria, the way I am. He was, for a little while, but he isn't any longer. And he can't stand scrimping and saving, or even the thought of them. It doesn't satisfy him to have security. He wants riches. He's got to have them, to feel he's succeeded." Aloud, she said serenely, "Michael, how would you like to go down to St. Peter's-at-the-Crossroads for a few days? I've been waiting for a good chance to suggest it, and this seems to be one. We could take the children and the car and have a little outing."

"All right, if you feel like it. I don't care what we do."

The next morning they were off, remaining in the country until the end of the week. On the whole, the visit at the old rectory was pleasant. Uncle Roger and Aunt Vinnie, who had both failed perceptibly, were pathetically glad to see them; Mamie Belle outdid herself in the array of delicacies which she set before them; the county families were all extremely cordial. When she and Michael went to Solomon's Garden, Daphne managed to have a few words alone with Honor Bright Stone who, in spite of the seclusion in which she now lived, was, as Ambrose Estabrook had said, still a great power on the Washington scene, both in her own capacity as a writer, and through her brother-in-law, John Stone, the Junior Senator from Massachusetts.

"Daphne, I do wish you'd spoken about this to me before!" Honor exclaimed regretfully—almost reproachfully, it seemed to Daphne. "You know that President and Mrs. Conrad have gone away on that Central American Goodwill Tour and that John has gone with them! They won't any of them be back in Washington this summer, unless there's some sort of a national crisis. Faith Marlowe might have been helpful too, but she's in Germany with her son. I could have said a word very easily to her—I've known her all my life—and it wouldn't have been much harder to approach Neal Conrad. He's an old friend too. I'll try writing, if you like, but personally I don't advise it. You can ask favors, in person, that sound all right. But when you try to ask them on paper, they seem aggressive or presumptuous."

"Yes, I know," Daphne agreed sadly.

"In the autumn, if it isn't too late—" suggested Honor.

Daphne thanked her, but in her heart she felt that endless as the waiting seemed, everything would actually be decided

144

long before autumn. She tried not to let her sense of depression and discouragement spoil her enjoyment. She had always been very fond of Solomon's Garden, as a place, and she was devoted to both Honor and Honor's husband, Jerry. But the interlude there was not wholly successful. She was kept aware that Michael was unstimulated by it. And when they left it, he was critical in his comments as they motored back to St. Peter's-at-the-Crossroads.

"I can't understand why the Stones should elect to live in such a god-forsaken place. It can't be a question of money with them."

"Oh, Michael, Solomon's Garden is a heavenly place! I think it's the most beautiful place in Virginia. And that's the way they like to live. Jerry always wanted to be a planter, from the time he was a little boy. And Honor would rather dig out old documents and make them over into thrilling historical novels than do any other kind of writing."

"Jerald Stone could have been a great public figure, like his father and his brother, if he'd only tried. He's got all the natural gifts and Lord knows how many millions. And his wife, before she sank into this state of desuetude that seems to go with the holy state of matrimony, as far as she is concerned, was a crackerjack. I'll never forget her 'Honor Bright' articles or her 'B. Ware!' column."

"But, Michael, Jerry didn't want to be a great public figure. He may have a talent for politics, but he hasn't any taste for them at all. And Honor was sick to death of the articles and ashamed of the columns, before she got through with them. They don't crave careers. They're too happy by themselves."

"You're not suggesting, are you, that I ought to be so happy, simply in being married to you, that I shouldn't care what became of my career?"

A few years earlier Daphne would have flared up, too, and there would have been a quarrel. Now she answered with infinite tenderness and patience.

"No, Michael dear, of course I'm not. You're more of a man than Jerry, in every way. You'll amount to more, you're bound to, it's essential that you should. And I'm not beautiful and gifted like Honor. I couldn't be to you what she's been to him, no matter how hard I tried. I haven't got it in me to fill a man's life to overflowing, as she has. I know all my own limitations. If only they don't hold you back!"

Instantly he was all contrition, as he invariably was when his Irish temper had flamed quickly out of control. But it got the better of him several times in the course of the next few days. He had always viewed Dr. Daingerfield's preoccupation

145

with the history of crossroads churches impatiently; now this proved excessively annoying to him.

"I should think your uncle would have gathered by this time that I'm not thrilled at hearing that they're characteristic of Virginia, that elsewhere churches were usually built in villages," he told Daphne irritably. "Especially since I've heard it now about fifty times. It doesn't thrill me either, to keep on hearing that St. Peter's-at-the-Crossroads is unique because the rectory adjoins it, that this wasn't the colonial custom—you told me that yourself, the first time I ever saw you! Or that parsons used to be paid in tobacco when that was cheap and in money when tobacco was high, thus insuring their poverty in either case! As far as that goes, I don't see that customs have changed very much—poverty seems to be the only attribute of a clergyman's life that is insured! I hate to see a man submit tamely to such conditions!"

"They've accomplished a good deal, first and last, even if they have been poor," Daphne remarked quietly. "They've been teachers as well as preachers and farmers at the same time. And some of them have been saints and scholars too. As for this history Uncle Roger's working on—well, I can see that would have real value."

"For whom? Who'd read it? Who'd publish it?"

"I don't know yet. But I think someone will, someday. Uncle Roger has the same sort of gifts my father had. They're diverted in different directions, that's all."

"I'm afraid they're buried in both cases, Daphne. You better make up your mind to it and turn your own attention to something more practical."

"I never pretended to be practical, Michael."

"I know it. And I don't want you to pretend now. I want you to buckle down to the idea in earnest."

Aunt Vinnie's predilection for the harp irritated him even more than Uncle Roger's preoccupation with history. Everytime that she touched the strings proved the occasion of a fresh outburst.

"My God, can't she let that thing alone? It sets every nerve in my body on edge!"

"I know it does, Michael, but I can't bear to tell her so. That harp isn't just a musical instrument to Aunt Vinnie. It's a symbol of sentiment. Her great-grandmother and her grandmother and her mother and all her elder sisters played on it. She believes that on silent nights she can hear them playing on it still. You know, Michael, that there's at least one ghost in every well-regulated Virginia household, and at St. Peter's-at-the-Crossroads there are seven of them—seven lovely ladies who play celestial harps."

"I wish you wouldn't talk such nonsense, Daphne."

"But I'm not sure it is nonsense. Sometimes I've thought I heard them myself."

"What!"

He was so visibly angry that she changed the subject quickly. But afterward, when he reverted to it himself, making sarcastic remarks about "seven silly, simpering sentimentalists," she rallied to the defense of the harp players.

"They may have been sentimentalists, but they weren't silly or simpering. They had lots of courage. They were good shots and they rode beautifully. They knew as much about hunting and horseflesh as they did about music and loved these just as much. During the War Between the States, when the Yankees were pilfering and plundering all through the region, some of their horses were stolen. So after that the sisters took turns at sitting beside the drawing-room windows all night, two or three of them at a time, with their fingers clutching at the reins of the horses which were crouching just outside. They saved nearly all of them that way. Silly, simpering girls wouldn't have had that much resourcefulness and endurance."

She could see that the story impressed him, she knew that mentally he was making comparisons between her and other women of her family to the advantage of both. Nevertheless he continued to give vent to the general irritation which the atmosphere of St. Peter's-at-the-Crossroads seemed to engender within him; and this irritation developed into actual antipathy against all his surroundings after Daphne unwisely persuaded him to attend the funeral of Mamie Belle's sister-in-law, Floretta.

Daphne knew that Jerry had come to share in Honor's feeling of affection and responsibility for the negroes on Solomon's Garden, and that he would not dream of absenting himself from any occasion, either sad or joyful, which affected them intimately. She saw no reason why Michael should not be capable of parallel assimilation. She felt that with his usual zest for weird impressions he would be intrigued by the strange spectacle of the barren little church in the "Hollow" where the colored people worshipped, when this had assumed funereal guise: The homemade coffin, the simple sprays of garden flowers, the preacher's prayers, the mourners' wailing, the sweet husky singing of "lined out" hymns—all these, she believed, would prove touching and arresting to him. She had not rightly reckoned on the degree of his apathy or realized that an experience which in a foreign land would satisfy his yearnings for the exotic would fill him with repugnance if undergone in his own country.

She saw him shrink back when their seats of honor, directly behind the casket, were designated; she knew that he was trying to avert his eyes from Floretta's still form and the uncanny color of her face, so different from the pallor which he had hitherto associated with death; and as the sermon progressed, she saw lines of loathing deepen around his mouth.

It was very warm and the church was very crowded. The itinerant preacher had come from a distance, and now that he had finally arrived, after a delay of several days, he seemed determined not to stint his audience. He dwelt at length on the virtues of the departed: even though she had never been baptized, he felt sure she would be saved; he had known that she was getting religion the last time he saw her, from the way she sang to him. As he enlarged upon this scene, and the untimely complaint which had followed it, the mourning of the congregation rose to a wail, led by the bereaved widower and Mamie Belle herself, with Floretta's twelve children joining in the chorus. The preacher could hardly make himself heard above it as he lined out the final hymn.

> *"Why should we trouble to convey . . .*
> *This body to the tomb? . . .*
> *For days the flesh of Jesus lay . . .*
> *And shed a sweet perfume . . ."*

By the time they had escaped, Michael was actually rigid with rage. Instead of breaking out into invectives which cleared the atmosphere, he did not speak at all until they were nearly home. Then as he stopped the car, it was only long enough to permit Daphne to descend alone.

"I'm not getting out," he said shortly. "I'm going to drive far enough and fast enough to get some fresh air into my lungs. Of course I won't presume to comment on the flesh of Jesus. But as to Floretta's flesh, after awaiting the arrival of the preacher throughout several summer days . . ."

All the next week his sarcasm was scathing. When eventually he saw Daphne coming down the stairs from the attic, laboriously carrying a small ironbound chest, he spoke to her with unwarrantable sharpness.

"Good God, what have you got there? A child's coffin, homemade like Floretta's?"

"I have my father's papers, Michael. Don't you remember I spoke to you about them a long time ago, and then again when we first came here this time?"

"I'd forgotten them—and I thought I suggested that you'd

better forget them too! What are you going to do with them now?"

"I thought I'd take them back to Alexandria with me, and look them over, evenings."

"Hell's bells, haven't you spent enough time with your uncle shuffling through old papers about churches and graveyards while you've been here! And haven't you got the Alexandria house full enough of junk already without dragging some more home? I'd say you had! There's nothing in it except the plumbing that isn't at least a hundred years old."

"Well, the plumbing is nice and new, isn't it, Michael?"

She did not argue with him about the little chest. But the next day, while he was out in the garden with her Aunt Vinnie, she tugged it down another flight of stairs and stowed it away in the trunk on the back of the new Ford. When Michael saw it they were already late about starting home, and though he exploded again, he did not bother to take it out. When they were halfway to Alexandria, he began to tease her about it, which was his way for apologizing for his outburst.

"So you put one over on me, Daphne, about that old chest?"

"Not really. You know I wouldn't do that, Michael, that I wouldn't deceive you. But I didn't want to have an argument about it and I did intend to take it. So I thought——"

"Quite a cagey girl, I'd say."

She was glad to see him in better spirits than in a long time, but she knew that his merriment was only ephemeral, that within an hour or two the depression which seemed to have become habitual would reclaim him. Her mind reverted to a Bible verse which she had learned as a child, as it so often did with her in times of trouble. "Hope deferred maketh the heart sick, but when desire cometh, it is the tree of life." Michael had been sick with deferred hope for many weeks now; only the signal success which he craved as a starving man craves food, could serve him on which to draw as a source of strength.

Daphne opened the gate which led into her own garden with a sense of thanksgiving that they were home again. In the flounder house they had, after all, every essential to happiness. Surely Michael must come in time to recognize the sanctuary it gave them, to feel not only contentment but fulfillment within its walls. And surely nothing could wrest it from them now. Fate would not again play false with them.

149

The house was hushed and cool as they entered it. There was a lantern burning above the front door, flanked on either side with ivy-covered walls; another light, more softly shaded, stood beside Michael's old secretary in the library. He walked over to this, and picked up the pile of neatly stacked mail which Susie had laid there for him. For a moment there was a sound of ripping envelopes and crackling paper in the still room. Then silence again, shattered at last by a harsh laugh, as Michael handed to Daphne a sheet surmounted by the letterhead of the Department of State:

"January 21, 19___

Michael Trent, Esquire
Vice-Consul Class I at Canton
On leave in the United States of America
Alexandria, Virginia
SIR:
   You are informed of your transfer to the
American Consulate at Yünnanfu, China,
where you will serve as Consul Class VI
of the United States of America.
   You are directed to proceed to China as
soon as practicable by shortest available route and you are authorized to charge
the actual cost of transportation and sub-
sistence while enroute between Washington
and Yünnanfu, in accordance with the
Government Travel Regulations. Upon com-
pleting this travel you will render an
account and draw a draft on the Secretary
of State at 15 days sight, to reimburse
yourself for the allowable expenditures
made.
   Upon your arrival at Yünnanfu, you should
report at once to the American Consulate
there, where you will be informed of your
duties.
   I am, Sir, your obedient servant.
      For the Secretary of State:
         AMBROSE ESTABROOK,
            3rd. Assistant Secretary of State"

CHAPTER 11

THE GREAT gate of the American Consulate at Yünnanfu swung slowly open on its hinges, permitting the Master, the Master's Wife, the Small Girl and the Small Boy to pass within it. The gateman bowed almost to the ground as he admitted them. The mafu who had been standing in the shadow awaiting their return, advanced and helped them to dismount from their strong, shaggy ponies.

The Master's Wife, the Small Girl and the Small Boy always smiled at the gateman and spoke to the mafu when they came in, and then stopped to give the ponies parting pats and lumps of sugar, before they went on to the inner courts, past the gateman's house and through the outer court where the chairs were kept, and where the chair bearers and the relief men patiently awaited their pleasure. But very often the Master did not speak or smile at all. He strode along to the offices which were located just inside the outer court, where the two Chinese clerks and the strange secretary who made up his staff awaited him. He entered the offices and laid down his riding crop and began the business of the day without saying anything at all except a brief good morning. It had been that way ever since he had come to Yünnanfu, four years earlier.

He had been royally welcomed on his arrival. The Consul whom he was relieving, Mr. James Jarvis, had come to the station to meet him, accompanied by Mrs. Jarvis and the Jarvis twins; and Mr. Jarvis had been in excellent spirits, proud and pleased to be able to tell his successor that he had just acquired title, on behalf of the American Government, to the palace of a former viceroy. This palace contained some thirty or forty rooms in all; it was surrounded by a beautiful botanical garden and enclosed by a high substantial wall: In Yünnanfu Mr. Trent would be lodged commodiously, whatever he had endured elsewhere—and the news had somehow seeped through to Mr. Jarvis that Mr. Trent had endured a good deal, here and there, first and last. He greeted Mr. Trent heartily, slapping him on the back, shaking him by the hand, and becoming immediately voluble on the subject of the viceregal palace. But none of this seemed to cheer Mr. Trent as much as Mr. Jarvis had expected; so then he turned expectantly to Mrs. Trent, who rewarded him by being more responsive, for which he was duly grateful. Doggone it all, he had done his darnedest—and it wasn't as if all those goldfish ponds and marble figures and flowering courtyards and painted pavilions were going to do *him* any good! He was hell bent for God's country, the sooner the sweeter.

Besides the Jarvis family, several other American families had come down to meet the train on which the Trents were arriving, which they had taken at Haifong, after their three-day voyage on a small French coastal steamer. The other

Americans had all taken the same steamer from Hongkong to Haifong and the same train when they had come to Yünnanfu themselves. So they knew how it all was: They knew how the customs officers made disembarkation an ordeal. They knew how the narrow gauge railway wound its way upward and finally reached the heights as if exhausted by its tremulous passage. They knew how welcome the crystalline atmosphere was to the jaded wanderers when they reached Yünnanfu, and yet how remote and intangible this always seemed to strangers. Surely an outsider's arrival was a time and an occasion when any American would hold out a glad hand to any other American, let alone a new Consul!

So they were all there: Mr. Means, who represented oil, Mr. Echols, who represented automobiles, and Mr. Perkins, who, in a sense, represented God, since he was a Methodist missionary. Each of these men came with his wife and children. Mr. Bowes, who was an aviator, and Mr. Clancy, who was a mining engineer, came alone, for they were unmarried; but they joined forces after their arrival at the station, as they were very good friends. These persons were all residents of Yünnanfu itself, so it was easy and natural for them to come to meet the train—they frequently did so, for it furnished a diversion. But there were several additional missionaries representing as many different denominations who were located hither and yon about the Province, and who had temporarily abandoned their battle with bandits and their struggle for souls in order to come into the city and welcome the new Consul.

Everyone was genuinely glad to see him. Mr. Jarvis had been popular, but platitudinous, and platitudes wore thin if you saw a man every day and several times a day. Moreover, the American colony understood his eagerness to get to the United States, and it would have been unbecoming to begrudge him his holiday at home after his years of exile. A new man, new business and social methods, new jokes, new mannerisms, would all provide variety so sadly needed in a place where the round of activities, pleasant as it was on the whole, was permeated with monotony.

Accordingly Mr. Means and Mr. Echols, as well as Mr. Jarvis, were hearty in their greetings, and Mr. Perkins murmured that he hoped the blessing of the Lord would rest on the new Consul's work in the foreign field. But before Mr. Bowes and Mr. Clancy could come crowding forward, it was evident that, after all, this was not an occasion for backslapping. Mr. Trent was courteous, but he seemed to be rather reserved; he did not invite familiarities and it might even be doubtful whether he would brook them. As for his wife, whom Mrs. Jarvis and Mrs. Means and Mrs. Echols and Mrs. Perkins had all been prepared to welcome warmly, she was lovely-looking but she was apparently rather shy, and her eyes had rather a hurt look, as if something had made her suffer, though she smiled very sweetly. Only the Trent children seemed wholly without restraint. The little girl, who bore such an uncanny resemblance to both her father and her mother, responded cordially to the overtures of the Jarvis twins; the little boy, who had a remarkably winning way about him, accepted with candid enthusiasm a ball which Tommy Means offered him, and bounced it up and down the entire length of the station platform, catching it as it sprang up to meet him.

In spite of the disarming friendliness of Rosemary and Richard, however, the American colony was conscious of a slight chill. It called, collectively and individually, at the imposing Consulate, and its calls were duly returned; but it hesitated to press conviviality on a couple which apparently shrank from this for some reason. The Trents attended the farewell parties given for the Jarvises as a matter of course, and went down to the train with the other Americans to see them off when they took their exuberant departure. But after that there was a hiatus in hospitality.

Mrs. Means was the first to make a determined effort to bring this to a close. Feeling inwardly a little uncomfortable, as if something she had eaten had disagreed with her, but outwardly appearing smiling and breezy, she called on Mrs. Trent a second time and invited her to join the Ladies' Bridge Club.

"You do play bridge, don't you, Mrs. Trent?"

"Oh, yes! Not as well as my husband, but I do play. I enjoy it very much. When does the Ladies' Bridge Club meet, Mrs. Means?"

"Every Wednesday morning at eleven."

"Then I'm afraid I'll have to say no, much as I regret doing so. You see, I teach Rosemary in the mornings. By the Calvert Method. I'm very inexperienced, and that makes everything so plain. We're shaking down into the routine nicely. But I don't dare tamper with it. I feel my only chance of succeeding is to keep regular hours and to make Rosemary keep them. I'm sure you'll understand."

"Yes, of course. I think you're awfully plucky to show so much initiative. I'm afraid Tommy is growing up a young savage; but I don't seem to have much knack about teaching him. And it's so easy just to drift along any old way in a place like this."

"Why don't you let him come here for lessons? I could

153

teach two children as easily as one—not that I know anything about teaching, as I've just explained, but I'll do my best. And the companionship and competition would be wonderful for Rosemary. Tommy's about her age, isn't he? Five?"

"No, he's over seven," Mrs. Means confessed, a little shame-facedly. "Why it's most awfully kind of you, Mrs. Trent! But I'm afraid it would be an imposition."

"Of course it wouldn't. And if there are any other children in the colony whom you think I could teach too, I wish you'd let me know. I'd like to start a little school at the Consulate. Of course, as I said, I'm not very capable—but perhaps it would be better than no school at all."

"Why, Mrs. Trent, I think you're simply wonderful! May I tell Mrs. Echols what you've said? Her Betsey is running wild just like my Tommy—and if you ask me, I think the six Perkins children are worse than either of them."

"Of course, tell Mrs. Echols—and there's something you could tell me, if you'd be so kind. Do you think I could get a French nurse for the children? It seems a shame, when it's being spoken all around them, for them not to learn it while they're little. Foreign languages come like second nature when you're young, if you have half a chance with them."

Mrs. Means answered impetuously. "Oh, Mrs. Trent, don't employ a French nurse!" she exclaimed in accents of alarm. "All the members of your Chinese staff would boycott her! They might even do worse. I know that Chinese are supposed to be perfect, as servants, but one or two terrible things have happened here. A man we know very well was stabbed to death while he was asleep by his number one boy, with whom he'd argued and made to lose face. Whatever else happens, you've got to let your Chinese servants save their faces and keep their squeeze."

"Yes, I know," Daphne answered with a slight shiver. "I've kept house in China already, you see, in Canton. And, of course, I realize that customs here are much more inflexible still. But I must think up something—I mustn't let the children lose such a chance. Would a governess be resented, do you think, or a tutor?"

"I wouldn't have a French tutor for a little girl," Mrs. Means said, still warningly. "But a governess—no, your servants wouldn't resent that, if she didn't do anything resembling work, if she didn't take the slightest physical care of the children, just taught them; and if she were rather haughty, that would be all the better. I think there are one or two wilted aristocrats here—but I'm afraid their titles would come high!"

"I think I could manage that part," Daphne said quietly. "I'm not short of money, just now."

"Well, I congratulate you," Mrs. Means answered, with a short nervous laugh. "Most consular families are so dreadfully hard up—it's a sin and a shame!"

"Yes, I know," Daphne Trent said again. "We have been too. But just now things are better with us—that way."

There was something in her voice which made Mrs. Means wonder if there were other ways in which things were not better with the Trent family than they had been, or indeed not as well. But though she resolved that eventually she would find out what these other ways were, she knew that for the moment she must not betray any curiosity. She realized that this shy, sweet young woman, who kept revealing qualities of submerged strength, would resent it if she did. So she rose to take her leave, casting an appreciative eye around her as she did so.

"What marvelous old maps, Mrs. Trent! I've never seen any just like them. It's hard, isn't it, to realize that 'Parts Unknown' ever ran to such limitless regions?"

"I don't know. Sometimes I think those are limitless yet.— But I'm glad you like the maps. They belonged to my father. Those and the breakfront bookcase."

"You've made this house perfectly beautiful. I wouldn't have realized that American colonial furniture would look so well in a Chinese setting."

"It seems to look well in almost any setting," Daphne replied, with the pleasant smile which did not obliterate the hurt look in her eyes. "I took it to La Paz first, and it simply transfigured one of the most hideous little houses I've ever seen. Then I took it to Canton, where we had a big cool plain house, and it looked well there too. And then I took it back to Alexandria, where most of it came from in the beginning, and—well, of course, it looked best of all in my flounder house there."

"Oh, have you a flounder house? I've heard about them, naturally, but I've never seen one. Alexandria is the only place where there are any, isn't it?"

"There are two or three in Fredericksburg and two or three in Charleston. But Alexandria is the only place where there are any number of them, where they're really typical."

"And you have one of them! You lucky creature!"

"I did have one. I sold it before I started for China this time. I had an exceptionally good offer for it, and my husband pointed out that it seemed silly to cling to it when there wasn't any prospect that we could ever live in it."

"But didn't you hate to part with it? A lovely unique thing like that!"

"Yes, I hated to part with it. But Michael helped me to understand that it was the sensible thing to do—and now you see there is plenty of money to have just the right French governess or whatever else is best for the children. That's more important, after all, than keeping the flounder house."

Daphne had found just the right French governess for the children soon after her talk with Mrs. Means. Mademoiselle Henriette de Hauterive belonged to one of the most illustrious of old Norman families. How she had ever happened to stray from the moated fortress on the plains of Caen which her ancestors had begun to build before the Conquest of England, had long been a mystery to the foreign colony of Yünnanfu. But it did not long remain a mystery to Daphne. Her approach to Mademoiselle de Hauterive was so tactful and so tender that the proud, lonely woman told Madame Trent, of her own free will, that she had a younger sister at the Carmelite Convent in Hanoi and that she had come to Yünnanfu in order to be comparatively near her, in order to see her as often as the rigid rules of the Order would permit. Their parents were dead; they were the last of their immediate family; she had not been able to bear the prospect of severing the slender tie which still bound her to Soeur Agnes des Anges——

"And your home?" Daphne had asked her gently.

"It is closed, Madame. The *gardien* and the *fermier* still live there, the place is watched, the crops are harvested. All that cannot be neglected, *bien entendu*. But the chateau itself is empty."

"As long as you haven't looked out on the garden, shining like a long channel of radiance, and known that you could never see it again. As long as you haven't heard the gate which leads to it clicking behind you for the last time; as long as you haven't had to sell it—" said Daphne, more gently still, and Mademoiselle Henriette, glancing at Madame Trent with swift Norman shrewdness, saw that there were tears in that lovely lady's eyes.

The Chinese servants had not resented the arrival of Mademoiselle de Hauterive on the scene. They were impressed by her detachment and her elegance, and they waited upon her, in the courtyard set aside for her exclusive use, with the same obsequious perfection which marked their service of the Master and of the Master's Wife. She left it very seldom, except to go to Mass, and to stay for a little while each morning in the courtyard which the Master's Wife had arranged for the use of the Stranger Children who came there to school. But after lunch the Stranger Children went home, and in the afternoon, when the Small Girl and the Small Boy had had their naps and their baths, their amah took them to the Teaching Lady's own courtyard and sat there while the Teaching Lady taught them and talked with them and sometimes played with them a little. But she did not feed them or mend their clothes or watch over them. She only taught them and talked with them more and more, so that the Master's Wife seemed content, and smiled oftener than she had done at first. Then the amah, who adored the Master's Wife, was content too.

After the matter of the Teaching Lady had been settled to the satisfaction of everybody, the Master's Wife took up the matter of the ponies. It would be well, the servants heard her saying to the Master, if he and she were to ride every morning, before he went to his office and she went to her school. The Small Girl could ride with them, and in a year or two more, the Small Boy also. It was she who learned, and told the Master, that if they were to have three or four horses they must have a mafu on purpose to care for them, that this service must not be asked of one of the regular servants, as it might be if there were one horse, or possibly two. It was she who found out where the mafu should be lodged and what he should be paid and where the ponies should be kept and what these should cost. It was plain to see that she was a careful wife, thoughtful of all such details, and that she did her husband honor.

After the Teaching Lady had been installed in her own courtyard and the mafu had been hired and the ponies bought, the Master and the Master's Wife began to do the things that other foreign persons did in Yünnanfu. They went out in their chairs, with the relief men running along beside the regular carriers, and paid visits. They went out to tiffin and out to tea and out to play tennis and out to play bridge. They went to dinners and to dances, to the French Club and to the English Club. And when it was suitable that they should do so, they gave parties themselves, big parties, like everyone else, so that the number one boy had to go to borrow the big ice cream freezer that had a strange squeak from one foreign family and extra china from another and extra silver from another. But this Master's Wife had more china and silver than any Master's Wife who had ever been at the American Consulate or at any other consulate in Yünnanfu. So now the American Consulate held a proud place in the city and reflected credit on the community. Its staff was satisfied, and the passing years brought no disharmony or disaster to it. But if the Master had smiled when he came in from his ride, and had stopped for a moment to speak to the mafu and the gateman before he went on his way to his offices, somehow the outer courtyard would have been a pleasanter place.

Michal Trent laid down his riding crop and spoke his crisp word of morning greeting. The two Chinese clerks responded courteously. The round-shouldered girl sitting in front of the typewriter futilely fingering the keys, did not respond at all.

"Good morning, Miss Lane," repeated Michael, his voice slightly edged with irritation.

The girl looked up slowly, and Michael repressed a harsh exclamation. Her dress was disordered and her hair awry. She was flushed and heavy-lidded. She had evidently been crying and her tears were still undried.

"Aren't you feeling well?" Michael asked, rather sharply.

"No, not very."

"If yot're not able to do your work, you'd better go and tell Mrs. Trent. She'll get in a doctor, if she thinks it's necesssary after she's talked to you."

"Oh, Mr. Trent, you won't send me to the hospital, will you? I haven't dared tell you I was ill, for fear you would. I've heard awful things of the way foreigners are treated there."

"Well, it's run by foreigners—both hospitals are. You know that. A foreigner ought to be able to get along in one of them. If you don't want to go to the English Hospital you can go to the French Hospital—that is, if you need to go to a hospital at all. But aren't you getting a little ahead of the game?"

"No—no—I'm sick and I'm frightened—terribly frightened. The English doctors don't want to bother with Americans or the French doctors, either. They don't want to provide proper food for us in the hospitals—they think it's too much trouble. And they don't want to care for us either. They know they can't experiment on us, the way they do on the Chinese."

"You're hysterical," said Michael abruptly. "Please leave the office at once and go to Mrs. Trent. You know that I'm extremely busy, that there's a report to get out this morning and that I'll have to typewrite it myself, since you're not able to do it."

He watched the girl drag herself out of the room, still choking with sobs and, turning toward the machine, began to copy the résumé of political conditions which he had

drafted the day before. There had been a good many communistic disturbances in the Province of late—so many, in
fact, that after making all his plans to spend his leave in
Ankor and Bangkok, he had abandoned the project. Daphne
had consented to go with him, leaving the children under
the suitable supervision of Mademoiselle de Hauterive. She
had been reluctant to do so, but he had over-persuaded her—
after all, he reminded her, Rosemary was nearly ten now and
Richard was seven—she could not continue to baby them
indefinitely! But in the end it was he who told her that they
must stay where they were after all. Brigands, like the poor,
were always with them, he said. He could not help it if a
missionary or two got mislaid while he was gone—they would
not be much missed, for that matter, if they did. But communists were something else again. He could not tamper with
a situation involving them. He thought, derisively, that
Daphne had not seemed sorry when he told her they were to
stay where they were. He would never have guessed, in the
beginning, that she would develop into so maternal a type.
But once she had learned how, she was certainly in her element taking care of children.

Besides, Daphne was contented in Yünnanfu, or would
have been, if she had not known of his deep dissatisfaction,
if she had not perpetually blamed herself because they were
there. For somehow, before they left Washington, the story
had leaked out that the Honorable T. Gilbert Morgan was
disciplining Michael Trent because the latter had criticized
the American system of shifting Foreign Service officers from
one part of the globe to another, comparing it unfavorably
with the British system of zoning. And when Michael had
turned on Daphne, fiercely demanding whether she had ever
repeated the complaints he had uttered to her, she could not
deny that she might have done so. She did not think she had;
however, it was possible. Her mind was still confused when
she tried to remember everything that had happened, everything she had done and said during those last awful months
on Shameen.

"You don't think perhaps you could have said the same
thing to anyone else that you said to me, yourself, do you,
Michael?" she had asked piteously, her lips trembling, her
face stricken.

"I know damned well I never did. It's only women who
go around bleating out things like that. And I thought you
were different, I thought you were going to be a helpmate
to me." .

She had done everything she could to make up for the
irreparable indiscretion which had condemned him again to

159

exile. In justice, he was obliged to admit that. At the end she had even been sensible about selling the house. There was no reason why she should not have been, but for a time it had looked— Well, anyway, that sentimentality was all over, and they were substantially better off because it was. And she had never once said that she herself had found it a wrench to leave Virginia, when she had just got settled down there, or shown any foolish fears about going back to China, either on her own behalf or on the children's. She had never said anything more about hoping that her next child would be born on American soil or indeed referred in any way to possible future children when he himself ceased to do so. And if their communion was not as close and as constant as it once had been, this was because he himself was now free from the sense of perpetual need of her and not because she had withdrawn a second time from him. She treated him with the same tenderness which she had revealed as a bride and, in spite of Michael's moods, managed to imbue their relationship with the spontaneity and intensity which had characterized it in the beginning.

It did not occur to him that his manner had become mocking and his mind misused as he continued to nurse his grievances. The corroding effect of these upon his sense of proportion and perspective escaped him entirely; and if Daphne was aware of the change which had taken place in his outlook and his nature, she gave no sign that this had caused her irritation or distress. Indeed, it was seldom now that she betrayed disturbance of any kind for any reason, that hot color flooded her cheeks or a startled look came into her eyes. The shyness which had characterized her as a girl had gradually been succeeded by attributes of serenity which seemed hard to shatter. She appeared to accept, without fear and without protest, all the circumstances of her existence with the same sublimity of spirit in which she had accepted the inevitability of the forces which in the end had precipitated her union with Michael.

Socially, she had achieved immense success in Yünnanfu. She ran her own establishment extremely well; and the fact that she had not rushed headlong into a meaningless round of morning bridge parties and similar vapid pursuits had enhanced her position instead of jeopardizing it. As soon as it was seen that her presence at a party was something which must be maneuvered, everyone strove to secure her as a guest. The Americans liked her simplicity, the English liked her distinction, the French liked her poise, the Chinese liked her tranquility. She was in constant demand among the foreigners, and her contacts with the native population were no less cordial. She did not live entirely shut off from this, as she had on Shameen. The wives of the Salt Commissioner, the Reconstruction Commissioner and the Commissioner of Education were her friends, and she went frequently to the homes of these functionaries. Occasionally, to be sure, a Chinese general passing through the city was tendered a dinner by the local governor at which no ladies were present, and consequently Michael went to it without her. But an episode of this sort was the exception rather than the rule. Usually it was she who was offered the more intimate entree.

It was almost never that she made any suggestions about Michael's schedule or trespassed on his preserves. From the beginning, she had realized that he did not care to consult her about his career or have her frequent his office; and since he had accused her of responsibility for his banishment, he had never spoken to her again about his work, and she had tacitly accepted the added rebuke which his silence implied. Her recognition of his resentment had been so complete and so comprehensive that he had never expected to find her intruding again; and when the consciousness that one of his clerks was standing beside him, bowing and repeating in a low voice the astonishing statement that Mrs. Trent would like to speak to him, he looked up with unconcealed amazement from the report he had begun to type when the tearful Miss Lane had laid it down.

"Do you mean that Mrs. Trent is outside, in the courtyard?" he asked unbelievingly.

"Yes, sir. She said she was sorry to disturb you, but that she felt it was unavoidable."

Michael pushed back the typewriter and rose. The clerk held the door open for him, bowing again as he walked out of the office.

"Well?" he said irritably.

"I'm awfully sorry, Michael. But I felt I had to find out— Did you ask Miss Lane, when you engaged her, to give you the date of her latest vaccination?"

"Good Lord, Daphne, you sound like a quarantine officer! No, of course I didn't. I didn't even ask her whether she'd ever been vaccinated at all. Why should I? I don't make out medical reports, you know—not yet. It may be the next thing required of a Foreign Service officer. It would fit right in with signing death certificates."

"I hope you won't have to sign a death certificate now, Michael."

"What are you talking about?"

"Well, Miss Lane came to me, as you told her to do. I could

161

see she was feeling very ill, so I turned the children over to Mademoiselle de Hauterive and got Miss Lane off to her own room. I took her temperature and it was a hundred and three. Then I persuaded her to let me help her undress and get her into bed, and I saw that her body was completely covered with a red rash. So I did ask her when she had last been vaccinated, and she mumbled something unintelligible and showed me a scar on her leg that might have been made by anything twenty years ago. When Dr. Lebrun arrived he told me what I suspected already—that she had smallpox and that she had it very badly."

"Smallpox! Here in this house!"

"She's been in this house, right along, Michael, you know," Daphne reminded him quietly. "She can't spread infection now, isolated in her own room, half as rapidly as she's been spreading it for days already, going from one courtyard to another. I don't really think there's much danger. The children are as immune as science can make them already, and most of the servants who are afraid of modern methods have had smallpox anyhow. I didn't come here to spread an alarm. I came to explain the situation to you and to ask you to send out chits canceling my engagements for the next week. I think everything will be all over by then."

"And what are you planning to do in the meantime?"

"I'm going to stay with Miss Lane, of course."

Her voice was as serene as usual. She went on speaking as if oblivious of the incredulous and angry exclamation with which Michael interrupted her.

"Dr. Lebrun thinks he can get a French nurse to help me—a Sister of St. Vincent de Paul. But whether he can or not, this is a responsibility I can't dodge. The girl is all alone in the world. When she came up here from Shanghai, in response to your advertisement, she was just about desperate. She's had a pitiful life. She's told me some of the details—she didn't dare tell them to you. And unless I'm terribly mistaken, she's going to have a pitiful death. I'm afraid there's nothing I can do to prevent that now. I might have, if I'd only known how ill she was a little sooner, if I'd only had sense enough to inquire whether she'd taken sensible precautions in this disease-ridden country." Daphne broke off suddenly, aware that Michael might construe her words as a reproach because he himself had made no such inquiries. "I know there isn't much I can do," she continued calmly. "But I've got to do what I can. I'm sorry you don't approve——"

"Don't approve! I absolutely forbid you to carry out

162

such senseless scheme! I shall send that crazy girl to the hospital as quickly as I can get her there!"

"I think this is the first time since we've been married, Michael, that I've done anything against your wishes or declined to carry them out. But I'm going to do both now. Miss Lane isn't going to the hospital. She's going to stay here in the Consulate. And I'm going to stay with her till she's either dead or well."

There was a strange commotion in the outer courtyard. The sound of it penetrated past the gateman's house and the place where the chairs were kept and reached the quiet offices beyond the inner courtyard. Michael turned savagely from his typewriter for the second time that morning.

"Will one of you please go and see what that infernal noise is about? I can't get anything done as long as it keeps up."

"I beg pardon, sir. It seems you have a visitor. And the gateman has told him that there is sickness in the house and that it would be wiser if he would go away. But he declines to do so. He does not seem to understand the gateman or the number one boy, who has also been summoned. He keeps on shouting that he wishes to come in."

"Well, go yourself and find out what he wants and bring me his card."

"He has no name paper and he declines to say what he wants. He only stands and shouts."

Michael shoved the typewriter away from him and strode across the room. He went past the gateman's house with the speed to which rage lends wings. Then in the outer court, he stopped suddenly in his tracks.

Before him, still bellowing with rage, clad in tumbled tweeds, a red spotted tie and a tropical helmet set about an empurpled face, rose the fantastic figure of Mr. Alonzo Loose.

CHAPTER 12

DINNER AT the American Consulate in Yünnanfu was invariably smooth of service and considered of cuisine; but since the mysterious withdrawal of the Master's Wife into the sick chamber of the Young Miss of Strange Scrolls, and the unheralded arrival of the Big Man with the Volcano

163

Voice, this repast had achieved a degree of excellence which bordered upon perfection. As if to make up to the Great Guest for the absence of the Master's Wife, the ten servants, each in his own way, had redoubled their efforts to please and to satisfy. All had been successful, but the cook had perhaps been most triumphant of all. As Mr. Loose drained his fourth glass of champagne, and pushed back the plate which, five minutes earlier, had been heaped with his second helping of *soufflé surprise,* he made a slight sound indicative of contented satiation.

"You live well, Trent," he observed, with a brevity which in no way belittled his appreciation.

Michael shrugged his shoulders. "Champagne comes in duty free, and it's so cheap that everyone serves it all the time. It's one of the few commodities which the French permit to pass without protest," he said nonchalantly. Then he added in the satirical tone which had become habitual, "Probably because they don't care to be deprived of it themselves—it's a different story when their own tastes aren't involved! As for the rest—well, asparagus has become almost as common as rice all over this Province, and the Chinese seem to have their own special flair for blanching fish and roasting ducks and whipping eggs into any kind of a sweet froth. It doesn't imply any special skill or vast expenditure."

He accepted the wet twist of hot towelling extended to him, passed it through his hands, and lighted a cigarette. Mr. Loose likewise accepted the final ministrations of the boy who had been serving them and selected a cigar from his pocket.

"I thought we might have coffee and liqueurs in the pavilion by the upper pool," Michael observed, still nonchalantly, as they rose. "It's pleasant there at this time of the evening."

"It's pleasant there at almost any time of day or night, as far as I can see," remarked Mr. Loose, still appreciatively. "I'd say, if you asked me, that you'd come a long way in the matter of pleasant surroundings since you lived on the Sopo-cachi, Michael."

"I admit that I have. But I didn't enter the Foreign Service specifically to seek pleasant surroundings—in a Chinese city where it takes fourteen days to get an answer to a letter sent to the seacoast, not to mention the length of time it takes to establish communication with the rest of the outside world!"

"Feeling a little out of touch with the good old U. S. A., are you, eh, Michael?"

"Well, how do you think you'd feel, if you'd lived in Yünnanfu four years?"

164

"Fed up, the same as you do—fed up with the whole damned business!"

Mr. Loose set down his coffee cup with such force that it clattered against the delicate saucer beneath it. Then, resolutely, he reached for the big blown glass in the depths of which a thimbleful of redolent cognac glistened, and tossed this off at a gulp, instead of slowly savoring its aroma.

"Listen," he said, wincing a little as the fine fire of the brandy darted downward, but still smacking his lips at the richness of it, "I told you the truth when I said, five days ago, that I'd come to China partly because I didn't have much of anything else to do, what with my business going along so well and my diplomatic talents unappreciated by the State Department, and partly because I'd got a touch of jade madness and wanted to add a few Buddhas and bowls and incensers to my collection of antiques. But I didn't tell you the whole truth. I didn't even tell you the whole truth when I said that incidentally I'd been sort of sick for a sight of you and Daphne, though that was true enough too. I liked her from the minute I laid eyes on her, and I liked you right away too, even if I did get your goat. And I know you've had a raw deal. I know that Morgan is keeping you sidetracked here because he's a sorehead and a spoilsport and because he's got the idea that when he clamps down on anyone that makes him a great guy, chock-full of power and glory, like Jehovah, if you know what I mean."

"Yes, I think I do know what you mean," Michael observed grimly.

"Well, then, here's something else maybe you don't know. Morgan has given me a raw deal, too. He knows I want to be Ambassador to England. He knows I rate it—that is, the same way most of the men do who've been sent there lately —because they've owned big newspapers which have supported the right man in a presidential campaign, or because they've been shrewd enough, with their shyster lawyer training, to call the British bluff and get away with it. I can play their game as well as they can, and I've been freer-handed with the money bags than any of them. But Morgan's blocked me. He doesn't want any more roughnecks at the Court of St. James's—he wants a few highbrows. He says he's 'seeking a new order of things in the Foreign Service.' What he means is, he wants to see an American Ambassador in London who climbs into a topper and tails every night even if the Chancery burns down and the Government blows up! A man who keeps his house icier than the drinking water he serves with his boiled turbot and roast mutton and cold shape—all to prove to our English cousins how

165

much of their culture we're capable of absorbing! Cold shape, my eye! What a name for a dinner dish! It sounds more like a description of a corpse to me. Though when you get right down to it, I don't know but what it would fit some of the representatives of this new order of things pretty close at that!"

In spite of himself, Michael laughed. It was not a very hearty laugh, but Mr. Loose immediately pounced upon it.

"It isn't so damned funny," he said furiously. "Morgan's poisoned the mind of one president after another against me, just so that he can get to dress up this potential boy doll of his in a topper and tails and set him down at Prince's Gate with strings attached to his behind reaching from there to the State Department, where Morgan can pull them at any minute! Shaw might have been handled, if it hadn't been for Morgan, or even Conrad, with the right approach—say through John Stone or Faith Marlowe! But Morgan has kept telling Conrad that I'm an 'unscrupulous industrialist,' and Conrad, who's playing up to the working man just now, has veered away from the idea of appointing me, like a frightened rabbit. Bland, who took to the tall timber the minute that toy revolution broke out in Bulgaria, and who'd have been court-martialed if he'd been in the Army instead of the Foreign Service, has smoothed everything all over and been appointed to Paris. *Paris!* He simply sat around Washington until Morgan got sick of the sight of him—hired the Royal Suite at the Mayflower and dug himself in. But Bland's a blueblood. Maybe that's why he gets such cold feet. Anyhow, that's why Morgan not only puts up with his little vagaries but promotes him."

"I suppose there's a chance that Morgan will topple from his own pedestal someday," Michael said slowly.

"Well, yes—there's a chance. But we may have to wait until hell freezes over for it to come! There are a few optimists who believe that with this rift in the State Department itself, which keeps getting wider all the time, there may be a new line-up, with Estabrook, instead of Morgan, standng in with the President."

"I've heard something of the kind myself. A little news seeps through, even to Yünnanfu," said Michael, still slowly. "Estabrook really does believe in promotion for merit, he really does want to see career men get a break. If he ever does come into power, I believe he'd see to it that I got a good post."

"Yes—if he ever does! But what are you going to do in the meantime—stay on here, dry-rotting, in your pleasant surroundings?"

166

"What else would you suggest that I should do?"

"Chuck it all! Clear out! Resign!"

"And then?"

"And then take over the direction of Loose Elixir, Inc. in Europe for me!"

"What!"

"That's what I said. That's what I came here to say. But you've kept me so blame busy, trotting me off to that week end picnic and those hill temples and around the French Club and the English Club that this is practically the first time I've had a chance to talk to you alone. Even when we've been at home, you've had a cozy little group of twenty or thirty here most of the time, lapping up champagne and shoveling in food. People here take a case of smallpox a good deal in their stride, don't they? You'd think they wouldn't venture within ten miles of this place, even if two or three acres of it are isolated and under quarantine, considering what's happening here. But these folks just laugh it off and come plunging along in. Not that I'm frightened myself, but you'd think——"

"You were saying just now——" Michael interrupted with a suppressed eagerness which did not for one moment escape Mr. Loose. The ex-Minister to Bolivia took up his theme again.

"Well, it's this way, Michael: The field for the Elixir used to be just a domestic one. Then it spread to Mexico and Central America and crept down the West Coast. You remember those trips I used to take from Bolivia, on the trail of antiques? Well, it just happens that I was on the trail of trade at the same time. Latin Americans are lapping up Elixir on both sides of the Andes now. By the quart. By the gallon. But Europeans haven't come to heel the way I'd hoped, and I believe it's because, so far, I haven't found just the right man to pour my product down their throats and make them scream for more. That is, unless I've found him here in Yünnanfu."

Michael did not answer. Mr. Loose, glancing at him from under heavy lids, which concealed shrewd eyes, saw that the muscles around his mouth had contracted, and that little beads of perspiration were standing on his upper lip.

"I could give you a pretty fair salary from the outset," Mr. Loose continued casually. "Say thirty thousand a year to start with—well, maybe I could push it up to forty. With commissions and expenses and office space extra, of course. And if you took hold, like I think you would, you ought to be worth double that five years from now. A man can do a lot, Michael, on a hundred thousand a year—not that I'd set any special sum as a limit."

Michael moved jerkily in his chair, and this time a smothered sound, not unlike a low growl, rose from his throat. But still he made no actual answer, and Mr. Loose went on speaking.

"When I asked you two days ago what an American Consul was good for anyway, in this neck of the woods," he said, "your answer wasn't so damned convincing to me. It sounded sort of vague. You said the post was a 'political one.' Political, hell. You said the French were watching the English and the English were watching the French and that you were supposed to be watching them both. Well, if you want to spend your life watching the French and the English I can fix it so it will be easy for you to do that without doing it in a place where you'll have to wait months to get a letter from home. You can have a house in London and another in Paris, just as well as not. You said something about watching communists too. Well, Moscow's an interesting place right now, and I believe the Russians would take to Loose's Elixir like ducks to water, if it were put up to them the way it could be—just the thing to warm them up on long cold winter evenings. When it comes to dry-nursing all kinds of missionaries, from Mennonites to Methodists, who want to preach to the tribespeople, like you're doing in the odd moments when you're not watching the French and the English and the Communists, I should think you could do without that part of the job and never miss it. As far as that goes, I shouldn't think you'd break down and cry if you never tried to make up another collection for a derelict who'd gone broke as well as native, or witnessed another shotgun marriage or settled another paltry estate or O.K'd another death certificate. When we went out to that little sandy cemetery yesterday, and you started walking around among the graves, and saying that every time you saw a new one it set you to thinking about the people who'd died out here, who'd been exiles for years and never'd had a chance to get home, it gave me the creeps. It set me to thinking too, the same thing you were—that there wasn't any guarantee you might not end up in that little sandy cemetery yourself. And it gives me the creeps to think of Daphne shut up in that stinking room, facing all the nastiness that a lady like her hadn't ought to even know about, much less see. All the parties and palaces in China don't make up for foulness like that!"

The violence of his voice smote raucously upon the encircling stillness. Almost imperceptibly, dusk had closed in

168

around them. The coffee cups and brandy glasses had long since been noiselessly removed with silent skill. It was not the custom of the boys to come back to the garden after they had performed this service; instead they left trays in the Master's bedroom and in that of his guest, set out with bottles, syphons and sandwiches; their softly padding footsteps would be heard no more until morning. Yet certainly someone was approaching through the gloaming. Before Michael could frame an answer to the outburst which had just been poured forth, both men were conscious of an intruding presence. Then they heard the sound of pebbles crunching under a light step, and saw a dim form in the distance.

"It's Daphne," Michael said hoarsely.

"Well, now, I'll be glad to see her! We'll talk to her about my little proposition, shall we? I'll bet you anything it'll make a hit with her. There's another thing you've told me that I've been turning over in my mind—that when you asked Daphne to marry you, she tried to put you off, not because she was afraid of what you'd probably run up against if you struck out together, but because she thought there'd be so many hurdles for you to heave yourself over that you'd find it hard to win through to the sort of success you wanted, if she was along, hindering you. I'd say myself that she'd been a good deal more of a help than a hindrance, even if she did do a little babbling once. Personally, I never believed that story. I though it was a good deal more likely that you let the cat out of the bag yourself sometime when you were mad clear through and a trifle tight and then forgot about it afterward. I've seen you when you were mad, Michael, and I know how you blow up when you're that way; and though I've never seen you drunk, I have seen you when you were carrying one cocktail too many and I know how that affects you too. Not that I'm blaming you, as far as that goes—I think you've done darned well by and large.—I wouldn't have been a mite surprised to find you soused half the time in a place like this—it gets lots of men that way; and looking around me, I'd say that one or two other members of the American colony had succumbed good and plenty. But while I'm not blaming you, I don't think it's fair Daphne should be blamed either. I'm still maintaining she's been a help and not a hindrance. But at that she was a pretty good prophet in some ways, wasn't she? What with all your physical and financial worries in La Paz, and that nice little massacre on Shameen, and this long drawn-out endurance test at Yünnanfu, you haven't got very far, have you, Michael, on your way to fame and fortune? Even if you don't have to limit yourself to the rations the State Department has doped out as 'sufficient' for a man and his wife and two children, with one servant, to eat in the course of a month, you could do with some expansion, couldn't you? Beyond ten pounds of butter and sixteen heads of lettuce and 'two large cans each of peaches, pears, pineapple, corn and peas'! Even if you don't get stabbed in the street, by some maniac to whom you've refused a passport, like that poor chap in Asia Minor, you could do with a little more security too, couldn't you?"

"Daphne has on a white dress," said Michael, still hoarsely.

"Well, I always thought white looked nice on her, didn't you? Not but what everything looks nice on her, she's so nice-looking herself. But if you'd ask me, I'd have said white favored her almost more than anything else."

"Yes. But she's been careful not to wear it in Yünnanfu. She knows the Chinese don't like it. It's the color of mourning here."

"You mean you think that sick stenographer she's been taking care of has died?"

"If she hadn't, Daphne wouldn't be coming out here now—in a white dress."

"Then there's another exile, isn't there, Michael, who didn't get home—even at the end? There's going to be another grave in that sandy little cemetery. Rather points up my argument, doesn't it?"

Again a smothered sound rose in Michael's throat. He was standing now, his eyes fixed on his wife as she came toward him. Gradually her figure, phantomlike at first, had detached itself from the dusk, and assumed aspects of radiance and reality. When she was quite close, she held up a warning finger.

"I think perhaps you'd better not kiss me or shake hands with me," she said gravely. "I suppose there's no danger really—I've bathed and washed my hair in disinfectants and nothing that I have on has been near the quarantined courtyard. But just in case—" She looked from Michael to Alonzo Loose. "I'm sorry that my welcome to you has been so long delayed," she continued. "But I know you realize it wouldn't have been, except for some very grave reason. May I greet you now as the hostesses in La Paz greet their guests, by saying, '*Esta es su casa*'? It's such a graceful way of telling a visitor how much pleasure his presence brings with it."

"Is the girl dead?" asked Michael abruptly.

"Yes—she died about three hours ago. It was pretty dreadful toward the end. But it's all over now."

"Everything dreadful is over now, for us," Michael said violently.

He sprang forward and seized her arm. "Listen," he said. "We're through. Through with scrimping and saving. Through with disease and danger. We've got a chance after all—the kind of chance I'd given up all hope we'd ever get. We can clear out of here tomorrow. We can go to Europe by way of Java and have that month there together that we've had to put off again and again. You can stop teaching the children—we'll send them to the best schools on the Continent—and we can have some more children, without wondering how we'll feed and clothe and educate them. You can stop economizing in little ways that don't show and in big ones that count a lot with you whether they show or not. You can stop managing and maneuvering so that you won't lose face before our servants and the French and the English—by God, we'll have our servants under our heels, and the French and English too for that matter! You can have beautiful clothes and jewels and luxury and leisure! Everything I've wanted to do for you, is coming to you at last!"

With no apparent effort, Daphne freed her arms from his grasp. "I'm not quite sure I understand," she said gently.

"Of course, you don't—you couldn't. It's one of those things that doesn't happen, except in fairy tales! And it *has* happened. Mr. Loose has come here to offer me a directorship in his company. With a house in London and a house in Paris and another in Moscow if I want it. With a salary of forty thousand as a starter—*as a starter!* With—with *millions* in the offing! That's why I told you everything dreadful was over, for us. That's why I said we were done with peril and poverty. Because we're through with it all. We're through with the American Foreign Service!"

"We're not through with each other, are we, Michael?"

He seized her arm again, and spoke to her loudly. "You must be crazy," he shouted, "to say a thing like that. Haven't I just been telling you what this is going to mean to you as well as to me?"

"You've been trying to. But you don't seem to see at all, what it would mean to me."

For the second time, still with no apparent effort, she freed herself from his grasp. "It would mean," she said, "that I'd feel all these years we've lived together had been wasted. We started out wrong, Michael. We started out feeling that the Consular Service was a means to an end—a means to our own ends. We thought, if you went into it, we would have a chance to see the world. We couldn't see it any other way, so we took the way we could. We didn't

171

think of putting anything into the Service, beyond what we had to; we only thought of getting all we could out of it; and we were rather resentful because we couldn't get more. We never stopped to think that perhaps one of the reasons the Service wasn't better paid and better placed was because it had somehow failed to make the American people and the American Government conscious of its worth and of its importance. We never thought of trying to *contribute* to its worth and its importance. We were selfish and grasping and—and desperately in love with each other."

She paused, but only for a moment, and when she went on she spoke as if she were entirely oblivious of the presence of Alonzo Loose.

"We looked at love wrong, too, just as we looked at life wrong," she said softly. "That is, in the beginning. We thought it was just a crying need of the flesh. But gradually we learned better. I love you a great deal more now, Michael, than I did at first. I love you with all my heart. And I believe you love me too. You haven't acted as if you did, for a long time, but I've never doubted that you do."

"Of course, I love you! I love you so much that——"

"That you want to give up a fight you've only just begun? If that's the best you can do, I don't believe you've learned much about love after all. And you haven't learned anything at all about what the Service really means, about what you must give it as well as what you want to get out of it. I've never forgotten the last words you said to me, when you sent me away from Shameen, 'Missionaries and soldiers and consuls don't desert their posts!' Are you a deserter after all, Michael? Are you the sort who can stand up under shellfire, because there's glamour and glory to that, but can't endure the strain of doing sentry duty alone?"

As if she had finally remembered the presence of Alonzo Loose, she looked from Michael to the other man. "You mustn't think I don't appreciate what you're offering," she said gratefully. "I know you are our friend. I know how kind and helpful you mean to be. I know how pleasant and profitable an association with you would be for Michael. I know how much such an association would be worth to him, if he were free. But he isn't. That is, it doesn't seem to me that he is. When a man promises to serve his country, to further its interests, to uphold its standards, to glorify its name, he doesn't do it with mental reservations. At least he shouldn't. He doesn't whisper to himself that what he really means is that he'd be glad to do all this in Paris or Budapest or Buenos Aires, but not in Megallanes or Newfoundland or Liverpool. His promise means more than that. It means

172

something like the marriage vow—'for richer for poorer, for better for worse, in sickness and in health, till death us do part.' "

Again she paused for breath. And again, when she spoke, it was to Michael, and as if she were oblivious of Alonzo Loose.

"There was something else you said to me on Shameen. You said I was to remember that whatever happened then, nothing could divide us after what had happened there. You meant we had become one spirit, just as we had long been one flesh. I told you in the very beginning, Michael, that I believed we were meant to be indivisible, that there was something portentous about the way we came together. I believe it still. That's why I asked you, when you began telling me that we were through with so much else, whether we were through with each other?"

"And I told you, when you asked me that, I thought you must be crazy! I still think you must be. We're not through with each other because I'm through with the Service—and all the disillusion and the wretchedness that it's brought me. You can dress it up in fine phrases if you want to, Daphne, but they don't mean anything. I'm not deserting a duty. I'm getting rid of a handicap. Why, men resign from the Service all the time!"

"Yes, I know they do! And I know why—and what kind of men. Well, then—that's the kind of man you are—and all these years *have* been wasted! But if you're getting rid of your handicaps, Michael, you'd better get rid of them all. Another thing I told you in the beginning was that you would travel faster if you went alone, and that I knew you'd want to travel fast. Perhaps that was a better prophecy than the one I made when I said we couldn't do without each other."

It was so dark now that he could see only the outline of her figure, not the expression of her face. Then he felt her fingers fleetingly, against his, and was aware that she had dropped something small into his hand.

"I'm not going to indulge in any more fine phrases," she said with calm finality. "If you feel the way you do, I think you'd better go to Europe with Mr. Loose. And I'll take the children and go back to St. Peter's-at-the-Crossroads. I want you to be perfectly free, Michael, to do exactly as you wish."

She moved away from him into the engulfing night, leaving him with her wedding ring in his hand.

PART V

Forbidden Fruit

CHAPTER 13

THERE HAD been rivalry between the Chateau de Hauterive and the Chateau de Blonville ever since the latter—a parvenu compared to its ancient Norman neighbor—had been built during the reign of Louis XIV by the first scion of the house to enjoy royal favor. Indeed, it was the opinion of the De Hauterives that the De Blonvilles' abode could not properly be classified as a chateau at all—it was simply an overgrown *manoir* with a mansard roof, a blank façade and long rows of gray shutters. Compared to the moated and turreted castle which had alternately sheltered the De Hauterives and disgorged them to do battle long before the Conquest of England, the Chateau de Blonville was indeed unimpressive. On the other hand, it emanated an air of elegant prosperity and well-tempered animation, which was more than could be said of the dilapidated Chateau de Hauterive, where the cobblestoned courtyard was bare, and the thick walls were covered with damp moss, and only one lone swan swam disconsolately about in the stagnant water under the great drawbridge. The gray shutters of the Chateau de Blonville were freshly painted every other year, and if a bit of stucco fell from its blank façade or a tile from its mansard roof, the damage was instantly repaired. It was surrounded by pebbled walks which were constantly raked, and by green lawns which were closely cropped, and by circular flower beds which blazed with variegated color but which were as neat as they were gaudy; while beyond the walks and the lawns and the flower beds was a long straight avenue bordered with tall straight trees which were mercilessly pruned every spring, but which by autumn had always regained their natural luxuriance, and which cast their pleasing shade so comprehensively that this covered even the

174

grilled iron gateway surmounted by a gilt crest and two fluted urns filled with geraniums, which opened from the highway into the estate itself.

It was not only because the Chateau de Blonville and its surroundings were well-tended, however, that they looked so attractive; much of their atmosphere of comfort and cheer was due to the fact that they were inhabited. The De Blonvilles had never been among those absentee owners who spent a scant month or two each year on their estates; indeed, the greater part of them spent only a scant month or so away from it. The present Countess, Vivienne de Blonville, who was a Parisian by birth, was an exception to this rule, and she contrived that both her husband, Victor, and her son, Xavier, should break it with her; but the more she gadded about, the more closely did her widowed mother-in-law, the Dowager Countess, and her two unmarried sisters-in-law, Charlotte and Gertrude, cluster around their ancestral hearth. Their cousin, Denise de Crequi, nèe De Blonville, also made the Chateau de Blonville her headquarters whenever her husband, who was a naval officer, was absent on sea duty; and she brought her three children, Marcel, Georges and Yvette to the country with her. So in this way the matter was more than equalized.

Taken altogether, the De Blonvilles presented a picture typical of a French provincial family in its more prosperous and aristocratic aspects. The Dowager Countess, invariably dressed in long and rustling black, wore her abundant gray hair, which was kept from sliding about by sidecombs, in a large knot on the top of her head, and was never seen without some very fine diamonds depending from her large, pierced earlobes, and others, equally fine, glittering on her blue-veined hands. In spite of the fact that her coiffure, her attire, and her ornaments were all so outmoded, however, she had a dignified bearing and an elegant figure, and was far more imposing in appearance than either of her daughters. Charlotte and Gertrude both had beady eyes and shining noses, and they wore drab sweaters which hung limply on their flat forms, over thin sagging dresses which only the most hopeful nature could possibly have visualized as being appropriate for the Norman climate. Denise was always trimly turned out in knitted suits which she made herself, her worsted work being constantly in her nimble fingers; and she kept her three well-behaved children neat too, knitting all their socks and all their pull-overs, besides seeing to it that their berets were worn at just the right angle and that their aprons were changed almost as often as if these had been made of white lawn instead of black sateen. But

Denise sighed in secret when she turned from Marcel, Georges and Yvette to look at Xavier. For the only son of Vivienne de Blonville, née De Cacé, had inherited both his mother's charm and his mother's chic; and since she herself had inherited a large share of the De Cacé fortune, she did not hesitate to buy everything that the boy wore from Sulka, and everything that was put on him he wore exceedingly well.

If it had not been for the De Cacé fortune, it is doubtful whether the Dowager Countess would have considered Vivienne a suitable match for Victor. She was lovely to look at and amusing to listen to, of course; and the Dowager Countess was only too well aware that so much allure seldom came coupled with a great name and a large dot. But Vivienne was frivolous. Her father had been successively Governor of Morocco and High Commissioner of Syria; her youth had been spent under exotic surroundings for which she had formed an unfortunate taste; she was fond of travel and unwilling to forego the excitement of it. She made it clear from the beginning that she did not care to stay in the country all the year around or even half the year and that she did not intend to be tied down by children. She adored Xavier and indulged him to a degree that alarmed all the rest of the family. But even the argument, constantly brought home to her, that he was the last in a direct line to the title, could not coerce her into producing another son to safeguard this.

Her attitude toward her mother-in-law had always been superficially as deferential as it was fundamentally defiant. She had insisted that the Dowager Countess should keep the most spacious suite in the chateau for her own, and that she should continue to sit at the head of the heavy table in the vast dining room. Vivienne never suggested that she would have liked to see one of the smaller salons, less ponderously decorated, used for the more intimate meals of the family, and—with still greater self-control—she refrained from remarking that a change of silver with every course and the elimination of napkin rings and toothpicks from the groaning board would have been pleasing to her. The De Blonvilles, like most Normans, lived in a lavish way when it came to food, though they were frugal in other ways, and the Dowager Countess had never sat down to less than a dozen dishes for either lunch or dinner in her life. Vivienne, with due regard for her figure, ate lightly, but she did not interfere with the menus either. In her own ultrasmart little Paris flat she arranged everything to suit her own fastidious taste. As far as the chateau was concerned, she could afford to bide her time. Besides, the less it suited her, the more she was inspired to make adroit her excuses to be absent from it.

She was a fine horsewoman and she spent most of her mornings in the saddle when she was in the country, coming in to luncheon with some plausible excuse for her lateness, when the others had already consumed their multitudinous hors d'oeuvres and their steaming mussels. In this way she was able to begin her own meal with the scallop of veal smothered in mushroom sauce—which she surreptitiously scraped off—or the chicken *à la Vallée d' Auge,* one of which was almost invariably the *piéce de résistance.* Then she smoked while the others ate *Pont l'Eveque* cheese on great hunks of bread; and afterward she selected one peach or one small bunch of grapes from the variegated fruits offered to her. She knew that her mother-in-law considered smoking in the dining room a *coutume barbare,* but this point was not discussed between them. The Dowager Countess was too proud to bring it up, and Vivienne was too tactful.

The cigarette was a two-edged weapon. It safeguarded her diet, and it offered her an escape from conversation. As long as she continued to puff at it daintily, she could sit silent. And this suited her also. She preferred to take no part in her mother-in-law's heraldic histories or the endless chatter of Charlotte and Gertrude concerning the Curé and his noble work in the village. ("If they had to be virgins, they should have been wise instead of foolish and have taken the veil," Vivienne often murmured caustically to herself. "It is only in the cloister, clothed in a becoming habit, that celibacy is charming.") Denise was less trying to her, for Denise had sense. But she was almost too noble and earnest for Vivienne's taste. You could never quite forget, in the presence of Denise, how fond she was of her husband and how faithful she was to him during his long absences, nor how hard she was trying to do her very best by her children, all on an infinitesimal income. Not that she ever referred to any of this, but it was evident just the same.

Victor did not bore Vivienne especially when he and she were in Paris. There, on the whole, he was adequate as a husband. But at the chateau he seemed less a husband and more a son and a country squire. He did comparatively little talking on his own initiative, and when he did speak it was of the soil and the crops and the herds, seldom of the stud or the game, which would have interested Vivienne far more. Xavier was always engaging and intriguing in conversation, but he was far too well brought up to intrude himself in the forefront of the scene. So on the whole, the abundant meals at the Chateau de Blonville, which seldom lasted less than an hour and a half, were sources of considerable tedium to Vivienne.

Slipping casually into her place one June morning, with her usual apt apology for tardiness, she suddenly decided that she could not endure the smugness of her surroundings any longer, that she must set off some sort of a bombshell in the self-satisfied circle into which, at the age of eighteen, she had somehow let herself be drawn. (Victor himself had never quite understood his good luck in winning such a dazzling creature for his own, and Vivienne had never enlightened him as to the real reasons for his success.) She helped herself sparingly to the *sole Normand* which, as it was Friday, had supplanted the scalloped veal, and made her startling announcement with nonchalance, in the form of a question.

"It is amazing, isn't it," she remarked, "to see the revolution which is taking place at the Chateau de Hauterive?"

She was conscious of a general gasp. The Dowager Countess was the first to recover power of speech.

"A revolution at the Chateau de Hauterive?" she inquired with suppressed astonishment. "I'm afraid I do not entirely follow you, my dear Vivienne."

"But surely you have been over there some afternoon lately, *chère Maman*, when you have gone out for your drive! I know that Charlotte and Gertrude always wish to hasten straight on to the village, in order to get to church in time for vespers, but I thought, of course, you had called before this, and I was wondering——"

"Vivienne, I am very much confused by your remarks. You know that the De Blonvilles and the De Hauterives have never been on terms of intimacy—such airs as that destitute, moribund family always gave itself, and for no reason whatsoever! But that is beyond the point. There has been no one at the Chateau de Hauterive upon whom I could have called, even if I had wished to do so, for a great many years."

"There is someone there now," said Vivienne, conveying a bit of fish daintily to her well-rouged mouth. "Of course, I do not know whether you will wish to call or not, but I think you might find it diverting to do so. I have."

"You have already called at the Chateau de Hauterive?" inquired the family in one voice.

"Oh, yes. Several times now. In fact I have formed the habit of dropping in, quite informally, every day or so this last fortnight."

"But is the place rented then? Who is there? The De Hauterive sisters were the last of their family, and Agnes, who became a Carmelite, died in Hanoi, while Henriette went into voluntary exile for her sake."

"Yes, as long as she lived. But now that Agnes has died, Henriette has returned. Under quite propitious circumstances, I should say."

"She has returned!"

"Yes. With a very acceptable husband and twin sons about two years old."

"A husband! Twin sons! But she was of an age——"

"The twins are perhaps *enfants de miracle*. But I doubt it. I do not believe she was really as old as she looked when she went away."

"It is easy enough to investigate her age, of course, in the *Almanac de Gotha*," remarked the Dowager Countess, her excitement by now quite unsuppressed. "But whom has she married then, Vivienne?"

"A gentleman by the name of Blake. I believe he is the Counselor of the American Embassy in Paris. And a great friend of that rich American industrialist whom everybody is talking about nowadays."

"I have no idea whom *you* are talking about, Vivienne," said the Dowager Countess with more irritation in her voice than she often allowed herself to betray. "I do not know anything about a rich American industrialist."

"Which proves, *chère Maman,* that you should permit us to persuade you to visit us more frequently in Paris, as I have ventured to tell you before. Because then you would know. This man is all the rage there."

"Which man? The Monsieur Blake whom Henriette de Hauterive has so unaccountably married?"

"No, no. The great industrialist, Michael Trent. He is very arresting—good-looking, amusing and even quite distinguished. He has bought himself a house on the avenue d'Iéna, which is about twice as big and twice as showy as the American Embassy, which it faces diagonally, and he gives the most elaborate and extravagant parties there that you can possibly imagine. Victor and I have been to several. He comes down occasionally for week ends here too, with the De Hauterives. It has occurred to me that you might like to invite him to dinner, considering how much hospitality he has offered us."

"Is he married, this Monsieur Trent?"

"I suppose so. Yes, he must be, for he has two charming children—a son and a daughter—who spend their vacations with him. Or rather they seem to be spending most of this one in Normandy, at the Chateau de Hauterive. He sees

179

them when he comes down here for the week ends to which
I referred."

"And his wife?"

Vivienne shrugged her shoulders. "I have not seen her or
heard any reference to her. Americans are very casual about
such matters."

"To think that such nonchalance should be part of their
national life!" exclaimed Charlotte in a shocked voice.
"Though, as we all know, this is scandalous. I am amazed,
Vivienne, that you should speak so lightly of divorce."

"But, Charlotte, I am not sure that there is any divorce!
Monsieur Trent may be a widower, for all I know—though
if that is the case, I should not say he was an inconsolable
one."

Her mother-in-law shot an attentive glance at Vivienne,
then changed the subject slightly. "The Chateau de Hauterive is hardly in a condition which renders it suitable for
the reception of guests," she said, in a tone which did not
suggest that its dilapidated state was the source of much
regret to her.

"But, *chère Maman,* that is what I have been trying to
tell you! Its condition has been undergoing changes which
amount to metamorphoses! Everything is being repaired and
restored! I never should have guessed that the Chateau de
Hauterive contained so many priceless pieces! When I went
there with Victor just after our marriage to return the De
Hauterives' bridal call, the place was positively moldy! But
the mold has disappeared as if by magic. The tapestries alone,
now that they have been well cleaned, would repay your
inspection—they are simply superb! The Salle des Chevaliers
has been transfigured into one of the most magnificent apartments I ever saw in my life. Henriette has her bedroom in
the largest tower, so that it is circular in form, with walls
a meter thick, and all its accouterments are sumptuous. As
for the garden, it is no wonder that the De Hauterive roses
used to be famous. They must cover almost an hectare of flat
surface, besides being festooned over countless arbors and
trellises. Even the chestnuts bordering the avenue are flanked
with rose trees."

"My dear Vivienne, you are becoming very glowing in
your descriptions. Is this Monsieur Blake, whom Henriette
has married, a millionaire then?"

"There is money in the ménage somewhere, certainly,"
interposed Victor, speaking for the first time. "And obviously, it does not come from poor Henriette de Hauterive.
Perhaps some of it is Monsieur Blake's. But I am inclined
to think it is Trent who is their banker. Henriette was his

children's governess when the Trents were in China and a great mutual attachment sprung up between them. Doubtless, it seems to Monsieur Trent a fortuitous arrangement to be able to have his son and daughter under her supervision still, in the absence of their mother."

"Are you certain that there is a financial arrangement in connection with this, Victor?"

"*Eh bien,* I am not certain, *Maman.* But it appears to me a logical one."

"To me, on the contrary, there is something irregular about it all," said his mother disapprovingly. "Such things do not happen in the best society. A governess whose estate is restored for her by a former employer—no, no, that is not done!"

"You are not suggesting, are you, *Maman,* that Henriette has been so exceptionally fortunate as to achieve both a presentable husband and a rich lover? I said she was younger than she looked, and it is true. Still she is not a *femme fatale.* I doubt whether she could satisfy the requirements of Monsieur Trent for a mistress. I believe these would be exacting."

"Vivienne!" exclaimed the Dowager Countess quite sharply. She turned from her daughter-in-law to her cousin, and made a suggestion, more smoothly. "If you have entirely finished your luncheon, Denise, perhaps you will take the dear children out on the terrace? It is such a lovely day that it seems too bad to keep them in merely because the rest of us have become involved in a prolonged discussion. They seem to be growing rather restless, and no wonder! We will rejoin you a little later, for our coffee and tisanes." Then, as Denise, whose alacrity in complying was both a credit to her good breeding and a betrayal of her subservience, shepherded her flock from the room, the Dowager Countess looked back at Vivienne. "You forget yourself," she said sternly. "I am sorry to be obliged to remind you that you are not, at the moment, mingling with the smart set in Paris whose society you enjoy so much, but that you are in the midst of a refined and sensitive circle. Such a remark has never been made at my table before, and I trust never will be again. I did not for a moment intend to cast reflections on the character of Henriette de Hauterive. I am sure that this is above reproach, and the fact that her family and ours have not always been in complete accord, does not prevent me from taking exception to the aspersions which you have made on the Norman noblesse as a whole in speaking slightingly of one of its members."

"You said yourself that the arrangement was peculiar," retorted Vivienne, a little sulkily.

"Yes. But not that it was vicious. No doubt Henriette will have some explanation to make of it that will be entirely satisfactory. At all events I shall go to see her, and give her the opportunity of doing so. No doubt she will be glad to take advantage of it."

The Dowager Countess rose majestically. "I think it would have been considerate of you, Vivienne," she observed, without giving any indication of unbending toward her erring daughter-in-law, "to have advised us more promptly that Henriette de Hauterive had returned to her ancestral home. Naturally, we would all have been glad to extend the proper courtesies to her, under the circumstances. And to her husband also, of course. That goes without saying. As far as Monsieur Trent is concerned, it appears that he is a very old friend of the Blake ménage. I do not see why we should hesitate to extend hospitality as far as he is concerned either. I shall call upon Henriette this afternoon and invite them all to dine with us tomorrow evening at half-past eight."

"And at the same time you will invite Rosemary and Richard Trent to come to goûter with Marcel and Georges and Yvette and me, will you not, Grand'-mere?" inquired Xavier, beguilingly.

The Dowager Countess gave a slight start. Her glance, which had once been unerring, was no longer as keen as it had been, and it had escaped her notice that Xavier had not left the dining room with his cousins, under the capable direction of Denise. She was not altogether pleased to find him standing near her, looking at her with that mixture of impudence and blandness which only a child of Vivienne could have achieved.

"Why should you wish to have these foreign children take goûter with you, Xavier?" she asked, trying to speak as severely as when she had addressed his mother, and failing. For Xavier was the darling of her heart.

"Eh bien, I do not, especially. But I thought perhaps you would not permit me to invite them to anything else. Of course, I should like it much better if you would let me take dinner with you, and invite only Rosemary, with her father. Would you, Grand'-mere? After all, I am old enough now to come to dinner when there is company—though naturally Marcel and Georges and Yvette are not. Nor is Richard Trent. We could ask him to take goûter some other time, with them."

"We will ask Monsieur Trent's little daughter to come at some other time, also, if at all," said his grandmother with dignity. "And you will have an early dinner with your cousins, as usual, when I am entertaining. We do not need to rush
182

into all sorts of innovations, merely because the Chateau de Hauterive is inhabited again."

She moved across the floor, her black garments rustling about her as she walked, and the large diamonds hanging from her ears quivering slightly. Her two daughters followed her, hunching their sweaters about their shoulders, for though it was a cool day, there had been no fire in the dining room, which was heated, if at all, according to the calendar and not according to the thermometer. Victor fell back politely, in order that his wife might precede him. But she gave him an arch glance and shook her head.

"I am not coming out on the terrace just yet," she said gaily. "I wish to speak to Xavier for a moment. Please do not wait for me, *cher ami*." Then as her husband closed the door behind him, she looked searchingly at her son, giving a light laugh as she put her arm around his shoulder.

"Eh bien, mon petit choux," she said, rather mockingly, "just what does all this mean? When did you contrive to meet *la petite* Trent? And where?"

"I didn't contrive, *Maman*. It was an accident."

"Oh, it was an accident! *Bien entendu*, but I should still like to know when and where it occurred—this accident."

"By the brook," said Xavier, softly. "About three weeks ago."

"And since then——"

He did not answer instantly. His mother's hand, straying from his shoulder to his neck, felt the warmth beneath his low collar, and knew that he was blushing. But when he turned to look at her, his eyes, which were level with her own, met hers coolly.

"Since then I have seen her every day," he said. "Not by accident. By design. Usually beside the brook. Sometimes in the woods. The place does not matter much. I should like it if *Grand'-mere* would invite her here, of course. That is the way I really want it to be. But whether she does or not, I intend to go on seeing Rosemary Trent."

Suddenly his voice broke, the bravado swept out of it. "You'll help me, won't you, *Maman*?" he said pleadingly, speaking like a little boy.

He had never appealed to her in vain. To a rare degree, he and she were bone of one bone and flesh of one flesh, and both were poignantly aware of the close tie which united them. But now Vivienne pushed her son away from her as she answered him.

"No, you little fool, I shall not help you," she said savagely. "I think you must be crazy. And I shall tell Rosemary's father, the next time I see him, that he had better

183

lock his silly little daughter up, and put a stop to all this nonsense."

"And where," inquired Xavier, pleasantly, "will you be seeing Rosemary's father the next time, *Maman?* Will it be in the same place that it was the last time?"

CHAPTER 14

LATE THAT afternoon, three members of the De Blonville family visited the De Hauterive estate under entirely different circumstances.

The Dowager Countess was the first to set out. She did not change her dress, but she added a few more diamonds to those she was already wearing, and put on a fringed pelerine, a plumed hat, and a pair of long gloves, all black, and all rather rusty with age. Then, armed with a small black parasol to shield her complexion from the menacing sunlight, she stepped into the Victoria which she had never discarded for a motorcar, and drove elegantly away.

Under ordinary conditions, she would have taken Charlotte and Gertrude with her, for she secretly sympathized with their starved existence and strove to brighten it for them; but she did not feel that the present conditions were ordinary. Quite the contrary. Her well-regulated mind was in a most unseemly tumult, and the harder she tried to correlate her thoughts the more difficult this became. It was strange enough to visualize Henriette de Hauterive as happily married and economically secure, without having two strange Americans mixed up in the story of her rehabilitation. And that one of these strange Americans should be separated from his wife but encumbered with a daughter added to the complications of the scene. She did not know which had disturbed her more—the secret satisfied smile on Vivienne's painted lips, or the impudence of Xavier's dancing eyes——

She saw, with a start, that she had arrived at the entrance of the De Hauterive property, and that a red-cheeked concierge, with two children hiding shyly behind her full skirts, had emerged from the lodge to open the gates. There were flowerboxes in all the windows of the little cottage, and its miniature garden was bright with them too; beyond, the rose trees between the driveway and the chestnuts which lined it, were already bursting into bloom. It was an unusual design for an avenue, the double rows of trees, one so fresh and fragrant, the other so tall and stately; the Dowager Countess could recall only one other place in Normandy where she had seen anything of the kind. But it was effective. She wished that some early De Blonville had thought of such an arrangement for his own estate.

"It seems to be possible to drive across the drawbridge in a carriage," she said to the coachman. "We will continue until we reach the courtyard."

There were a dozen or more swans swimming slowly about in the moat where the water was now clean and high, she observed; and presently some fluffy cygnets floated past in the wake of their mother, who arched her snowy neck with pride as she glided along. There were ducks too and ducklings in the pond, and two dogs were frisking about on the velvety lawn; they all seemed symbolic of the new life which was flowing into the old place. And there were flowers, flowers everywhere. As the Victoria entered the courtyard around which the castle was built in a hollow square, the Countess saw that there were great jars and urns filled with them even here, and that the old well in the center of the area had been opened and cleaned and decorated with fresh trailing vines. Before her aged coachman could descend from his seat and ring the bell for her, the iron-hinged doors of the main entrance had swung open, and a liveried servant appeared in the dark aperture, bowing respectfully.

"If Madame la Countess will be pleased to give herself the trouble of descending, Madame Blake will come to greet her in the small *salon* at the instant."

If this were the small *salon,* the Countess reflected, as she seated herself on a Louis Quince sofa, what must the large one look like, the great Salle des Chevaliers of which Vivienne had spoken? The tapestries at which she was gazing were the best that Beauvais could produce, the thick carpet under her feet, a soft toned Aubusson, the vases on the mantel, priceless Sèvres, the portrait above it an exquisite Nattier! In the cabinet between two of the long windows draped in brocaded velvet, was a collection of jeweled snuffboxes; and in another which faced it from the opposite side of the room, between two buhl cabinets, was a collection of medals and miniatures. As the clock chimed, a small door underneath the dial flew open, and some porcelain figurines emerged and danced gaily about in a circle. The Countess was so intrigued with them that Henriette de Hauterive was beside her before she became aware of her hostess' presence.

"My dear Countess, how very kind of you to call! I told your charming daughter-in-law, only yesterday, how much

I wanted to see you! And now, as if in answer to my wish, here you are!"

Henriette leaned forward, smiling cordially, and kissed her visitor on both cheeks. The Countess was conscious of a sense of considerable shock; and inadvertently the thought crossed her mind that if a transfiguration such as she was now beholding could take place, something might still be done for Charlotte and Gertrude. When she had last seen Henriette, the poor creature had looked as lank and limp as they did. Now her figure was stately, her manner serene, and her face fresh. Her hair was becomingly arranged, and her powder-blue dress, modishly made, brought out the clear color of her eyes. She was the personification of mellow bloom and mature fulfillment.

"It is indeed a happy surprise to find you installed here again, and so pleasantly, my dear Henriette," the Countess murmured. "If you do not feel I am too curious, may I ask you to tell me something about your seeming good fortune?"

"I owe it all to the Trent family," Henriette said simply. "After my sister died, I should have been completely alone in the world, as you know, except for them. But Mr. Trent, who was then American Consul in Yünnanfu, was more helpful to me that I can possible tell you, and I had become deeply attached to his lovely wife and to his two delightful children, whom I had already been teaching for several years. They all insisted that I must make my home with them in the future."

"So Providence took a hand——"

"Indeed, yes— For it was in their home that I met their friend, Jerome Blake. He had stopped off in China to see them, on his way to Siam, where he became First Secretary of Legation, after having been for a long time stationed in Tegucigalpa. From there he was transferred to Algiers as Consul General, and after that to Paris as Counselor—imagine, after years spent in far corners of the earth, in humble positions, what it meant to him to come to Paris as Counselor!"

"Indeed, yes!" exclaimed the Countess in her turn, using the awed voice of one who speaks of having seen a sinner attain a high seat in heaven.

"But meanwhile—meanwhile he had written me of his affection for me. He had declared his heart. And I must confess that he had already won mine—he is so sincere, so kindly, *enfin*, so good, I cannot begin to tell you! And since at that moment it appeared that the Trents would no longer require my services, I joined him in Algiers. We were married there."

"I am very much touched, Henriette, at your tender recital. But how did it happen that the Trents——"

"Monsieur Trent had decided to retire from the Service," Henriette said easily. "A very remarkable position had become available through another friend of his—a Monsieur Loose, a Croesus among *commerciants*. Monsieur Trent thought he must take advantage of such an opportunity, which brought him to Paris, before we reached here ourselves. Unfortunately, at the same time, Madame Trent was impelled to return to the United States because of the delicate health of the aunt and uncle who had reared her. She took the children with her, and thus I was free."

"But since then——"

"Since then Madame Trent has unfortunately been detained in America by the continued ill-health of her relatives," said Henriette firmly. "But naturally, she does not wish to deprive her husband of seeing their children. Therefore they join him in France—where he is detained by his business—during their vacations."

"But—" began the Countess again. Henriette interrupted her, deferentially.

"I think I can guess what you are about to ask me—what the part is which the Chateau de Hauterive is playing in all this. I scarcely need to explain, since anyone as discerning as yourself readily understands that persons who are constantly under great strain, like my dear husband and Monsieur Trent, feel the need of a diversity of occupation, of relaxation and repose, though without too much extravagance. It therefore occurred to them to form a company and start a stud and stock farm. Normandy is, of course, the ideal region for such an undertaking, and I was pleased to be able to put my estate at their disposal. We have every reason to believe that the results of our venture will be satisfactory. Meanwhile, I am experiencing the untold joy of being in my own home again. We have an apartment in Paris, of course, as well. But this will be our real center in years to come, and already our friends are fast finding their way to it."

Henriette leaned back, beaming and slightly breathless. The Countess regarded her speechlessly, relief and envy struggling for the mastery of her mind. In spite of the regrettable absence of Madame Trent, there was nothing in the least shocking or scandalous about this amazing *ménage à trois*. Instead, there was a sound and congenial partnership in which one person concerned furnished the capital, another the plant, and another the prestige. It would, no doubt, augment the immense fortune of Monsieur Trent still further and enable him to make a magnificent provision for his children; at the same time, it would afford complete security for Henriette and her husband. The Countess was well aware of the potential fertility of her neighbors' neglected hectares, of the eminent suitability of the estate for the purposes to which it was now being put. If Victor had only done something of the sort with their own property, instead of frittering away his time in Paris, to what realms of wealth might he not have soared! But Victor, she thought contemptuously, was satisfied with what he had, besides being completely under the dominion of his frivolous wife. If she could have foreseen, on the day of his baptism, what a poor weak creature he would prove to be, she would never have consented to the name which had been given him. For her, Victorine had been appropriate. How could she guess that Victor would be so inappropriate for her son?

Other aspects of the association of the Blakes and Monsieur Trent began to flash before her dazzled eyes. Between them, they would create a social center of the highest importance at the Chateau de Hauterive. "Already our friends are fast finding us out here," Henriette had said. And among these friends were undoubtedly financial magnates, distinguished diplomats, perhaps even French cabinet officers and foreign princes. The Countess saw the local pre-eminence of the Chateau de Blonville already beginning to totter.

It was a blow, a heavy blow, but she managed to take it bravely. "I cannot tell you how delighted I am at everything that you have imparted to me," she said with well-simulated fervor. "And I hope we shall see a great deal of you from now on, and of your husband and Monsieur Trent, also. In fact one of my purposes in coming here today was to ask if you would not all dine with us tomorrow evening, *dans la plus stricte intimité.*"

"But we shall be charmed! That is, if you will permit us to bring with us the Italian Naval Attaché and his wife and Mr. Loose, who are coming to spend the week end with us."

It was then as the Countess had feared. The invasion of personages had already begun. She continued, however, to rise to the occasion.

"Naturally, my dear Henriette. We shall be having only a very simple little dinner, but your friends will be welcome to it as well as yourself."

"You are too kind. And now may I not offer you a cup of tea?"

"No, thank you, my dear Henriette. I am quite well. Indeed my health has never been more robust."

"Some Calvados then, to drink to our reunion. But I

insist. It will refresh you after your ride. And you must let me show you my sons. I know you will agree with me that they are cherubs."

She rose, gracefully, and reached for a bell pull. As she did so, her attention was attracted by a flash of color outside on the terrace.

"And not only my sons, but my wards," she said smiling, and opened the window. "Rosemary!" she called after a slim vanishing figure. "Rosemary, my dear! Will you come back here for a moment, please?"

The Countess rose in her turn, and looked out over the terrace. A little girl had wheeled about and was coming obediently toward them. The Countess was aware, at first, only of the unusual litheness of movement, and of beautiful unbound hair shining in the sun. Then, as the child approached, the effectiveness of her coloring, enhanced by the yellow dress she was wearing, became more startling. Never, as far as the Countess could remember, had she seen anythink quite so striking as those hazel eyes with that pale amber skin. Involuntarily, she caught her breath. Henriette was not a *femme fatale,* that was true enough. But this child—what would she be in a few years—a very few years? Was she a child after all? She did not seem to be so young as she had looked from a distance, as the Countess had somehow taken for granted——

"Did you want me, Aunt Henriette?" the little girl asked pleasantly, in perfect French.

"Yes, Rosemary. I wish to present you to my friend and neighbor, the Dowager Countess of Blonville, who lives on the next estate."

Rosemary curtsied. The Countess, blinking a little, realized that the curtsy was faultless also; and as the little girl's hand slid into her own, she felt the child's soft fingers curling confidently into her own.

"How old are you, my dear?" she heard herself asking, unexpectedly.

"I am fourteen," said Rosemary, and raised trustful eyes to the Countess' face.

They did not make her stay very long in the salon, Rosemary was thankful for that. After the darling twins had arrived with their nice nurse, and liqueur and little cakes had been brought in by Jacques, Aunt Henriette asked her where she had been going before she had been called; and she said, to the arbor beyond the rose garden to find Richard, and see if he would not like to walk down to the river with her before *gouter.* So then Aunt Henriette had told her she might run along, and she had curtsied again to the queer old lady who was, unaccountably, Xavier de Blonville's grandmother and had said *au revoir*.

She had not told a story—that is not a real story. She did mean to go to the arbor to find Richard. And she did mean to ask him to go to the river with her. But she knew beforehand that he would decline. Because whatever she suggested to Richard nowadays, he said no, he couldn't do it, he was writing a poem.

It had all begun the winter before, when Mother had opened a little horsehair trunk which once belonged to Grandfather Daingerfield, and started reading poems. Rosemary had seen that trunk carried to China and back again, but she had never seen it opened until that cold night just after Christmas, when they were sitting around the fire in the rectory just after Sunday supper, with nothing special to do. Jerry Stone, and his wife, Honor Bright, who wrote books and things, had come over from Solomon's Garden, where they lived, to spend the evening, and suddenly Mother asked if they wouldn't like to hear some of Grandfather's poems. And just like a flash, Honor had said yes, she would love to, and Mother had started reading.

The poems were very beautiful, so beautiful that some of them made you cry, though of course some of them made you laugh too, and others made you think and others made you see places to which you had never been. And pretty soon Honor had exclaimed, "Daphne, why on earth don't you get these poems together and have them published in book form? I'll help you if you like!" Mother had thanked her, in a voice that shook a little, and said it would mean a great deal to her if Honor would do that. She hadn't dared attempt it herself, because she was afraid she didn't have just the right "feel" for poetry. She had tried to write it herself, over and over again, but she had always failed. So somehow——

Well, the next day Honor had come over again, and she and Mother had started putting Grandfather Daingerfield's poems together. And while they were working, at the big table in the library, Richard had come in and had handed Mother a little smudgy piece of paper, with just a few lines scrawled across it. But when Mother had seen it, her face had begun to shine, and she had handed the paper to Honor. Then Honor had read it too, and made a funny little sound in her throat, and said, "Well, Daphne, even if you haven't got a 'feel' for poetry yourself, I reckon you've given it to your son. This is *good* for a kid to have written. I'm going to send it straight off to Mr. Meacham."

Mr. Meachan was an editor Honor knew who had a big

paper in New York, and he had published Richard's poem and sent him five dollars in a nice letter. So ever since then Richard had kept on writing poetry. He did it partly because he enjoyed getting checks for five dollars and nice letters from a man like Mr. Meacham, and partly because he could see right away how much it meant to Mother to have him do it, for Richard would rather do something to please Mother, than make a million dollars, like Daddy. Every time he wrote her a letter from France, he wrote a poem to send along with it. But it wasn't only to get checks and please Mother that Richard wrote poetry. He wrote it because there was something inside him that made him want to, just as there was something inside her that made her want to go to the river and meet Xavier de Blonville——

Perhaps it had been wrong for her to pretend to Aunt Henriette that she thought Richard would like to go to the river with her, that he was only waiting to be asked; but she hadn't been able to help doing it. She felt very guilty, so when she stopped at the arbor she tried to act insistent. But Richard only gazed at her with a far-off look in his eyes.

"Can you think of anything that rhymes with satin?" he asked her.

"Latin," she said; but Richard told her that wouldn't do and when she went on urging him to come for a walk with her he was cross. Well, not exactly cross, Richard was never that, but she could see he was tried.

"The *Ile de France* sails day after tomorrow, you know," he said; and Rosemary knew that meant Mother's letter and the new poem must get off on the *Ile de France*.

She ought to be writing to Mother herself, but she didn't know just what to say to her. She hadn't mentioned Xavier de Blonville at the beginning, and now it seemed rather awkward to do so. She couldn't very well write, "Dear Mother: About three weeks ago I happened to meet a boy named Xavier de Blonville down by the river. I liked him very much, so ever since then I have been meeting him there nearly every day. Other days we have gone walking in the woods together." Mother would at once wonder why she hadn't told Aunt Henriette about Xavier, why he hadn't been invited to the chateau, why it was all a secret. (She didn't understand, herself, why she had felt so shy about mentioning it, but there it was—a sinking sensation in her stomach every time she tried to speak of it.) Mother might even cable. Then Aunt Henriette would reprove her, gently, of course, but still it would be a reproof, and afterward tell Daddy. "Michael, I think perhaps you ought to know that Rosemary is meeting a strange boy every day down by the river." And Daddy, who did not seem to approve of any boys, if they so much as looked at Rosemary, would be terribly fierce, and storm around and shout that there would be plenty of time for all that ten years from now, and how would she like to be shut up in a convent school for a change?

If Mother had only been there, she might have understood, because Mother was good at understanding when you talked things over with her, though it 'was much harder to explain them in a letter. She might even have quieted Daddy down and made him listen to reason on the subject of boys in general and Xavier in particular. She had had great success, in China, when it came to quieting Daddy down about lots of things.

It complicated life for a girl when she met a nice boy like Xavier and couldn't tell her parents about it. This was just another instance, the worst one yet, of how inconvenient it was having Mother in Virginia and Daddy in France. She did not blame Daddy for not wanting to live at St. Peter's-at-the-Crossroads, where there was not even a telephone and where absolutely nothing ever happened. On the other hand, she did not blame mother for not wanting to live in that great gaudy house on the Avenue d'Iéna, which looked like something Mr. Cecil de Mille might have seen in a nightmare, when his rest was disturbed because he was trying to plan the setting of a new super-movie. But certainly there must be some sort of a happy medium between the two, like that lovely flounder house they had had in Alexandria, for instance, where they could all be happy together, as they had been there. Rosemary felt sure that Xavier would have been made welcome in the flounder house, and that he would have liked it.

She sighed, and a little choking feeling came into her throat. But just then she caught sight of Xavier standing on the river bank, looking eagerly in the direction from which she always came. He had on a white shirt, which was open at the throat, and white shorts, and fuzzy socks which did not come quite up to his knees. There was something about Xavier's bare throat and bare knees that affected Rosemary very strangely. She loved to look at them, just the way she loved to look at his dark eyes and his straight nose and his laughing mouth. She felt that she would like to stroke them, very gently, with the tips of her fingers. She had met lots of boys before, but this was the first time she had felt that way.

Suddenly Xavier saw her. He called to her in a glad voice, and then he came running to meet her, bounding over the long grass by the river bank in quick easy leaps. But somehow she did not feel as if she could run too and meet him halfway. She stopped where she was, and looked down at the ground, and did not answer when he shouted. She knew he would be disappointed, because she had never stopped like this before, and still she could not help it.

"Eh bien, te voilà!" he said joyously, when he was quite close to her. He sounded as happy as if he had been waiting for her all his life, and had found her at last.

"Yes. I wasn't sure I could get here today. Your grandmother came to call, and Aunt Henriette sent for me. But fortunately she did not make me stay in the *salon* very long."

"Grand'-mere did not say anything unkind to you, did she, *cherie?"*

"No—no. It was queer. I felt as if she didn't want to like me, but that she did, after all."

"Of course, she did! So everything is all right then."

"Yes, I suppose so."

"But you seem so sad, Rosemary!"

It was all too true. The choking feeling had come back into her throat and her lips were trembling.

"Voyons, voyons! What can be the matter?"

"I don't know," said Rosemary. She sank down in the long grass and covered her face with her hands. "I am so lonely," she said in a strangled voice.

"Lonely! When you and I are going to have two long hours together?"

"Yes. But I want my mother," she sobbed. And then she burst out crying.

She might have known that Xavier would be wonderful. He did not argue with her at all, or try to force her to explain why she was acting so foolishly, as Daddy would have done. He sat down beside her and put his arm around her shoulder, and patted it a little every now and then. But he did not talk to her at all. By and by, when she felt a little better, and began to grope for a handkerchief which she could not find, he slipped one which was cool and clean into her hand. And when she had mopped her eyes and looked up at him, she saw that his expression was not faintly mocking, the way it sometimes was, but very gentle and tender.

"Voyons," he said again, at last. "It would be delightful, of course, if *Madame ta mère* were here. But since she is detained by duty to her aged relatives, we must not quarrel with the situation, must we? No! On the contrary, we must make the best of it as it is. And I believe it can be made very pleasant after all."

He smiled at her in the nice way he had, and there was something so reassuring in the way he looked, that Rosemary slipped her hand into his and squeezed it gratefully.

"Do you really think so?" she asked with renewed cheerfulness.

"I am sure of it. Indeed, it has been pleasant already, has it not, *chérie?*"

He squeezed her hand in his turn, and Rosemary looked up at him and smiled too, though there were still a few tears left on her cheeks.

"Yes," she said shyly, "it has." She knew that she was coloring, she could feel her blush burning even at the back of her neck, and still she did not look away from Xavier again.

"*Eh bien,* it is going to be pleasanter and pleasanter all the time. Because pretty soon, when you start home again, I am going with you. I am going to tell your Aunt Henriette that we happened to meet, and if I do not say it was three weeks ago already, that is neither here nor there, is it? Then she will invite me to stay for *goûter* with you and your brother. And by and by your father and Monsieur Blake will be motoring in from Paris for the week-end. And before the evening is over, we shall all be on the best of terms."

As Xavier outlined this agreeable plan, it sounded so simple that Rosemary wondered why she had not thought of it herself, long before.

"And tomorrow," Xavier continued, "early in the morning, you will get a little note from my grandmother asking you to dine with us tomorrow night. I know it was in her heart to write this note, from the moment she looked at you. But because she thinks perhaps you are a little young to be invited to a formal party, it will probably not be until late this evening that she will actually do so. It will arrive, however. And you will put on the new dress you told me about, the white net with the rosebuds, and your little string of pearls. And then you will come to the Chateau de Blonville looking just like the Princess in the fairy tale."

"Who has gone to meet Prince Charming's family?" Rosemary inquired.

"Yes, Rosemary. And the Prince, of course, and all his family will be waiting to give her their warmest welcome."

He spoke so earnestly, that for an instant, Rosemary was startled again. But as she tried to draw away from him, Xavier leaned over and kissed her very gently on the lips.

Then she knew that nothing in the world could ever frighten or hurt her again.

Vivienne, standing beside the open door of the hunting lodge, lighted her twentieth cigarette and looked at her watch for the hundredth time.

She was in an excessively bad temper. In the first place, she had not recovered from the nasty jolt Xavier had given her after luncheon. It was bad enough that he should have had a chance to make such a fool of himself—if it had not been for the slow convalescence which had kept him at home after that inopportune attack of typhoid fever, he would still be safely confined in his *Lycée* at Evreux! But it was infinitely worse that he should have had a chance to discover that she had been playing the fool too, in a more serious way. A fine mess they were in now—mother and son, father and daughter! She intended to tell Michael Trent exactly what she thought of him for letting Rosemary run around loose, the instant he arrived.

But he did not seem to be arriving. Half-past four, that had been their understanding! And here it was after six! In another hour she would have to start back to the Chateau de Blonville, since she had rather a long way to go on foot, and must be in her room early enough to dress for dinner, in order to avoid rousing further suspicions. If she consumed all the time that was now left to her in recriminations, there would be none left for anything else.

Not that Michael Trent ever required much time for his purposes. He did not invite surrender, lovingly and lingeringly. Instead, he took what he wanted, boldly and brutally. At first, this ruthlessness had appealed to Vivienne irresistibly. She had found it thrilling to be seized and subjugated. Now, she had begun to feel that Michael's methods lacked finesse. She would have enjoyed a preliminary period, in the course of which she could coyly postpone the inevitable climax of their meetings by all sorts of playful arts; and afterward, she would have been glad to relax in a series of satisfied caresses. She had gone so far as to intimate as much to Michael. But he had laughed shortly, and answered her with equal curtness.

"This isn't that kind of a love affair," he told her. "In fact it isn't a *love* affair at all. You know that, Vivienne, as well as I do. But anytime you want to put a stop to it, that'll be quite all right with me."

She did not want to put a stop to it, she could not bear the thought that it might end. For the first time in her life she had been completely overwhelmed by passion, and this was still unslaked. It was better, far better, to let Michael dictate the terms of their intrigue than to give him up, better to consent to brief hole-in-the-corner meetings, to sudden onslaughts and careless leave-takings, to long delays and bitter disappointments, than not to see him at all, not to feel the sweep of his vitality all around her, not to be forced under his magnificent domination——

It was growing dark in the woods around the hunting lodge. Michael had never been so late before. Perhaps this was to be one of the times when he failed to come altogether, after leaving her for hours a prey to uncertainty. There had been instances of such nonchalant neglect, several times lately, and when she had reproached him for them, he had only shrugged his shoulders and made the reply which she so greatly dreaded.

"I'm a busy man. I can't always tell when I'll be free—or whether I'll be free at all. If it annoys you to wait for me, we better call these meetings off."

"If you leave me in the lurch once more, we will" she had retorted angrily. But the next day, as if to test her, he had done so; and still she had come to their hide-away again, and waited.

This time, she decided now, was the last she would ever do so. She would tell him, when he came, what a fool his daughter was making of herself, and then she would laugh at him and leave him. Without even giving him a chance to touch her. Without——

"Well, Vivienne, I seem to be late again."

She had been so absorbed in her angry thoughts that she had not heard him come up, and it was so dark that she had not seen him. Now his inflexible arm was already around her, pressing hard against her breasts. She tried to shake herself free.

"Let me go," she said furiously.

"Don't be absurd. What do you suppose I came here for—and what did you wait here for?"

She would have to be very quick. In another instant she would be too late.

"I know what you came here for. But I doubt if you know what I waited for. I have a surprise for you."

"Then you better relieve my mind by telling me what it is at once. I'm in a hurry."

"I'll tell you at once but I don't think you'll be much relieved."

"Well, good God, Vivienne, what is it?"

"We've been found out. By my son."

She felt the pressure of his arm slacken. It was an instant before he answered her.

"I'm very sorry," he said with genuine regret in his voice. "He's just a boy—isn't he? And extremely fond of you? He must be very much upset to find out that his mother——"

"He didn't speak to me about it as if he were upset. He used his discovery as a threat—a threat to make me receive your daughter. It seems that for the last three weeks, he's been spending most of his time with her, down by the river bank. I found *him* out first. So you see——"

She never finished her sentence. Michael Trent struck her straight across the mouth. When she recovered from the impact of the blow, he was gone.

CHAPTER 15

MICHAEL ALWAYS averaged a hundred kilometers an hour on the smooth Norman roads. To be sure, he did not see much of the countryside as he did so. The loveliness of "the fragrant snow of spring" which made its orchards such a blooming mass in May, the luxuriance of the multicolored roses which clambered over its walls and arbors in June, were alike lost on him. So was the quaintness of the half-timbered houses and sturdy stone churches in the provincial towns, the grace of the small scurrying rabbits which leaped like little white phantoms across the pathway of his car, the poignancy of the tall stark *Calvaires* rising along the roadside. As far as all these were concerned, he might have been driving blind. But he never failed to see his son waiting for him at the gateway through which he entered the drive to the Chateau de Hauterive.

He did not know what had possessed Richard to make a practice of coming and standing there in the twilight, watching for his father to swing into sight, far off in the distance, on the long straight road. The boy never seemed to be out of patience if he were late, or resentful if he were surly or silent. Richard accepted his father's habits and his father's moods unquestioningly and uncritically. On the trustful assumption that sooner or later the big racing car would loom up on the horizon, with Michael at the wheel, and that meanwhile there was nothing to do but wait until it did, Richard stood and bided his time. There was the same expectancy in his face, the same immobility in his bearing, that there had been in Daphne's when she had stood beside the churchyard gate at St. Peter's-at-the-Crossroads, years before.

The resemblance and the recollections which Richard's

vigilance evoked where alike provocative to Michael; but though he had told the boy, more than once, not to "bother" to meet him, he could not bring himself to the point of speaking sharply, even though he did speak shortly. That strange quality about the child which, from his infancy, had surrounded him like an aura, was too disarming.

However, Michael hoped, as he swung savagely along after his encounter with Vivienne, that for once something would have happened to detain the boy at the chateau, for this time he certainly would not be able to curb his tongue or conceal his temper. What a fool, what a colossal fool, he had been to embroil himself with Vivienne! And having done so, to what still more prodigious heights he had permitted his folly to mount in not breaking with her before she drove him to committing the still more unpardonable offense of laying violent hands upon a woman whom he had held in his arms over and over again! But did history repeat itself? Did folly run in the family? Was Rosemary, at the river's brink, already on the point of an irreparable misstep? That little girl! That graceful golden child! It was unthinkable! Yet it had also been unthinkable that her mother——

He groaned between clenched teeth. No, certainly he could not stand it tonight if he saw the slender young figure of his son silhouetted, motionless, against the massive portals. If Richard had come racing down the road, and had catapulted himself into the car, breathless and beaming, that would have been different. He could have understood a youngster of that type, and could have coped with him, in a rough and ready fashion; he might even have derived real satisfaction from the impetuousity and virility of a boy like that. But this silent little sentry, with his mien of mystic watchfulness, was alike baffling and bewildering.

There was no escaping him, however. He was there, as usual. Michael could see him, half a kilometer away. The long gloaming had already set in; but this had a clarity all its own, unlike the brilliance of sunshine, yet even more luminous. For another hour yet, its strange lambency would lie over the land. It was a light uniquely suited to Richard, who loved the time of day when it appeared better than any other; to Michael it represented only one more unfathomable foreign factor in French life.

He jammed on his brakes, and without shutting off his engine, flung open the door of his car. His son came toward him, gazing across the space which divided them with a radiant face.

"I'm so glad to see you, Father."

"Hello, Richard. Climb in."

"I'll just walk through the gate and close it after you. Then I'll get in. I think Alphonsine is putting the baby to bed. Anyway, I'm sure she didn't see you or she'd have come out of the lodge."

"She's supposed to watch for me, not you. She's paid for it."

"Yes, I know. But don't you think, Father, that sometimes it is the people who aren't paid to do things for us, who do the most?"

Michael, putting the car into motion again, did not answer. The boy's thought, and his manner of expressing it, had been uncannily like Daphne's. Resentment surged through him afresh.

"You better get in. I'm in a hurry."

"Yes, Father, I will, now that I've shut the gate.—You don't feel too hurried to have me tell you something, do you, while we're driving up to the house?"

"No, not if you tell me quickly."

"I've written another poem. About a lady in a satin dress. I thought of it when I saw Aunt Henriette coming down the dim stairway in the candlelight last evening, wearing powder blue and silver."

Again Michael did not answer. This mania for versifying which Richard was developing, irritated him unspeakably. Yet because it was Richard, he still hesitated to put his irritation into words.

"I believe it's the best one I've ever done," the boy went on cheerfully. "I thought I'd like to read it to you before I put it into Mother's letter and mailed it."

Michael pressed his foot down harder on the accelerator.

"May I read it to you, Father?"

"Yes, if you want to, by and by. But you know I don't care much about poetry, Richard."

"I thought you used to like it, when Mother read it aloud to you evenings. Or was it just having Mother read that you liked, not the poetry?"

"I don't believe I analyzed the situation, Richard. Besides, that was a long time ago."

"Yes. That was one of the reasons I thought you might like it if I read to you. Because it was so long since anybody had."

"I don't want to hurt your feelings, Richard, but I can think of a good many things I'd rather have you do than read poetry—or write it, for that matter. You're my only son. I'm very ambitious for you. Most students and poets have been failures."

"Have they?—Just what is a failure, Father?"

"Well, I can't go into that now either, in detail. Generally speaking, a man who doesn't make money is considered a failure."

"You're a great success then, aren't you, Father?"

"Oh, yes! I'm a tremendous success!"

Richard glanced at him questioningly. The irony in his voice, though confusing to the boy, was inescapable.

"I want to see your sister," Michael said shortly, shutting off the engine and slamming the door as he got out. "Find her for me, will you? Tell her I want her to come to my room at once."

"I think she has company, Father. She came in from her walk just before I went down to meet you, and a neighbor of ours, Xavier de Blonville, was with her. Aunt Henriette invited him to stay for *goûter*. They asked me to have it with them, but I wanted to go to meet you. I think they're having it now, in the rose garden. Shall we go out there together and join them? I'm sure you'd like to see Xavier. He's one of the nicest boys I've ever met."

"I haven't the slightest desire to see Xavier de Blonville."

"Well, but if you want to see Rosemary right away, you'll have to, won't you? I mean, I couldn't go out into the garden and ask her to leave a guest, in the middle of *goûter*, even to come and speak to you, could I, Father?"

"Well, do you suppose it would be asking too much if I should intimate that I should like to see your Aunt Henriette, instead?"

Again the sarcasm in his voice was inescapable. The radiance faded from Richard's face, leaving it troubled.

"Why, yes, of course, Father, if you need to see her very much. I'll find her for you and tell her, shall I, that you've come home, that you're waiting to speak to her?"

"Very well. I don't see though, with all the servants there are on this place, why they shouldn't run errands and carry messages. But as usual there isn't one in sight."

"Jacques is at the door, Father. I know he's only waiting to open it for you and take your hat and gloves, before he goes out to get your bags. Of course, he'll tell Aunt Henriette, if you'd rather."

"I don't cáre who tells her. There's no use in making a mountain out of a molehill. But I do want to see her at once."

"Then how fortunate! For here I am, Michael, come out on purpose to greet you!"

Michael swung around. Henriette, again wearing the powder blue dress which had inspired Richard to verse, was standing beside him, smiling serenely.

"I am so glad you could get here tonight," she said cordially. "Jerome has been held up at the Chancery—this fluctuation of the franc is too annoying! He telephoned that he and Capomazza cannot get down until tomorrow. But Mr. Loose has already arrived. I have put him in the tower apartment next to yours. He is not looking very well and he said something about wanting to speak to you, before dinner."

"He'll have to wait. I want to speak to you first."

"Ah— Then let us come into the small salon, where we shall be undisturbed. Richard, will you go to Rosemary? She has been waiting for your return to cut the strawberry tart.—There— Now that the dear child has left us, Michael, tell me why it is that you are so upset?"

"What's the meaning of this French cub's presence here?"

"The meaning? Of Xavier de Blonville's call? I'm afraid I do not quite follow you, Michael. His family lives on the next estate to this. It is a family of some standing in the community, though it is not one of the oldest—I know very little of its history prior to the seventeenth century. However, since then there has been nothing to its discredit, except that some of the male members have married slightly beneath them, for mercenary motives. Xavier's grandmother, however, is a *grande dame* of the old school. She was here earlier this afternoon, to see me, and indicated that other members of the family would follow. She has very kindly invited us all to dinner tomorrow night."

"I hope you had the good sense to decline!"

"But why should I, Michael? It is exactly the sort of invitation that you have always urged me to accept. And the De Blonvilles are exactly the sort of persons with whom you have been most eager to establish connections."

"Nothing will induce me to dine with the De Blonvilles tomorrow night. You'll have to make some kind of an excuse. And if you don't get rid of the boy at once, I shall. In a way that will leave very little doubt in his mind whether it will be wise for him to return."

"I am sure you would not be so unwise yourself, Michael."

Her voice was still unraised, her manner still unruffled. Nevertheless, in spite of his rage, Michael was aware of an adamant aspect to both.

"I think Rosemary is having her first rosy glimpse of romance, Michael. You wouldn't dim the vision for her, would you?"

"Meeting a young roué by stealth! Spending hours with him alone by the river!"

"Who put it to you that way, Michael?"

"It doesn't matter. I know that's what she's been doing. I thought I could depend on you to take better care of her!"

"You may depend upon me now, as in the past, to take the best care of Rosemary that anyone can, except her mother. But even I cannot interfere with fate. Rosemary is not stealthy, but she is shy. If I am not mistaken, shyness is a characteristic she has inherited from Daphne. And she is very young—only a child. I think she could not bring herself to speak of a meeting which meant much to her, which in a sense was a revelation to her—that she did not know how to speak of it. As for Xavier, no doubt it would have been more conventionally correct if he had withdrawn the moment he happened to catch sight of her and had waited for a proper presentation before speaking to her. However, that does not seem to be the usual procedure in such cases. If I am not mistaken, the first time you saw her mother, you walked across a ballroom and asked her to dance with you, did you not? Without any sort of introduction whatsoever?"

"That is beyond the point. I don't intend that Rosemary——"

He broke off abruptly. Henriette, who had been sitting at ease on a brocaded sofa while he paced up and down the room, rose and moved quietly toward the door.

"I really do not think there is anything further for us to discuss at the moment, Michael. If you absolutely decline to dine with the De Blonvilles, I can always send a note saying that you have been recalled to Paris. But in that case you would actually have to leave at once, which would be an affront to the guests you have invited here for the week end, and I believe that later you would greatly regret having taken a step which the De Blonvilles would certainly also interpret as an affront. As for Xavier, if it displeases you to have me receive the grandson of an old friend in my own house, I will tactfully try to discourage further visits on his part. But I believe such a course of action would almost certainly result in a resumption of the clandestine meetings which have so displeased you, whereas, if Xavier is made welcome here, there will be no occasion for any more of those. You must decide these matters for yourself, of course. But they cannot be decided hastily. And for the moment, I feel you would be very well advised to find out what it is that so greatly concerns Mr. Loose."

Michael mounted the stairs in a state of increasing fury. At every turn he seemed to be baffled and balked. Richard with his visions and his verse! Rosemary with her secrecy and her stubbornness! Henriette with her impenetrable poise and her irrefutable logic! They were all against him. And Loose was against him too—Loose, who was always complaining that he hadn't brought enough "tone" to his position, no matter how fast the money came rolling in! Loose, who hadn't gone back on the extraordinary offer which he had made in Yünnanfu because that would have been contrary to his code, coarse though this was, but who had never let Michael forget that in making it, he had taken Daphne's presence and the prestige which went with it for granted, and that he had been let down——

By the time Michael had reached the North Tower, his sense of injury and irritation was overwhelming. Without preamble, he turned the handle of the door leading into the great medieval guest room.

"Henriette says you want to see me," he observed abruptly.

"You bet I do! But not so much that I expected you to walk in on me without knocking!"

"Sorry! I've had an upsetting day. My mind was on something else when I opened the door."

"On something else, was it? Sure it wasn't on some*body* else? Wasn't on a hellcat named Vivienne de Blonville?"

"Look here——"

"Look *here!* It's about time you looked—not here, but *out!* When you get so careless with your correspondence that it's easy for your own secretary to turn spy, I'd say you better watch your step. 'If you can't be good be careful, and if you can't be careful be as careful as you can.' I said that to you the first day I ever went into your house, and you gave me a pretty dirty look for quoting such a low-down proverb. But it was good advice then and it's still good advice. I haven't interfered with you much, Michael——"

"There's been no reason why you should. Except for this one infernal slip—and I don't for the life of me know how that happened—I've always made good."

"You mean you've always made money. I didn't hire you to make money—I had all I knew what to do with of that already. I hired you to put class into my concern. That's where you've fallen down, from the very beginning. And now, if you ask me, I'll say you've fallen down hard!"

Mr. Loose banged with both fists on a buhl table which stood beside him. Then, as if in smiting it, he had given partial vent to his long-smothered resentment, he spoke in a voice that was surprisingly gentle, almost pleading in tone.

"I suppose you think I haven't got much call to set myself up as a mentor," he said, "considering that you didn't think it was safe to leave your wife alone with me for five minutes,

203

back there in La Paz. I know I've got a bad reputation myself. I'm not as black as I've been painted, but there's some truth in what's been said about me. That's just the point. I knew I never could live down the impression that my morals were as loose as my name, any more than I could live down the impression that I was a pretty slick business man. And I finally got reconciled to the idea that everyone thought I was a bum and a bounder. Because I thought you'd make it up to me. I thought I'd live to see you climb to the places I couldn't reach, and that in a way I'd get to them with you. You needed money and I could help you make it. That was easy. I had more than I knew what to do with, as I said before, and you had everything else. A good education and a good appearance and good manners and a lady for a wife. Lord! The picture was perfect! I could see you sitting right beside the throne, at the Court of St. James's, once you'd piled up the cash that would ease you into the seat.

"Of course, I didn't reckon on Daphne feeling the way she did about the Service. I didn't think it had got under her skin so. She knew you wouldn't get an ambassadorship until kingdom come, at the rate you were going. So I didn't think she'd mind if you took a short cut to one. Still, I'm bound to say I admire her for the way she stuck to her guns. She thought an awful lot of you, Michael. It nearly killed her to leave you. But she figured that if she threatened to you'd stay in the Service, and when she found she was wrong her pride was so hurt there wasn't anything left for her to do but clear out anyhow. And I figured you'd do so darned well, with the chance I was giving you, that pretty soon you'd get her back again, and then we'd all be headed straight where I meant we should go. Well, I was wrong too. Daphne and I were both mistaken in you. You haven't got it in you to make good, either by the long rough road or the short quick cut."

"If that's the way you feel—" began Michael furiously. But Mr. Loose raised a warning hand.

"Yes, that's the way I feel, and you might just as well hear me out, Michael, because I mean to finish what I started to say. I didn't expect, either, when I said you could have a place in Paris, that you'd fix it up to look like a casino, all chandeliers and staircases. I thought you'd have a house with Daphne's furniture and flowers in it. That's what would have gone over really big here. Of course, this chateau's handsome, I'm not saying it isn't. But as far as the French are concerned, this is a Hauterive house, like it's been for a thousand years already. My money may have gone into it, but it's still Henriette's name that's made it what it is, and

204

you don't enter into the picture at all. What you needed and what I needed was that you should have a house of your own."

"If—" began Michael again. But again Mr. Loose interrupted him.

"I know too, though I'm not what you'd call a student of the Bible, that it isn't good for man to live alone, and I wouldn't have held it against you if I'd heard you were slipping off now and again to places where men don't advertise their presence if they can help it. I'd have hoped Daphne'd never hear about it, because it's such smutty business, and there's something so fresh about her, like her own flowers. But I'd have understood myself. I'd have winked at it. What I can't understand, what I can't wink at and don't intend to, is that you should risk an open scandal by getting mixed up with a shameless hussy like Vivienne de Blonville. I wouldn't put it past her to brag about her affair with you, at the top of her lungs, if she thought there was anything to be gained by doing it. On the other hand, I wouldn't put it past her to turn around and scream that you'd seduced her. She'd demand that her honor be avenged if she thought you had the slightest idea of dropping her. And believe me, there'd be plenty of people springing up with swords in their hands if she did that! She's a slut herself, but her father's a Colonial Governor, and she's a relative of almost every prominent person in France! What's more, she's the wife of a decent fellow who's been your own guest over and over again! She's the daughter-in-law of Henriette's oldest friend! She's the mother of the kind of boy Daphne always hoped Rosemary would marry! Well, I may be a bum and a bounder, as I said before, but I've never done anything so downright dumb or as downright dirty as you did when you took her on!"

The gentleness had vanished completely from his voice. He brought his fists down on the table again, and this time the force of the blow overturned it.

"Leave it lay there!" he shouted, as Michael mechanically leaned over to pick it up. "It isn't any flatter than my hopes are! They've toppled over, the same as that table has. It won't matter, Michael, if you make fifty million now. I'll never live to see you an ambassador after this!"

CHAPTER 16

NEVER, DAPHNE thought, had any June been as beautiful as this one was. Day after day a bright sun rose in a blue sky; yet there was still a crystalline quality in the air, almost autumnal in atmosphere. Even at noon the heat was never oppressive; and in the evening, freshness rose from the earth and mingled with the zephyrs which stirred the trees. In the garden at St. Peter's-at-the-Crossroads every trellis and arbor was overhung with roses; in the churchyard every grave was garlanded. The ivy shone with fresh gloss; the crepe myrtle fell in snowy cascades; the lemon lilies were lifted, like fragrant chalices, on their slender stalks.

During the daytime, Daphne spent several hours in her uncle's library. It was a peaceful place, lined to the ceiling with mottled, leatherbound volumes. She loved the shabby look and smooth feel of them; even the scent, mellow rather than musty, which rose from their pages when she left them lying open on the table where she worked, seemed sweet to her. The task of sorting and assembling her father's papers and poems was almost finished; in another week or so they would be ready to send to Brooks & Bernstein, the publishers who were to bring them out. Honor Bright had helped her with the compilation, and when Honor was with her, everything went forward in a brisk and businesslike way; there was nothing slack or amateurish about it, and the finished product would profit by her professional touch. But in Honor's absence, Daphne often sat spellbound, turning over the typewritten sheets which someday were to be transformed into a bound volume, and dreaming of the potentialities, still unrevealed, which they embodied.

For she knew now that their appearance might do much more than bring tardy recognition to the strange suppressed genius of her erring father; it might also pave the way to the recognition of the fresh and budding genius of her gifted son, the discovery of which had been precipitated by rummaging through the contents of Larry Daingerfield's trunk. Daphne did not doubt that through one of those inexplicable though not infrequent tricks of heredity, her father's talents had been reincarnated in Richard, after lying latent throughout a generation. But in the case of the child, there was to be no tardiness and no tragedy; he had had co-operation and encouragement from the beginning; and now Mr. Brooks had gone so far as to say that if the Daingerfield collection went over well, it might not be a bad plan to follow it up with a slim volume of verse by Richard. From the advertising angle, such an arrangement would certainly have an appeal all its own.

"We'll have to find just the right title," he had told Daphne, when Honor brought him to the rectory to talk the matter over. "A number of years ago, a book was brought out that was called 'Poems by a Little Girl.' It did very well. We want to follow out the same idea, though we wouldn't do anything as plagiaristic, of course, as to call this proposed collection 'Poems by a Little Boy'—we'd find something original and provocative—something that would link it with his grandfather's verse. Give the matter some thought, Mrs. Trent, in your leisure moments. You might have an idea yourself."

So Daphne gave the matter thought, as she sat surrounded by old books, turning the pages of a new one. Very often she did little else, until the long shadows slanting across her desk roused her to a realization of the lateness of the hour. Then she put everything into place, and stepped quietly from the library into the garden.

Her work there had already been done, before the sun, which was now setting, had been high; the early morning hours were always given to weeding and watering. This, on the contrary, was her period of relaxation and rest. She was able to close her consciousness to thoughts of the portentous book during the fragrant twilight, as easily as she had closed the door of her study on her own escaping figure. But her interval of idleness was seldom protracted. Following the casual custom of the county, visitors came constantly to the rectory: The Carter Tayloes from Barren Point never let a week go by without stopping in for supper. Honor Bright and Jerry Stone motored over every day or two from Solomon's Garden, bringing with them the prominent politicians who frequented their plantation. The President used it as a retreat from the cares of office and a center for confidential conferences; and Jerry's elder brother, John Stone, the Majority "Whip" in the Senate, was a ringleader in the group closest to him. Another outstanding member of this group was Ambrose Estabrook, the Under Secretary of State.

He had aged a good deal, Daphne reflected, since he had first befriended her and tried to befriend Michael, during the months when they had been living in the flounder house at Alexandria. His own period of "hope deferred" had been an arduous and anxious one; it had taken heavy toll of his vitality and endurance. The "retrenchment program" which had deprived four hundred students of the opportunity to matriculate for the Foreign Service was one of the governmental "economies" against which he had fought tooth and nail; and the fact that his fight had been a losing one had eaten into his very soul. Deprived of children himself, he had lavished upon these postulants all the solicitude of vicarious fatherhood; his protests over their plight had been as heartfelt as they were vigorous.

"The poor youngsters know well enough there's a depression going on," he kept reiterating. "They don't expect positions right away. All they're asking for is a chance to prove they're fitted to have places eventually. Most of them have spent years getting ready to prove it. There isn't a law school or a medical school in the country which would decline to let its students take their examinations at the end of their course. This doesn't mean the boys are guaranteed practices or patients; but it does mean the efforts which have seemed to them so endless won't in the last analysis, seem futile to them as well! I won't be responsible for spoiling the whole outlook on life of four hundred boys, all for the sake of saving a few hundred dollars—which, as a matter of fact, they're willing to take out of their own pockets!—especially when we're squandering millions in other directions at the same time!"

But in the end, he was obliged to accept this responsibility, or appear to do so; and as one bewildered and embittered young man after another left his office, after arguments and expostulations which led nowhere, the lines grew deeper and deeper in his cultured face, and the habitual control of his manner settled into a still more self-protective reserve. It was during this period that he began to seek out Daphne Trent, not occasionally, as he had done heretofore, but with increasing frequency. At first he was only aware that he found at her side such solace as had nowhere assuaged him since the loss of Constance, the wife of his youth. Daphne's presence was infinitely restful to him, infinitely consoling. He expected nothing, he wanted nothing, beyond the sense of tranquility and healing which she gave him, and he felt no impulsion toward a continual experience of this. But as time went on, he found his attitude toward her changing, almost imperceptibly. He began to miss her when he did not see her for several consecutive days; then he began to yearn for the sight of her whenever he was separated from her. And soon the sight of her was not enough. He wanted to cover her hand with his while they sat talking together, to brush back the soft hair from her white brow, to kiss her

208

transparent eyelids. At last he faced the fact that he was deeply in love with her.

He tried to face it squarely, without illusions and without excitement. He knew that she had never thought of him as a suitor, far less as a lover. He was years older than she was, a reserved and unromantic figure; he doubted whether the idea of divorce had ever crossed her mind, and he felt sure that the alternative of an intrigue would be even more repugnant to her than it would be to him. Yet he knew that the moment could not be indefinitely postponed when he would ask her to accept inclusion in the secret places of his heart and home.

Meanwhile, as he tried to bide his time until this moment should become propitious, the political crisis, so long predicted, came to pass; the Honorable T. Gilbert Morgan toppled from his place in the seats of the mighty and Ambrose Estabrook was promoted to his position. After that, the next move upward had come swiftly and easily, and now he was Secretary of State in practically everything except name.

He had long since ceased to lead a lonely life, and the demands upon his alleged leisure were incessant; but still he managed to be at Solomon's Garden for almost every week end, and to come over to the rectory from there, with the President and John and Jerry and the others, to drink Daphne's mint juleps or to consume great mounds of Mamie Belle's waffles. He also managed, very often, to come to the rectory during the week by himself, when the others knew nothing about it—unless, as he shrewdly suspected, Honor Bright was undeceived as to the true state of his feelings and the persistency of his course. He was a rather slow and cautious driver; yet he contrived to cover the ground between the Department of State and St. Peter's-at-the-Crossroads in approximately two hours. He could usually reach his destination by seven, sit for an hour in the garden with Daphne before Mamie Belle called them in to supper, and then return to the arbor for another hour afterward. Even so, he was back at the Cosmos Club by midnight. On cool evenings, supper was earlier, and after Mrs. Daingerfield had played a selection on the harp, which Estabrook enjoyed as greatly as Michael disliked it, she and the rector retired to their own room. Then Ambrose Estabrook sat by the hearthstone in the study instead of by the pool in the garden.

"I know that actually you do a great deal of diversified work," he told Daphne once. "Yet somehow you always contrive to give the effect of sitting quietly about, waiting without impatience, for something to happen or someone to come. It's immensely restful, especially to a man who is constantly confronted with women who are springing round and round in a squirrel cage."

Daphne laughed. "I'm not impatient," she said. "I never have minded waiting. Something always does happen—and someone always does come."

"The man who came first was certainly very fortunate," observed Ambrose Estabrook dryly.

Daphne flushed. Her color still came and went easily under provocation, as it had when she was a girl.

"I'm afraid he wasn't," she said. "*I* was fortunate, and I think he was happy—for a little while. But afterward— Perhaps it would have been better if he hadn't come at all, or if he had come here in vain."

"No man has ever come here in vain," Ambrose Estabrook told her, "no matter how little you found it in your heart to give him. As for Michael Trent, and your infinite bounty to him—" He saw that Daphne's flush had deepened and that her eyes, which she was averting from him, were full of tears, and changed the subject easily. "How is the book coming on?" he asked. "I have great confidence in that collection. I feel it's going to be an immense success."

"It's nearly done. I have confidence in it too."

"What are you calling it?"

" 'The Smothered Spring.' Do you think that's a good title?"

"Yes. Very vivid, very original."

"I'm so glad."

"I may have some news for you, myself, about the time you tell me your task is finished."

Daphne looked up at him inquiringly, the tears gone from her eyes. But he did not seem inclined to say any more, and curiosity, like impatience, was still alien to her. Instead of asking questions, she began to trace the quaint lettering of the tomb on which they were sitting, and to read aloud:

> " 'Here, Lyes, the. Body.of.
> MARY TRIMBLE, who De
> parted, This.Life Feb. 18th in the
> Year of. Our Lord.1770.
> All. you that. Come. My.Grave.to See
> As, I am. Now. So Must You Bee
> Repent. in. Time. Make. No. Delay
> In the Bloom. of Youth. I was
> Snatched Away.' "

"It seems to have been quite the fashion for lovely ladies to die young in those days," Daphne remarked whimsically.

"Men, on the contrary, lived to a ripe old age, wearing out two or three wives along the way! Listen to John Trimble's epitaph.—It is ever so much more cheerful:

> " 'In
> Memory of
> JOHN TRIMBLE
> Who Died the 22nd of April, 1824
> Aged About 82 Years
> He Lived Beloved and Died Lamented
> His Hospitality was Unbounded.' "

"The place still lives up to the old traditions," Estabrook remarked. Unlike Michael he was not averse to lingering in the old churchyard. But a savory smell was issuing from Mamie Belle's kitchen and he realized that he was healthily hungry. Besides, the sooner that supper was over, the sooner he would have Daphne to himself. "Aren't you going to ask me in to sample the latest specimen of unbounded hospitality?"

Daphne finished putting the manuscripts she had assembled into their final form on the first really oppressive day of the summer. It was after six o'clock when the last clip was adjusted and the neatly typed pages slipped smoothly into the big manila envelope, already addressed in heavy ink, to Brooks & Bernstein. She had meant to take it to the post office, three miles distant, as soon as it was ready to go off. But it was too late for that, this evening. However, one night's delay would not matter much after delay of over thirty years! She laid the packet squarely down on the blotter, and throwing up the windows, which had been closed during the day to keep out the heat, looked out toward the shimmering garden; but it still seemed so hot that, after a moment's hesitation, she decided to bathe and change into fresh clothes before she went into it, even for a breathing space. When she came downstairs again, half an hour later, she saw that Ambrose Estabrook had forestalled her and that he was already sitting beside the pool.

"Have you been here long?" she asked, as she went forward unhurriedly. "I'm sorry if I've kept you waiting! But I felt so soiled and sticky when I left the study— It's terribly hot—I'm afraid we're going to have a storm."

"I'm afraid so too. It's bad weather for the flyers."

"The flyers?"

"Daphne, do you let the world drift by you entirely, now

211

that you're down here? You knew, didn't you, that some experimental transatlantic flights were to be made this week? Under the direct sponsorship of the Department of Commerce, but with the indirect supervision of the Department of State? They're to blaze the way for an established route."

"Ye-es—I've read about them. But I wasn't vitally interested. I've never been up in a plane, never wanted to go. And all this experimentation seems to me so futile and foolhardy! Why should anyone wish to fly across the ocean, especially now that you can go safely by boat in five days?"

"Someone might wish—or need—to get there in less than that, even though the idea seems to you so fantastic. Besides, the progress of aviation is part of the inevitable march of time. We may not like it, but we've got to keep abreast of it, or fall into utter desuetude."

"I'm not sure that I should mind that. I'm not sure that I want to keep up with anything so ruthless as the march of time.—The men won't be allowed to start on their flight, will they, if there's a storm?"

"No, of course not. No one wants them to take unnecessary risks. One more slight delay won't matter much, after all these years."

Daphne laughed lightly. "That's what I reminded myself, a little while ago, about 'The Smothered Spring,'" she said. "I finished editing the book this afternoon, but just too late to take it to the post office."

"Then it's done! And its completion coincides with my promotion, as I thought it might."

"With your promotion——!"

"The Secretary of State has resigned. He's been very feeble, very fragile, for a long time, as you know. He's had to be relieved of a great many of his responsibilities. I've had a hand in the relief. The President has seen fit to show his appreciation of my services."

"You mean——"

"I mean I'm the actual Secretary of State now, not the Acting Secretary any longer—or that I shall be as soon as the Senate has confirmed the appointment which was made this afternoon. Will you be the first to congratulate me, Daphne?"

He seldom spoke banteringly or tritely. Daphne guessed that the reason he did so now was to ease the strain of a moment which would otherwise have been tense.

"I will indeed! I don't know when any news has made me so happy!"

"Then perhaps you're in a mood to impart joyful tidings as well as to receive them?"

There was still a jesting note in his voice. But there was a serious undertone too, which she could not fail to recognize.

"I've imparted my joyous tidings already. I've told you about the book. There's nothing else for me to say."

"There's a great deal else that you might say, Daphne, if you only would."

"What? A dull old matron like me!"

"You know perfectly well that you're not old, that you're not dull and that you're not matronly."

"I've been married nearly sixteen years!"

"You mean that you were married when you were very young and that you lived with your husband twelve years, but that you haven't lived with him now for over four."

"I don't live with him. But I'm still married to him."

"It seems to me a very unsatisfactory arrangement all around. Is it one which you have thought of prolonging indefinitely?"

"I haven't thought. That is, I've tried not to. I've just waited. You've told me yourself, Ambrose, that I have great capacities for waiting."

"Yes. But in this instance, what are you waiting for? Do you think Michael Trent will humble himself and come back to you?"

"No."

"I trust it has not occurred to you that you might humble yourself and go to him?"

"No."

"Then I'm afraid I don't understand your plans or your program."

A muffled noise, like that of menacing thunder, rose slowly and rolled away in the distance. Daphne followed the direction of the sound anxiously with her eyes. Then she looked down at the slim hands which she was alternately locking and unlocking.

"I haven't any plans. I haven't any program. I only know that some events are inevitable, that some acts are final, and that you have to accept the consequences of these, whatever they may be. My marriage with Michael was one of them."

"An inevitable event? Or a final act? They're not synonymous, you know."

"They are for me, as far as marriage is concerned."

"Are you sure of this, Daphne?"

"Yes. I'm very sure."

A vivid flash, followed by a sharp report, clove through the ominous clouds. These parted, as if the bolt which had pierced them had actually rent them asunder. Daphne shivered, in spite of the heat.

"Shall we go in? The storm seems to be coming closer."

"No, I prefer to stay here, if you're not afraid. There is something else I wish to say to you, and I don't believe it is going to rain immediately. In fact, it looks a little brighter."

"Is the other thing you wish to say about marriage also, Ambrose? Because if it is——"

"No, it is about something quite different. You have convinced me, against my will, that it is futile to continue a discussion of that subject. So I am prepared to drop it—at least for the time being. However, I hope to convince you that we might profitably pursue the discussion of another subject, though I'm afraid it may be against your will in this instance, too."

Daphne did not answer. Her head was lifted now, as if she were listening for another thunderclap, but she continued to clasp and unclasp her hands, instead of holding them, according to her custom, quietly folded in her lap.

"Did it ever occur to you," Ambrose Estabrook asked slowly, "that diplomacy is not necessarily a masculine prerogative? That some women might be suited for such a career also?"

"No—yes—that is—several girls have taken and passed Foreign Service examinations already, haven't they? I thought two or three of them were serving as vice-consuls."

"I wasn't referring to that. I was referring to the fact that there is no real reason why a woman should not receive a political appointment, as minister, if she were fitted for it, and the President and the Secretary of State were agreed concerning her fitness."

"I don't suppose that there is. But do you know any such woman, Ambrose?"

"I think I do, and the President subscribes to my opinion. It has occurred to us both that under all the circumstances, such an appointment might appeal to you. If it would, the President is prepared to make it."

"The President is prepared— Ambrose, I don't understand what you are saying!"

As if impelled to physical flight from the dazzling proposition which had been hurled at her, she had sprung unconsciously to her feet as she spoke. Ambrose Estabrook stepped swiftly into the path before her and grasped her hands.

"Listen to me, Daphne," he said forcefully. "You know that if Michael had only been possessed of half your patience, I would have done everything in my power for him. He was told, over and over again, that all he had to do was to sit tight and wait. But he wouldn't listen. He wouldn't even look at the handwriting on the wall. It was written, clear as

214

crystal, long ago, that Morgan's days were numbered, and that when he came to the end of them, mine would begin. Anyone who ran could read."

"Yes, I know. But Michael——"

"Men are made by the East, or broken by it, Daphne. I don't need to tell you which are the strong men and which are the weak ones. Michael let it break him. Just compare his attitude with Jerome Blake's, exiled in Tegucigalpa! And look where Blake is now—in a position Michael would give ten years of his life to hold! Yet Michael and Jerome, in the last analysis, both got their deserts."

"Yes, I know," Daphne said again, more hurriedly. "But the East—it didn't break Michael, not really. It was only——"

"It was only that Loose came along at the psychological moment, I suppose. But Michael could have listened to you instead of to Loose, if he had to listen to someone, if he hadn't the strength of character to stand on his own feet and make his own decisions! If he'd listened to you, if he'd stayed in the Service, he'd have been sent to Berlin as second secretary the minute Morgan was out—that was the post I always wanted Michael to have, the post I was sure he was fitted for. Later it would have been easy to get him shifted to some less vital point as first secretary, to arrange a 'career' appointment for him as minister to some small country. It wouldn't have been done primarily for Michael's sake, of course. He's a capable man, but there are at least a dozen I can think of, offhand, who are just as good or better. It would have been done for *your* sake! Because you *are* exceptional! You're an asset and an ornament to the Service! You're the sort of woman we can't do without! So now that the time has come for me to act independently, I'm going to do what I please with my public life, even if I can't do what I please with my private life. I'm going to use my power to give you the post your husband might have had!"

The control of his manner, the calmness of his voice, had completely vanished. Still holding Daphne's hands, he had drawn her down on the bench beside the pool, speaking with such mounting intensity as he did so, that the roar of the thunder coming closer and closer, seemed only an accompaniment to his words. Daphne, struggling to free herself as from catastrophe closing in upon her, wondered if presently she would hear her own voice rising in a scream.

"Ambrose—please—please— don't act like this! Don't speak to me in such a way! It's all so foolish, it's all so fantastic! I never was an asset, I never was an ornament to the Service—I never could be! You've reproved me yourself,

215

over and over again, because I didn't take enough initiative, because I didn't try to meet influential people and go to important functions——"

"Years ago, before I realized that history would be made in your own garden and at your own fireside, wherever you established yourself!"

"But all I do is to sit and listen! I rarely make any comments, hardly ever a suggestion!"

"And what do you think we want our diplomats to do?—stand on street corners shouting into megaphones? If a few more of them would sit and listen to what is going on around them, instead of perpetually making comments that don't amount to anything and suggestions that aren't wanted, the American Foreign Service would have a good deal more prestige than it's got at present!"

Daphne drew a deep breath, so deep that it sounded almost like a gasp. Estabrook seized upon her stupefaction.

"It's only the second raters who need to struggle and strive for prestige," he said vehemently. "But it's the natural perquisite of people who really count—like yourself. Don't you see the significance of having the President in your house every week? Don't you know there isn't a woman in the world, not even Honor Bright, in whom John Stone puts more dependence than he does in you? And John Stone is going to be President himself, someday! Doesn't it mean anything at all to you that the Secretary of State——"

"But I'm so confused—I'm so completely stunned! It isn't an hour since we were speaking of the flyers and you asked me if I let the world drift by me completely——"

"Because it's been your *choice* to let it drift—not because you weren't *capable* of doing otherwise! You're capable of anything! And tonight you're going to make a new choice. You're going to choose the country to which you'll be sent as Minister Extraordinary and Envoy Plenipotentiary!"

Daphne gasped again, and again Ambrose Estabrook went rushing on.

"Shall I help you to make it? Shall I tell you where I've loved to visualize you?"

"I— Ambrose, please stop, please let me think, please listen to me!"

"I love to visualize you in Athens. 'The violet-crowned!' That wouldn't be just the city, it would be you too! You're a Greek yourself, Daphne, you've been told that before. Even your parents must have realized it when they named you! Even Michael must have known it when he pursued you! You'll be going home, going to a land of which you're essentially a part, to a country which will claim you as its own! Its very language won't elude you long——"

He stopped abruptly, struck by a sudden thought. "Or will it elude you at all?" he asked imperatively. "Your uncle is a scholar as well as a saint; he taught you himself, didn't he, for the most part, when you were a girl? Didn't you delve into the classics with him? Haven't you studied Greek already?"

"Yes—yes—I have. But that wouldn't help, would it, in talking? I mean, modern Greek must be so different——"

Estabrook put back his head and laughed. "Don't be childish, Daphne. You know the characters, don't you? The grammar, the groundwork? If you've forgotten those, partially, your uncle could help you brush up on them again—you may be sure he's never forgotten them! Why don't you ask him to go with you, and your Aunt Vinnie too? They're getting old, they've lived leanly all their lives. You could give them a glimpse of paradise on earth, if you showed them the Isles of Greece!"

"I—I know. I thought of Uncle Roger the minute you began to talk. He's said so wistfully, so many times, that if he could only see Greece before he died——"

"He shall see it! You'll make it possible for him to see it! And when you do, you'll feel, for the first time in your life, that you've partially repaid him for all the sacrifices he's made for you, all the kindness he's shown you! And with him to help you, how long do you think it will take you to correlate the Greek you know already with what you need to know? A few weeks probably, a few months at most! You'll be unique, you'll be invaluable! And to think I wasn't even considering this added advantage when I first considered you for Greece—or rather Greece for you!"

This time she did not even draw a deep breath when he stopped. She was completely dazed by the spell which he was weaving around her.

"You'll have a white house, on a hill, in an olive grove," he told her passionately. "You'll make it beautiful, as you make beautiful every house that you inhabit. You'll have a garden with warm roses and white lilies in it, you'll have an orchard and a vineyard too. You'll pile your table with glowing fruit and fill your goblets with sparkling wine. You'll set silent statues among the stately trees and then breathe life into them. You'll glorify everything you touch. Daphne—Daphne—I can see it all!"

His words were coming in a torrent now. Daphne, summoning strength at last to brace herself against the impact of them, spoke very slowly.

"Could I—are you sure I could do all that—in Greece?"

"All that and much, much besides! I haven't begun to tell you, Daphne, what you can do—what you will do!"

"And it would mean a great deal—to Greece—and to this country—and to you—if I went?"

"More than I can possibly tell you!"

"Then—if I say I'll go—if it's so important that I should go—will you let me do it in my own way?"

"But, of course, you're going—and of course, you're doing it in your own way!"

Without warning, the latent lightning suddenly zigzagged through the churchyard and darted down among the tombs. As the reverberating crash which followed it shuddered slowly into silence along the garden wall, Ambrose Estabrook heard Daphne speaking again, speaking as serenely as if no ruinous storm were upon them, as if no tense and terrific scene had taken place between them.

"Very well. If you really mean that, I'll go to Greece. I'll take Aunt Vinnie and Uncle Roger with me and find a little home for them near my own. I'll speak the language and learn to know the land. I'll try to be wise and do good. I'll live in a white house on a hill and cultivate a vineyard and set statues among the trees. But I won't live there alone. I'll live there with Michael. Because I won't be the Minister. He will. Because you'll send a cable to him and offer him the appointment. And when he's accepted it, when he doesn't feel humiliated and injured any longer, but full of pride and purpose again, he'll ask me to come back to him. And I'll go. I'll go gladly and quickly. And we'll never let him know you offered the appointment to me and that I declined it. We'll never let him know I suggested that you should ask him instead. He's been hurt enough already. We won't hurt him any more. But we'll have a secret, you and I. Something we share, something of our very own instead—instead of other things we couldn't have and couldn't share. I'll be your emissary to Greece, Ambrose. But no one except you and I will ever know it."

She was standing again, her hands freed, her figure poised for fleet-footed flight. The rain, released at last from the massive clouds, had begun to fall in sheets of silver all around her.

"We can't stay here any longer," she said swiftly. "I'm going to run—I can still run as fast as when I was a girl! I'll race you to shelter. I dare you to try to catch me! Will you accept another challenge from me, Ambrose?"

She had disappeared completely when he reached the

house, himself. Indeed, a strange quiet rested over the rectory, the more uncanny because of the turbulence of the storm outside. Daphne's Aunt Vinnie invariably sank into her bed at the first thunderclap, and lay there, clutching at her husband's hands, until the elements were quiet again; although he was undisturbed himself, the rector was too tenderhearted to leave her alone, a prey to her fright; so he also was in seclusion. Mamie Belle accepted storms even less philosophically than Mrs. Daingerfield, for she shared in all the superstitions of her race. With an agility amazing in one of her size, she dove into her own cabin, and sinking on her knees, moaned and beat upon her mountainous breast with her big black hands.

"Oh, Laud, lissun! We is pore miserable sinners, but we ain't done nothin' much wrong after all. Not this time, leastaways. Oh, Laud, save us!"

Estabrook went into the deserted kitchen, took off his coat and shoes and placed them near the fire. Then he sat down and waited for them to dry, his brain still seething. He had amazed Daphne, as he had expected and intended; but he had not reckoned on rushing headlong into a form of recklessness which was completely out of character both for a mature man and a sober statesman; nor had he dreamed that Daphne would turn the tables on him by supplementing a surprise with a shock. He had made a headstrong offer from which he could not now withdraw. But she had delivered an ultimatum which he could not avoid accepting.

And if he did accept it, what then? Why then Michael Trent, the failure, the deserter, would triumph after all! Michael Trent with his futile record in the Service and his millions made in patent medicine! Michael Trent who stood for everything that Estabrook, bent on advancing the "career" man, had sworn should be uprooted and destroyed! No Presidential appointment, precipitated solely by the expediency of scattering political plums among campaign supporters more grasping than deserving, would smack of greater favoritism and scanter justice than this. Yet how could the Secretary of State, having pledged his word to the woman he loved and who so richly merited his regard, retreat from the position in which he had placed himself?

There was no answer to such a question. Estabrook rose and began to pace up and down the floor. The ancient boards, wide and loose, creaked under his weight as he walked. Mrs. Daingerfield's harp, gleaming in its corner, began to give forth strange sounds. A quivering chill crept along Estabrook's spine as he listened to them. It was futile for him to argue with himself that the harp stood insecurely on the

219

uneven floor, that its strings vibrated because they were shaken by the storm. He could have sworn that they shook because ghostly fingers were touching them. The stories of a haunted house which Daphne had told him no longer seemed fantastic. He himself could feel phenomena at work and sense the nearness of supernal beings.

The atmosphere was becoming momentarily more and more oppressive, more and more uncanny. He was tempted to go and tap on Daphne's door, to ask her to come out of her room and listen reasonably while he talked with her rationally—for this time he would be rational. The storm was still raging outside; the very air was electric; but his own mind was beginning to clear at last, his own spirit was growing calm again.

He had almost reached the staircase, bent on carrying out his purpose, when he was startled by the sound of the heavy knocker. Someone was pounding on the front door so violently that it had begun to shake; the uproar in the midst of the dimness and silence was uncanny. He turned down the hall, his new-found sense of tranquility completely shattered, and flung the door open.

Honor Bright was standing in the entrance, cloaked and hooded in red cellophane, with the rain pouring down in streams from its smooth transparent texture. Her face, framed by the heavy braids from which the covering had partially slipped away, was very pale; almost instantly Estabrook realized that it was not only the storm which had made this so wet, but that there were tears on it too.

"What has happened, Honor?" he asked sharply.

"A frightful accident. A cable has just come in. Thank God it came to our house!"

The world seemed suddenly to come to a standstill. Estabrook spoke thickly.

"You mean that Michael——"

"*Michael!* I mean that *Richard's* been terribly injured, that he's probably dying! And there isn't another boat, another boat that makes any kind of time, till next Wednesday! The *Europa's* just gone, and the *Aquitania*— I looked in the *Tribune* while Jerry got out the car. Ambrose, it will kill Daphne if Richard dies and she——"

"Richard won't die.—And I'll be with him, in France, tomorrow evening!"

They turned, aghast. Daphne had come down the stairs so swiftly and silently that they had not heard her. Now she stood between them, her eyes fixed on Estabrook's face.

"There are the flyers," she said. "The transatlantic flyers

220

you told me about. Even if there is a storm, even if it's peril-ous, one of them—one of them, at least, could start tonight! You said you meant to use your power. You can use it now. You can send out a man and you can send me with him!"

PART VI

Blazing the Trail

CHAPTER 17

IN SPITE of the storm, it was not really rough. For over an hour, Daphne had sat tense in the copilot's seat, fearful lest the slightest movement on her part would upset the precari-ous balance of the plane. Clive, the pilot, had unconsciously augmented her terror by the terse orders he had issued as he took her leather belt from her trembling fingers and fastened it firmly about her.

"Don't fumble with that again," he said curtly. "You might get it unbuckled. And remember to keep your feet off the rudders and your hands off the control wheel and the in-struments. They're not meant to play with. We're bound to do some bucking. But it isn't healthy to get hysterical, no matter how much we rock around. Are you ready?"

She had not answered, because her lips were quivering and would not form words. So Clive had repeated his question, speaking more sharply the second time. Then he had glanced at her and had seen that she was inclining her head, that her mouth was moving pitifully, even though no sound came from it.

"Scared stiff," he had muttered to himself. "Probably she'll be sick as a dog too. Well, it can't be helped now. After all, she brought it on herself—and on me. She knows as well as I do that we've got to see this through or die in the attempt. And that's not maybe, either."

He pushed the throttle wide open. Never before had he "given the gun" to his ship with such sudden ruthlessness. The huge metal monoplane began to shudder violently, like some imprisoned monster striving to shatter the chains which bound it to the earth. The ground beneath it was a viscous mass of mud; its wheels sunk deep into the slime and stuck there; for a long time they revolved as futilely as a wheel in a squirrel cage. At last they responded convulsively to the motive power above them and moved feebly forward; but as they did so, the ship sank heavily upon them, retarding their halting progress still further; the great tanks in its fuselage, installed to supply extra fuel, weighed it down unyieldingly.

"What is the matter?" Daphne whispered, her unmanageable mouth finally responding to her will.

She was rigid with terror. All the friendly faces with which she had been surrounded to the end were now blotted out of sight. Even Honor Bright had disappeared. It was Honor who had taken the situation in hand from the beginning, who had sent Daphne and Estabrook speeding on their way to Washington with the assurance that she would attend to all details and catch up with them before Daphne left the field. It was she who had prevailed upon the Department of Commerce to get the final permit necessary to authorize a transatlantic flight. It was she who had telephoned the airport to ask for a volunteer pilot. It was she who had got in touch with the State Department and the White House. She had thought of little things too, as well as big ones. She had remembered that Daphne would need a flying suit, that she could not start across the ocean in the white lace dress she had put on when she left the library to go into the garden, and which she had still been wearing when she flung herself into Estabrook's motor, without even stopping to throw a scarf around her shoulders. So Honor had mentioned the flying suit in the course of her telephoning, and thanks to her foresight it had been secured in approximately the right size. She had thought of food also, she had remembered that Daphne would be hungry when she had recovered from the first shock of her grief and her fright. So Honor had filled thermos bottles and made sandwiches and brought them with her in a little leather case when she and Jerry left Solomon's Garden and went flashing through the storm over the "Richmond Road" that led to Washington.

Jerry had been wonderful too. It was strange that so many people misjudged Jerry, that they sized him up as superficial because his manner was so easy and graceful and his expression so irresistible. Actually, when it came to a showdown, Jerry was almost as dependable as his brother John; yet it was the apparent lightness of his approach to the crisis through which she was passing that had redeemed it of some of its horror in Daphne's tortured mind. While

Jerry could still smile at her, while Jerry could still talk to her in his friendly facile way, there was still a beam of radiance in the engulfing darkness. She saw that this was so and drew on the sight for succor. John was standing by too, and Ambrose Estabrook had indeed "proved his power." Moreover, at the last moment, one of the great shining limousines bearing the White House crest came swaying onto the muddy field and the President himself had stepped from it. He had grasped Daphne's hand warmly, had told her there was nothing, absolutely nothing, which would be left undone to assure the safety and success of her venture. But none of these eminent men had sustained her as Honor did. There was no man who could. In this supreme moment, her spirit yearned for the support which only another woman could give her, for only another woman could fathom the grief of a *mater dolorosa*.

Honor had seen that this was so, with that uncanny sixth sense which she had always possessed, and Honor had not failed her. But now Honor was gone. Or rather, Daphne herself was gone, leaving Honor behind. Honor and Jerry and John and Ambrose Estabrook. Everyone in whom she could place dependence, everyone on whom she could pin her faith. She had left the safe earth and her true friends and was strapped into a hard narrow seat beside a stranger, a stranger who at first spoke to her harshly and now would not speak with her at all. Either he had not heard her faint voice above the sound which roared around them, or else he did not think her question was worth answering. Still he could not be altogether indifferent to her anguish. After all, he had consented to undertake this wild hazardous flight. He had not declined, like the other pilots who had been approached, to start out in a storm.

There was some light in the cockpit, about as much as in the front seat of an automobile when the dashboard was lighted. Daphne tried to turn her head, without moving her rigid body, and look at the man beside her, the man who had been willing to try to take her to Richard, and who was now absorbed in grappling with the great metal monster which could not disentangle itself from imprisoning mud or prevail against its own unnatural load. She noticed that though he was a big man he was lean, and lithe in his movements, in spite of the clumsiness of his flying suit. His face, for all its healthy color, had a chiseled look; the profile was aquiline; there were lines around the lips. She guessed, rather than saw, that his eyes were gray, and knew them to be keen and questing. His hands were remarkable. As she watched them moving over the controls, she had almost the feeling that he was using them to rescue the helpless ship from its morass, to lift it up miraculously and set it free. The fantasy had hardly taken form in her consciousness, when the plane leaped a little. It fell back, but when it leaped a second time, it gave a bigger bound. For an instant it swayed, as if sunk again. Then it swept up into the air.

The rain was beating hard against the windows, hitting them in pellets and then streaming down them in rivulets which met and merged. In spite of the coating these made on the glass, Daphne thought she could see the curve of the Potomac, outlined with lights, and the gleaming dome of the capital. But she was not sure. Perhaps this was only part of the same fantasy which had made her feel that Clive was lifting the ship with his own hands; and afterward she saw nothing else for a long time. She had always thought the trip between Washington and New York a dull one when she had made it on the train; now she was amazed to realize that under less harrowing conditions the flight would be dull too. She had imagined, beforehand, that in a plane there would be an omnipresent sensation of insecurity, because there could be no feel of solid ground beneath the machine, as there was in a motorcar. Now she found there was no predominating awareness of any such lack, that the air supplied the same support as the earth.

Clive had not uttered a syllable since the take-off. Once he had turned on the dash lights, apparently to check some of his instruments; and from time to time he appeared to be trying to tinker with an obstreperous radio. But aside from these intermittent activities, he was wholly preoccupied with his flying. The human silence, in the midst of the mechanical din, was uncanny. Daphne longed to have it broken, yet she did not dare try to divert the fixed attention of the man at her side. Then suddenly he spoke to her.

"New York," he announced briefly.

Again she turned her head toward the window at her side. The downpour was not quite as heavy as it had been; there were only little trickles of rain coursing down the glass, with clear spaces between them. Through these she could see the city quite plainly, though it did not look like a city. It looked like a strange illumined universe. She had ceased to listen for the thunder, because the noise of the engines, roaring all around her, made distant sound unreal and unalarming in comparison. But the lightning still startled her every time it flashed through the obscurity; and now that she saw it darting down to meet the uncanny radiance that shone beneath it, it took on new aspects of danger.

"I— Are we all right?" she gasped.

"Yes. Everything's O.K. so far. Arrangements were made before we started for Station R. C. A. to broadcast weather reports to me every hour on the hour and for me to broadcast back every hour on the half hour. That hasn't been possible yet because of this electric storm. Won't be until we run out of it. The static's very bad. You've heard that sputtering, scratching sound, haven't you, every time I've tuned the radio? But don't worry. I can check as far as Boston by the 'beam' and after that by the coastal cities and the lighthouses until we're out over the ocean. Then I'll fly a compass course across the ocean."

She did not know what he meant when he spoke of the "beam." But apparently it was something reassuring. And his comments, extensive compared to any he had made up to then, had given her so much comfort, after the long interval of ominous silence, that she decided not to run the risk of annoying him by asking questions. It would be better, she concluded, to wait for him to speak to her of his own accord.

Again the period when he said nothing, seemed endless. Occasionally he lowered a map case which was rigged over his instrument board and studied its contents carefully, or leaned forward to make computations on a writing pad spread out across his knees. But all this was incomprehensible to her, and after she had watched him at work for a few moments, the sight of his scrawls and scribbling ceased to distract her. The flight had become a progress of awesome but unbroken monotony.

"It hasn't any end to it," Daphne murmured desperately to herself. "It's going on like this—and on and on—and I shall never get to Richard. This is what people mean when they talk about eternity. Not death, not nonexistence, but something that doesn't stop, that can't stop. I've got to make it end, I've got to find a way to stop it. Oh, God, what shall I do?"

In spite of her desperation, the monotony was making her drowsy. Suppose Clive were to become drowsy too? Then he would lose mastery of the plane, and they would go dashing down to destruction in the ocean. The thought appalled her; it began to obsess her. She dug her nails down deeply into her palms and bit her lips to keep from screaming. For this was not another fantasy in which she was gripped. They *were* dropping, they were falling with hideous velocity, as men fell from high buildings when they committed suicide. The air had withdrawn its support. There was only a vacuum between the ship and the sea, and presently the slender strip of space which divided these two would be gone. They would be plunged into the icy water, they would be drowned, they would be dead——

"We'll be going up again presently," she heard Clive shouting.

She did not believe it. There was no bottom to this pit into which they were falling, except the relentless waves. Any instant now she would feel them breaking in cold billows over her braced feet. But still she bit her lips and kept her hands clenched. Even though she died in the effort to hide it, she would not reveal her terror to this stranger who was going to his own death with her. It would not be very long now. There was to be an end after all, though not the end she had sought. It would not have mattered much, if only she could have reached Richard first——

"That down draft was pretty bad. You took it like a Trojan."

" 'Down draft'?" she spoke stupidly. It amazed her to find that she still had the power of speech. This, by all rights, should have been gone.

"Yes. 'Air pockets' some landlubbers call them. We dropped about fifteen hundred feet in a few seconds. But we are flying at six thousand again now."

"Will— Are we likely to fall again like that?"

"We may. But it never seems so bad the second time. Anyway, we're running out of the storm. We've got that to be thankful for."

She tried hard to be thankful. When destruction had seemed so imminent, she knew that she should be thankful. But it took time. She had been so galvanized with terror that she was still numb. And she could not readjust her mind to the idea of safety. She was conscious only of reprieve. But Clive was calling out to her again, quite cheerfully this time.

"Nova Scotia!"

She tried to look out of the window, as she had done before. She could see nothing but an opaque mass of white, dense out of all proportion to its delicacy.

"Fog," explained Clive. "There's nearly always fog around Nova Scotia and Newfoundland. But the land is there, underneath us. I've just checked my charts." He paused. "We can go down, if you want to. It's our last chance. There's only open ocean after this."

"Yes. I—I know."

"And you want to go on?"

"Yes. I want to go on."

She had not realized, until they were spoken, how irrevocable the words would sound. She must say something else, something in lighter vein, that would relieve the strain, just as Jerry's facile speech had relieved the strain at the airport before she started. Now that she was used to the noise it did not bother her so much. She could hear better, and her own voice did not sound like a scream.

"Is there anything at all I could do? It's hard, sitting so still, and just thinking——"

"You don't need to sit so still, if you don't want to, any longer. I'm afraid I gave you the wrong idea when we started, but I couldn't have you bucking around at the take-off.—Any time you want to unfasten your belt, while the course stays smooth, and go back into the fuselage, that'll be quite all right. There's enough light to see by, and space to squeeze between the tanks. The lavatory's in the rear."

He spoke casually and unselfconsciously, as an elder brother might have spoken to a younger sister making a long journey in his care. A wave of appreciation for his solicitude swept through the numbness in which Daphne had been engulfed. She unbuckled her belt and struggled to her feet.

"Take it easy. You're bound to be cramped. When you come back, you must try to relax. You're not in a dentist's chair, after all."

Surprisingly, the deep lines around his thin lips were curving upward a little.

"You could help me to navigate, indirectly, if you'd care to."

"Help you? How?"

"I'll show you. But take your little trip first, and on the way back to the cockpit, get out that leather case of yours from the compartment where the tools are. It's just behind us, between us and the fuel tank. I think the contents of that case will taste pretty good to us. Maybe you didn't realize it, but it's breakfast time. This fog is so thick we couldn't see the sunrise. But it's broad daylight down below us."

"I'm sorry we missed the dawn. There—there would have been something symbolic about it for us, wouldn't there?"

"We'll see it tomorrow, over the Channel. That'll be a darned sight more symbolic. Go get that coffee now, won't you?"

The coffee Honor Bright had put up was piping hot and thick with cream. The sandwiches she had made were loaf-width, cut thick, with the crust still on. The slices of bread were liberally buttered, and between them lay large tender pieces of cold roast beef.

"Food does make a difference," observed Clive. "Stow away what's left, we'll be glad of that too, later on." Then as she returned to the cockpit a second time, he asked, "Ready for a lesson?"

"Yes. I'd like one."

"Well, the automatic pilot actually does a good deal of the work——"

"The automatic pilot?"

"Yes. The device that controls the rudder and stabilizer and keeps the ship on its course. But the course has to be changed at half-hour intervals to compensate for our own change in position along the great circle, in relation to the North Pole. You can help by looking at the compasses occasionally, to see that they check with the numerals I give you at the time of the changes. For instance, they're set at 63° now. See that they stay there until I reset the course."

Daphne turned her eyes toward the board and began to stare at it with fascinated attention. Clive followed her gaze with approval.

"That's the idea. And there are two other instruments you can watch. The oil pressure gauge and the fuel gauge. If the needle of either should suddenly fluctuate, call my attention to it at once. Of course, I look at these instruments myself, instinctively. But if I find you're good at grasping details, I'll feel freer to devote more time to calculations and observations. My copilot would have helped me with these, if we'd made the flight as we'd planned it. Now I have to do them alone."

"I see. I hope you'll find I'm good at detail. My husband used to think I was."

"Have you been a widow a long time?"

"I'm not a widow. But these last few years my husband and I have been separated a good deal, I'm sorry to say. That's why I said he *used* to think I was good. I mean there's been no chance for him to see it lately."

Clive nodded without answering. He had felt no personal curiosity about the woman who was to be his passenger, when the call had come through asking for volunteers to make the flight. He had regarded the hazardous experiment merely as the means toward an end—an end which in his case meant sure fame and possible fortune in his chosen career. Vaguely, he had supposed that Mrs. Trent must be Ambrose Estabrook's "lady friend," since it was the Secretary of State who had precipitated this crossing at her request. But he was not interested in the affairs, either public or private, of the Secretary of State. He was really interested, in the last analysis, in only one thing, which was flying.

"Are you married too?" Daphne inquired, her eyes fixed fast on the compasses.

228

"Hell, no!"

"You don't seem to think it is a good plan to get married."

"Not for an aviator. If he wants to reach the top, he mustn't be hindered."

"You agree with Kipling then. You believe that 'he travels the fastest who travels alone.'"

"I've never read Kipling. But I'd say he had the right idea."

The lines around Clive's mouth relaxed again and he looked at Daphne with renewed attention, less impersonal than the casual glances which he had hitherto cast in her direction. Well, she was a pretty woman, there was no denying that: Lovely color, nice features, pleasant expression; probably a good figure too, though it was hard to tell about that, wrapped up the way she was. He'd like to see her sometime in a light dress, guessed she'd be easy to look at. And she hadn't been sick after all. There had been no nausea and all the mess that made, to bother with. No hysterics either. She'd been scared, like he'd known she would be, but she'd sat tight, she'd kept a stiff upper lip. And now, if he wasn't mistaken, she was beginning to take things easier. Besides, she had something above the ears. Quoting Kipling and all, six thousand feet up in the air! That took presence of mind. He was all for brains in a woman, himself. A doll baby was all right in her place, or a vamp. But a plane wasn't the place for either——

"How would you like to try your hand at keeping the log?" he heard himself asking, unexpectedly.

"I'd like to. What shall I do?"

"First, get it out of that metal case there beside you——. It's a little leather-bound book, pretty mangy-looking——. That's it. Now write what I tell you: Time 8 A. M.——"

"8 A. M.!"

"Sure. What did I tell you about watching the instruments? Look at those three chronometers. One's set at Eastern Standard Time and one at Paris Time; the third one shows the actual length of time we've been in the air. Now go ahead and write: Time 8 A. M. Speed 180 m. per hour. Temp. 36°. Foggy. Storm over. 6,000 ft. Gas 39 gals. per hr. Position estimated just past lower tip of N. S. 750 m. out."

She scribbled hastily, trying to think in terms of abbreviation. Clive glanced over her shoulder.

"That's the idea. I'll give you some more data by and by. In the meantime, if you think of anything you'd like to say on your own initiative, jot that down too."

She nodded in her turn, and for the first time smiled, herself. Well, of course, she was worried to death about her son; otherwise she would never have taken this desperate chance.

229

She could hardly be expected to go grinning over the ocean. But certainly it did brighten things up, to have her look like that. If she'd only hold it! She must have thought of something funny. "If there's anything you'd like to say, on your own initiative—" Gosh, that was it. She was going to try to set down her own impressions of this flight. It might make good reading. He would have a look at that log, directly he woke up, twenty-four hours after they got to Paris——

The smile vanished, but the look of strain and sorrow had certainly eased too. Daphne continued to hold the logbook in her hand, her fingers between the leaves. Every now and then she scribbled in it with the stubby pencil. But for the most part she kept her eyes on the instruments. The chronometers, which she had overlooked entirely at first, seemed to enthrall her. Well, that was easy to understand too. Every revolution which they made marked the minutes which were taking her nearer to her son——

It was bitterly cold, flying at eight thousand feet. Clive, chilled to the marrow himself, knew that Daphne must be nearly frozen. Her face had lost its delicate color, it had begun to look blue, the fine features blurred, the soft cheeks pinched. She was still holding the log, still looking at the chronometers; but she had ceased to scribble, and her gaze, instead of being intent, had become fixed. Clive wondered if she noticed that the engine had begun to spit and sputter. He hoped she had not, for he knew that if she did the sound would alarm her. *If* she did—. Well, there was no use trying to dodge it—*when* she did. For the spitting and sputtering did not stop. The noise it made had been merely disagreeable at first, something that annoyed you, like a wasp or a file. Now it was ominous, spelling out danger as it spat and sputtered.

Daphne turned to look at it, though she did not speak. It was as though she had sensed the superfluity of speech. But her eyes pleaded for the word of explanation which her lips did not entreat.

"Ice."

That didn't help, he must tell her more than that, when he could. He must tell her where the ice was. He must say that the wings were coated with ice, that there was ice in the carburetor. But he couldn't now. Because he must keep the motor going. That was the first essential—the only essential. The controls were "loggy," they were sticking. A new kind of vibration had set in. The compass was oscillating. The ship was shuddering; at any moment it might go into a spin. He called out one curt order, as he focused all his strength on the pressure pump.

"Watch the altimeter! We've got to keep clear of the water!"

The altimeter! He had not told her about that! But she understood, and her understanding was no longer riddled with fright, but clear and calm. They were falling again, not suddenly, as they had in the down draft, but with a quivering movement, like that of a top losing momentum. Only this time it was the other way around. They were gaining momentum; at any moment they would begin to twirl. Daphne's gaze swept over the instrument board, fastened itself on a whizzing needle.

"5600—4300—2800——"

The light had turned to tingling gray. In it the wings of the ship were still visible, but nothing else. Flying had ceased to be a physical sensation. It was only a mental process, something that still went on at the base of the brain, in spite of everything.

"1700—950—600——"

They were coming out of the thick cotton batting clouds, there were winking green waves below them—barely visible —clearly outlined—very close. Daphne could see them rising and falling, rising and falling. But she could see Clive's hands too, those wonderful hands that moved about over the controls with the same delicacy with which a surgeon wielded a scalpel. She felt that they would not fail her.

"460—380—225——"

"All right. We're out of it. On the up grade again!"

It was true. The shuddering of the ship had stopped, the compass had ceased to oscillate, the needle no longer whizzed. It was mounting again, pointing at 300, at 400, at 500. When it reached 600, Clive began to drive steadily ahead.

"Thawing her out," he explained. Yes, by God, he could explain now, and that game girl had an explanation coming to her! There had been pretty close to thirty minutes when he had thought the motors would cut out altogether, that the show was over. And, of course, she had thought so, too. But she had gone right on watching the altimeter and calling out the numbers, hadn't faltered for a second. By God, he would never forget the sound of her voice when she said 225——

"Have to get the ice off the wings," he went on. "And out of the carburetor. Can't risk another spin with this load of ours.—Did you know that we had seven tons of gas aboard when we took off? Part of that's gone now. But we're still overloaded."

They were skimming along smoothly over the winking

231

waves which rose and fell with such rhythmic regularity. The ship and the sea seemed to be in harmony with each other.

"I'm not afraid of the ocean any longer," Daphne said slowly. "I like looking at it."

Clive nodded. "I know what you mean. I do too." There was harmony between them also, he had begun to feel that, and wondered if she had. "We'll keep to this course for a while."

It was an hour later when he began to pull the nose of the ship gradually up again, an hour in which no words had been uttered, but when the sense of companionship had deepened steadily. When he finally spoke to Daphne again, it was in the voice of a man addressing his partner.

"Got to have more altitude. It's safer in the long run. And we can make better time high up. At least fifteen miles an hour more."

The awful opaqueness of the fog was gone. It was thinner when they came into it this time, flying over a double layer of tufty clouds. There were rifts in it too, between light showers, and moments when it melted away altogether. Then suddenly it grew iridescent. They were encircled with a frame of multicolored light.

"Clive! Are we in heaven? Look at that!"

He chuckled with appreciation. But the next instant a little forking flame of feeling darted through him.

"It's a rainbow," he said briefly. "They're round, you know, when you get to see them up this high. No break in the circle. How's that for symbolism? You haven't had to wait to see dawn—" He stopped abruptly, too much moved to go on. "Listen," he said, "I'm going back to the navigation table for a few minutes. You take the stick. This is your flight. It's your ship too."

It was impossible, but it was true, like so many other things in life. She had held her hands on the wheel, she had felt its response and its power. Now Clive had come back again, but he had not instructed her to relinquish the controls. Instead he was leaning over, with his arm around the back of her seat, and his face so close to hers that he did not have to raise his voice when he spoke to her.

"Would you like to hear from your son?"

She turned swiftly, uncomprehendingly, with a little startled cry. Clive went on quickly.

"Steady there! You're not going to pieces on me at this late hour, are you, after everything we've come through all right? Maybe I shouldn't have asked you like that, without any warning. But it's this way: I've got the position of sev-

232

eral vessels at sea. I think I might be able to establish communication with one of them in code. Of course they've all been informed of our flight, by now. Their operators will be standing by. Slip back into your own seat again and let me see what I can do. I won't have any trouble with the radio, this weather. Look at that sun, blazing away up there!"

She slid slightly over to the right, her shoulder brushing against his as she did so. Then she listened breathlessly. Almost instantly she heard a click, followed by sharp staccato notes. "Dah-dit-dit-dah-dah-dah-dit-dit-dit-dit-"

"I think I've got the *Europa*."

"The *Europa*!"

That was the boat she had told Estabrook was fast enough for anyone, less than twenty-four hours earlier. And now she was passing over it in mid-ocean, now she would soon be leaving it far behind, plodding its way through the waves while she flew swiftly on. It would not reach Cherbourg for three days yet while, before another noon, she would be seated at Richard's side. That is, if Richard——

"Did you hear?"

"Hear what?"

"Didn't you know I was getting a message?"

"Yes, of course. But I don't know what it is!"

"I'm going to tell you. In just a second now."

Clive's hands were moving rapidly over his writing pad, though he continued to listen intently to the poignant patter of the radio as he decoded.

"The—boy—still—lives," he read slowly, as if he were reciting a litany. "Signal—your—own—safety."

"Oh— *Oh, Clive!* Signal—'We are safe ourselves and we are speeding to him.' If—if that's all right?"

"It's O.K. by me," said Clive, gulping down the lump in his throat.

She did not know just where she was. It was queer to feel so cold and cramped, in a big warm bed. That is, she supposed she must be in bed, for it was dark, and she had been sound asleep. Even now, she was only half-awake. But the bed did not feel natural. She must have thrown off the quilt, she must have slipped down on her pillow. She tried to reach for her coverings, to pull herself up. Then she realized that it was a man's coat she had over her, that her head was resting on a man's shoulder——

Michael! Miraculously she must have found Michael, since it was only against Michael's shoulder that she could have slept. They were together again. Nothing should ever separate them again. What was a career compared to a marriage?

233

Someone—she could not think who—had asked a long time ago what it profited a man to gain the whole world if he lost his own soul, and that was what she had tried to ask Michael, in that dreadful far-off day in Yünnanfu. That and nothing else. But she had not made it very clear. Otherwise, he would have understood. Otherwise, he would not have left her. Otherwise, she could have held him. Although someone else had said—and though she could not think who this was either, it was not so very long ago in this case—that if a man wanted to get to the top, he mustn't be hindered. Of course she had said something of the sort herself, when she had given Michael back his ring. But she hadn't meant it, not really, she hadn't expected to be taken at her word.

The other person who had said it *had* meant it. Who could it have been? Drowsily, she tried to think. But the speech did not seem to fit anyone to whom she tried to attach it. Michael had never said it himself. Even in his most desperate and discouraged moments, he had never failed to make her feel that she was necessary to him, in one way or another. Alonzo Loose had never said it. The loneliness of his life was a constant crucifixion to him; he sought to escape, not to achieve isolation. Jerome Blake had never said it. He had pined, patiently, for a home and a wife and children; his acquistion of them had turned him from a pitiful, thwarted creature to a happy and triumphant man. Jerry Stone had never said it; he owed everything he had and was to Honor Bright. And Ambrose Estabrook had never said it; he wanted to merge his life in her own. But wait, she was coming closer. Estabrook had not said it himself. But someone who was mysteriously linked with him had done so. The aviator—that was it! The aviator who had answered Estabrook's summons.

She sat up, suddenly wide awake. Another unbelievable thing must have happened. After she had heard that Richard was alive, she must have sunk down, relaxed and relieved, against the shoulder of this stranger whose full name, even, was unknown to her, and gone to sleep from sheer exhaustion. How long she had slept she had no idea.

"Where are we?" she asked in confusion.

"Heading toward Ireland. I veered slightly to the north to touch its lower tip. It's a safety measure. I want to have as much land as I can underneath us in case we have more engine trouble or run short of fuel. Not that I think there's any cause for anxiety."

"Do you mean we've almost *reached* land?"

"Yes. We'll be over Ireland in another hour or so. Then, of course, we've got to cross it—Ireland and England too.

And afterward, the Channel. Though the Channel doesn't amount to anything. Fifteen minutes will cover that."

"What time is it?"

"Almost 2 A. M. Look at your chronometers, lady! I told you we'd greet the dawn in France. It's been a gorgeous night. But the moon's gone, and the stars will begin to get dim pretty soon.—Would you feel like holding the sextant and the octent for awhile? I don't believe I'll need them anymore, and if I do, I can ask you for them. I've found out, you see, that you're good at detail, and I'm getting a little stiff myself. I want to shift around."

"You should have waked me up. I might have really helped, during the night. Astronomy is one of the few subjects I know something about."

"Astronomy!"

"Yes. I couldn't afford to go to school much when I was a girl. So my uncle, who is a scholar and a saint, taught me himself, mostly. He didn't bother about a curriculum. He taught me whatever he enjoyed and whatever he thought I might enjoy, myself."

"Astronomy, for instance?"

"Yes. And—and Greek."

She closed her eyes again. For a moment she seemed to see a white house, set upon a hill, in the midst of a Grecian olive grove. She would never see it now, she knew, except in fancy. She would never taste Hymettus honey or set marble statues in a dim grove. But she was on her way to Richard. She was almost there. The dream had been beautiful. But the reality was magnificent.

"Will we be able to see the coast of Ireland?" she asked, resolutely opening her eyes.

"Probably. Why?"

"I've always heard it was so wonderfully verdant. I've often wondered if perhaps it didn't inspire the poem that begins:

> " 'Thou wast all that to me, dear,
> For which my heart did pine:
> A *green isle* in the sea, dear,
> A fountain and a shrine—' "

Her voice trailed away, and was swallowed up in the sound of the ship. She was startled to feel Clive touching her.

"What's the rest of the verse?"

> " 'All wreathed with fairy fruit and flowers,
> And all the flowers mine.' "

235

"I'd say you ought to get your share, and if you don't, I'll know the reason why, myself," Clive remarked cryptically.

They did see the coast. The stars had faded almost completely when they sighted it. But the sky, translucent as a moonstone overhead, was already rimmed with rose at the horizon. The land lay lush and lovely beneath them. Then, in sparkling splendor, the cliffs of Dover reached up toward them. . . .

The plane was beginning to descend. It was swooping about in circles, and as each circle was completed, there was a drop, not sudden and startling like those which had occured in the air pockets encountered during the night, but gliding and gradual. The red roofs of small rectangular houses came into view, the flattened tops of clustering trees, green and golden fields, roads unrolling like straight white bands of ribbon. Then the roofs looked darker, they were closer together, there were fewer trees, but a great field where multitudes of people seemed to be gathered. Clive nudged Daphne with his elbow.

"Le Bourget," he shouted briefly, above the roar of the engine.

The plane dove smoothly, touched the earth, bounded lightly away from it; then settled on it again, and skimmed over it with a scuffling sound, still moving in circles, but more and more slowly. Its roar became a rumble, a soft growl, a whisper; there was a creak, and the sound ceased altogether, just as the final curve came to an end. A great shout went up from the waiting multitudes, cries of *"Bravo!"* —"*Dieu soit benit!"*—"*Vive Clive!—"Vive les Etats-Unis!"* The doors were wrenched open, and the multitudes surged forward, pressing against the police and the photographers. Daphne could see the *agents'* blue capes and swinging batons, could hear them saying, good-naturedly yet authoritatively, *"Voyons, voyons! Attention aux ailes! En arrère!"* She could see the cameramen's black-hooded machines perpendicularly poised; could hear the clicking noise that they made, almost like a soft patter of machine guns, as they were trained upon her. Someone was grasping her numbed hands competently, someone was sliding solid steps under her cramped feet. Then Rosemary's strong young arms were around her bent neck, Rosemary's soft lips were against her cold cheek——

"Mother! Mother, *darling!* This is the most wonderful thing that's ever been done, ever in all the world——"

"Richard?" Daphne managed somehow to ask.

"Richard's holding his own. I believe he knows you're on

the way to him, though he seems unconscious. I believe that's what's kept him alive."

"And—and your father?"

"Daddy couldn't leave him, of course, even to meet you. Naturally, it's harder on Daddy than on anyone. He always watched for Richard, when he drove toward the chateau. But it never occurred to him, when he was recalled so suddenly to Paris, that Richard would know he was troubled, that Richard would be waiting at the gate to say good-by to him. Richard had never done that before. But this time he knew something was the matter, he wanted to comfort Daddy if he could."

"It was—it was your father who caused Richard's accident?"

"Yes, Mother. You'll be kind to him, won't you—for Richard's sake?"

She must not scream, she must not faint, she must not let the multitudes see behind the veil that hid her horror from their prying eyes. She bit her lips and tried to focus her gaze on the scene which was lurching about before her. It continued to sway for several moments. Then her vision cleared and her agonized mind with it. She saw that Rosemary, who still clung to her reassuringly, was not alone. Beside her was standing a tall spare woman, dressed in dingy black, who wore a grotesque hat perched on top of a gray pompadour and enormous diamonds in her long ears; while beyond this strange but somehow distinguished figure, stood a graceful boy, bare-headed and bare-kneed, whose hair was crisp around his forehead, and whose eyes and lips were mobile.

"Everyone will be so kind to you, it will be easy for you to be kind also," Rosemary was saying. "Everyone has been so kind to *me!* It would have been terrible if I had had to come to Paris alone, and Aunt Henriette and Uncle Jerome thought they shouldn't leave the chateau either. But my friend Xavier came with me—Xavier and his grandmother, the Comtesse de Blonville. They're here with me, Mother, waiting to welcome you."

PART VII

St. Martin's Summer

CHAPTER 18

MICHAEL WAS obsessed with the fear that Richard would call him, and that he would not be close by.

At first, of course, Richard had not called anybody. He had been limp and lifeless in his father's arms when Michael had picked him up in the driveway and carried him to the chateau. He had still been limp and lifeless when the doctor, whom Michael himself had gone to the village to fetch—because that was quicker than trying to reach him by telephone—bent over the small prostrate form in the *Salle des Chevaliers.*

The doctor had looked exceedingly grave. He was a robust, ruddy little man, with beady black eyes and a black pointed beard, whose countenance, it was plain to see, was ordinarily cheerful to the point of merriment. He wore a glittering watch chain, a frock coat which had seen better days, and a frayed red satin cravat. Yet in spite of these incongruous details, which were somehow obtrusive out of all proportion to their importance, even Michael was impressed by his directness and capability. He took the situation in hand swiftly and simply.

"Your son is alive, Monsieur. I can hear his heartbeats. You may listen to them yourself, through the stethoscope, if you wish. And as you can see, the blood from the wound in the head is spreading. Do not let that alarm you. It is a good sign. We will check it, and meanwhile we will send at once for an ambulance. We must take this little fellow to the hospital at Caen."

"Couldn't we keep him here?"

"That would be most unwise, Monsieur. In fact, it might be fatal. We must have X-rays taken at once to determine whether there is only concussion of the brain or whether there is a fracture of the skull. Also whether there are other fractures. In accidents of this type, there is nearly always severe injury to some of the extremities."

"Then couldn't we take him to the American Hospital in Paris?"

"That also would be most unwise, Monsieur. We must get him under observation immediately. But if you have reason to feel that he is not getting the best possible care, you can send for specialists from Paris. I assure you that the local physicians will welcome consultations."

"The ambulance is on its way," remarked Henriette, quietly. Michael had not noticed that she had left the *Salle des Chevaliers* at all. His eyes had been fastened on Richard's white face all the time the doctor had been talking. But, like the doctor, Henriette had capably assumed control of the situation. "Remember that we are not in an uncultured country, Michael. Caen is a university city. The hospital there is excellent. And as Dr. Norchais has reminded you, consultants can get here quickly from Paris. In fact, while telephoning Jerome, I have suggested that he should bring two doctors down with him—a brain specialist and an orthopedist. By the time the X-rays have been made and developed, or very soon afterwards, they will have arrived."

Apparently everything had been taken out of his hands. Apparently there was nothing he could do for his son, stricken down by his own rash act. Nothing except to wait, which he had never learned how to do. Nothing except to stand by, with no one at his side. If only Daphne had not deserted him! No, not that. In this hour of anguish, the pretense which hitherto had saved his pride would not serve. It had been swept away, like everything else which had made him self-sufficient and arrogant and ruthless. If only he had not driven Daphne from him! She would have been steadfast, her loving kindness would have sustained him. But Daphne, like Richard, was lost to him forever.

Even when he was told that Richard would live, even when he heard that Daphne was on her way to him, it did not seem to make much difference. How could he believe the doctors when he looked down at his son, and saw that Richard was still motionless, still unconscious, still white with that strange unearthly pallor that had a quality of transparency to it? They kept assuring him that a broken thigh was the only fracture, that this would heal in four or five months, that aside from this there were only bruises and lacerations and a mild concussion with which to cope. *Only!* Only complete withdrawal, only unfathomable silence on one side; only blind despair and corroding remorse on the other. That was all there was left of the mystic yet mighty relationship between him and his son.

And if this were all there was left between him and Richard, what of the ties that had bound him to Daphne? She herself had repeatedly said that they were indissoluble, that there was an inevitability about their union. Yes, it had been inevitable—he could still see that. The forces which had drawn them together had been overwhelming. But they had lacked indefinite power after all. Otherwise, how could he have let her go, that time when they had both taken their self-willed way from Yünnanfu? Otherwise, having had the folly to let her go, how could he have failed to speedily reclaim her? Otherwise, how could he have offered to marriage the supreme insult which his intrigue with Vivienne represented? Such questions were unanswerable.

When Daphne arrived at the hospital, Michael had been sitting on a small straight chair outside his son's room, waiting to be allowed to go in and wondering how a man greeted his wife when he had not seen her for over four years and meanwhile had lived with another woman? And Daphne had come up to him as naturally as if they had only parted the day before, as if neither scandal nor tragedy lay between them.

"Michael! My dear!"

She had held out her hands and raised her lips. In the presence of the doctor and the sister who had brought her in, he could not choose but make some show of response. Daphne must have felt the detachment of it. Nevertheless she gave no sign that this was so.

"I'm afraid you must be exhausted," he managed to say, inwardly cursing his own inadequacy.

"No. I slept for several hours in the plane. And it was a marvelous flight. I'll tell you all about it tomorrow. And I want you to meet Clive, the man who brought me, to whom we both owe so much. Shall we go in now and see Richard together?"

When she saw Richard, he felt sure, she would break down. A human being could endure just so much, and no more. After that, something snapped. But as they went into the bare little room, and stood side by side at the foot of their son's narrow bed, a miracle seemed to happen. There was a change in the atmosphere, as if a sudden warmth, a sudden perfume, had swept through it. Michael could have sworn that for an instant, another presence had pervaded it. Then the illusion, if it were an illusion, passed. But with its passing came another miracle.

Richard turned his head and half-opened his eyes. His fingers moved slightly, as if he were feeling for a familiar hand. Then he spoke.

"Father," he said softly. "Father, are you there?"

After that he drifted off again, almost instantly. But there was a difference in his immobility. It was slumber which engulfed him now, profound, but natural; the quality of abnormality had vanished from his unconsciousness; and there was a faint tinge of color in his face. Daphne spoke of these symptoms encouragingly.

"Shall we leave him for a little while now, Michael? He's sound asleep."

"He might call me again."

"He will, of course. But not right away. How long is it since you've slept yourself, Michael, or eaten?"

He had no idea. Still in a daze, he heard Daphne give swift instructions, and presently some cider and bread and cheese were brought in and offered him by a lay sister, and he accepted them. Then he stretched out on a cot in a vacant room, with Daphne sitting beside him.

"I'll wake you right away, Michael, if Richard should wake himself. The doors are open—I'll hear him if he calls. Well, anyhow, I'll *know* if he calls. Don't you remember the time in Canton when you heard me? Well, this will be just the same."

Strangely enough, it was almost the same. He waked without any clear sense of time or place, but with the assurance that Richard wanted him, as urgently, as poignantly, as Daphne had once wanted him. He stumbled to his feet and felt Daphne's arm around his waist, supporting him.

"Don't worry, Michael. You'll get to him before he actually does call you. He hasn't yet."

Daphne was right. They had been in Richard's room for several moments before the boy said "Father" again. This time his voice was clearer. And presently he went on speaking.

"Everything is all right, isn't it? I mean, you didn't go back to Paris after all?"

"Yes, everything is all right. No, I didn't go back to Paris after all."

"You're not going, are you?"

"No, I'm not going."

Richard seemed completely satisfied and once more he drifted off into untroubled slumber. The next time he roused, he recognized Daphne also.

"I knew you'd come. But how did you get here so quickly? Or wasn't it quick?"

"Yes, it was very quick. I flew."

"Across the Atlantic? Oh, Mother, you didn't!"

"Yes, I did. I'll tell you all about it."

"I want you to. And I want to see Rosemary, please, and Xavier. Only now I'm sleepy."

He recognized all his friends; he was glad to see them all, as gradually they came in one by one for a moment. But he did not ask to see any of them a second time. It was only for Michael whom he asked repeatedly, and Michael, self-hounded and hollow-eyed, waited unceasingly for the summons.

At the end of ten days, the condition of concussion had cleared. Richard had begun to evince interest not only in all his visitors, but in his general surroundings. The traction apparatus in which he was confined intrigued him. He talked to Michael about it.

"Why do they call this a Balkan frame, Father?"

"I believe because it was originated during the Balkan War in 1912."

"Have you ever been to the Balkans?"

"Yes, I was in Sofia for a few days last autumn."

"Tell me about it."

Michael related everything he could remember about Sofia, which had not greatly impressed him. He was aware that his recital was colorless. But Richard listened to him with breathless interest.

"I'd like to go there. Perhaps we can go together sometime, Father."

"Of course, if you like."

"But in the meanwhile we'll have a nice time at the chateau. You knew, didn't you, Father, that the doctor had said I could go back to the chateau sometime in August? I'll be out of the Balkan frame by then, though I'll have to stay in bed for two months longer. I think I'll sort of miss all these pulleys and ropes and weights at first. They're awfully amusing."

After they had gone back to the chateau, the fear that Richard might call him and that he might not be close by, ceased to obsess Michael and he began to see his son in proportion to the general situation instead of as a dominating figure on a scene which was otherwise vague. Up to that time, Daphne had given him balance and hope, but she had remained consistently in the background. It was only when he turned to her for comfort that she emerged from the shadows, and once she had given him the reassurance he needed, she seemed to retreat, as if she took it for granted that all his solicitude should be centered in Richard. She herself made no demands upon him, or indicated, in any way, that she expected him to be concerned about her. If she were worried or weary herself, she did not show it; she looked surprisingly well. She was installed in a quiet hotel close to the hospital and came and went between the two. Nominally, Michael was installed there also, but actually, he almost never left the hospital. Eventually it occurred to him that she might be lonely. When he questioned her, however, she denied this.

"After all, I'm there only during the evenings and for my meals. And I generally have company for those. Everyone has been wonderfully kind and cordial."

"Company?"

"Why, yes. Of course, Rosemary comes over every day, and someone always comes with her. The *jeune fille bien élevée* doesn't go tearing around the countryside alone, in Normandy, even now."

Michael, recalling his rage because he had felt that Rosemary was doing something rather like that before her mother's arrival, opened his mouth to say so, and with unusual self-restraint, closed it again. After all, the question of Rosemary, like many other questions, could be settled later on, when Richard was further on the road to recovery. A mutual self-defensiveness, almost an antagonism, had sprung up between him and his daughter. There would have been an explosion long before this, if it had not been for Richard. But Daphne was apparently unaware of any such strain.

"Jerome very often brings her," she continued. "He's been a tower of strength, Michael. Do you remember how kind he was to me when I was sick in La Paz? Well, this has been just the same."

Michael wished that Daphne would not keep referring to past incidents and saying that some present episode was just the same. It seemed to indicate that she still believed in a union which he realized was ruptured. But he could not talk about this either.

"Henriette can't keep leaving the twins," Daphne went on, "but Mr. Loose comes to see me two or three times a week. I think Richard might like to see more of Mr. Loose, Michael. You should encourage him to go to the hospital.— And then there have been the de Blonvilles."

"The de Blonvilles visit you?"

"Oh, yes! Not the young Countess, who I hear is so

pretty. It seems she is in Paris just now, and that she is planning a trip to the Near East. But the Dowager Countess, and her cousin, Denise de Crequi, and her grandson, Xavier, come frequently. And the Prefect of Caen and his wife and several other officials have called at their instigation."

For the third time in the course of the same conversation, Michael found there was nothing he could say; and he did not again attempt an intimate talk with Daphne while they remained in Caen. But the consciousness of his dependence on her and his need for close communion with her gradually took on form and substance. Now that Richard was getting better, now that he himself was no longer almost annihilated by anguish, he found his paramount concern shifting, slowly, almost imperceptibly at first, from his son to his wife. He listened, with increasing attentiveness, when she talked. Her mind had matured amazingly; she was acquainted with men and movements, she observed and interpreted trends and theories. He could not help wondering how she had learned so much, considering the seclusion in which she had lived; and then, apprehensively, wondering if she had always been wiser than he had consented to admit? In a relationship which had seemed so complete had he overlooked or ignored one of her finest attributes?

After all, it would not have been strange if he had. She would never strike any man, primarily, as an intellectual woman. He watched her covertly, as she moved about, or sat, in repose, at Richard's bedside. If anything, she had gained in grace during their years of separation; her figure was flexible, and very slender still. But curves had come into it that had not been there before, and her flesh looked softer and warmer. Submerged in her dignity was a desirability which was deeper than ever. He must have been blinded not to have seen this sooner. But now that he saw it, what could he do? Ask her to take him back? Take her without the asking? The memory of Vivienne mocked him as he asked himself this.

He had not forgotten Alonzo's warning of Vivienne's probable reaction to a break in their relationship; and at last, goaded into fresh fears by her insidious silence, he took a desperate initiative and sounded his superior out on the subject. It was the first time since their return to the chateau that he had gone to the room from which he had been driven on the day of Richard's accident; and he found that Mr. Loose was not disposed to make his mission easy in any way. Indeed, the manufacturer regarded his general manager with thinly veiled contempt as Michael, with an awkwardness rare for him, strove to express himself.

"I guess I get you. You think this hellcat may cause trouble for you and you want to make sure she won't. You want a good deal, don't you, Michael?"

"I suppose I do. I suppose I always have."

"Well, it's something if you've got around to admitting it. Not much, but something. Myself, I'd say you'd got more than you deserve already. Your boy's going to get well."

"Yes, thank God!"

"You'd better thank God. And while you're thanking him, I wouldn't ask him for anything more, if I was you. I wouldn't push my luck."

"I'm not sure I know what you mean."

"Oh, yes, you do! You're thankful your son's life is saved, but you're not thankful enough so's you can be satisfied unless you can get your wife back too. And after you get her back, you won't be satisfied unless you get something else."

"I'm glad to hear you speak as though you thought I had a chance of getting her back."

"Well —Women are queer. I never could see what Daphne wanted you for——"

"Perhaps for some of the same reasons you wanted me yourself."

"Perhaps. I'm not saying you haven't got a way with you, Michael. And unlimited brass. If you didn't have brass, you wouldn't be talking back to me the way you are now."

"I don't feel particularly brazen. It must be just a habit. I'll try to get rid of it."

For the first time Alonzo looked at Michael with something resembling sympathy. He answered with less brusqueness.

"Well, I wouldn't try too hard. Brass has its points. Some people call it self-confidence, and self-confidence gets you things and takes you places. But as I was saying, I wouldn't push my luck if I was you."

"I won't push it. I'm not going to force myself on Daphne, if that's what you're afraid of. But I can't help hoping that someday I can make her see how much I care. I can't help hoping that someday I can make her understand how hard I'll try this time. All I'm asking for is one more chance. Is that too much to ask for?"

The confidence had gone from his voice. He stood stripped of all self-assurance, humbled in the presence of the man who had magnified him, fearful in the face of his own wrongdoing, hurt almost beyond endurance. It was too much for Alonzo Loose.

"Well, now," he said huskily. "Well, now— Things have

245

sort of changed since I talked to you about this the last time. I don't believe Vivienne's going to make trouble for you now, Michael. I guess she knows it would be a boomerang if she tried to. There's too much feeling in favor of a man when he's down to make it healthy to start something else going against him. And you have been having a tough break, there's no denying that. With Richard and all I mean. I haven't said much, but I know what it did to you, running over that boy. I'm sorry, Michael, if I've rubbed you in the raw——"

He paused, and looked inquiringly at Michael, as if expecting some response. In the absence of one, he went on again.

"What's more, whether you like the reason for it or not—and I don't suppose you do—I figure Xavier kind of has the whip hand over his mother, hasn't he? That is, if she started to tell all, her way, couldn't he tell a lot more, his way? Not that I think he would. Xavier looks like Vivienne, and that's about as far as the resemblance goes. He belongs, when all's said and done, to a different breed. But she hasn't got the sense to realize that. She's a lot more afraid of Xavier, Michael, than you are of her. That's why she's on her way to Syria, if you ask me."

He rose, and laid his fingers on Michael's arm.

"Give me a helping hand, will you?" he said. "I don't walk so easy, these days. You've been a big help to me, Michael, don't ever let me or anyone else give you the idea you haven't. I don't believe your usefulness to me is over, either. More likely it's only just begun. We all say lots of things we don't mean when we get mad. I'd like to take back most of what I said the last time you came to this room. And I guess you'll get your second chance. That is, if you don't push your luck. Let's go and have a look at Richard, shall we? After that I believe I'll turn in."

CHAPTER 19

IT WAS so warm that Richard's bed had been wheeled out into the arbor at the end of the terrace. From where he lay he could see the chateau, looming majestically over the deep moat, and the garden, still bright with cosmos and chrysanthemums; or else, by turning his head, he could look beyond the laden orchards and the fallow fields to the river and the

246

undulating countryside that extended beyond it. Whichever way he looked, he saw imperishable beauty. But sometimes it seemed to him that it was when he closed his eyes that he saw the most beautiful of all visions, the visions which afterward took form and substance in his poems.

There was a bell by his bed, and he could summon anyone he wished to his side in an instant. His mother was seldom out of sight, never out of hearing; she had been sitting with him most of the morning, reading aloud to him from "The Smothered Spring." The book had been published several weeks earlier and it had met with instantaneous success. It was splendid to know that people appreciated it; but it was even better to be able to hold it, in finished form, in one's own hands, or find favorite passages on a printed page. After Mother had closed the book and passed it over to Richard, she had talked to him for a little while about his grandfather, Larry Daingerfield, and about what this success would have meant to him, if it only could have come during his lifetime. Then she began to talk about what it would mean to Richard himself.

"Mr. Brooks told me in the beginning, that if 'The Smothered Spring' did well he would like to follow it up with a book of verse by you. I've just had another letter from him. He said that anytime you felt well enough——"

"But, Mother, you don't have to feel well to write poetry!"

He thought he had seen his mother wince, he thought a shadow had fallen across her lovely face. He strove to reassure her.

"You know that when Grandfather wrote his poetry he was wretched, he was poor, he was in exile."

"Yes—and I wanted it to be so different with you!"

"It is different with me, Mother. I'm not wretched, I'm happy. I'm not poor, I'm rich. I'm not in exile, I'm at home—at least, I think that Normandy seems more like home than any other place outside of Virginia, don't you, Mother?"

"Yes, Richard, I do."

He knew that she was telling him the truth, that she was beginning to love this land of their accidental adoption as much as he and Rosemary loved it already. His heart bounded at the thought.

"Well then— You see how different it all is. And this is the very best time for me to write poetry, when I'm not chasing around.—Will you send word to Mr. Brooks for me, Mother, that I'm sure I can have enough verse ready for him by Christmas time, to make into a book?"

247

"Yes, darling, I will.—Have you thought of a name, Richard, that you would like to give your book?"

"I thought I might call it 'A Spring Released.'"

"'A Spring Released,'" Mother had repeated after him very slowly. Then she had leaned over and kissed him on the forehead and he had felt tears falling on his face. "We thought we had given you a great heritage, Richard," she had said at last, "when we gave you the name of one of your grandfathers. But God gave you a greater heritage still. He gave you the grace which he had withheld from your other grandfather."

After that Mother had left him for a little while and next Xavier and Rosemary had come to see him. Xavier was at his *Lycée* now near Evreux, but every now and then he came back to the Chateau de Blonville for a brief holiday, most of which, after all, he seemed to spend at the Chateau de Hauterive. This was the holiday of All Souls and All Saints— that is, Xavier called it All Souls' and All Saints', though Richard himself had always called it Halloween, and had associated it with ringing bells and putting candles in pumpkins rather than with going to church. He was immensely interested to find out how different celebrations were in Virginia and in Normandy, and he and Xavier discussed these differences by the hour.

"But you have Indian Summer in Normandy, anyway, at this time of year, even if you do call it All Saints' instead of Halloween!" he had remarked triumphantly.

"Indian Summer! But this is *St. Martin's* Summer, *mon cher!"* Xavier retorted gaily. He put back his head and laughed, showing his splendid white teeth, and then he told Richard all about St. Martin of Tours, an intrepid and dashing knight, who divided his beautiful red cloak with a beggar.

"He was a very gallant saint. He is highly thought of throughout France and it is fitting that we should have named this fine weather of late autumn after him. But, of course, in Normandy, we do not have to turn toward Touraine for a saint any more than we have to turn there for anything else. We have our own, we are self-sufficient."

Then Xavier talked for a long time about Thérèse Martin, who had become a Carmelite nun when she was fifteen and had died when she was only twenty-four and had been canonized as Ste. Thérèse de L'Enfant Jésus. It seemed that she had lived quite near by, that members of her family were still living near by—for she would not be a very old woman if she had lived, even now. Xavier thought his grandmother had actually seen her in Lisieux, when they were both young girls. At all events, as soon as Richard was on his feet again, they would make an excursion and go over to Lisieux themselves and have a look around the city of Ste. Thérèse. It was a very pleasant place, Xavier said, and it would be agreeable to lunch at the Maison de la Petite Marquise, an inn over five hundred years old, where the *pâté de maison* and the cider were both very good.

"So I shall be eagerly awaiting your quick recovery," Xavier said, springing up, "which no doubt Ste. Thérèse herself will expedite. What do you say, Rosemary? Shall we walk down to the church in the village, and put a candle in front of her shrine, and make sure that the flowers banking her statue are fresh, before all the other worshipers begin flocking in for the fete?"

He had given Richard a merry look, as much as to say, "Of course, you understand perfectly, *mon cher,* that while it is all very well to light candles for a saint, that is just a pretext in this case, because what I really want is to walk to the village with your charming sister." He had put his arm lightly under Rosemary's and led her away. Xavier was always gay whatever he did. Richard realized that an American boy would not have been so frank about his feelings for a girl, any more than he would have talked unselfconsciously about saints and miracles, as if they were a natural part of everyday life, instead of something solemn and secret, which nobody thought about, much less mentioned, except in church. Richard did not think that Xavier was especially religious; but he evidently recognized the place of religion in a well-organized life, accepting it and welcoming it as he did other manifestations of civilized and enlightened existence. Otherwise he would not have been typically French, for the French set great store by all forms of culture and graciousness; Richard realized that. And he realized also that Xavier was typically French, from the top of his crisply curled head to the soles of his slender feet. But still, he had begun to seem almost like one of the family too——

Because Richard liked Xavier so much and had so greatly enjoyed his conversation, it seemed natural for him to speak about both to his father, who was his next visitor. He repeated everything Xavier had told him, with due credit, about St. Martin's Summer and Ste. Thérèse's roses and so on.

"Xavier said, St. Martin took his sword and cut his cloak right in two— Xavier said, there are carvings and stained glass windows in Tours showing just how it happened, that are simply marvelous.—Xavier said, Les Buissonets, where the Martin family lived, is a lovely place and you can go there anytime.—Xavier said, Thérèse wrote a book, after she

249

became a nun, that you can buy anywhere. Will you buy it for me, Father?"

"Yes, of course, Richard, if you want it. Do you think it is the sort of book that would be interesting to a boy?"

"Well, Xavier said it was *very* interesting and, of course, he is a boy! And I think he has very good taste, don't you, Father?"

"No doubt. I haven't had any occasion to observe. What is the name of this book Xavier de Blonville recommended and that you want?"

Father was puzzled, Richard could see that, because Xavier had talked about saints instead of sports, or something else of the kind, this beautiful autumn day. So he tried to explain to Father what he had just analyzed, himself, about Xavier's diversified but well-balanced views on life. And presently he was aware that Father was not puzzled any longer, but very much interested, and that they were discussing grown-up subjects together as man to man. Father stayed with him a long time, and it was one of the very best visits they had ever had together.

Later in the afternoon Uncle Jerome came to see him. It was Saturday so Uncle Jerome had half a day free, though he was obliged to spend most of his time at his office, in the Chancery of the American Embassy at Paris. He worked very hard there, though on the whole he liked his work. Sometimes things happened that bothered him, and he told Richard about those; and sometimes things happened that amused him, and he told Richard about those too.

"Delegations of ladies have been coming to the Chancery all day," he told Richard this time. "Of course, they all want to see the Ambassador, but Mr. Bland has one or two other things to do, besides receiving delegations of ladies. So one of the vice-consuls welcomes them in the outer office and then he brings them in to see me. I thought the season for delegations had almost closed—July and August is when those are at their very prime—but it seems it isn't over even yet. The Women's International League for Peace and Prosperity is holding its biennial convention in Paris right now, Richard. Its members are prosperous, all right. They're stopping at all the best hotels. But peaceful! Well, that's something else again. Why, they're indignant about everything! They're indignant because they're sure they're being gypped in the shops! They're indignant because there's not enough steam heat in their rooms! They're indignant because the President's wife hasn't come to any of their meetings! They're indignant because the Ambassador hasn't given a reception for them!"

"He will though, won't he?"

"I hardly think so, Richard. He is very much occupied."

"Ye-es. But it doesn't take much to occupy Mr. Bland, does it? What I mean is, I have never seen a great deal of him, naturally, but he never seemed very busy to me. That is, *really* busy. He seemed to be sort of standing around at ceremonies, with a lofty expression on his face, wearing spats and a pearl gray tie. You know he never comes down here, even for overnight, without a valet, and Rosemary said once he was the sort of man who looked as if he had never put in his own cuff links. I see just what she means. Now ambassadors are supposed to give receptions and things, aren't they, when their country's people come to the capital where they are stationed? Isn't it part of their job? Mr. Bland gave a huge reception for Honor Bright last year. He had plenty of time to do that. And it sort of seems to me that when ladies are lovely-looking, like Honor, and belong to old Southern families, and have senators for brothers-in-law and presidents for friends, that he always has time to give parties for them. It is only when they're sort of plain and Midwestern and have connections with grocery stores and organizations that he's so terribly occupied."

"It isn't like you to be so critical."

"Yes, I know, Uncle Jerome, but you have to look at things squarely, don't you, even if you do write poetry? And I can't see what good Mr. Bland is doing anybody, I really can't. If he were busy with all kinds of drudgery and detail, it would be different. But he isn't. You do that part for him. Now if Father were the Ambassador to France, you know how he would have acted with the Peace and Prosperity delegates. You know he would have had all those ladies to *luncheon* and given them the feeling that he was terribly glad to see them and that what they were doing was *important!* He'd have sent one of the vice-consuls to find out about the steam heat, and he'd have gone himself to the Elysée and asked the President's wife if she wouldn't come to a *special* meeting at the Embassy, as a gesture toward the marvelous Franco-American fellowship, dating from the glorious days of Lafayette, that we are so mutually eager to maintain. And she would have come running."

"You have a great admiration for your father, Richard."

"Well, hasn't everybody? You've told me yourself, lots of times, that it was simply wonderful to see how he took hold, when he first came to La Paz, just a youngster, reorganizing the office and getting work out of the Indian clerk and all

251

that. And then Mother told me how wonderful he was in Canton, brave and resourceful and uncomplaining. And I can remember him in Yünnanfu myself. He was only a consul, but he made the Chinese look up to him as if he'd been a great lord. He knew all about 'face,' he kept a big establishment, he did everything in a lavish way even if there wasn't much money to work it out with. The French and the English admired him too, because he was so efficient. And since he's had a chance to make money, just see how he's piled it up! Why, of course, I have a great admiration for Father, Uncle Jerome! He's exactly the sort of man every boy wants for a father!"

Last of all, before his nurse came to wheel his bed back into the chateau for the night, Mr. Loose came to see him. Richard felt very sorry for Mr. Loose, who always seemed lonely, no matter how many people there were where he was, and discouraged, no matter how much money he made. He never talked very much. He sat and stared, at nothing in particular, though there were such lovely things to look at all around. So Richard did the talking himself. He began just where he had left off with Uncle Jerome, talking about his father. Mr. Loose did not say anything for a long time, in fact not until he got up to leave, rising in the slow lumbering way he had as if his weight were an encumbrance to him. There were big dark pouches under his eyes, but the eyes themselves were bright and he looked at Richard hard with them from under his shaggy brows as he spoke.

"So that's the way you size your father up, is it?" he said.

"Yes, sir. That's the way I size him up. And I ought to know, oughtn't I? I know him better than anyone else does, because I'm his son. We talk things over together."

Daphne sat in the turret room which she used for a study, with all the poems Richard had ever written arranged in piles on the ornate Empire desk in front of her. It had been quite a task to get the desk up the stairs, which were narrow and winding and steep; but somehow it had been done. Jacques had heard Madame admiring the desk, the week after her arrival at the chateau, and he had given his henchmen no peace until they had helped him to install it in the apartments which she had chosen as hers.

She was deeply absorbed in what she was doing, so deeply that she did not hear footsteps on the steep stone stairs, or indeed any sound at all, until she was startled by a knocking noise on her door and realized vaguely that it had been going on for some time. Then she laid down the sheets of paper she was holding and said, "Come in"; and when she turned she saw that Michael was standing on the threshold.

"Am I disturbing you?" he asked rather formally.

His manner toward her was still strained, though she had been in Normandy for over four months now. Indeed this was the first time that he had spontaneously sought her out.

"Not at all. I am just looking through Richard's poems, getting them ready to copy before I send them to Brooks & Bernstein. But there is no hurry. I am very glad to see you."

She spoke sincerely. She herself had experienced no sense of strain in seeing Michael again after their long separation. She had been told that explorers' wives were often very shy with their husbands, when these men came home after years of absence in the far corners of the earth. But though she herself was so essentially shy, she had not shrunk away from Michael. The sympathy she felt for him would have engulfed every other feeling, even if it had not seemed natural and logical to her, as it had from the beginning, to be with him. If he had come into her chamber the night after her arrival, she would have taken him into her arms, and pillowed his head on her breast, and comforted him. But he had never come into her chamber. He had never even come to her study before this.

"It was about Richard that I wished to see you. He seems to be very much better."

"Won't you sit down? Shall we have a little fire? A fire is very pretty, under that big stone hood, and it is always so cheerful.—Yes, I believe he is better."

She leaned over and touched a match to the logs that lay neatly piled on the hearthstone, swung her own chair around to face the fire, and pulled another close to it. Then she opened a small carved box to reveal cigarettes, and poured Calvados into some delicate glasses from a crystal decanter.

"You've kept your gift for homemaking, wherever you go, I see, Daphne."

He still spoke formally, but appreciation and admiration were in his voice. Daphne warmed to his praise.

"I have been wondering, however, now that Richard is so much better, whether you have been longing for your real home, whether you had been thinking about returning to Virginia."

"Only in a general way. And only because——"

She hesitated momentarily, then went on with her old confident candor. "Only because the flounder house is on the market again, and I'm afraid it may not be, very long. The people who bought it haven't been contented in Alexandria. They think it's a dull place. So they're leaving. But lots of

253

other people are coming in, more and more of them every day.—And I thought, now that I have a little extra money from my father's book—I would have to mortgage the house, very heavily, of course. But still I believe I have enough for the first payment and perhaps I could arrange through some bank—I've always loved it so, Michael, and when Uncle Roger is gone, which may be any time now, the rectory will pass into other hands. I'll have to have a center somewhere——"

"You'd have to *mortgage* the house very heavily! You believe you could *arrange to finance its purchase through some bank!* You'd cross the ocean just to do that!"

"Why, yes. When Richard is well enough to take with me. And Dr. Norchais feels that before so very long now——"

"Don't you realize, Daphne, that I'm a millionaire, that I can buy you a dozen houses if you want them? Or aren't you willing, even now, to accept anything at all from me? It was I who robbed you of the flounder house, by forcing you to sell it against your will. Won't you let me give it back to you?"

The strain was gone from his voice at last. It was vehement and vibrant. Relief, like a great wave, swept over Daphne at the sound of it.

"I didn't realize, truly. I've thought so little about the money you were making, Michael—except to sense, vaguely, that it was something which had come between us, as poverty never did. But, of course—if you want to give me back the flounder house, it—it would make me very happy to have you do so."

She stretched her hands out toward him impulsively. "I suppose," she went on, "that you would know how to arrange everything by cable, that it wouldn't be necessary for me to go back to Virginia on purpose to buy it. And I'd be immensely relieved, because no matter what the doctor says, I don't believe Richard should have the excitement of a voyage for a time yet, and still I couldn't bear to be separated from him."

"That is what I came to talk to you about. I can't bear to be separated from him either! He—he means everything in the world to me. Just today—talking with him, I— *Daphne, do you have to take him away from me again?*"

It was a cry of anguish, straight from the soul. He had snatched her outstretched hands, he was gripping them hard, as a drowning man might have gripped at a raft. Infinite compassion overwhelmed her.

"No, Michael," she said quietly, "I don't have to take him away from you. I know fathers and sons ought to be to-

254

gether, that men can bring up boys better than women can. There is no reason why I shouldn't leave him with you when Rosemary and I go back to Virginia."

"But Rosemary seems bent on staying in France herself!"

Daphne smiled slightly, still without apparent perturbation, in spite of the rapid beating of her heart. "There does seem to be a mysterious attraction about it for her," she said. "Or shall we be frank, and admit that it isn't mysterious at all? That it's comprehensible and natural and lovely?"

"You—you wouldn't mind if she married this—this French count?"

"There isn't any question of marriage, there won't be for several years yet. Not just because Rosemary is so young, but because French people go about such things cautiously and carefully, you know that. I can't imagine Xavier's grandmother countenancing, much less encouraging, any other method. And with his parents in Syria, she's the person to whom Xavier is most directly responsible—indeed, I reckon she always has been in any case. She's a grand old lady, Michael. I can't tell you how much I like her, how easy I find her to get along with. She reminds me so much of my own relatives, in King George County. And Denise is simply the salt of the earth. Yes—when the time comes, I shall be very glad if Rosemary——"

Her smile deepened. Her voice trailed off in tranquil silence. She sat gazing into the fire as if she could see rosy visions amidst the flames.

"You wouldn't say that, Daphne, you couldn't, if you knew everything——"

She looked back at him, her face still untroubled. "But I don't," she said. "We never do, Michael, do we? Aren't there always some 'parts unknown' in every human being's life, just as there are in every obscure corner of the world? We can't carry our discoveries beyond a certain point. There are always some secrets and some silences. It's probably better that there should be."

"But—" he said hoarsely.

"I'm very sure of that, Michael."

She pressed her hands reassuringly against his. Then she leaned forward.

"Let's not talk about that any more just now," she said softly. "Let's talk about the flounder house. I do want you to buy it for me, Michael. I do want to go back to it— sometime. Perhaps we'll all go back to it together. We might even go by way of Java—at last! But for the present—since you are settled in France, and Richard belongs here with you, and Rosemary is beginning to feel that she belongs here too, there isn't any real reason, is there, why I should hurry back to it alone? Don't you think, Michael, that on the whole it would be more practical—and infinitely pleasanter—if I stayed on here with the rest of you?"

It was so dark in the village church that when the leather door swung shut behind Xavier and Rosemary, she could not see anything clearly at first. It was cold too—much colder than it had been outdoors; a chilly draft had rushed out to meet them when they opened the door. But in spite of the chill and the dark Rosemary did not feel at all frightened. She felt that the small stone church was a friendly place.

"The shrine to the Little Flower is just over here, on the left."

Xavier led her straight to it, through the darkness. He knew exactly where it was, as she had felt sure he would. And when they reached the corner where the statue of the young Carmelite was ensconced, they found candles all around it, giving it warmth and light, and flowers banked about it, so sweet that the stale scent of incense which hung elsewhere over the church was engulfed in their fragrance here.

"I think my aunts have been here already. I think they have brought these fresh flowers. Poor souls, that is their main distraction, to come to this village church. Still it is not such a bad idea after all. Shall we light some candles ourselves, Rosemary?"

He slipped two five-franc pieces through a small slot in a metal box, and they tinkled as they fell to the bottom of it, making a cheerful sound in the stillness. Then he lifted two long tapers from a rack and gave one of them to Rosemary.

"We stand them up so, just in front of the altar. *Voilà!* And then we say a prayer to Ste. Thérèse for Richard's recovery. Do you see those little marble tablets back of the altar with inscriptions of gratitude and thanksgiving upon them? They have all been placed there by persons who have cause to be grateful to Ste. Thérèse. No doubt we shall place one there ourselves someday. It looks to me as if Richard were beginning to recover already. Thérèse probably had something to do with it."

"I'm not sure that it's proper, Xavier, for a Protestant to light candles and erect tablets to saints."

"Nonsense! Of course, it is proper. That is, it is proper enough. Who wants to be too proper? Besides, you will not be a Protestant long anyway if you stay in Normandy. So you may as well begin to get used to Catholic customs."

"Is it a Catholic custom to talk like this in a church?"

"Naturally! You do not think the *bon Dieu* would wish

256

us to pretend that we are strangers to each other, do you, just because we are in His house? Or Ste. Thérèse either? Remember they are both very friendly to us."

He slipped, unselfconsciously, to his knees and crossed himself. Rosemary sat still for a moment and then she knelt down beside him. It did not seem as strange to her to be doing so as she had thought it would. She did not bend her head, but looked up at Ste. Thérèse smiling down at her beyond the candles and the flowers. Xavier was right. The saint had a very friendly face.

"If we are going to pray for Richard," suggested Rosemary, "I think we might pray for Mother and Daddy and—and ourselves too, don't you, Xavier?"

Henriette and Jerome Blake and Alonzo Loose were having dinner together in the small *salle des armes* which they frequently used instead of the vast *salle à manger,* when there were not many guests or when they were alone. It was served with a flourish by Jacques, and it was an excellent dinner, with partridges and Pommard and *Pont l'Eveque* as its mainstays, though there were various lesser dishes as well. Henriette and Jerome always had good appetites, and Alonzo Loose, though food had often revolted him lately, did full justice to his meal tonight. In fact, he called to Jacques, after that willing soul had left the dining room for good, to bring him another slice of cheese.

"And I'll take a little more wine with it, Jacques. Just a drop."

The Pommard was the product of a prize vintage. Mr. Loose sipped it slowly, savoring it as he did so.

"Richard is getting better," he said at last, breaking in on the comfortable silence with his statement.

"Yes," Jerome answered. "I noticed it myself today. He talked to me about Mr. Bland."

Alonzo Loose chuckled. "I'd like to hear Richard's opinion of Bland," he said. "I shouldn't be a particle surprised if it was about the same as mine."

"He talked to me about his father too."

"Well now, I'd like to hear what he said to you about Michael."

"If you two will excuse me," Henriette remarked, "I think I will have a look at the twins, before they settle down for the night. I'll see you again later, in the small *salon.*"

They rose, and Jerome held the door open for his wife as she crossed the floor and left the room. When he turned, Alonzo Loose had lighted a cigar, and was puffing away at it thoughtfully.

"It looks, from what Richard said to me," he finally remarked after another long comfortable silence, "as if Michael Trent was all set to stage a comeback."

"It looks to me," observed Jerome drily, "from what Richard said, as if Michael were well along on his comeback already."

PART VIII

Presidential Progress

CHAPTER 20

"WELL, THAT seems to dispose of the Canadian Trade Pact, at least for the moment, doesn't it, Ambrose? I think we might call it a day— After all it's nearly seven, and you and I have both been hard at it since before nine this morning. Stay and have a swim and a snack with me. The place is so torn up, you'll probably get supper on a tray in my study. But there's still plenty to eat, even if the kitchen is being remodeled."

"It's very kind of you, Mr. President. Of course I'd be glad to——"

"You'd be 'glad to but'— Is that what you started to say? Well, go ahead and say it! Surely you and I don't need to stand on ceremony! But Anne and Nancy are in the country, and Ned's off on some racket of his own, as usual, so I thought——"

"Why not come out with me, instead of having me stay here with you? It would do you good, after being cooped up all day, in this heat."

"Where were you planning to go, when I extended my inopportune invitation?"

"To the Trents' in Alexandria."

For a moment Neal Conrad drummed with his fingers on the cleared desk in front of him. Then he asked a casual question.

"I take it there's been a complete reconciliation in that quarter?"

"Yes. Apparently."

"Rather upsetting to some of your own plans, isn't it?"

"I've succeeded in readjusting those, Mr. President."

259

"I see. Well, I've no objection to going out to Alexandria with you. I've always liked Daphne Trent immensely, as you know. I seem to see her better in her country setting though than in Alexandria—and without a husband. What do you think of Trent, anyway?"

"I believe I've told you before, Mr. President. I think he did good work and got a raw deal in the Service. He made millions, both for Loose and for himself in business. And he was predestined to succeed as a lawyer, starting out as general counsel for all the Loose interest. What's more, he's connected, through his wife, with almost every influential family in Virginia. He found his practice there ready-made."

"We could do with a few influential connections ourselves in Virginia, Ambrose."

"I know it. And I'd say you couldn't do better than to seek them out through Michael Trent."

Conrad drummed on the desk again with his fingers. Then he asked another question, still casually.

"Trent's entirely lost interest in diplomacy now, I suppose? That is, you sounded him out on Greece, didn't you, a year and a half ago, and found it didn't appeal to him?"

"Yes, Mr. President."

"Then he'd have no special incentive to making himself useful?"

"It's never safe to make that as a positive statement, is it? But I think I may venture to say that I don't believe the prospect of a post in any secondary country would tempt him very much."

"I see. Well, shall we be on our way?"

"By all means. And when you see Daphne Trent in Alexandria, I think you will agree that she fits in there as naturally as she does at St. Peter's-at-the-Crossroads—and as naturally as she did in La Paz and Canton, for that matter. Her flounder house and her walled garden are both charming. And she's renovated the old 'Quarters' at the rear, and made those distinctive too. In fact I imagine we'll find them the center of the party tonight, with an overflow into the garden. She's converted the entire ground floor into two big rooms, with a serving pantry at the side nearest the kitchen end of the house. And she's filled them with Victorian furniture that belonged to Michael's mother. It may sound like an anachronism. But as a matter of fact, it's extremely effective."

As the gate of the white picket fence in front of the flounder house swung open to receive them, the President found that he was not disposed to dispute the opinion of his Secretary of State. The scene which met his eyes was not

260

only picturesque and pleasant; illumined as it was by the sunset, it seemed to have captured the essence of the sky's rosy glow. Beyond the double galleries which flanked the house he could see men in white flannels and women in filmy dresses seated at little tables scattered about through the garden. Some of them were intensively playing bridge and others were engaged in leisurely conversation; but all of them had tall frosted goblets in their hands and trays of fancy canapés at their elbows. From the "Quarters" beyond came the sound of music, and through the open doorway leading into these, dancing figures which drifted lightly to and fro were dimly visible.

At the sound of the clicking gate, Daphne detached herself from a group standing near the old millstone and came gracefully forward. She was wearing a full-skirted dress made of flowered chiffon and finished with a lace fichu; the effect was as quaint as it was cool. When she saw Estabrook's companion, she quickened her footsteps and approached them swiftly, pausing at one of the bridge tables to lay her hand on her husband's shoulder and murmur a word in his ear.

He glanced up with the look of startled indignation typical of the expert bridge player resentful of interruption. Then, recognizing the cause of this in a flash, he put down his cards and leaped to his feet. As he approached the President, Conrad was instantly aware of his magnetism and vitality; indubitably, Trent had limitless resources of both mind and matter on which to draw. He moved quickly, even lithely, with the springing step and easy action of a young man. His shoulders were broad, but his thighs were narrow; together they enhanced the general effect of elastic strength which he emanated. His crisp hair was still untouched with gray, his skin fresh, his eyes clear and keen. Conrad remembered suddenly that he was a tennis champion as well as a bridge champion, that the rarefied atmosphere of La Paz had not prevented him from winning numerous golf tournaments, that he never took a train between two points which were connected by plane and that he drove racing cars better than many professionals. It all seemed significant and portentous.

"Good evening, Mr. President. How good of you to come out! You're a bridge player, I know. Shall we make up a table? And I'm sure you'll want one of Daphne's mint juleps."

"I shall indeed.—How is the mint here, Daphne, compared to what you grow in King George? Yes—I'd be glad of a rubber or two. I've heard rumors though, Trent, of what you do to your opponents."

261

"Someone must have been maligning me. However, we might play together in a set game."

"I can't think of anything I'd like better. Will you join us, Ambrose? And find a fourth? Tyler perhaps?"

"We'll be lambs led to the slaughter— But just as you say. I'll take a look at the Secret Service men, to see if they're satisfied with arrangements, and then I'll be with you."

The company as a whole had risen, and with Daphne at his side, Conrad moved from one group to another, shaking hands and stopping here and there for a brief chat as he made the rounds. His small talk had always been good; it was no effort for him to meet people in this way; and he was amazed to find that he knew almost everyone present already. The gathering was both diversified and distinguished. A dozen or more members of the Diplomatic Corps were foregathered, and as many members of Congress, with their wives; three or four outstanding journalists; two "cave dwellers" who seldom condescended to mingle in heterogeneous festivities; a number of Alexandrians with historic names; a few "county" couples who lived on famous estates; and an aviator whose name was more famous than any of these. Apparently Daphne had achieved the American equivalent of a *salon* and adapted it to her own surroundings and her own tastes.

"Shall we go out to the 'Quarters' too? My daughter would be thrilled at the thought of presenting her friends to you, and of course it would be a red-letter day for all of them if you came to their party. But I don't want to bore you——"

"It wouldn't bore me. I'd like to see the youngsters."

His fatigue had dropped from him like a cloak. His geniality was spontaneous. This was the sort of thing he ought to manage to do oftener. Already the Executive Office and all its problems and burdens seemed a hundred miles away.

"We're very much pleased that your son enjoys coming to these informal little dances. I hope he's given you good reports of them."

"Ned? He never reports anything to me! Do you mean to say he's here tonight too?"

"Why, yes! I thought of course you knew!"

Daphne had scarcely finished speaking when a golden-haired girl, dressed in apple-green organdy, appeared in the doorway of the "Quarters" with four young men who were engaged in jocular dispute, following closely at her heels. The President recognized his son as the most importunate among them.

"You promised me the next dance, Rosemary."

"The next but *one*. If you wouldn't cut in before that. And you did."

"I say, that isn't fair."

"It is too. Atta girl, Rosemary."

"I'm not going to dance with anyone right now anyway. I'm going into the garden."

"We'll sit this one out then, won't we, Rosemary?"

Daphne broke in upon the tumult. "My dear, I'm bringing a guest to the 'Quarters.' I know you'll wish to be the first to welcome him."

The young girl met her mother's gaze and then turned toward the visitor unselfconsciously. She gave a bright smile and came down the steps without either haste or hesitation.

"Good evening, Mr. President. You *are* the President, aren't you? Of course you're much more friendly-looking than your pictures, but I recognize you just the same. I think I saw you, through the door, too, at St. Peter's-at-the-Crossroads. Only in those days I was always being shunted off to bed. I'm so glad you came to our party. Ned, why didn't you tell us your father was coming out?"

"Apparently Ned and I have not divulged our plans to each other as fully as we might," the President said a little dryly. He glanced from the girl in green to his son and back again, permitting his eyes to rest reflectively on the charming picture which she made. Then he smiled in his turn. "But I should say that no great harm had been done either way," he added. "Your mother told me that I might come in and see the 'Quarters,' Rosemary. You're going to show them to me, aren't you?"

Confound it, he was confused. It had been a surprise, in the first place, to find the cream of the capital crop ensconced in the Trents' garden as if thoroughly and agreeably familiar with it; and it had been something of a shock to discover that Ned was quite at home there, and that—unless all signs failed—he had every intention of entrenching himself still further. Now it was still more startling to sit face to face with Michael Trent across the bridge table and see what happened. Conrad was a good player himself, and he had long maintained that a game of cards offered the best possible chance of sizing a man up. Well, if this were true—and Neal Conrad was not given to doubting his own axioms—then Trent was both a plunger and a winner and it was high time that he was put to the most effective use. Indeed, it was past time, through some lamentable oversight or lack of judgment, and Conrad hoped, with a twinge of apprehension, that it was not altogether too late. He gathered that Trent had a temper, but that was an asset as often as a drawback, and it did not spend itself on his game. His mobile face, from the moment he picked up his cards, became as masklike as the countenance of a professional gambler. He played rapidly, recklessly, and with extraordinary skill. He knew all the rules, but he disregarded them entirely when it best served his purpose to do so. There were moments when he lost heavily; but he recovered himself, and won for long successive stretches. A man who played bridge like that would play politics in just the same way. The question was, could he be persuaded to do it?

"Grand slam in hearts, doubled and redoubled," Neal Conrad heard Michael Trent saying evenly. "That seems to give us another rubber. Shall we stop for supper, Mr. President, or would you prefer to go on?"

Neal Conrad was all in favor of stopping for supper, not only because he liked his food, but because he wanted time to get his breath and correlate his thoughts. The meal was brought out to the garden, which had been skillfully lighted, and served at the little tables, temporarily transfigured with embroidered cloths made of grass linen: cold salmon, sizzling chicken, creamed samp, spoon bread, green salad in a big wooden bowl; then strawberries as big as plums, powdered with sugar and scooped from a deep dish, angel cake pulled apart with a fork, coffee dripping from one glass cylinder into another. The President talked, spasmodically, with his host as he did full justice to everything set before him, almost overlooking everyone else in his absorption.

"You play a good game of bridge. I don't know whether I've ever seen a better one."

"Thank you, Mr. President. But I'm afraid it's due to force of circumstances rather than natural aptitude."

"Yes? I don't quite follow you."

"Well, when I first played, that is, to any extent, it was in La Paz, and the Bolivians are probably the best card players in the world except the Chinese. I needed to be good to beat them. And I had to beat them or I couldn't have paid my bills. I was a Vice-Consul then, with a sick wife and a salary of twelve hundred a year."

"I see."

"Afterwards, of course, I had a chance to play with the Chinese too. For nearly eight years. If I hadn't killed time, the last half, I probably should have killed myself. Of the two, the former seemed the lesser evil. Though there were moments when I wasn't so sure. But fortunately life in the foreign field is all behind me now."

"Michael, I believe the President might enjoy seeing the house. We haven't been indoors at all, except at the 'Quarters.' I want him to see my maps so he can describe them to Mrs. Conrad. And it's lovely and cool on the upper gallery. If you and he would care to take your cigars there——"

Yes, Daphne had made it very easy, very easy and natural for him to sit in the upper gallery, which was quiet and secluded, and talk with Michael Trent while the other guests went on with dancing and card playing. No one interrupted them. Once he heard Ned's voice, which was very like his own in quality, rising above the sound which came to him merely as a melody or a murmur. "Is my old man still there? Golly, I guess he means to spend the night! But it's all right by me!"

A few minutes later, he came tardily to the realization that none of the other guests could go home until he had taken his own departure, that some of those finicky ambassadors and moldy senators were probably not as much pleased with his protracted stay as his son, or with as much reason. What was more, he'd been rather casual in his behavior towards them, sneaking off like this. They'd resent it if he didn't make it up to them somehow. The first he knew, he'd be hearing about some more trade agreements, and some patronage. The Secret Service men too would be getting restive. They would like to see him tucked into the Lincoln bed every night at ten o'clock, with a sedative inside him and a sentry at the door. Well, he'd have to make it up to them too. Good grief, it was two o'clock in the morning! But anyway, he'd had his talk with Trent. They understood each other. That is, he thought so.

He and his host went back into the garden together. He had feared that he might find signs of dejection and weariness there. Very often people drooped when they were kept up too late, or bristled with thinly veiled irritation. But nothing of the sort had happened this time. Charades were being played, with the garden wall for a background and the upper terrace for a stage. Actors and audience appeared to be alike alert and enthusiastic. In the "Quarters," the youngsters were still dancing exuberantly.

He accepted an easy chair and a Tom Collins and settled back to watch the show. It was a good one, a political take-off. Even Estabrook had a part in it. Strange that a highbrow like Estabrook should shine in comedy. And yet, it wasn't so strange after all. Many things which had confused the President, earlier in the evening, were clearer to him now.

The tableaux came to an end, in a storm of applause. Neal

265

Conrad rose, reluctantly, and made the rounds again, with his hostess at his side. This time he lingered a little longer with each group, jested with some of the guests, invited two senators to have luncheon with him on a tray the next day, told a journalist that a story might be breaking in the morning. Everyone was in high good humor when at last he turned toward the picket gate.

"May I come again sometime? On the quiet like this?"

"We'll be tremendously honored. Next time I hope our son will be at home. He's spending the week end with my aunt and uncle, at St. Peter's-at-the-Crossroads: Uncle Roger is doing the final polishing on his book about Colonial churches, which Brooks & Bernstein are bringing out in the fall, and Richard has written some incidental verse for it. They're enjoying their collaboration immensely."

"Well, give them all my kind regards when you write."

"Thank you, Mr. President. I will."

"And remember that you and your husband and that pretty daughter of yours are coming to the White House often after this."

"Yes, Mr. President."

"Is that a promise?"

"Yes. It's a promise."

He and Estabrook were off, jolting over the cobblestones which the Hessian soldiers had laid a century and a half before and which the Alexandrians had so stubbornly declined to dislodge for concrete. He did not speak until they had swung out into the Memorial Highway, the Secret Service men speeding along behind them. Then rather cryptically he addressed his Secretary of State.

"I don't know how much of that you engineered, Ambrose, and how much of it just happened. But you needn't bother to explain. It's all right either way. In fact, it's a damn good thing."

CHAPTER 21

"IT's TWO minutes past six. The train's being held."

"Your watch must be fast. This train isn't held for anyone but Mr. Big himself, and he's out on the rear platform, posing for the cameramen with the missus on one side of him and the offspring on the other, while he waves a heartfelt farewell and utters a few well-chosen words to the cheering populace. I filed my story, describing the moving scene minutely, two hours ago. So I can sit back now and have a drink."

"I thought you were on the wagon."

"I am. But I just fell off. I've got to have something to strengthen me, so I can climb back on."

Chris Stearns, the brilliant but undependable representative of the Cleveland *Times,* grinned and pressed the button between the seats. Bert Scruggs, of the Associated Press, shot an apprehensive glance at him, and then looked away again. After all, it was none of his business. He liked Chris, they all did. But if Chris took one drink, he was apt to take a good many. And it was a matter of common knowledge that there had been some slight hesitation on the part of his paper, about sending him across the continent on the presidential special. The *Times* had put up with a good deal from him, because of his unparalleled flair for ferreting out facts, and the exceptional magnetism which made him personally popular in circles where this could be translated into terms of scoop and circulation. But just the same he had been given a pretty sharp warning. If he broke over before the train was actually out of the station——

"Alfonso isn't even on the car yet. It won't do you any good to ring. I tell you the train *is* being held. It's an outrage."

Gus Graham, of the Kansas City *Courier,* spoke with his habitual ferocity, as if the delay were an affront to him, which he could not possibly overlook. He was a huge unkempt man, whose mane of heavy hair was never combed, and whose beard always showed black through his swarthy skin, even when he shaved twice a day, which was not his habit. He was acting as host, having been assigned to the drawing room because of his immense size; his boon companion, Aubrey Warren, of the Boston *Observer,* who adored all which Gus anathematized, was sharing it with him. He spoke soothingly now.

"Don't rip up the upholstery, Gus. It cost the Pullman Company plenty. We're off anyway. And the culprit's coming down our own alley."

As he spoke, the sound of a pleasant feminine voice, marked by a modified but unmistakable Southern accent, filtered through the smoke-laden atmosphere. "One hat box, one dressing bag, two suitcases—yes, that's all, Alfonso," the unseen lady was saying. "I think I have compartment 'C.' That was a close shave, wasn't it?"

"Yes, *ma'm,* Miss Honor, I'll say it was. I'se mighty glad

you made the train though. I shore would have been sorry to see you left behind. Dey's lots I could spare better than you."

The four reporters had leaped to their feet simultaneously. Before the Pullman porter had finished speaking, they were crowding around the newcomer, shaking her vigorously by the hand, propelling her in the direction of the drawing room, plying her with questions.

"Well, for the love of Mike, see who's here!"—"What do you mean, Honor Bright, putting one over on us like this?" —"What ye done with Jerry?"—"Look here, Honor, did ye bring along some mint from Solomon's Garden?"—"What do you know anyway?"

She disengaged herself, laughingly, from their friendly clutches, slipped to a seat on the sofa, and took off her hat, running a slim hand through the shining masses of her hair as she did so.

"I didn't mean to spring anything on you, really," she protested. "Mr. Meacham telephoned me just two hours ago to say that Ted Ellsworth had broken his leg, and begged me to take his place. I couldn't let the *Enterprise* down in an emergency like that. Even Jerry agreed that it wasn't to be thought of. He's going up to New York on some racket of his own while I'm away."

"Go on, Honor Bright, you know you've been itching for an excuse to get back to us. And ever since those pieces of yours about the Clive-Trent flight were syndicated, you were a marked woman. Say, that was a scoop what *was* a scoop!"

"I don't deserve any credit for those pieces. All I did was to use Daphne Trent's notes."

"Oh, yeah? Well, I'll tell the world you used them pretty damned well. Say, it looks like you're the proverbial answer to prayer. Maybe you can solve the mystery of the moment for us: How come Daphne Trent and her husband are on this train? Drawing room in the staff car and all that? What's up? Who is this man Trent anyway? What's he got? What does he want?"

"He's got about everything. I don't know what he wants. Nothing maybe."

"Oh, yeah?" jeered Gus Graham a second time. "Come clean now, Honor, you're among friends."

"Honestly, Gus, I don't know what he could possibly want that he hasn't got already. He's a tremendously successful lawyer with an established position. He has a beautiful home and a charming wife. His daughter's in love with a French count. His son's a poetic prodigy, without any of the obnoxious qualities that usually characterize both poets and prodigies. In fact, Richard Trent is everything that one could wish for in a son."

A slight trace of wistfulness had crept into her voice. Gus, who adored Honor and knew that the lack of a son was the greatest grief of her life, spoke gently as he answered her. But at that he was not to be diverted.

" 'Saw right. I've seen the boy myself, he's a grand kid. But just the same, you can't tell me Michael Trent isn't out after something. And he's got me foxed. Two years ago nobody in Washington had ever heard of him. And now he practically lives at the White House. 'Cause why?"

"He and the Secretary of State—" began Aubrey Warren.

"*He* and the Secretary of State! Aw right, aw right! You don't need to crack one of my ribs, Bert with your elbow. But say: Here's a fellow that quits law to go into the Foreign Service and then quits the Foreign Service to go into the patent medicine business and then quits the patent medicine business to go into law again. Sounds to me like he couldn't stick to anything, like he couldn't succeed at anything. But here he is, eating out of the President's plate and——"

"Well, Honor's not responsible for that, is she? Instead of baiting her about Trent, why don't you get her to go back to the observation car and dislodge her brother-in-law from his seat beside the throne? If she'd bring him back here so that we could ask him a few questions, that would be constructive."

"Say, that's a swell idea! Come on, Honor, get going."

Gus and Chris both had her by the hand, pulling her out of her seat. Again she tried, laughingly, to disengage herself. But this time the two men held her fingers firmly.

"All right, I'll go," she said lightly, "though I'm not promising I'll bring John back with me. He might keep me there in the observation car instead."

"You wouldn't go highbrow on us, would you, Honor? Like that fellow the Baltimore *Banner* wished on us in the last campaign? The man who spoke only to the President and God? It's bad enough to have a socialite like Aubrey around, without your putting on side."

"You know I've never put on side," Honor said earnestly. "I'll do my best to get John for you, I will really. And I want to set you right about Michael Trent too. He isn't a quitter. Every time he's made a change, it's been because that represented a step upward. And when he left the Loose Elixir Company as General Manager in the Foreign Field, he became its leading counsel. Mr. Loose felt, himself, that Michael would be of more use to him in that capacity, once the European business had been built up. Michael turned it over to his successor in marvelous condition, and still keeps an eye on it, of course. He's got a part interest in a Norman chateau that serves as a swell centre for that. But he knew Daphne would rather live in Virginia than in Europe, and he——"

"So you do know something about that situation after all, do you? Well, we'll hear about that later on then. Now go along and bring back the boy friend. And at the same time you might ask Rushmore when he's going to get the President's Chicago speech to us. He's always late with his releases, darn him."

Honor's absence from the press car was protracted. Several hungry secretaries and secret service men who had had no time to get any lunch, in the last-minute rush before departure, were already in the diner wolfing down their evening meal, and they hailed her as she went past. So did the steward, Charlie Macomber, with whom she had traveled many times before. Like the waiters and the porters aboard, he was regularly attached to the Presidential train. He knew the tastes and habits of all his passengers, from the movie men and radio operators up front, to the senators and cabinet members in the rear. He catered to each with equal skill and equal interest.

"I've got something very special for you this evening, Miss Bright. Guinea hen, young and tender. About what time do you think you'd like it?"

"I can't tell you yet, Charlie. Probably I'll have dinner very late, in the press car."

"Anytime and anywhere you say, Miss Bright. I'll see that you're satisfied."

She nodded to Charlie and passed down the car, responding only with a smile and a lifted hand to the other greetings showered upon her until she reached the table where Patrick Rushmore, one of the President's private secretaries, was bolting down a club sandwich. Then she paused and leaned over.

"The boys are beefing already, Pat. They say you're always late with your releases."

"They lie," remarked Rushmore cheerfully. "But then everyone always does, in your nefarious trade." He grinned cordially. "They'll get the speech all right," he said. "Ostermeyer is just putting the finishing touches on it now. I'll bring it up to the press car myself later on. Any other good news, Honor?"

"They've sent me back to get John. And they're all agog over Michael."

Rushmore nodded understandingly. "Yes, I gathered that,"

he said. "Queer, isn't it, Honor, how we can nearly always tell, down in the President's car, how they're feeling, up in the press car? And vice versa? Rage, relief, amusement, anxiety—they all communicate themselves. It's uncanny. This time, on the whole, I think everyone's starting out in good spirits. Don't you?"

"Ye-es. But this is going to be a ticklish campaign, Pat."

"Nonsense! The election's in the bag already."

"You know better than that. You know that with the foreign situation what it is, and labor raising such a row, and above all this question of a third term——"

She stopped, observing that Senator Slocum, who was seated three tables away, was eating his dinner with the elaborately unconcerned expression of the more or less involuntary eavesdropper. Senator Slocum's wife, the former Sadie Tighe, was not a favorite of Honor's, and she had not stopped to speak to them. Now she retraced her steps.

"Sit down, sit down," Senator Slocum said heartily, as Sadie began to gush and coo with delight. "Have a highball with us. No? A cocktail then——"

"Just a glass of dry sherry while you tell me how things are looking in North Carolina."

Half an hour had elapsed before Senator Slocum finished reviewing the local political situation. Then Sadie began assuring Honor for the fiftieth time that everyone, literally *everyone* in North Carolina hung upon her slightest word and devoured all the periodicals for which she wrote.

"You're not going to be *cruel* to us, are you, and make us go a whole *year* without a new novel?"

"No, Mrs. Slocum. There'll be another novel out next spring. Unless I spend the entire summer trailing the President."

"It *is* a long trail when he starts out, isn't it? And an uncertain one. I'll never forget the last campaign, when he went across country and couldn't decide from one moment to the next what route he wanted to take. Nobody knew which route he *would* take, up to the very last moment, not even the train dispatchers! The superintendent couldn't so much as issue a ticket! Finally we went from Gary to Peoria and down to St. Louis, then zigzagged back and forth through Illinois and Wisconsin as far as St. Paul and all the way southwest again to Omaha."

"It wasn't very direct. But then, of course, no one who doesn't like the way the President travels is obliged to accept an invitation to go with him."

Honor spoke with the smoothness which sometimes roused

271

Sadie's suspicions. Senator Slocum, scenting trouble ahead, hastened to intervene.

"I agree with my wife that Conrad's very unreasonable when it comes to routing, as he is about a good many other things," he said pompously. "I have been connected with several railroads in various capacities and I know it isn't necessary to keep a train jumping over cow pastures to make suitable connections between given points."

"No, naturally not. But perhaps he isn't thinking about cows as much as he is about votes. I'm sure he needs a master mind like yours to direct him through the green pastures and beside the still waters."

Honor rose with a suitable show of reluctance. "We must talk about this again sometime," she said. "I know it's important. I'm sorry that I have to be off now. I was in pursuit of John Stone when I stopped to speak to you and I must continue the chase. I am always in pursuit of John, you know."

Since it was very generally understood that it was John who had long been in pursuit of Honor, and that far from giving him any encouragement, she had persisted in marrying his brother instead, she left her hearers even more puzzled than she had found them. As she entered the staff car, she ran into the object of her search.

"My first piece of real good luck," she remarked, kissing him cordially. "And I need one, after Sadie.—I was just coming to get you, John."

"I haven't had a mouthful to eat all day, Honor. The Senate was still in session when I left and——"

"Well, you can eat with us pretty soon in the press car. But not right now, in the diner. This is one of the times when I have to come back with my shield or on it."

"I'd have been better off if Ellsworth hadn't broken his leg," John said, with his slow smile. "I can see that you'll victimize me, Honor, all the way across the continent."

"Wouldn't you rather have me victimize you than to have someone else victimize the President?"

"Of course. You're right, as usual. And you know I'm glad to serve as a shield for you. Lead on, Macduff."

As Majority Leader in the Senate, John Stone was greatly respected and admired by the press, though his own reserve prevented him from obtaining the kind of popularity which flowed so naturally in the direction of his younger brother, Jerry. He could not tell a slightly smutty story with ease, or call men and women instinctively by their first names; he never became hail-fellow-well-met with them. Nevertheless the welcome he received when he entered Gus Graham's drawing room was sincere and hearty, not only because he represented an authentic and important source of news, but also because he was genuinely liked for himself.

"Sit down, Senator. Have a highball. How's everything on the Hill?"

"Thanks. About as usual, I think."

"Meaning that Congress is going to keep on blocking everything the President wants done?"

"I wouldn't say it was quite as bad as that."

"Well, how bad is it?"

"That depends on which end of the telescope you're looking through, doesn't it?"

"All right, from your end?"

"From our end, I'd say things were looking pretty well. The President's popular, personally. Even the extreme isolationists like him."

"They don't act as if they did."

"But they do. When it comes to a showdown, they'll support him."

"How do you mean, support him? Let the Navy Appropriation Bill pass, or let him have another term?"

"I believe the Navy Appropriation Bill will pass all right. Even the isolationists admit the need for it, with the foreign situation looking the way it does now. I think the Farm Bill will pass too. That eases the strain over the other."

"Yes, that ought to placate the Middle Westerners about armaments. But will it make them swallow that third cup of coffee?"

"I hope so. Off the record, I believe so."

At this point the drawing room door, which had been only slightly ajar, was thrown open and a short fat man hurled himself in upon the conference. He was almost as broad as he was long, and he was wearing a black and white checked suit of unconventional cut, set off with a bright red tie, fastened in a careless bow. Above these shone a round and ruddy face and a mop of unruly yellow curls. He seized upon Honor, swung her to her feet, and twirled her about with unbelievable skill and swiftness. Then sweeping the others with a jovial glare, he bellowed out an indignant question.

"What's become of the President's speech? How's a fellow to write a column if he don't get his handouts?"

"Keep your shirt on, Alf. We're all in the same box. But the fleet-footed messenger whom we dispatched to Olympus brings back the tidings that Jove's thunderbolts are even now having their spark plugs adjusted. You know Senator Stone, don't you?"

"Pleased to meet you," panted the portly columnist, without any show of extraordinary pleasure. "So they've got you running errands already, have they, Honor? How is the Mr. Big anyway? The rumor around Chi these last few days is that he's a mighty sick man, that his heart's giving out, that he'll never be able to stand up under the strain."

"He looked pretty well to me the last time I saw him, and that was this morning."

"Anyone looks well to you, Chris, after you've had your fourth. Thanks, I don't mind if I do. Well, anyway, what's this I hear about the President's new pet?"

"Pal, Alf, not pet. This President doesn't have pets. That was two or three Presidents back."

"Well, pal or pet, it's all one to me. What about him?"

"We all want to know about that too. Honor says he's just a great philanthropist, working for the good of his country, with no thought of sordid gain for himself."

"No, she didn't."

"Shut up, Bert. You take things too literally. And you take Honor too seriously. Doesn't he, Honor?"

"Of course not. It might be a good thing if some of the rest of you had Bert's outlook, if you'd wake up to the fact that life is real and life is earnest. Since you don't take any stock in my analysis of Michael Trent, why not ask John about this?"

"That's the idea. Tell us about this mystery man, Senator."

"Mystery man?" The Majority Leader raised his eyebrows slightly. "I can't imagine anyone less mysterious than Michael Trent."

"Well, I don't know anything about him except that his wife's a stunt flyer who stands in well with the Secretary of State and his son's an infant prodigy."

"You'll know more before the trip is over," remarked John Stone, cryptically and a little dryly. "Will you excuse me now, gentlemen? As I told my sister-in-law when she asked me to join you, I haven't had anything to eat all day——"

"Well, of course, you'll stay and eat with us! We were just going to ring for Alfonso! Sit down, Senator, sit down."

Without actually forcing his way out of the drawing room, John had little choice but to comply. Alfonso, white-coated and beaming, was already blocking the doorway.

"Listen, Alfonso. We need another syphon and we need some more glasses and we want a menu. Get Leonard in here from the diner."

"Yessah, Mr. Warren."

"Listen, Alfonso. Mr. Macomber says that guinea hen's a

special tonight. Please ask him to tell the chef to start cooking it anytime now."

"Yessum, Miss Honor, I shore will."

"Listen, Alfonso. I want you to take a note to the President's secretary, Mr. Patrick Rushmore. You know Mr. Rushmore, don't you? Now this is very important. You understand?"

"Yessah, Mr. Stearns, I understands."

"There's room for another person in here," Honor observed, as Alfonso started on his willing way. "That is, there will be, if we can crowd Alf up into the corner. Don't the rest of you think it would be a good plan to get hold of that new man from San Francisco who's been put on—Durham I think his name is—and ask him to join us? He must be somewhere around. He'll tell us what the gossip is on the coast. Whether they're saying that the President beats his wife or that he's responsible for the shipping strike. Whether they think he's gone too far or not far enough in standing up to Japan. Whether——"

"Whether they'll support him for a third term or not. We get you, Honor. All right, let's have this Californian in to dinner. I think it's a risk though. He may be able to tell us something about Michael Trent, but the chances are he won't talk about anything except the climate."

Charlie Macomber was a happy man. The Middle West might be boring to some people, but to him it was beautiful, for there was no part of the country where the heavy diner rode so smoothly with the train going at top speed, as over the prairies. His passengers could enjoy their breakfast there, with no risk of spilling their orange juice or slopping their coffee around. And now that the President's wife had come into the car, he would have been really troubled if there had been jolts and jars, as there sometimes were on the mountainous stretches, or in places where the roadbed was bad.

He had always liked Mrs. Conrad. Not merely, as he often told people, because she was the President's wife, but because she was such a pleasant-spoken lady. Always had a kind word for everyone and never forgot anyone. He had been steward in charge of the diner on the Conrad Special when Mr. Conrad was still in the Senate, going through his first Presidential campaign. Mrs. Conrad had looked like a girl then, hardly older than her own daughter and pretty as a picture. She hadn't had anything to worry about that time. But the second one had been a good deal harder. Charlie had seen Mrs. Conrad look troubled a good many times, during the course of it; he knew it was wearing her down. He'd

275

been glad, for her sake, when it was over; though personally, he'd reveled in every minute of it, proud as punch that he'd been promoted to the Presidential Special. It was all one to him that he never could close the diner, that passengers came in demanding food every hour of the day and night, or kept ringing to have it sent to their compartments. The waiters didn't complain either. They'd all been buoyed up with the excitement too. He guessed they would be this time. Except that a third term— Well, that was something else again to worry about.

He held out Mrs. Conrad's chair for her, saw her comfortably settled in the sunny corner that she liked. Her son and daughter and secretary were all with her. Made a nice group. Refined, that was the word for it. Mrs. Conrad was a very refined lady, and everyone around her had to meet her level. He wrote down the order carefully.

"I'll have just dry toast and black coffee, please, Mr. Macomber."

She couldn't be dieting. He'd never seen a woman of her age who'd kept her figure better. She—why, she must be nearly fifty, though she didn't look a day over thirty-five, even now. Worry, that was what made her lose her appetite. Worry and strain. Well now, he must see if he couldn't tempt her with something.

"The melon is very nice this morning, Madam."

"I'll have some tomorrow for lunch."

"I want some now. Melon and oatmeal and honey and muffins. And a big glass of half and half."

"Yes, Miss Nancy." This girl wasn't dieting, or worrying either. A good healthy appetite. It was a pleasure to serve her.

Probably it was just as well Mrs. Conrad wasn't hungry, for she couldn't take so much as a sip of coffee or a bite of toast, Charlie noticed, that she wasn't interrupted. First one thing and then another. Every few minutes one of the telegraph boys came down from the front car with a message for her. Every few minutes someone stopped at her table and spoke to her—that gushing Mrs. Slocum, for instance, had acted as if she were glued to the aisle. Then at Englewood a covey of photographers and local reporters got on. The photographers all wanted shots of Mrs. Conrad, eating her breakfast. The reporters all wanted to know if she didn't think Chicago was the finest city in the world, and whether she had any special message for the farmers' wives, and if she'd enjoy living in the White House four years more. She posed and smiled for them but she didn't say very much.

She had good sense, a level head on her shoulders. Charlie Macomber had always known that.

There had been a little disturbance when the train stopped at Englewood. A delegation of well-wishers, marshaled by a local politician, had come to the station, bent on getting aboard the Special and shaking the President's hand. Mr. Rushmore had been obliged to leave his coffee to cool while he went out on the platform to explain that he was very, very sorry, but that the President was just putting the finishing touches on his speech and couldn't be disturbed at the moment. Charlie Macomber knew as well as anyone that it was Ike Ostermeyer who put the finishing touches on the President's speeches, and that this one was all done anyway, because the reporters who had been beefing about it the night before had it now, and were sitting turning the pages of it while they ate their breakfast, beefing some more. Gus Graham and Aubrey Warren were quarreling over it, Gus shouting that it was just a sop thrown to big business and Aubrey insisting that on the contrary it represented a shameful concession to labor. Chris Stearns was telling Bert Scruggs that there was nothing there to get your teeth in, and Bert was saying seriously that he thought it was a sound, straightforward speech and that it would go over big in the Middle West.

It seemed to Charlie Macomber that the diner was full of rows that morning. Tim Flaherty, who was on the Mayor's Council, and one of the biggest political shots in Chi, *had* got on the train at Englewood, and had landed on Mr. Rushmore like a ton of brick, giving advice, issuing warnings, making complaints. He was telling Mr. Rushmore about the dust storm that had just swept over the prairies, in a manner that indicated his conviction that the President was responsible for this, that he had stirred it up on purpose to annoy the Middle West, and that coming on top of the drought, it was peculiarly unfortunate. He was talking about the colored vote and the German vote, as if he felt that both had been jeopardized. He was saying, for God's sake, not to let the President get mixed up with that crafty crew he had played around with the last time he was in Chi; the President was smooth, all right, but that particular crowd was slick. On the other hand, there were some men he had slighted before who had got to be appeased; a few well-placed promises would help, and some soft pedaling on the foreign policy. And if Mrs. Conrad could see her way clear to staying at the home of Senator and Mrs. Stevens, that would be a good plan. Mrs. Stevens was quite a leader, she had a big acquaintance among influential women. She would

277

like to be able to brag that Mrs. Conrad had stayed with her and it would be a good thing if she did——

Mr. Michael Trent came into the diner with his daughter Rosemary, and Ned Conrad, the President's son, got up from his seat beside his sister and went and sat with them. He had finished his breakfast really, but he thought he'd have another cup of coffee and a cigarette. Mr. Trent greeted him very cordially, and presently he and Ned had their faces close together; they were talking confidentially. Charlie Macomber couldn't hear what they were saying, but he knew the signs. Ned, whose real name was Neal, like his father's, but who had been nicknamed to avoid confusion, was shrewd and farseeing. The President was inordinately proud of him, put a great deal of dependence in him, had become quite insistent that older men should admit him to their councils. Mr. Trent seemed willing enough to do this, though Charlie knew there was resentment about it in some quarters. But in this case, Charlie wasn't so sure that Ned himself wanted to talk politics. Charlie thought that maybe Ned had changed seats so that he could talk to Rosemary.

Now there was a girl who could give even Nancy Conrad cards and spades. Of course Nancy was pretty and pleasant like her mother. But this girl—well, there was a shine to her and a finish. Charlie couldn't quite define it, because he'd never seen anything just like it before. Her clothes were simple enough. No fluffy ruffles to them at all. But they had an air; she sure did know how to wear them. And there was something about her coloring——

"If you and Ned will excuse me, Daddy, I think I'll go back and sit with Mother."

"Won't you join us, my dear, for a moment first? You can take Ned's empty seat—that will give him and your father a chance for a nice quiet talk."

Mrs. Conrad was speaking very cordially, well you might say affectionately. And, of course, Rosemary Trent did what she had suggested, at once. But Charlie thought some of the light had gone out of her face.

"The President was saying to me this morning that he wanted to see more of you, Rosemary. Perhaps tomorrow evening, when we're en route for Denver, you'll dine with us in our own car."

"Thank you very much, Mrs. Conrad."

"And meantime, while we're in Chicago, we'd be pleased to have you sit with your father and mother on the reviewing stand for the parade and on the platform in the Auditorium for the President's speech. Mr. Rushmore has made arrangements for an extra ticket."

Charlie saw Mr. Trent glance sharply across the aisle at his daughter, as if he were afraid she were going to decline Mrs. Conrad's invitation, and wanted to give her a high-sign so that she shouldn't. Certainly there was something wrong. Most girls would be tickled to death to have that much attention from the Presidential family, especially when there was a good-looking young man involved. But this girl seemed to be really unhappy about something. She had lots of self-control, she didn't whimper or whine. But as Charlie opened the door of the diner, so that she and Mr. Trent could go back into the staff car, he heard her say to her father, "Daddy, you know I wanted to accept that invitation from the French Consul General and his wife while we're in Chicago. You know they're friends of Xavier's."

"I'm sorry, Rosemary. But I have other plans for you this time—plans that are more important than any depending simply on personal pleasure. You have a great opportunity. I know I can count on you not to lose it."

Well, somehow Charlie didn't feel as happy as he had earlier that morning, after he had watched them go out of the diner together. It was a fine day, the weather would be perfect for the parade, there was no doubt of that. But some of the sunshine had gone for him. It made him miserable to think of the look on Rosemary Trent's face—like she wasn't seeing the President's son at all, but gazing way off into the distance at something that meant more to her. And still, being perfectly polite, not letting her father down.

Charlie would have liked to be able to tell Rosemary what a grand girl he thought she was, and to say, on the side, that she mustn't let politics wear her down. He'd seen a lot of them, first and last, and they weren't worth any girl's happiness. Not even Presidential politics.

There was tension in the staff car, and the feeling of it extended, not only into the observation car, but into every part of the train. As Pat Rushmore had told Honor, it was uncanny how the mood of a single group could spread until it had affected the temper of them all.

Everything had gone swimmingly at Chicago. The Special had arrived just at lunchtime, when the stores were disgorging shoppers and employees by the thousand and when the huge hotels were sucking in thousands of others. The great commercial center of the Loop was always teeming at this hour, and with a procession thrown in for good measure, the effect was one of an overwhelming ovation for the President and a clamorous demand for his re-election. The procession itself was stupendous—Chicago did things of this

279

sort well. Bands and banners were alike bright and blatant; civic organizations turned out to parade in full force, adorned with badges and belts; there were floats, and detachments of mounted police; the line of march was miles long. When the grandstand had finally been emptied after a prolonged exchange of greetings and promises, endless wringing of hands, and much general joviality, the President and his party wedged their way through massed multitudes which were cheering to the last man as he rode triumphantly out of sight, waving his silk hat and bowing left and right from his open motor.

He spent the afternoon closeted in conferences, and this time he saw none of the wrong people. Meanwhile Mrs. Conrad and the ladies who were traveling with her were entertained by Mrs. Stevens, who gave a large reception in their honor in her palatial though hideous house on Lake Shore Drive. The effect produced was admirable. There was only one slight hitch in the proceedings, and that was of a personal and private nature, and fortunately never even came to the attention of the preoccupied Presidential pair.

Rosemary Trent had been standing beside her mother when the grandstand group dispersed, looking her very loveliest, and responding without either shyness or awkwardness to the genial welcome extended to her by the political elect of Chicago. Daphne's own attention had been momentarily distracted by glad-handing coming from another direction; and when she turned to speak to her daughter again, Rosemary had disappeared.

For an instant Daphne's heart stood still, as visions of kidnapers and abductors swam before her agonized eyes; in a flash she remembered all the evil she had heard about Chicago. Then she felt a hard little square of paper pressed into her hand, and heard a reassuring voice whispering in her ear.

"Don't worry about your daughter. She's well looked after. She asked me to give you this."

Daphne could not even see who it was that spoke to her. She unfolded the hard little square of paper with trembling fingers. She read in Rosemary's delicate finished script:

Dear Mother—
Please do not worry about me or feel that I have been wilfully disobedient to you. But I felt I must take the early part of the afternoon to call on Madame Delacroix, for Xavier's sake. I have found a friendly policeman who has promised to pass me through the lines, and he will

also see that I get back to Mrs. Stevens' house before anyone but you can miss me.

Love from
Rosemary.

P. S.
A member of the press who hates Ned Conrad has helped me to make my arrangements, but I have promised not to tell which one.

Rosemary was as good as her word. She appeared at Mrs. Stevens' monstrous dwelling, sweet, smiling and deferential, before anyone except her mother had missed her—Ned was "in" on the conferences that afternoon, so for once it was easy enough to elude him. But Daphne, during the interval of her daughter's absence, found that her habitual tranquility had completely deserted her. It was torture for her to play her designated role before Mrs. Stevens' gushing guests while all the time her anxious thoughts were centered on her "one ewe lamb." In praying that a fairy prince might come for Rosemary, she had not dreamed that Providence would take her quite so literally; a French count might conceivably have come within the scope of her petition, but the only son of a President was something else again; and the complications presented by the rival claims of these suitors were appalling. She was sure that Rosemary had left her heart in France; but one of the principal reasons why Michael had been willing to sever his connections there and return to Virginia had been because such a step would mean separating Xavier from his daughter. Now that a potential alliance with the White House was looming up on the horizon, as a result of his return, his satisfaction was supreme. He talked about it with Daphne lightly, almost jestingly, in a way that he thought might win her over.

"You know you'd be the proudest woman in the world if you could see Rosemary walking down the aisle in Christ Church on Ned's arm, wearing that white brocade wedding dress you inherited from your great-grandmother."

"Ye-es. If I were sure she was happy. If I were sure that at the same moment she wouldn't be imagining what it would have been like to walk down the aisle of the Cathedral at Bayeux on Xavier's arm. Don't put any pressure on her, Michael. Let her decide for herself."

"Pressure! It ought not to be necessary to put any pressure on a sensible girl in a case like this."

281

"Girls aren't always sensible, Michael, when they're in love."

"You're not getting personal about this, by any chance, are you, Daphne?"

"Of course not, dear. But everyone doesn't like Ned Conrad as well as you do. I've happened to hear that in the press——"

"The press had better play up to Ned, if it wants to stand in with the President. And so had Rosemary, if she wants to please her father."

Leaving the question of Rosemary entirely aside, Daphne knew that she would never forgive Ned Conrad if he were to reopen the rift, so recently healed, between Michael and herself. And that was what she feared, desperately, might happen. When she returned to the Presidential Special, after the exercises in the Auditorium, she was prostrated by the strain she had undergone during the day. Michael found her utterly unresponsive to his jubilant mood.

"There wasn't even standing room in that place—not a square inch—and it holds eight thousand. I never saw such enthusiasm."

"There wasn't the equivalent of what the French call a *claque,* was there, Michael? I thought, once or twice, that the applause was just a little—well, I wouldn't say mechanical, but perhaps adroitly directed."

"Of course not! It was all absolutely spontaneous. The President could have been carried off the platform on the shoulders of supporters, in the good old-fashioned way. They would have taken him to the train, shouting and singing as they went. He told me himself, when I said good night to him, that his reception in Chicago had surpassed his every expectation. And look at the press he got!"

"Have you had a chance to talk to Honor?"

"No, she went off somewhere with Bert Scruggs after she filed her story. Why?"

"She wants you and me to have lunch with her in the press car tomorrow, to meet some of her 'crowd', as she calls it."

"Tomorrow's a full day. We've got an operating stop at Omaha and a small unscheduled detour—the President's decided to go and see an elderly cousin of his who lives at Swink, Nebraska. It's a good move. He may get out and run a threshing machine for an hour or so too. He hates being cooped up all the time and that's also excellent build up. So I'll be busy with all this, too busy to make a definite luncheon engagement. Besides, I'm not yet sure I want to be a joiner as far as Honor's crowd is concerned. John Stone seems to be able to run with the hare and hunt with the hounds, but I don't believe I can."

"Honor does that herself, Michael. She and John work from opposite ends, that's all. She'll be very helpful."

"Rosemary can be a good deal more helpful.—Did she behave herself all the time in Chicago?"

"Oh, yes, beautifully."

It was one of the few fibs she had ever told Michael. As the train slid swiftly along toward Denver in the darkness, Daphne lay and worried about it and about the underlying causes for it. She slept very little and the next morning she had a bad headache.

"I think I won't get up, Michael, if you don't mind."

"But I do mind. What's the matter with you anyway, Daphne? You're usually a better sport than this! You don't let little things like headaches knock you out."

She did not attempt to argue with him, and after she had had her coffee, she rose, rather dizzily, and dressed. She was just slipping a smart new print over her shoulders when Michael re-entered the compartment, obviously upset.

"Senator Templeton has died—ether pneumonia after an exploratory examination. The President thinks he ought to attend the funeral. That means changing our route, cutting our stay in Denver short and heading north for Montana. Everyone's more or less upset."

"Then perhaps I could lie down again——"

"Good Lord, no! Come out and pour some oil on the troubled waters. You're good at that generally. I suggest you begin with Mrs. Slocum.—If I had my way I'd shove her off the train at the next station."

Daphne found that the buxom blonde was, indeed, in an extremely peevish frame of mind when she tapped on the door of the Slocums' compartment and asked pleasantly if she might come in. The Senator had gone forward to the club car—to escape, Daphne suspected, from the recriminations of his spouse, for it was too early in the day for him to be really thirsty. So Sadie was alone, turning over the dog-eared pages of a movie magazine. She looked up with a petulance which she made no effort to conceal.

"Why, yes, come in, Mrs. Trent, if you'd care to. This is a dreadful journey, isn't it? I'm sure the thermometer will register a hundred in the shade before the day is over."

Daphne murmured something about the advantages of air-cooling.

"Yes, in the train! But how much air-cooling will there be, I'd like to know, at Swink, Nebraska? Or out in the middle of a wheat field? I'm not surprised, Mrs. Trent, that

283

the South isn't altogether in sympathy with the President's program. Such antics aren't dignified. The South sets great store by dignity."

Daphne, remembering that Sadie herself had originally hailed from the great open spaces of the Middle West, forbore, with restraint especially commendable in a Virginian, from reminding her companion of this fact. Instead, she asked a casual question.

"But surely you feel, Mrs. Slocum, that on the whole the South *is* sympathetic toward the President?"

"Well, I don't know. Of course, Senator Slocum is doing everything he can, *everything*. But it's uphill work. The South isn't as solid as it used to be, and as everyone knows, North Carolina's a doubtful State nowadays. And the President doesn't take the trouble to confer with Senator Slocum about the peculiar problems there, which my husband understands so much better than anyone else. All his time seems to be taken up with *newcomers*. Can you believe it, Mrs. Trent? The Senator and I haven't been asked into the observation car for lunch or dinner or even tea since we left Washington."

Flushing slightly at the reference to newcomers, Daphne pointed out that they had all been in Chicago for both lunch and dinner the day before and that the trip was hardly under way yet.

"Still, I've heard a rumor that the President has asked some *young people* to dine with him tonight. I can't understand such inconsistency on his part. Unless there's some reason *we don't know about* for his doing so, when his seasoned advisors are being neglected."

The hint of a romance, Daphne felt sure, would have placated Sadie, who belonged to the type that fattened on these. At the very moment, she gave the effect of panting for tender tidbits. Daphne looked resolutely out of the window.

"It'll seem good to be among the mountains again tomorrow, won't it?" she said. "I don't dislike plains—in fact, they're infinitely restful to me. But I miss hills and valleys when I don't see them for long stretches of time or distance. I wish it were possible for us to see something of the Rockies in the vicinity of Denver. I've always heard that Cripple Creek Canyon was superb."

But Sadie was not intrigued by the idea of superb scenery. Balked in her quest for a love story, her attention was diverted toward mystery instead, as two unobtrusive-looking men walked quietly down the corridor.

"Do you suppose there's been a threat on the President's life?" she asked eagerly—almost hopefully it seemed to

Daphne. "Every time I turn around, I step over a secret service man. I think it's really ridiculous to have so many of them quartered here in our car. Surely they'd be just as well off with the radio operators and the photographers."

"They would be. But the President might not. After all, the photographers' Pullman is quite a distance from the observation car."

"Then you do think there's danger?"

"I don't know of any special danger, I'm glad to say. But it isn't possible to have too many safeguards."

"Have you heard," inquired Sadie, her torpid mind roused at last, darting off in another direction, "that the President may actually go up Cripple Creek? Isn't that the name of the canyon you were speaking about a moment ago? It seems that a new motor road is being built up over the old Georgetown Loop, and Senator Etheridge has wired asking if Mr. Conrad wouldn't like to see it. I suppose this wretched funeral may make a difference, but if it weren't for that we might all have a chance for a little diversion. I thought Chicago was awful, didn't you? Just so much meaningless pandemonium! And to go from that to Butte, Montana, seems simply too much!"

"It's very sad about Senator Templeton."

"Sad! You know the old saying, Mrs. Trent, that cloture might help some, but that what the Senate needs most is a few well-placed funerals."

As Daphne had heard this witticism at least twenty times, she did not rally very enthusiastically to it now. Her head certainly was splitting—and she had not seen Rosemary to talk to her that morning—and she wondered if the thermometer really would register a hundred in the shade at Swink, Nebraska.

It did. To be exact, it registered a hundred and two. And the President's aged cousin, whom he had stopped to see, was not really very much pleased about his visit. She was a very old woman, a good deal of a recluse, and she did not agree with his political views, which seemed to her dangerously progressive. She had just had all her teeth out, she did not wish to pose for cameramen, even with a relative—whom she had incidentally not seen in twenty years—who was a presidential candidate. She did not like to have all these strange people clambering over her neat little porch and prying into her closed parlor. She agreed with everything George Washington had said when he declined a third term and therefore had nothing in the way of a modern catchword about one to give to the press. It was a matter of much gen-

285

eral relief when the greatly publicized visit was over, and the Presidential Special had resumed its progress across the prairie.

If Swink had been disappointing, however, the threshing machine was aggravating. No sooner had the President climbed upon it and obligingly posed for his picture, than it became evident that something had gone wrong with the thresher's mechanism. It would not budge, and therefore motion pictures, representing it as moving majestically forward in the midst of the ripe grain under the skillful guidance of the President, could not possibly be taken. A delay ensued, during the course of which a series of consultations took place: Would it be better to send out for another machine, or move to another field, or resume the interrupted journey, abandoning the bucolic feature altogether? It was finally decided that the last course would be the wisest, all things considered; if the stay in Denver were to be curtailed at one end, certainly it would be better not to dock it at the other also.

No one's temper had been improved by standing about in the heat, and Pat Rushmore, who as usual had done more dashing around than anyone except Bert Scruggs, suddenly sagged down on the burning ground, a victim of sunstroke. Bert and Ike improvised a stretcher and carried him back to the train; and Dr. Hornaday, the President's physician, looking grave when he came out of Pat's compartment, said that the secretary must have watchful care and complete quiet. This meant that Ike had to take over Pat's duties as well as his own; and since his own included the completion of the President's Denver speech, for which the press was already howling, Ike was finally goaded, through desperation, into telling the press exactly what he thought of it. In return, the press profanely voiced its own opinion, none of which got anybody anywhere.

Retreating to his own quarters, in a state of explosion, after his encounter with the fourth estate, Ike was suddenly succored from an unexpected source. His blind rush to cover was halted by the quiet and pleasing figure of Mrs. Trent, who made a suggestion which caused Ike's jaw to drop open.

"Mr. Ostermeyer—I don't want to seem pushing or presumptuous—but I wonder if I could possibly help you? That is, the President's speech is drafted already, isn't it—I mean it's practically complete except for a little last-minute revision and polishing? I edited all my father's papers—with Honor Bright's help, of course—and I learned something about putting material into final form. Then I work all the time with my son—he's very talented, but not very strong,

286

and, of course, immature and inexperienced. And there was that book about the flight Clive and I made—I didn't do any of the actual writing, except for the notes in the log which Honor used in her articles, but I did make suggestions and redraft certain passages. Clive doesn't pretend to have any literary ability at all. But all this has had such good results that I thought perhaps——"

For a moment Ike stared at her with such stupefaction that he neglected to close his mouth. She was kind, of course, to make such an offer, and after the merciless badgering he had undergone, Ike was grateful for kindness in any form. But the idea that dickering with a few old musty documents and some doggerel written by a kid would fit her to fix up a speech of the President's was so fantastic that it wasn't even funny. He was afraid he would laugh right out in Mrs. Trent's face. Then suddenly he shut his jaws together with a snap. For somewhere at the back of his photographic mind rang the remembrance of the cultured voice of the Secretary of State, in earnest conversation with the President. Ike still seemed to hear Ambrose Estabrook saying, "Mr. President, there isn't a woman in the country who knows more about national and international affairs than Daphne Trent, or who can express herself on public questions better, in a simple way. The reports Michael Trent sent in, during the course of his consular career, were models of their kind, and she had a hand in almost every one of them. And since Michael's connection with the Loose Elixir Company—that is, during the latter part of it, when he and Daphne have been together—she's been helpful in every kind of build-up imaginable. A woman like that, Mr. President, with great courage and great trustworthiness added to her gifts and graces, is simply invaluable to the country——"

"Well, you might try anyway," Ike said, bringing himself back to the present, and speaking with a gruffness that veiled his gratitude. "The Big Boss can't do anything more to it himself today—that's one sure thing. If Pat hadn't passed out cold, I suppose he would have known how to keep that Nebraska Committeewoman away from the President. But she slipped by me like an eel, and in a moment of weakness, the Big Boss told the secret service man not to stop her when she started climbing over the railing of the rear platform. She must have given him an earful since."

It was all too true. The President had begun to regret his moment of leniency before Mrs. Thaddeus B. Coffin, National Committeewoman for the State of Nebraska, was so much as well-launched on the tale of woe she was bent upon unfolding. Everything, it appeared, was wrong in her state, from the distribution of patronage to the condition of the crops. The farm on which the threshing machine had broken down belonged to her cousin, Elmer Coffin, which was one of the reasons why the train had been routed past it; and certainly, to the uninitiated, it appeared to be in prime condition. But its appearance, according to Mrs. Coffin, was deceptive. The buildings had all been given a fresh coat of paint in anticipation of the President's visit; but this did not alter the fact that there was a blight on the beans, that the strawberries had been attacked by cutworm, and that the foreclosure of the mortgage was imminent. Under these circumstances, if the President could see his way clear to appointing Elmer to some lucrative office it would be very helpful.

Unfortunately, the President was aware that there was more involved than a question of what might be helpful to Elmer. There was also the question of what might be helpful to him. Mrs. Thaddeus B. Coffin was a pest, but she was also a power. She ranked high in the Rebekahs and the Grange and she was a past Grand Matron in the Eastern Star. She had been one of the first active suffrage workers, and her party zeal had never abated. Neal Conrad had a vigorous constitution and a strong mind, but eventually Mrs. Coffin wore him down. He ended the interview by promising her cousin an appointment, and by asking her to remain for dinner.

It had been no part of his original plan to let in a miscellaneous mob for the evening meal; Michael, Daphne and Rosemary Trent, and John Stone had been invited to the observation car; they, with Anne, Ned, Nancy and himself would make an agreeable group, almost a family party. Now another man must be asked for the benefit of Mrs. Coffin; and this man, the President decided, might as well be Gus Graham as anybody. Gus had to be invited sometime, and Mrs. Coffin did not rate anybody better. But the presence of Gus almost automatically indicated that of Aubrey, and this meant still another woman. The President instinctively turned to Honor Bright.

When word to this effect was sent forth, Gus had just settled down to an all-night poker game with Alf, Bert, Chris and Durham, the new man from San Francisco, who had given them all a pleasant surprise, both personally and professionally. The air was blue with smoke and profanity and permeated with great good will. As Gus rose and pulled down his shirt sleeves, he swore with a savagery which had no relation to the genial oaths he had just been uttering.

"Why the so and so and so and so and so couldn't he have

288

landed on Aubrey instead of me?" he demanded of the company at large. "Aubrey likes to eat all the way from lobster cocktail, to salad swimming in nectar dressing, with terrapin and a small steak alongside, and nothing but a little sherry and sauterne to wash it down with. I don't. I hate it like hell. I want roast beef and whisky. I still don't see why he didn't pick on Aubrey."

"He did. Aubrey and Honor Bright," Ike Ostermeyer, who had brought in the message, answered rather tartly. "They were having cocktails with Senator and Mrs. Slocum when I told them. And they weren't any better pleased than you are. They were all set to have dinner with the Slocums and play bridge afterward and, incidentally, find out just how hard the solid South is cracking under its veneer. As for the Slocums, who haven't been invited into the observation car at all yet, they're fit to be tied. But you better not do so much crabbing. It's not often that Mr. Big invites any of you journalists in to dinner with him."

"Well, that won't stop us from crabbing. I wonder you dared show that handsome mug of yours down here again, without bringing us the President's speech. Didn't we tell you, two hours ago, we'd punch it for you if——"

"It's all ready. Bring it to you in a few minutes," Ike announced astonishingly, as he disappeared down the corridor.

With the coming of night, the pall of gloom which had lain over the staff car all day seemed to deepen. Mr. Lyme, the Postmaster General, and his wife had been affected by the heat, though not in the same way as Pat Rushmore; they were confined to their compartment by cramps and colic. Poor Pat was tossing restlessly from side to side, pressing his ice bag more closely down upon his throbbing temples. Senator Slocum was consuming one planters' punch after the other, as Sadie continued to tell him just what she thought of the Conrads and why. The telegraph boys walked limply to and fro, instead of bounding with spirit on their errands. Even the secret service men seemed less alert than usual. Daphne, feeling still more exhausted than the night before, had returned to her compartment alone. Honor Bright had hurried back to the press car as soon as the dinner party broke up, and Mrs. Coffin, placated with promises and replete with food, had been deposited at a convenient way station. Rosemary had been induced to inspect the moon from the rear platform; and the men, with the exception of Ned, had remained deep in conference with the President, who seemed disposed to break his usual rule of getting to bed by eleven.

But again Daphne could not sleep. She lay listening for Rosemary's light step in the adjacent compartment, for Michael's firm tread on her own threshold. But when her door was finally flung open, it was by her daughter and not by her husband.

She could hear Rosemary breathing fast before the girl snapped on the electric light; then she saw her, flushed, disheveled and tearful.

"I hate him. I loathe him. He tried to kiss me. I slapped his face. I'm going straight into the press car and tell the boys and Honor to announce my engagement to Xavier in the morning papers and put a stop to all this before it goes any farther."

"My dear little girl, I implore you to be reasonable. You can't announce your engagement to Xavier without the formal consent of his family. A Frenchman isn't free to act on his own initiative in regard to marriage until he's twenty-five years old. You know that. And you know perfectly well that the Comtesse has not given her formal consent as yet. She has only said that when you and Xavier were old enough she would be very pleased to consider——"

"Very well then, I'm going to ask Bert to put through a cable for me, telling her that I'm being persecuted by the President's son, and asking her if she won't consider immediately."

"Darling, you must listen to me. You mustn't mention Ned's name to Bert, publicly or even privately. You must be patient, you must be polite——"

"And have that contemptible cad put his dirty hands on me again? Mother, how can you? How would you have felt, when you were in love with Father, if——"

She had begun to sob, convulsively. Daphne slipped out of bed and put her arms around Rosemary, trying to steady her. The girl was shaking from head to foot.

"Dearest, for your father's sake——"

"For my father's sake! You're willing to see me go through hell for Father's sake! You don't care what happens to me, as long as Father——"

"Rosemary, you're all unstrung, you don't know what you're saying. You know I love you dearly, that I desire your happiness above everything."

"You don't! You don't! You desire above everything that Father shall get what he wants—whatever it is!"

"Darling, I—I don't know, but I am very much afraid that there is some special reason why Father would rather

290

you didn't marry Xavier, why he'd be glad to see you interested in someone else. Not Ned necessarily. Any suitable young man."

"Isn't Xavier suitable?"

"Yes, of course. I mean, any suitable young man besides Xavier."

"Well, why *besides?*"

"Rosemary, I can't discuss that with you. I don't *know*, only I'm afraid——"

Daphne had begun to tremble too. Mother and daughter, clinging close together, were each appalled at the other's plight.

"Mother, what *is* it? What is the trouble?"

"Nothing—nothing. Only try, Rosemary—try to be nice to Ned for the rest of this trip. I'll see that you aren't left alone with him again. But if you don't do anything rash now, it may mean that in the end——"

"That in the end I'll marry Xavier? Say yes, Mother, and I promise you I won't do anything rash—that is if you promise me you won't leave me alone with Ned again——"

Daphne repeated the promise feverishly, hoping that the intensity with which she spoke would make up for the vagueness. For she had not said yes in answer to Rosemary's question, and though the girl had not protested or entreated any more, she had gone uncomforted to her own compartment.

Daphne was still trembling herself when she got back into her berth, and as she lay still, trying to regain her self-control, the darkness seemed to take on a more and more menacing quality. It was very quiet in the car, unnaturally so. She hoped that poor Pat was getting some sleep, and reproached herself because she had not been in to see him. How essentially selfish almost everyone was, she reflected, placing personal troubles over those of others, and imagining them to be unique or paramount. Pat must be stricken because he had failed his chief at a crucial moment, he was suffering intensely besides. Daphne was half-minded to dress and go to see him after all, late as it now was. But he might be asleep by this time. If he were, it would be a shame to disturb him.

She must have dozed at last, in spite of her distraction. She was roused by the sound of a soft and steady tapping. As she groped for her dressing gown, it was with the impression that someone was knocking on her door. Then she realized that it was on Rosemary's instead.

The lights had already been turned down in the corridor. When she stepped into it, she could see that a man was standing at Rosemary's door, but she could not tell who it was. She spoke tersely, in a hushed and vibrant voice.

291

"What are you doing? What do you want?"

The man turned, his finger on his lips. As he faced her fully, she saw that it was Bert Scruggs. A great wave of relief swept through her. Though she could not understand what Bert was doing beside her daughter's door in the middle of the night, she knew that whereas his visit might be shrouded in mystery, it was not a portent of evil.

"May I come into your compartment for a minute?" he asked in a hoarse whisper.

She nodded and retreated swiftly. He followed, shut the door after him, and stood with his back against it.

"We may all be barking up the wrong tree," he said, "but we've sort of got the idea up in the press car that Rosemary— that Ned— Well anyway, I was afraid the kid might not sleep so well tonight and I came back here to tell her something. I'll tell you instead, Mrs. Trent, and you can give her the message, if you think best. I just wanted to say that if Ned bothered her again, she might ask him what he was doing in Agua Prieta five years ago and whether Concha Gomez and her son are still living in the same place on the Calle Esmeralda."

The President, running through the pile of papers on the table beside him, was displeased, and felt he had ample cause for displeasure.

He had always enjoyed the luxury and seclusion of his own room on the observation car—the big bed, the comfortable chairs, the commodious desk, the well-adjusted lights, the glimpse, through a mirrored door, of the gleaming bathroom beyond. His upbringing had been too austere for him to accustom himself easily to the ministrations of a valet; but with the passage of years, Crawley had become almost a second self to him—a second self which prevented the other self from following a line of least resistance, from sleeping late and omitting some of the rituals of exercise and massage and bathing in consequence. With Crawley at his pillow promptly at eight every morning there was no loophole left for personal slackness, and Neal Conrad had come to count on Crawley's disciplinary measures as much as on Crawley's impeccable service.

This was, however, the only sort of discipline to which he did take kindly, and he was becoming increasingly sensitive to trends of public comment as he recognized their portentousness. Besides, the passage through the snowsheds of Nevada made reading doubly difficult. Neal had always hated this part of the transcontinental trip, with its endless tunnels, its swiftly alternating moments of darkness and light. But all due allowance for the annoyance caused by these conditions could not account, in full, for his mounting sense of exasperation. These pieces by Alf Schnitter now! It was ridiculous, on the face of it, for a big metropolitan daily to send out a comic writer on the Presidential Special. He would have protested against it long ago, if the Chicago *Free Press* had not been such a powerful paper. But he intended to protest now. An entire column consumed by a distorted description of his visit to his cousin in Swink, Nebraska! Another column consumed by a distorted description of the threshing machine episode! And still a third devoted to details of his disastrous trip up Cripple Creek, with a cartoon depicting him hanging by his suspenders, caught on a small scrubby tree jutting out at right angles from a precipitous peak, his legs waving widely out into space over a swiftly flowing river, and the whole captioned "Dangers and Difficulties of the Third Term."

Of course Alf had come close to the truth in every case—too close for the President's comfort. Neal was willing to admit himself that he had acted ill-advisedly in accepting the invitation of Senator Etheridge to inspect the unfinished mountain road—well, not ill-advisedly exactly, for he had declined to listen to advice of any kind. But darn it all, he had been caged up for so long! Those futile stops in Nebraska didn't count, when it came to a question of getting out in the fresh air, and certainly the funeral in Butte didn't. He had a slight twinge of conscience, realizing that the faithful secret service men, who had protested against the Cripple Creek trip, had been the ones to bear the brunt of the blame for it—they'd be cashiered now, very likely, when they got back to Washington, instead of being promoted as they'd been justified in expecting. They were responsible for his safety, and this had been jeopardized. Well, he'd make it up to them later, when the campaign was over. That is, if everything turned out all right in the campaign——

Naturally everything was going to turn out all right. But even so, he hadn't cared for the character of the wires and the radio reports that had come in the night before. He had gathered from these that his opponent had been making deep inroads into sections where he had assumed that he himself was safe. Now the morning papers seemed to carry out the same damaging impression. The rival candidate for Presidential honors might be a mossback or a mountebank—as a matter of fact, Conrad considered that he was both; nevertheless he somehow contrived to have a good press. Conrad found nothing that was encouraging and little that was consoling in the pile of periodicals beside him. Scruggs's dispatches were wholly satisfactory—there was one man at least upon whom he could depend: steady, earnest, hard-working, intelligent. No tricks in his bag. And Honor Bright had done her usual brilliant type of writing. No detail seemed to escape her, and she had the faculty of giving glamour and importance to little things. Her material was accurate too, as well as attractive. Her words carried conviction; she had an immense following. But the *Enterprise*, excellent as its news features were, Honor's foremost among them, was still luke warm editorially. Until this part of the paper could be jacked up, until its owner and its publisher came out flat-footed for the President, the *Enterprise* was hitting on only half its cylinders, as far as he was concerned.

Gus Graham and Aubrey Warren were both damning him, as he had expected, for different reasons, and he could not minimize the influence of the former in the Middle West and the latter in New England. Both could be offset, of course, by a different attitude on the part of the *Enterprise*—with New York City in the bag, Boston and St. Louis could both go hang! But the Cleveland *Times*—now that was something else again. Chris Stearns, so far, had given unqualified praise to only one thing—the Denver speech. That had gone over like a million dollars, better, infinitely better, than the one in Chicago, where the President had been undeceived by the surface clamor. Chicago, he knew, was not yet sure of itself or of him; Denver, on the other hand, would have rallied wholeheartedly to him, if he had not brought about an anticlimax himself, by taking that foolhardy ride. Well, on the Coast there would be no stunts and the speech must be a pushover. With Durham, this new man from San Francisco on the job, he could count on co-operation there. Durham's dispatches had been the most satisfactory of all, aside from Scruggs's and Honor Bright's. He must speak to Ostermeyer about Durham, see that he was shown some special attention.

The President touched his bell, and his secretary stood before him. "Good morning, Ike, good morning," Neal said, with more heartiness than he actually felt. "How is Pat coming along?"

"He's much better, Mr. President. I think he'll be up later in the day, for a while."

"Good. That'll give you a chance to devote yourself to the San Francisco speech. You did a fine job on Denver, Ike, I must congratulate you. Caught my idea exactly, and carried it through to a smashing finish. I'm counting on you to

294

do even better this time. If everything goes well on the Coast——"

"Mr. President, I think I ought to tell you——"

"Tell the Postmaster General I want to see him about that appointment for Mrs. Coffin's cousin. It slipped my mind yesterday, but I mustn't let it slide. Better say I'd like to have him and Mrs. Lyme lunch with me. And the Slocums. And Durham. And the little Trent girl without her parents. That'll be all for the moment, Ike. My appointment with Senator Stone is for ten-thirty, I believe? All right, bring him in anytime now."

"Mr. President, if it wouldn't inconvenience you, Mrs. Trent would like to see you for a few moments sometime today."

"Mrs. Trent!"

"Yes, Mr. President. She called me into her compartment directly after breakfast and said it was something very urgent and strictly private."

"Very urgent!"

"Yes, Mr. President. Perhaps you could arrange to see her before luncheon, after Senator Stone leaves you."

"You think this really is important, Ike?"

"I'm certain of it, Mr. President. Mrs. Trent isn't the type of woman who'd impose on your time if it wasn't. And I think I ought to tell you, Sir—in fact, I started to when I first came in—it was she who did the last revision of your Denver speech. You see, when Pat passed out and——"

"Daphne Trent wrote the final draft of the Denver speech!"

"Yes, Mr. President. And she's working on the San Francisco speech now."

Neal Conrad stared at his secretary. Ike, having shot his big bolt, remained silent.

"You know you shouldn't have taken a step of that sort without consulting me," Neal said at length, coldly.

"I know, Mr. President. But you were very much preoccupied. And the press was raging for its handouts. Something had to be done."

"Well, perhaps so. And the end seems to have justified the means. We'll let it pass this time. But see that it doesn't happen again."

Having dismissed his secretary on this note, Neal Conrad turned his attention to John Stone; but throughout the conference, the distracting thought of Daphne Trent obsessed him and upset him. There was every reason, he argued with himself, why it should obsess him under the circumstances; but there was none why it should upset him, if Ambrose Estabrook knew what he was talking about; and though no man was infallible, the Secretary of State usually did know. "There isn't a woman in the country who knows more about national and international affairs—she's been helpful in every kind of a build-up—a woman with great courage, whom you can trust implicitly—" The words echoed in his ears, as they had in Ike's——

"I'm sorry, John. You were saying you thought New England was perfectly safe, in spite of all the mischief Aubrey Warren's done there by writing about my socialistic tendencies?"

"Yes, Neal. I think I have that situation in hand all right, and Slocum feels pretty sure of North Carolina too, in spite of all the crabbing he's done. I'm glad you asked him in to lunch today."

"Well, if you only had some good news to bring me from New York City——"

"I think I have. I take it you haven't seen Michael Trent yet this morning?"

"No, not yet."

"Has he an appointment with you anytime today?"

"No. I've been seeing a good deal of Trent lately, as you know, John, and some of the Old Guard feel——"

"Oh, I know what they feel. It doesn't seem to make any difference that Trent has put half a million into the campaign already, and that he'll put in a million more anytime you need it. Or that he holds the employees of every one of the Loose Elixir factories in the hollow of his hand. But I think he'll give the old fossils something they'll have to bite into now. After all, it's more or less of a family matter, so I don't believe I'll be violating a confidence if I tell you Trent's latest news, myself. He and my brother Jerry have bought the *Enterprise* together."

"What!"

"Yes, they've been negotiating for it, on the quiet, for quite a while. Jerry's wanted Honor to have a newspaper that she could control herself, if she cared to. So when Trent suggested going in with him, Jerry leaped at the idea. As you know, they're neighbors in King George County, and they've always got on together like a streak. Jerry went up to New York to close the deal the same night that Honor started off with us. Michael just got a wire from him. It is closed."

"Your brother and Michael Trent are joint owners of the New York *Enterprise!*"

"Yes, the announcement will be made almost immediately. Of course, they'll keep Meacham on as managing editor—there isn't anyone who can touch him in that capac-

296

ity. And Honor will do what she pleases with her end of things, naturally. I haven't had time to discuss the matter with her fully yet, but I imagine she'll want to expand the scope of her activities a good deal. Also, that she'll try to get Scruggs back on the *Enterprise*, which ought not to be difficult. And I know she's already suggested to Michael that he should let Daphne have some hand in the editorials. Daphne has rather a gift in that direction—not that she'd ever sign her name to anything. But it wouldn't surprise me if she had something drafted already.—Of course, they'll come out with a two-column editorial, supporting you, right away.

"I'm glad to see Jerry getting into the newspaper game," John went on reflectively, as the President continued to stare at him without comment. "Really getting in, I mean. Of course, he's controlled the stock in a number of Virginia papers for some time already. Didn't you know that? Well, Jerry realizes that when you go down to Solomon's Garden you don't want to talk shop all the time, and not any one of these papers is important in itself. Taken altogether, however, their circulation's quite imposing. What I was getting at, though, was that I'm glad to see him getting into the game in a big way. It's time he had something besides his plantation to occupy him."

"You and Jerry aren't figuring that these newspapers might come in handy for you, four years from now, are you, John?" the President asked pleasantly.

His eyes were twinkling again, his lips twitched agreeably. He rose and slapped the Majority Leader jovially on the shoulder.

"We'll talk about that later on," he said with immense geniality. "You know you can count on me, John, to the limit when the time comes that you want my help. And when I say the limit, I mean just that. Meanwhile, I want to see you and Michael together directly after lunch—sorry, but I'm completely tied up until then. However, I'll keep the afternoon clear. We'll map things out. Honor and Daphne will join us, I presume, whenever we ask them in?"

"I'm sure they'll be very glad to," John said gravely.

If he felt any surprise at seeing Daphne, who was entering the observation car as he left it, he did not betray this. There was something about her expression which reminded him of the way she had looked when she started on her ocean flight —as if she knew she was taking desperate chances without counting the cost, because the end she envisioned justified the perilous way which led to it. Such a look was on her face now, and it was both puzzling and provocative. But John

297

had the wisdom to make no comment on it. Instead, after greeting her with customary cordiality, he said he had told the President their good news.

"I'm on my way to see him myself, now," remarked Daphne, with her usual disarming candor.

"I thought you might be. Well—good luck—to both of you!"

The President made Daphne very welcome. He spoke at once about the purchase of the *Enterprise*, he thanked her for her invaluable co-operation in regard to the Denver speech.

"I have the typescript of the San Francisco speech here with me, Mr. President. I think it's splendid. But you'll see that I've penciled a few suggestions along the margins. And I've brought along a draft for an editorial in the *Enterprise*, announcing that we are supporting you for a third term. Michael and Honor think it's all right, but, of course, we want your O. K. on it also. We're planning to run it next Sunday, if that would fit in with your views." She handed him a sheaf of neatly typed sheets. As he looked up from them, his satisfaction shining in his face, she extended still another piece of paper.

"And did John happen to mention that a little while ago I came across a copy of a rather interesting letter written by Washington to Lafayette? The existence of this letter isn't very generally known. I think we might choose a psychological moment and give it considerable publicity." Neal had hitherto regarded Daphne's predilection for historic research with amused condescension. Now he seized upon the photostat which she offered him. He read—

"*—There are other points on which opinions would be more likely to vary—*

As for instance, on the ineligibility of the same person for President, after he should have served a certain course of years.

Guarded so effectually as the proposed Constitution is, in respect to the prevention of bribery and undue influence in the choice of President, I confess, I differ widely myself from Mr. Jefferson and you, as to the necessity or expediency of rotation in that appointment. The matter was fairly discussed in the convention, and to my full convictions; tho I cannot have time or room to sum up the arguments in this letter.

There cannot, in my judgment, be the least danger that the President will by any practicable intrigue ever be able to continue himself one moment in office, much less perpetuate himself in it—but in the last stage of cor-

rupted morals and political depravity; and even then there is as much danger that any other species of domination would prevail. Tho, when a people shall have become incapable of governing themselves and fit for a master, it is of little consequence from what quarter he comes.

Under an extended view of this part of the subject, I can see no propriety in precluding ourselves from the services of any man, who on some great emergency, shall be deemed universally, most capable of serving the public."

His mouth was twitching slightly, his hand shaking, as he finished reading. He looked across at Daphne without relinquishing his hold upon the photostat.

"You've made a great discovery for me," he said hoarsely. "I'm overwhelmed with gratitude. And I shan't forget what you've done. You know that the time to break this is when that editorial you've written comes out. And you know the editorial itself ought to be altered to meet the exigencies of such a situation."

"Just as you say, Mr. President."

"Please don't call me 'Mr. President', Daphne, any longer. We've been friends for a long time, we're better friends than ever now. We shouldn't stand on ceremony with each other. Besides, we're almost relatives."

His keen eyes were twinkling again, the corners of his handsome mouth twitching. But Daphne continued to look grave, to speak formally.

"Perhaps you guessed, Mr. President, that it was on a family matter I wished to speak to you. Not about the *Enterprise*. Naturally Michael will want to talk to you about that himself."

"Yes, naturally. But I hope you'll sit in at the conference—you and Honor Bright. I've just told John so. In the meantime, if there's anything I can do to be of assistance in this family matter, as you call it, I'm entirely at your command. Of course, you know I'm tremendously pleased at the turn things have taken."

"It's very good of you. Michael's pleased too."

"But aren't you?"

"I'm not sure, Mr. President. I know it sounds presumptuous of me to say that, but——"

"Nonsense! What's the matter? Don't you like Ned?"

"I've liked what I've seen of him very much. He's attractive and agreeable. There's a great deal of you and of his mother about him, and you know how much I admire you both. But Rosemary's my only daughter. She's infinitely precious to me. You can appreciate that. You can understand

299

that I want to see her do more than make a great alliance. I want to see her make a happy marriage."

"Of course, and so do I. She's a fine girl, an exceptionally fine girl, Daphne. I don't know when I've seen one that I've liked any better. But why shouldn't she be happy with Ned?"

"I don't know of any special reason. But his first wife wasn't altogether happy with him, was she?"

The room had suddenly become very still. When the President spoke again his voice was cool and guarded.

"I'm afraid I don't follow you, Daphne."

"I'm sorry if I've raised a sore subject, one that's better forgotten. But under the circumstances——"

"I must repeat that I'm afraid I don't follow you."

"Of course, it's possible that I'm mistaken. You're quite sure that your son has never been married, Mr. President?"

"Naturally I'm sure. The idea is fantastic. He's had his little affairs, I suppose, like other young men, but——"

"He didn't marry a girl named Concha Gomez in Agua Prieta five years ago?"

"He— There was a time when he did live briefly in Agua Prieta. He went there on temporary business. I have never heard that he formed any sort of an attachment there, but it is possible that he may have done so—a transitory attachment, I mean."

"Not an attachment that led to a ceremony? A ceremony at which there were witnesses?"

"If you've been listening to a blackmailer, Daphne, it's beneath you."

"I haven't been listening to a blackmailer. There is no question of blackmail. I've told you already how sorry I am to speak of this, I've begged your pardon for hurting you. But I've got to protect my daughter. I've got to do more than that. I've got to protect your son. I've got to protect you."

He saw that she was telling the truth. The strength of her sincerity filled the hushed room.

"I don't believe Ned willfully did wrong," she said earnestly. "I think if there actually was such a ceremony, it does him great credit. I think he probably went through with it to defend a girl who would otherwise have been defenseless and—a still more defenseless child. A great many young men, caught in a jam like that, would have abandoned them to their fate. And later on, I understand there was a divorce. I don't think for a moment that Ned has gratuitously insulted my daughter by asking her to marry him when he wasn't free. I believe he thought he was. But the divorce,

300

like the marriage, seems to have been Mexican. One is just as liable to misconstruction as the other in the United States. Ned couldn't marry Rosemary, he couldn't even admit an engagement with her, that the danger of this misconstruction wouldn't arise. As long as he doesn't take any such step, the other persons most concerned will probably be only too glad to keep quiet, as they have in the past. But if he did, the whole affair might be brought out into the open. Nothing is a secret if more than one person knows about it. Nothing is safe if more than one person is aggrieved. And we couldn't risk a lack of secrecy and a lack of safety just now, could we?"

"No," he said hoarsely. "We couldn't."

He tried to go on, to ask her the source of her story, how much of it she had guessed and how much of it she really knew; to find out who, besides herself, knew the secret and where the greatest danger lay. But the words did not come. There was so much to face already, so much with which to contend. If he added one more burden to those he was already carrying, the load would be too heavy for him to bear. He must stop short of the ultimate weight.

Suddenly he slumped down in his chair, his ruddy face drained of color, the muscles around his mouth working. Daphne did not seem to notice. She went on talking with the same earnestness and the same gentleness that had characterized every word she spoke.

"I know this is an awful shock to you. I know you didn't visualize the situation at all. It's dreadful for me to have been the bearer of such bad tidings. But let's be thankful you and I have learned the truth before it was too late—too late for Rosemary and too late for you. And after the election's over—why then, of course, you and Ned will thrash this thing out together, you and he will do whatever you both think is best—and right. For the time being don't let him know what you've heard—him or his mother either. Just tell him you don't think the moment is propitious for an engagement between him and Rosemary. Tell him you need his undivided time and attention through the rest of the campaign. Tell him—you'll know best yourself, Neal, just what to tell him."

She rose slowly and held out her hand.

"We are going to keep on being good friends, aren't we?" she asked. "It is to be—Daphne and Neal, isn't it?"

"Yes, to the end of time!" Neal Conrad answered. And gripped her outstretched hand.

CHAPTER 22

Editorial—New York Enterprise.

WE'RE FOR CONRAD

The New York *Enterprise* believes that President Conrad should be re-elected for a third term and will do all it can to help him win.

The only real argument against him—we don't call it a reason because it doesn't strike us as being reasonable—is that his re-election will break the American tradition against third term presidents. The horrendous specter of Neal Conrad suddenly becoming a dictator on January 20 next is waved in our faces. Pardon us if we fail to shudder.

If President Conrad should again take that solemn oath to "preserve, protect and defend" the Constitution—which, incidentally, says nothing about a third or any number of terms for the President—it will not be as the result of a march on Washington or a *Putsch* or a bloody revolution. He will take it because the American people went to the polls as usual and elected him to Congress to make the laws he executes.

But we are being fed again the doctrine—so convenient always for the forces of reaction—that the founding fathers and George Washington had already looked a hundred and fifty years into the future for us and given us all the right answers to our problems, including, of course, an unalterable edict against a third term President.

We don't suppose the truth will ever catch up with the ancient myth but the fact is George Washington was NOT opposed to three or even more terms for Presidents of the United States. True, he did not want a third term himself. But in a letter to General Lafayette (See Ford's writings of Washington and our news story on Page 1) the first President said he did not see "the least danger" that any President could perpetuate himself in office.

He went further. He said he saw no reason why the country should rob itself of the services of the best man for the job when some great emergency arose. We agree with him—we think the great emergency is here and we should not allow ourselves to lose Neal Conrad.

To us the issue is simple. Europe and Asia are in a mess. Their peoples are fighting a new kind of religious war—always the most bloody and savage variety of conflict. This time, differing doctrines of government are at stake in place of the religious dogmas that were the excuse for battle in the old days. The President has kept us out of their brawls and we think will continue to do so.

But our people want change too and show no signs of relenting in their demands for a more equal distribution of this country's wealth.

It has been our good luck that the differing groups and their ambitious leaders were able to make the President their common commander. If that commander now throws down the baton of authority, we shall be at the mercy of the quarreling captains.

Then the fireworks will start. If the radical leaders press to the hilt their pet notions, we'll probably get communism. Or the reactionaries, driven by fear and violent opposition to the radicals,

302

may put into action what has so long been their whispered thought: "What this country needs is an American Mussolini."

We think either alternative would be tragedy for Americans. Of course, we can't help worrying about ourselves too. We don't think the *Enterprise* would fit into the picture of the yes-man press common to communistic and fascistic countries. And we're personally very poor about saluting.

On either side, lies tyranny. In a center of safety are President Conrad and a third term. We don't find the choice difficult.

Front page spread—New York Enterprise.

CONRAD WINS! CARRIES 38 STATES; THIRD TERM TABOO IS SHATTERED

America chose Neal Conrad tonight to serve a third term as President, shattering a tradition that has prevailed since the birth of the infant republic in 1789.

The President carried thirty-eight states. He lost Maine, Vermont, Massachusetts, Delaware, Kentucky, Maryland, Pennsylvania, Utah, Wyoming and North Dakota. At the same time the voters swept into office a Congress in which the President will have clear-cut majorities to carry out his policies. His strength will be greater in the Senate than during his last term. In the House he lost fifty seats but will still hold a comfortable margin of support.

Fifty million free-born Americans marched to the polls under sunny skies to record the historic endorsement of the feasibility of a third term originally outlined by George Washington. It was apparent in the early returns that the old tradition was doomed and the Conrad victory certain.

Decisively rebuffed in their bid for a return to power, the opposition party and their candidate face a superhuman task in rebuilding and re-forming their shattered lines.

Just before midnight when victory was assured, President Conrad pledged the nation that his third term would see him fighting for the objectives of peace and prosperity as he has fought for them in the past eight years.

From the porch of his Belford home, while a chill wind from the White Mountains ruffled his graying hair and a throng of faithful neighbors cheered, the President broadcast this message to the people:

"America has proved that it cannot be frightened by the bogeyman of dictatorship. It has re-elected a President, peacefully and constitutionally. This great victory assures our people that for the next four years we shall move forward along the same orderly path toward the same objectives to which we dedicated ourselves eight years ago."

As the President re-entered the house, a message conceding defeat and extending congratulations was handed him from his rival. The President immediately wired his thanks.

Today's result conclusively proved two facts:

1. The anti-third term tradition no longer has a hold on the American people.

2. The personal popularity of President Conrad transcends party lines and geographical divisions.

Embattled conservatives mustered the forces which lost the New England states, Pennsylvania and Delaware to the President. Factional party strife and personal jealousies are blamed by administration leaders for the loss of Kentucky and Maryland. The President's defeat in the trio of western states—Utah, Wyoming and North Dakota—is

303

attributed to opponents of his trade policies and heavy re-armament program:

| The election picture by states: | . . . . . . |
| . . . . | |

News Item—New York Enterprise.

TRENT CONFIRMATION VIEWED AS CERTAIN AFTER STONE DEFENSE

Washington, D. C., Jan. —. An excoriation of our "clique, not career" Diplomatic Service bubbled from the lips of Senator John Stone today in the course of a sturdy defense of Michael Trent, President Conrad's unexpected appointee to the Court of St. James's.

The Majority Leader, ordinarily even-tempered, angrily asserted that a "contemptible" attempt was being made by disappointed "pets" within the State Department to picture Trent as a mere "fat cat," whose large contributions to the Conrad campaign led to his securing the prized appointment.

Instead, asserted Stone, Trent was an experienced career diplomat whose brilliant work in difficult posts in South America and the interior of China went unrewarded for long and dreary years. Finally, Stone said, Trent entered profitable commercial pursuits, driven to it by the necessity of providing for his family.

"It is not his fault, but ours, that he had to wait until now to receive his just due," Stone charged. "We are lucky—though we don't deserve it."

The consensus of the Senate tonight was that in the face of Stone's belligerent defense of the Ambassador-designate, few, if any, voices will be raised against his confirmation either in the Judiciary committee or on the floor. The Senators declined to be quoted, but a few explained off the record that they had been questioning Trent's qualifications simply because they didn't know him. They pointed out that the elixir millionaire's diplomatic service

admittedly took place years ago and that he had since spent much of his time abroad.

The Senate galleries quickly filled when Majority Leader Stone suddenly interrupted debate on the administration's farm bill to go to Trent's defense. The Senator began soothingly enough with a sketch of the prospective Ambassador's early background, reminding his colleagues that Trent started his career right there in the Capitol as secretary to Congressman Horatio L. Tittmann, from his home state of Missouri.

"Then, trained in the law, he entered the Foreign Service, an enthusiastic, brilliant young man anxious to do his best for his country," said the Senator, his voice beginning to take on a sharper edge. "He did do his best for his country. In La Paz he handled a difficult financial situation with credit. His reward was the task of moving his young and delicate wife into a post into the interior of China, where they lived through revolution and real danger. Trent stayed at his post under shellfire, acquitted himself nobly. His reward was to be moved deeper into China. He submitted. But finally his patience gave way.

"He accepted a responsible business position with the Loose Elixir Company, and in no time at all the same qualities which he had placed at the disposal of his country with so ill a return earned for him a fortune and high place."

The President, Stone said, felt extremely fortunate in having a man like Trent to send to the Court of St.

304

James's, and indignantly refuted the idea that any amount of campaign contributions could secure for an unqualified man so vital a post.

Senator Stone's attack on "clique" diplomacy was rarely bitter and outspoken even for the highly privileged Senate.

Some observers predicted tonight the Secretary of State would have to take cognizance of it, might even make formal reply, though the well-known friendship between Estabrook and Stone would rob this of all actual sting.

Editorial—New York Enterprise.

OUR NEW AMBASSADOR

President Conrad has appointed Michael Trent, General Counsel for the Loose Elixir Company and part owner of this newspaper, to be Ambassador to the Court of St. James's. This poses a nice problem to the editorial writer—whether to act as if he didn't catch the name and write a few platitudes about the importance of the post which everybody already knows, or whether to let his conscience be his guide. The valiant never taste of death but once, so we'll proceed.

Mr. Trent did contribute a million dollars to the Conrad campaign fund. He has indeed been the driving power behind the Loose Elixir Company and we don't suppose he grudges the gagmen their wisecracks about his providing soothing syrup for Europe's headaches in his new job.

But there are other facts even more pertinent to the case of Mr. Trent. He is a trained diplomat.

As a young enthusiastic and idealistic lawyer, he began at the bottom and tried to make a success in our Diplomatic Service by the hard way of work and patience. His trouble was that the bustling bureaucrats in the Capital—we don't suppose they're any worse in the State Department than elsewhere—were too busy in their treadmills to pay any attention to him.

So he quit in a quite understandable huff and began to make money to provide for his wife and family. Eventually he made a lot of money and now he is about to go to the Court of St. James's where he'll undoubtedly do a fine job.

And everybody's happy and the country gets a break. Of course we still think it would be swell if the country had a real career service and didn't have to lean on luck quite so heavily to get a good Ambassador.

PART IX

"When Desire Cometh"

CHAPTER 23

"NINE O'CLOCK, madam. And as fine a May morning as you'd ever wish to see, milady."

It was useless, Daphne had discovered, to try to persuade Trotter not to call her milady. All Trotter's previous employers had been personages of title, and force of habit caused her to continue the form of address to which she was accustomed. She might start a sentence with madam, but before she had finished it she forgot and lapsed back into her old ways. Besides, as she often told her husband, who was the Ambassador's valet, she'd never seen a duchess, nor a princess either for that matter, who could hold a candle to Mrs. Trent when it came to being a lady.

As Trotter spoke, she busied herself with the cords of the cream-colored brocade curtains. They parted, and a pale, cool sunshine suffused the great room. It had none of the splendor of the Southern sun that Daphne loved so much; but there was clarity to it, and cheerfulness. After all the fog of the winter and all the rain of the spring, it was doubly welcome.

Trotter adjusted the lace-edged pillows behind her mistress and wrapped a chiffon bed jacket, trimmed with swansdown, around Mrs. Trent's shoulders. Then she placed the breakfast tray carefully down on the bed. It looked very attractive, set with flowered china. A fresh rose lay across the small folded napkin, and the fragrance of this blended agreeably with the delicate aroma of China tea and the pleasant scent of hot buttered toast.

"A secretary telephoned from the Spanish Embassy, madam. He said that the Duchess de Serreno would like to have you come in at eleven for one more rehearsal, if that would be perfectly convenient. Some of the new diplomats' wives don't feel too easy about their court curtsies even yet, milady. At least that was what I gathered."

Trotter's manner inferred that Mrs. Trent was not among this timorous and inadequate group, that *she* would know how to curtsy beautifully, even if she was doing it for the first time. Daphne smiled.

"Thank you, Trotter. Of course, Miss Larch said that I would be very pleased to go? She may bring in my mail anytime now. Did you tell Miss Rosemary about the extra rehearsal?"

"Certainly, madam. She's gone out riding now in the park, as usual. But she told me to say she'd be home at ten, milady, in case you should wish to see her about anything before starting for the Spanish Embassy."

"Thank you, Trotter. Did the Ambassador go with Miss Rosemary this morning?"

"No, madam, he went to the Chancery quite early. He said he didn't wish to disturb you, seeing as how it had been so late before you all returned from Marlborough House. A most beautiful ball, he gave me to understand, and Miss Rosemary quite the belle of it, I'll be bound. It was Master Richard that went riding with Miss Rosemary, and isn't he the fine figure on a horse, madam? I declare there was tears in my eyes as I watched the two of them start out together, there was, milady. They're such a grand-looking pair."

There were tears in Daphne's own eyes as she listened, but they were tears of joy. Richard on horseback again, Richard leading an active, joyous, untrammeled life. He would be punting on the river at Oxford the following fall, probably playing cricket the next spring, and meanwhile delving deeper and deeper into the treasure trove of the English poets. How he loved them all—Keats, Shelley, Byron, Browning, Wordsworth! Hardly an evening passed that he did not come to her, when she was getting ready to go out, and sit down beside her dressing table, his finger marking a place in a leatherbound volume he held in his hand.

"I've found the most beautiful passage, Mother. May I read it to you? And I've written a few verses myself today too, if you'd care to hear those."

A hundred years from now some other boy would be bringing a leatherbound volume into his mother's room and saying, "May I read you something Richard Trent wrote when he was young, Mother?" Daphne was certain of this. Not that she had ever had any doubt herself of her son's genius. But whether the world would recognize it as immortal, she had sometimes wondered, in the earlier days of its discovery. Now she knew.

Miss Larch came in with the mail. There were a few appeals for charity, a few announcements of openings and exhibitions, but for the most part it consisted of invitations. Daphne took the stiff coroneted cards in her hands, penciled small notations on them. "Accept—accept—ask the Ambassador—decline, with much regret, owing to a previous engagement to dine at the Polish Legation—decline, with much regret, owing to a previous engagement to spend the week end at Castle Rhodes—ask the Ambassador—accept—accept." She did a little dictating, gave a few general directions for the dinner she and Michael were giving, themselves, the following evening, dismissed Miss Larch graciously. Then she turned to the correspondence which she wished to look over at her leisure, correspondence that was personal and private in character.

Several radiograms lay on top. One was from Jerome and Henriette, now in Capetown; one from the Perrys whom she had first met in Panama, now in Peru. Honor and Jerry, Cousin Tyler and Uncle Roger, had all remembered her. And underneath the cables was a pile of letters. Most of them she glanced through more or less casually, smiling as she did so. But one she held in her hand for a long time, gazing gravely at the brief unsigned message which it contained:

"Remember that we still have a secret, something of our very own that we share, to make up—in some slight measure—for what we couldn't have and couldn't share. You are my emissary. My faith in you is unbounded and my life is dedicated to your service."

"If you please, Milady, your bath is ready."

Yes, of course, Trotter would have the bath prepared by now. She always drew it while her mistress went through the mail, shaking sweet-smelling salts into the water that bubbled and foamed in the big marble tub. Daphne, resolutely emerging from her abstraction, saw that Trotter had lacy lingerie laid out, silk stockings, polished pumps, a *tailleur* that Schiaparelli had just sent over by air express from Paris—Rosemary was standing in the doorway, still wearing her riding habit, flushed with exercise, laughing from the sheer happiness of being alive——

"Heavens, Mother, are you that far along already? And we mustn't be late at the Spanish Embassy, must we? Well, I'll have a shower and spring into my own suit and be with you before you can get downstairs."

It was not quite as quick as all that, but still there was very little delay. Rosemary was sitting beside Daphne in the limousine, they were riding through Prince's Gate into the park, down Piccadilly, turning into Berkeley Square. The

Spanish Embassy was located in a palace and it was full of priceless treasures which the Serrenos had brought with them from Spain. Both the Ambassador, Don Sebastian, and his wife, Doña Dolores, came from very great families, rich as well as ancient. There were gorgeous tapestries and somber pictures hanging on the walls, there were massive dark furnishings and heavy silver ornaments scattered about and lights cunningly contrived to enhance the effectiveness of these. The Ambassadress herself, in spite of some concessions to current fashion, gave the impression of having stepped out of a Goya portrait as she came forward to greet her guests.

"*Seya las bien venidas!* Did I incommode you with my so late, so inopportune call? *Lastima!* It is the little Lett who is anxious about her curtsy, so I thought it kinder that we should all assemble, that we should not let her know she alone had been stricken with fright."

There were a dozen of them in all, wives and daughters and sisters of new diplomats, gathered at the home of the *doyenne* of the corps to practice their curtsies one last time before the first Drawing Room of the season: The frightened little Lett, a blonde impassive Norwegian, a hawk-faced Turk, two handsome Hungarians, a bevy of dark South Americans from five different countries. These, with Daphne and Rosemary, made up the diversified group. A servant was dispatched to the Chancery to summon the Ambassador. He arrived, suave and smiling, kissed the hand of each of the ladies with a word of graceful greeting, and then took his place beside his wife on a great sofa of crimson brocade, with a gesture that implied he was adjusting a crown and fingering a scepter.

"I don't believe the real King will be half so stunning," Rosemary whispered to Daphne. "Don Sebastian has what it takes, hasn't he, Mother? He must have been a smoothy when he was young."

"He's a smoothy still," Daphne whispered back, smiling at her daughter. Her mood was merry. It was easy to jest on such a day as this.

Five members of the Embassy staff had also been pressed into service—sleek-haired, liquid-eyed undersecretaries, who impersonated the Lord Chamberlain and Gentlemen-in-Waiting, entering into the spirit of the rehearsal with the same zest as their chief. Slowly the line of ladies advanced toward the "King and Queen," some with real, others with mock solemnity. They kept at a careful distance from each other, so that they would not tread on each other's trains, and made their bows with such state as they could muster.

The Norwegian was stiff, the Lett rather limp; both the Turk and the Hungarians had the air of being slightly defiant; but the South Americans moved with languid grace, and bent their slim supple bodies without visible effort.

"They are good, very good," Doña Dolores murmured to her husband, her eyes following the lovely Latins. "But it is Mrs. Trent who has the most dignity, and her daughter who has the most charm. They are *encantadoras.*"

Liveried servants came in bringing dry sherry in silver goblets, small biscuits on silver trays, and *marzapan* in silver dishes. The arrival of these refreshments created an agreeable interlude. Then it was agreed that perhaps it would be well to go through the ceremony once more. Afterward, with an exchange of courtesies, the group disbanded. As they went out into the pale sunshine again, Rosemary suggested shopping before lunch.

"Shopping! What can you possibly want to buy, darling, that you haven't already?"

"Oh, nothing special! But it seems so festive to go shopping in London on a spring day! Let's, Mother—for just half an hour anyhow!"

"You know that Mr. Loose is flying over from Paris this morning, dear. We mustn't be late for lunch."

"We won't be. There isn't anyone else coming for lunch, is there, Mother?"

"I haven't heard of anyone. But you know perfectly well what your father will do if any stray Americans who look lonely drop in at the Chancery this morning."

"Yes, Mother, I do. Is he still being pestered, do you think, by ladies who want to be presented?"

"I'm sure he is. There had been over five hundred applications, the last time I heard, with openings for only fifty. It's too bad there should be so many hurt feelings."

Daphne sighed as she spoke, but Rosemary declined to be depressed. "They deserve to have their feelings hurt when they come snarling at him like hungry wolves," she said severely. "Think of that dreadful creature who offered him ten thousand dollars if he would only 'arrange it,' and who fairly foamed at the mouth when he told her invitations to court weren't for sale. Personally I'm sorry he gave in about Mrs. Coffin.—You wouldn't think, would you, that if she were so terribly hard hit as she made out when she climbed aboard the President's train, she'd spend money coming to England on the *Queen Mary* and staying at Claridge's and buying clothes from Revelle's? There seems something fishy about it to me. But I'm glad he got Mrs. Crofts on the list. I like her—she's so perfectly straightforward about going

310

after what she wants, not pretending at all, and yet never seeming to push."

They were a little late for lunch. Rosemary saw a perky little hat in a shop window, which she felt she simply must try on; and then the saleswoman brought out one or two others, just in case. But fortunately Michael had staved off the lonely Americans who had come to the Chancery that morning, suggesting tea the following afternoon instead of lunch that day. He and Mr. Loose were alone in the library when Daphne and Rosemary came in.

"I've almost decided to resign in your favor, Daphne, you've so completely overshadowed me," he said laughingly. "When I came home and asked about messages, I was told there weren't any—for me. Two or three court photographers and two or three court hairdressers and two or three court dressmakers had called to check on their appointments, but all these appointments were with Mrs. Trent. And where do I come in at the big show tonight, I'd like to know?"

"As if you hadn't 'come in' at a big show when you presented your credentials and at the first levee!—Shall we go down to lunch? I'm sure we're all starving!"

Ladies always lay down in the afternoon, Trotter told Daphne firmly, on the day that they were presented at court. Daphne did not feel at all tired, but she had learned not to argue with Trotter about non-essentials, so after lunch she suffered herself to be secluded in her room, with the curtains drawn, and surprisingly she went sound asleep. When she woke up it was teatime, and the court hairdresser was waiting for her.

There was not much he could do with her hair, she told him apologetically; she realized that it was just hair, so she never went to a *coiffeur*. The court hairdresser protested, and when he had finished with her, he had made her soft dark head look very lovely and very distinguished after all, and had half-convinced her that if she would put herself in his hands, he could work wonders for her. But when he saw Rosemary, he did not protest at all. He gave an exclamation of delight, and then he brushed out her curls and began piling them, in shining ripples and ringlets, on top of her head where they shone like molten gold.

"It seems funny, doesn't it, Mother, to put on a veil and feathers at this hour of the afternoon, before we've put on evening dress?"

"It seems funny to me to put a veil on anyway, Rosemary. I've never worn one before."

"You've never worn one before! Why you must have, Mother—when you were a bride!"

"No, darling, I didn't. You see I didn't have a real wedding, just—just a service. That's why I want your wedding, when you have one, to be so perfect and—and complete in every way."

The court hairdresser had gone, they were having their tea together in front of the fire in Daphne's sitting room, for there was an English chill in the air, even though there had been English sunshine intermittently through the day. Daphne had meant to say more than that to Rosemary, and Rosemary had meant to say more than that to her mother. But just then Michael and Richard came in and joined them and stayed with them until it was time for them to get ready to go to Buckingham Palace.

Michael had chosen Daphne's dress for her—cloth of gold with a cloth of gold train. And he had given her a beautiful parure of topazes and diamonds to wear with it—a tiara, necklace, a brooch, earrings and bracelets—that had once belonged to an empress. The feather fan she was to carry, with topazes and diamonds set in the amber sticks, was a present from him too—he had had it made to match the parure; and the cloth of gold coat, with the deep cape and wide sleeves of Russian sable, had been made, by Revelle, at his suggestion, to match the dress.

Daphne did not tell him that she herself had visualized her first court dress as a pale silk, that she would have liked to wear her grandmother's string of seed pearls and no other ornaments with it. She knew the cloth of gold was what he wanted, what he had pictured her for years as wearing; and when she put it on at last, knowing that he was pleased, she was pleased herself. But when he had suggested a similar costume for Rosemary, saying that she had always been his "golden girl," and that now she must have a golden dress, Daphne had protested. In the end they all agreed that since Michael had chosen Daphne's dress, Richard should choose Rosemary's. And Richard had chosen a creamy satin, not stiff and heavy, but soft and supple, with golden lights in the folds. He had chosen a scarf of lace made by nuns, light as a gossamer and mellow with age, to serve as her train. He had suggested that since Mother was not going to wear her seed pearls Rosemary might do so instead, and that as Mother was going to carry a fan, Rosemary should carry flowers— pale yellow roses and snowy lilies with yellow stamens. Since Mother was wearing sable, Rosemary should wear ermine. Michael had laughed at his son, saying that only a poet would dress a girl like that; and Richard had laughed back, saying that only a plutocrat would dress a lady as Father was dressing Mother. And they were all very happy about it.

Now at last the night had come when Daphne and Rosemary were to wear the dresses which Michael and Richard had chosen, and it was time to start for the Palace, though it was broad daylight still. The motor moved slowly forward through the parkway, between long lines of police and crowds massed on the sidewalks—crowds which commented, freely and audibly, on the occupants of the cars as these filed past. Daphne, drawing her wrap more closely about her, shrank back a little into her corner, stricken with the consciousness that she was conspicuous, that strangers were staring at her and shouting about her. But Rosemary leaned forward and smiled and waved her hand gaily when she saw that someone was waving to her.

"Isn't it fun, Mother? Isn't it all wonderful?"

It was an ordeal for Daphne, but she did not say so. After all, the worst was over. They had halted at the outer gate of the Palace; the footman seated beside the chauffeur had held out their invitations for inspection by the waiting officer; they had reached the gray inner courtyard; the big doorway, blazing with light, was swinging wide open. Then they were swallowed up in the huge dressing rooms, baronial in size, and friendly attendants were coming forward. "The train over the *left* arm, if you please, madam. There now, you have it exactly right—and quite lovely I'm sure. Can I do anything else to help you? Thank you, madam."

Now they were mounting the wide, soft-carpeted stairway, where Palace guards, gorgeous in trappings of scarlet and gold, were stationed on either side. The sparkle of jewels, the sheen of satin, the softness of velvet, were all about them. Misty veils streamed out, and snowy feathers stirred lightly in the flowerscented air. Men in knee breeches, men in splendid uniforms, more men in knee breeches, were mounting with them; women in silk, women in silver, women, like themselves, in gold. They were borne along, part of a great glittering wave, toward the Throne Room. They found their places amidst the tiers of seats, covered in red brocade, which rose on all four sides of the open space in the center, a pipe organ at one end, the crimson-draped thrones at the other. On the walls behind them, priceless tapestries were hung. From the center of the ceiling a crystal chandelier was suspended. Its prisms sparkled with iridescent light. Its radiance was dazzling.

The sound of the national anthem rang out, the signal that the royal progress through the State apartments had begun. The Lord Chamberlain and other officials, carrying

313

their staffs of office and walking backward, were preceding Their Majesties to the place where the Gentlemen-at-Arms were stationed around the two thrones. There was fanfare of trumpets. The King, dressed in the uniform of an Admiral of the Fleet and wearing the Orders of the Garter and the Bath, had ascended his throne. The Queen, dressed in sparkling sequins and wearing the Koh-i-noor diamond, had ascended hers. The royal family grouped itself gracefully about the sovereigns. The diplomatic presentations were about to begin.

"Being presented, the Duquesa de Serreno— Being presented, Madame de Crequi— Being presented, Frau Stoltzberg— Being presented, Mrs. Michael Trent."

The lights had been turned low in the library, and when Daphne entered it, she thought that Alonzo Loose, who was sitting sunk in a big chair beside the fire, had fallen asleep there. Then she saw that he was watching the doorway, that he was waiting for her.

She walked slowly across the room, her court train dragging its gorgeous length behind her. When she reached him, he was just struggling, in his lumbering way, to his feet. It had become increasingly hard for him to manage his unwieldy body. She put out a hand to help him.

"Tell me about it," he said, almost as a child might have asked—an unpopular but pathetic child—to hear about a birthday party to which he had not been invited. Then he sat down again to listen.

She began to describe the court, dwelling on every detail. "The ladies who are being presented enter the Throne Room by a door at the right of the organ," she told him. "They walk slowly past it and out of a door at its left, into a corridor. Then they re-enter the Throne Room by a door at the left of the thrones. Each candidate pauses while two Gentlemen-in-Waiting take her train and spread it out carefully at exactly the right angle. Afterward she hears her name being called out in a very loud clear voice at the precise moment when she curtsies before the King. Next she takes three or four steps to the right and curtsies before the Queen. It's all very simple really. When I felt my train being gently laid back over my arm, I could hardly realize that the presentation was over!"

"That's interesting, Daphne. That's all very interesting. What else can you tell me about it?"

She continued her minute description. Occasionally Alonzo Loose interrupted her with an eager question; occasionally he nodded his head and smiled, as if some aspects of the spectacle had proved particularly pleasing to him. When at last Daphne could think of nothing more to say to him, he sat for some moments staring into the fire, almost stolidly, and silence fell between them. At last, with an obvious effort, the old man roused himself.

"Where's Michael?" he asked.

"He's gone upstairs already. He didn't think you'd wait up for us. But I had a feeling you might."

"Where's Richard?"

"Asleep, I imagine, hours ago. I'll look in on him, to make sure, before I go to bed myself."

"And where's Rosemary?"

"She's in the garden."

"In the garden!"

"Yes. When we came back from the Palace we found we had another guest. Xavier came over on the Golden Arrow. It's cold and it's late, but I have a feeling neither he nor Rosemary will notice! Michael is in a mellow mood tonight. He told them, before he went upstairs, that they might plan to be married the end of June. Probably the plans will take some time to perfect."

She smiled, and though Alonzo Loose could not see her expression, he knew what it was like without seeing it. He smiled himself, and once more struggled slowly to his feet.

"Probably they will," he said with a slight chuckle. Then he added more laboriously, "But I guess it's time an old fellow like me went to bed."

"You take the banister and let me walk on the other side of you. It'll be easier for you that way."

"You've—you've always made things easier for me, Daphne."

"I'm so glad."

"You know, don't you, that—that——"

"Yes, my dear good friend, I know."

He paused painfully on the threshold of his room.

"This is the happiest night of my life," he said; and two big tears trickled slowly down his furrowed face.

Daphne leaned forward and kissed him lightly on the forehead.

She was very tired, so tired that before Trotter finally left her she felt she could not endure the weight of her own exhaustion. But she knew that the old servant, like the old promoter, had been waiting hopefully for hours to hear her account of the court. Again, in minute detail, she described

315

everything she had seen and done since she left Prince's Gate at seven o'clock.

"I never shall forget the graciousness of the Queen when she acknowledged my curtsy, Trotter. I couldn't take my eyes off her face—she's so much lovelier than I realized. And I shan't forget the Yeoman-of-the-Guard who was stationed outside the Throne Room either. He carried a spear and wore a stiff uniform that bulged with puffs. I hardly dared ask him the way to the supper room, he looked so huge and medieval. But he was very friendly too and helpful."

"And the supper, milady? Sumptuous, I suppose?"

"Oh, very! And I was so hungry, Trotter, that I ate a real meal. Of course, I hadn't had any dinner——"

It seemed to her that there was no end to Trotter's enthusiasm and Trotter's curiosity. But again she suffered, without visible impatience, the postponement of the blessed moment when at last she could be alone. She knew that it had not come yet. She knew that after Trotter had left her, the door between Michael's room and her own would open and that Michael would come to her, claiming communion with her. It was something deeper than desire which drove him to her now. It was a fundamental need to draw on her strength and her spirit. Without the solace which she alone could give him, he could not persevere and prevail.

She did not have long to wait. She heard the door click quietly, heard his firm tread across the soft carpet, felt his hand against the covering that lay over her. But it was not until he had her in his arms that he spoke to her, and when he did, his voice rang with triumph.

"I told you," he said, "I told you—in the very beginning, didn't I—that in the end I would make everything up to you? And I have—haven't I?"

She knew he was asking for the final assurance that everything for which he had striven had meant as much to her as it had to him. The events of the day that had just passed were to him the outward and visible signs of an ultimate and supreme success. He had always gauged achievement by the material and the manifest. He always would. And now that he had reached the pinnacle which he had sought so long to scale, it needed only a word from her to transform him from a suppliant to a conqueror. He never had known, he never could know, what the ascent had meant to her, what she had missed, what she had lost, what she had suffered, through it all. She must not tell him, she could not tell him now. And as the certainty of this swept through her, the conviction that after all there was nothing to tell, flooded her being. Again, as in the beginning, her own prodigality proved her own fulfillment.

"Yes, Michael," she said softly, *"you've* made up to me for everything."

THE BIG BESTSELLERS
ARE AVON BOOKS!

The Secret Life of Plants Peter Tompkins and Christopher Bird	19901	$1.95
The Wildest Heart Rosemary Rogers	20529	$1.75
Come Nineveh, Come Tyre Allen Drury	19026	$1.75
World Without End, Amen Jimmy Breslin	19042	$1.75
The Amazing World of Kreskin Kreskin	19034	$1.50
The Oath Elie Wiesel	19083	$1.75
A Different Woman Jane Howard	19075	$1.95
The Alchemist Les Whitten	19919	$1.75
Rule Britannia Daphne du Maurier	19547	$1.50
Play of Darkness Irving A. Greenfield	19877	$1.50
Facing the Lions Tom Wicker	19307	$1.75
High Empire Clyde M. Brundy	18994	$1.75
The Wolf and the Dove Kathleen E. Woodiwiss	18457	$1.75
Sweet Savage Love Rosemary Rogers	17988	$1.75
I'm OK—You're OK Thomas A. Harris, M.D.	14662	$1.95
Jonathan Livingston Seagull Richard Bach	14316	$1.50

Where better paperbacks are sold, or directly from the publisher. Include 25¢ per copy for mailing; allow three weeks for delivery. Avon Books, Mail Order Dept., 250 West 55th Street, New York, N.Y. 10019

RRB-74

ROSEMARY ROGERS

Author of the tumultuous epic bestseller
SWEET SAVAGE LOVE

THE WILDEST HEART

A rapturous tale that spans three continents, following beautiful young Lady Rowena Dangerfield from the shimmering palaces of exotic India, to the rich splendor of the Royal Court of London, to the savage New Mexico frontier, where Lady Rowena finally meets a man with a will as strong as her own . . . and their powerful, all-consuming love towers to the limits of human passion!

20529/$1.75